Blood of Rome Ret
John Salter

Copyright John Salter 2014
First Edition

The author has asserted their moral right under the Copyright, Designs and Patents Act 1988, to be identified as the author of this work.

All Rights are reserved. No part of this publication may be reproduced, copied, stored in a retrieval system, or transmitted, in any form or by any means, without the prior written consent of the copyright holder, nor be otherwise circulated in any form of binding or cover other than that in which it is published and without a similar condition being imposed on the subsequent purchaser.

Blood of Rome Retribution
John Salter

For My Family

Previous Books by John Salter

Blood of Rome Caratacus

Blood of Rome Retribution
John Salter

Prologue

In AD 43, a vast Roman invasion fleet landed on the shores of Britannia intent on conquest. Many tribes on the huge island did not resist, some surrendered without even drawing a sword, one, however did not. It was led by a man named Caratacus.

With his brother dead, he led the Catuvellauni in their resistance against the legions of Rome. During the first few days, two major battles took place at the Rivers Medway and Thames, where superior weaponry and tactics won the day for the invaders.

Forced to abandon his tribal capitol Camoludunum against overwhelming odds, Caratacus led his warriors west to the mountains of the Silures, a fierce and warlike tribe, who joined the resistance, with him as their chieftain.

Three years have passed and Caratacus has established a stronghold in the mountains and valleys from where he and his warriors launch deadly attacks upon those who have come to take his land, his people, and his life; for him surrender is not an option.

The mighty Roman Empire that had conquered virtually all who stood before it, were now uncertain of victory as their march westward faltered on the misty, windswept and mystical island of Britannia. This is what happened next in the life of

Caratacus of the Catuvellauni

This is his story

Blood of Rome
Retribution

Chapter One

    The two men sat in the coracle watching their fishing lines as the breeze and current gently lifted them up and down in the water. The weather had been mild over the winter months and was once again kind as the day's sun reflected glistening light off the shimmering water. They had become like brothers over the past three years, living and fighting together through victories and defeats against a common enemy, resisting the men intent on bringing about their destruction. Today however, wasn't a day for fighting, setting out before dawn, they had wanted to get an early start knowing that the fish would bite and hoping their haul would be good. Six large fish already lay at the side of the small boat, eyes unseeing, waiting to be smoked later.
    From a distance the small vessel was a mere speck on the water in the valley as it floated freely allowing the current to move it as was it's want, this way and that, gently rising and falling. From the shore a war band of fifty warriors watched on, as their leaders fished, keeping guard and making sure they weren't disturbed by unwelcome visitors. Caratacus wore a thin sleeveless green tunic with light woollen breeches; his dark blue and claret coloured woven cloak was folded over neatly in the base of the boat with his long sword at his side.
    Gone was his long hair of a few years before, taken by the lime he had applied so often before going to war against the foreign aggressors. His head was now clean shaven and shone with perspiration and a close cropped beard covered his face. He gave his line a gentle tug, but there was nothing there. The skin over his muscled arms was quickly browning again in the early spring sunshine as he sat enjoying the warmth and the company of his close friend and companion, his cousin Ardwen. Blue Celtic swirls and patterns were tattooed on both men's arms reaching up to their shoulders and

necks as was the fashion for the warriors of Albion. Ardwen still had a full head of hair that reached down to his shoulders and beyond, he wore only his beige breeches; so warm was the weather. His other clothing had been thrown in a heap next to his cousin's cloak.

"It'll not last." Ardwen announced, suddenly bringing Caratacus out of his day dream. He looked up at him knowing full well exactly what he meant.

"What won't last? What are you talking about?" He asked.

"The peace," Ardwen replied, "the peace won't last," He stared at Caratacus, "and you know it. We can sit here for weeks, a month maybe more but now the spring is here, they'll come again." Ardwen looked around at the water, "With winter over, our friends at Isca will be preparing to come and ruin our tranquillity once again it's just a question of when."

Caratacus looked back at the fishing lines, "I'm sure you're right, I wonder who they will send against us this time, one thing's certain, it won't be the great General Vespasian. I heard that after he returned to Rome he retired from the military and went to the country to lick his wounds but was called back to the Senate where he now builds his career as a politician. They will have many more competent generals to send into the hills to die, maybe one commanding the Second Augusta, although after the mauling we gave them, some of their men will be hesitant."

"I still can't believe all the tribes in the east just rolled over and bent their knees, fucking cowards the lot of them." Ardwen said hawking up phlegm and spitting it into the water, where it landed with a splash and then floated.

"Steady on, we don't want the fish diseased through the scrapings of your nose eh?" Caratacus said. "I don't want to find that in my food either, I wouldn't be in any condition to fight if I ended up swallowing that thing."

Ardwen smiled and looked to the tree covered shore. "Did you think they'd be here this long?" He asked.

Caratacus followed his gaze, "Albion? I don't know, I've never really thought about it too much. The tribes in the east seem to have allowed them to settle in, although we still hear reports of unrest from time to time. I think most of the chieftains are content to have a quiet life. Initially they were happy to take their gold and bribes but now they are the ones paying the price through taxes, slaves and having to give high quotas of their crops to feed the legions. I couldn't have lived that way but I think some of the people were glad to see the back of us Catuvellauni to be honest." He felt his line tug and go taught, he pulled quickly, smiling as he hauled in another thrashing fish. "I often think about Camoludunum and those we left behind. What must they think of us, of me for abandoning them?" He corrected himself.

Ardwen removed the hook and put the still struggling fish with the others. "You didn't abandon anybody if you remember. You left so that you could continue to fight. Anyway they could have come with you if they'd wanted to but they chose to stay there, so fuck them." He looked at the fish again as its struggle slowed and finally it stopped its mouth wide as if still searching for breath. "The place won't look the same anyway now or the people. It will be full of square stone buildings and that temple to Claudius that we heard they were building. That tells you something about the man! He actually thinks he's a God or something, just like the others before him."

Caratacus put some more bait on his hook and threw the line back into the water. "He's no God, that's for sure. I'd like to see him take my sword through the stomach. That would prove he's just a man. I'd thrust it in so far his ancestors would feel it. There wouldn't be any divine intervention, just a dead fool." He watched as Ardwen laughed and pulled in another fish.

"Thank you fish, I couldn't go back with less of your friends than this fellow here." He counted the catch, "That will do for today won't it? There are enough juicy ones here for a feast tonight after we've given them a little smoking."

Caratacus replied, "Yes I suppose your right." Then he looked back at Ardwen.

"What is it?" Ardwen asked, "What's the matter?"

"Do you remember some time ago, you said that I should give up my name because you thought it sounded too Roman?"

"Yes I do remember, and yes it does. I think your parents must have been too influenced by all the trade with Rome or something, maybe all that wine went to their heads, so what about it, what are you saying?" He asked.

"I think you were right. I don't want to be known as Caratacus anymore, I want to cast it aside." He looked to the shoreline where he could just about make out the war band baking in the sun. "When we get back to shore, my name will be Caradoc. That is the name of the man who will lead the fight for our people. Caratacus, we leave behind for the water to take."

Ardwen smiled, "Good it's about time as well." He picked up an oar from the floor of the small boat, "Right then, Caradoc it is, come on," he nodded at the other oar, "time to row. You may have changed your name but that doesn't mean that you can just lounge about and let everyone else do all the hard work does it?"

They slowly made their way to the shore where they stepped out of the small boat and dragged it onto dry land. Ardwen handed the fish to one of the waiting men, who slid two thin sharpened wooden stakes through their heads and then strapped them to the side of his saddle for safe carriage back to the settlement. It would take a few hours to get back to the mountain hideout but the journey would be safe and uneventful. Although the Second Augusta had attempted to make a major incursion into their territory a few years before, they had not been seen since. Trapped and isolated, the men of Vespasian's legion had sought refuge on a mountain top after their column was ambushed in the valleys below. The battle had raged on for days until the Twentieth Legion came to their aid and the Britons eventually withdrew. With a high casualty rate and men running out of ammunition for their bows, few javelins left and virtually no food, the Twentieth had arrived just in time as the Britons pushed for a complete and all out victory.

The Catuvellauni and the Silures had withdrawn from the region almost entirely initially but on seeing the Roman army retreat all the way back to Isca Dumnoniorium, they had returned and had now established full control of the mountains and valleys to the far west of the country. At Isca Dumnoniorium, the Second Augusta were replenished of the men killed or so badly wounded that they were retired from the army altogether. Legionaries were taken from other legions in Britannia and within a few months, they were back to full strength, five thousand men. With small revolts occurring in the south west, they were kept busy enough and had not yet returned to challenge Caradoc. After two years those rebelling against the occupation in their region were put down and a fragile peace began.

Work on the garrison at Isca Dumnoniorium had also continued and now where initially there had been a relatively small fort where soldiers had lived in tents, it had been replaced with wooden and concrete structures as more permanent buildings were erected. The new garrison town now dominated the land for miles around. A forty two acre site made Isca Dumnoniorium one of the largest Roman fortified installations in the country and slowly trade began to flourish. A permanent sea harbour had also been constructed a few miles from the garrison, where galleys and supply vessels could be seen off-loading supplies bound for the growing town and surrounding regions.

Relationships with the local people had also developed as they began to see some of the benefits from the occupying force but a few were still yet to be convinced that they could live with the men who had come from afar bringing with them traders and even civilian settlers. There were still problems however, and every once in a while a dispute would end in violence between the indigenous populations and the new arrivals, but overall, life was beginning to settle into a routine.

    The same thing could be said of the mountainous region where Caradoc now found himself with the Silures. Tribes in the region had heard of his success against Vespasian's legion and some had joined their growing number after they were given captured soldiers to use as slaves or as their people saw fit. Word had spread that the Roman's had reached as far north as the southern lands of the Brigantes during the last campaigning season. Those who had not joined Caradoc now watched with interested eyes to see how this would affect him and his allies. If the rumours were true it meant that all those living in the west would effectively be cut off from the east and the north. If the abstainers chose to fight Caradoc knew full well that it could determine the overall outcome of the occupation. The question now however was on whose side would they fall if any. Consequently, he and Ardwen had spent a lot of time talking to the councils and elders of the other tribes, trying to win their swords in the event of a further Roman incursion.

    Caradoc also knew that having eyes and ears in Roman occupied land was vital not only to their survival but also in order that he could plan a strategy of attack. His intelligence network had already outlined where they had built new forts and had constructed roads as they spread their boot prints over the country. Not long after he had arrived in the mountains, he had sent out spies to live and work the land near all Roman military encampments and settlements. Crofters, carpenters, shepherds, butchers and ironsmiths were now deeply in-bedded so that he had a good understanding of the enemy, what they were doing and most vitally, what their intentions were.

    The lands to the south west had seen the occupiers build large stone buildings that he understood were called villas. These places were where important and influential Roman families lived, those who had followed their army intent on plunder and theft. Some were isolated and those that weren't, only had small forts nearby for protection. Cavalry patrols monitored these areas, visiting these places fairly often but he knew they could not be at all places at all times. As they became more confident and assured of their safety, the villas began to spring up even further into the countryside, so the aid from the forts became less reliable and some were literally hours from help. Caradoc had asked his spies to provide him with drawn plans of these buildings and maps detailing their whereabouts. He had studied them carefully and knew they were tempting targets as he found various weak points. If he could attack and successfully destroy even a few of these places, other Romans would think twice before trying to settle there again and it would provoke their military into action, which is what he wanted.

The previous years had given him time to reflect on his defeats and he had come to realise that unless he had overwhelming numbers and even then, changed his tactics, it would be foolish to face them again as he had at the Medway and Thames, when they had first arrived. A better strategy was called for and a different way of thinking and striking terror into the hearts of those who had come to enslave the people of Albion.

With the war band mounted, they set off into the hills and rode towards one of their major settlements high in the hills, along narrow twisting paths and tracks.

"So what of Dumnoc?" Asked Ardwen. "Have you heard when he intends to attack the villa we discussed?"

"We'll know soon enough but I'm sure it will be long after it's actually happened and those who live there are all dead." Caradoc answered as he swung his cloak over the rump of his horse. He had chosen his first target as autumn had begun the previous year. He had to temper the urge to attack as soon as he had identified a likely dwelling, and realised that waiting would be better and would cause more damage to the minds of others when it did occur. A slow trickle of attacks would soon turn into a tide; one that he hoped would force the intruders back. A high ranking civilian official was residing there with his family and slaves far to the south west of the country in the land of the Dumnonii. It was a large agricultural region and ran down to the toe of the map, south west of the River Exe. The Romans had already begun to become complacent as they constructed their fine buildings with pictures on the floors and walls as they settled further and further away from any military assistance.

Caradoc had been told that the occupiers intended to show the Britons that they were not the demons they had been described as and were willing to live amongst them with their families, side by side, working together, prospering. The civilian official who 'owned' this land was said to have come from Rome itself and was intent on constructing large vineyards on Dumnonii land, where the weather was warmer and the climate kinder. He lived there with his wife and three daughters, all thought to be under twelve years of age. The household consisted of ten slaves and fifty others who worked the land. They were overseen by what the Romans called freedmen. There were twelve all told and they wore swords at their sides but would be easily overcome by determined warrior's intent on their destruction.

"That's good, the sooner we start spreading the poison of terror into them the better." Ardwen replied. "What will Dumnoc and his people do afterwards, come north?" He asked.

"I've told him to make sure they vanish back to their crofts and settlements and carry on as if nothing happened. They'll wait until things are quiet and then strike again when the time is right. Three of the slaves at this particular villa have even said they want to help during the attack if they can, they want to join us; they will escort their families north afterwards." Caradoc said.

"What of the Roman children?" Ardwen asked.

Caradoc looked at him with hard determined eyes, "I've told Dumnoc to take them if possible and have them brought here, they will make good slaves and their taking will horrify any other families who are trying to show that they are the same as us. If that is not possible, they are to have their throats cut and will burn with those who resist."

"Is that wise? Ardwen asked. "They will want retribution."

"Should we concern ourselves with what they want or what they may do? It is for us Ardwen to take retribution, they are the ones who betrayed us. Catuvellauni heads stare out at people on the outskirts of Camoludunum on poles as we speak. If we are afraid to attack these people because of what they may or may not do, we will never rid ourselves of them." Caradoc replied. "We will attack them when we can, where we can and as often as we can and we will not concern ourselves with their thoughts except one, fear. We will make fear eat away at them, until it is the only thought they have until they are gone. Remember my friend, we did not start this war and it was not us who invaded their lands, butchered their people and broke treaties, stopping trade that had been carried out for generations. We just wanted to be left alone, to live in peace but they wanted more, they wanted it all, everything. They have brought this upon themselves and we must make sure our hearts are black when dealing with them, whoever they are, no matter how old."

Ardwen pressed his lips together but did not answer or make another comment as they rode on. He knew Caradoc was right but wished things were different, they all did. By late afternoon they had reached the first roundhouse of the settlement as they emerged from the trees blanketing the valley they had climbed. Five dwellings were surrounded by twined fencing in a family group, beyond that was another and more as they rode on. There were many such ringed habitations sprawling along the valley, all linked by fencing and gates. Children ran out to greet them as dogs barked and wagged their tails excitedly as they saw the men approach.

Riding along the perimeter, Caradoc said, "We'll have to start building a defensive wall around the outskirts of the settlement. I'm sure that once the Romans start to bleed again, they'll come looking for those responsible and we have to be ready. I don't want them walking straight in like they did at home." As they entered the fence line through a large open gate, he jumped from his horse and handed the reins to a young man who came running forward. He led the horse to an area where others were corralled, chewing grass under the spring sunshine.

"We'll make a start on the walls tomorrow." Ardwen said. "We'll build ramparts two men high, maybe three and as straight as we can, it will make them harder to climb." He handed his horse to the young man. "It will also help keep that biting wind out in winter, although we'll lose the view." He nodded towards the valley laid out below them. Caradoc followed his gaze and looked down the tree line; it truly was a peaceful and beautiful place. Only the track disturbed the thick trees but it soon vanished below the green leaves as it wound its way snake like down the valley. It would be a difficult place to attack, with its natural defences of mountains and valleys but Caradoc knew the enemy were organised and determined, professional fighters. He didn't want to leave anything to chance. "Make the walls three men high." He said. Ardwen nodded.

They had discussed their plans at council meetings with the chieftains and elders and knew that they would have advanced warning of any future Roman intrusions into their territory. Men, women and children had already agreed to help build the walls that would surround the roundhouses as it was acknowledged that the way things were the enemy would simply walk straight in.

"Come, let's get some of that brew you're so fond of and relax while those fish smoke and become extra tasty." He said to Ardwen. "Let's talk of these problems no more for the day."

Ardwen smiled, "Good idea."

As darkness began to fall many miles to the south, Dumnoc was lying down under the cover of a large oak tree and watched as the slaves began returning to the villa, after their days toil in the fields. He counted them off as they trudged back after a day digging and tilling soil, preparing the ground for yet another row of young trees for their master's vines. When the last of them was inside and the large gated doors were closed behind them, he nodded to Drustan, who turned and went to where the others waited.

Dumnoc had been watching the villa on and off for a few weeks, so carefree were the occupiers who lived there. They had never noticed the solitary figure who would ride past nor had they paid him any attention, he was just another traveller on the dusty roads in this rural area. They had no suspicion of his intentions. Over two years before, he and some of his war band had gradually travelled south and taken occupations in and around garrisons and marching forts, some even working for Roman families providing them with food or had trained them how to hunt in the land they had come to. Others became shepherds or tanners, smiths, anything so that they could blend in unseen. They, the Romans, had no clue that some of the men and women they believed to be of the Domnonii tribe were actually Catuvellauni intent on revenge.

From watching the villa he knew what time they awoke, where the slaves and the freedmen went during their daily routine, when they tended the small rows of trees or dug new land, where they worked and what time they returned to the villa late at night. He knew what resistance he could expect from those who resided inside and suspected which of the slaves he could trust and those that would help when the attack came. Some had been openly badly treated, beaten and even whipped while he watched on, waiting for an opportunity to strike.

He had waited a long time for this moment, this opportunity to take the lives of those who had more than likely celebrated when his people had died a few years before, and had looked on eagerly wanting to take their land. His own family, two sons and his wife, had been wiped out during the battle at the river Medway and now as he waited for complete darkness, he felt his heart begin to surge and slowly pound as blood coursed through his veins as his battle rage grew.

Smoke billowed out of the villa's two chimneys and rose into the darkening sky as the occupants prepared fires to cook food after a hard day working, the slaves at least he thought. The compound was a large pale rectangle from this distance, with an open space in the centre. The slave's quarters were to the south, adjoining them at a sharp right angle was another wall, behind which the horses were stabled. Attached to that block was another long straight wall that contained the gates and then came the part of the building where the occupiers lived with their household slaves in a small building beyond.

His mind showed him images of how the structure would look in the morning, burnt and ruined, with corpses lying outside, dark blood staining dead bodies. He felt no sympathy for what was to come or those whose lives he would take, just hatred, cold, black hatred, even the young would die if it came to that. He watched and waited until the last candle was extinguished from behind the window skins and then waited again. When after a while all was quiet, he searched the building with his eyes one final time to make sure no guards had been posted, there were none, how arrogant and at ease were these fools? He stood up, stretched his aching limbs and then joined his warriors beyond the bank, a short distance away where they waited.

"Is it time?" Drustan asked. Dumnoc placed a hand on his friends shoulder and smiled. "It is my friend."

Some considerable miles further north-east at Isca Dumnoniorum, Centurion Varro secured his cloak with a brooch bearing the Second Augusta insignia engraved on it. It was usually positioned over his right shoulder when he was out in the field and held his deep red cloak in place away from his sword arm. Today it was above his sternum over the centre of his chest as he wasn't expecting to fight within the heavily fortified garrison. He checked the leather laces of his boots, pulling them tight and then left his bunk. He was the officer of the watch and found himself once again going out to check the men who stood guard on the garrison's walled perimeter. He would be glad when the campaigning season started again and he could leave the walls behind and the duties that he found himself performing. Like all other soldiers and officers, when they weren't engaged in active duty, the routine of military life took over, guarding, maintaining equipment, drilling, training and more training. After a while it became monotonous but it was necessary as he well knew.

Consequently the winter months had brought nothing but training, hibernation and yet more training and he yearned to get back out into the fresh air on his horse and doing what he did best, scouting for information and intelligence. The repeated training although at times a chore, he knew was vitally important and believed that he was more competent with his spatha cavalry sword, than ever before. He had also practised for hours on end with heavy and light javelins and had extended his throwing distance by at least three paces. As a centurion, he could also choose other forms of training and had spent time with the archers and had now become quite proficient with the curved weapon that could kill from a distance. As a consequence he had ensured that all the men in his tent party were equally as good with a bow. He now felt better prepared for the months ahead, months that he would be spending with a relatively new scouting group.

The men that he had originally arrived in Britannia with a few years before, were all dead, they had been replaced by other members of the Second Augusta. He had mourned his comrades for some time especially Decimus, who had been killed at the hands of Brenna, a woman he had shared an intimate relationship and his heart with. He had not been able to avenge his friend's death because of the circumstances at the time but he still felt an almost physical pain whenever his thoughts drifted to her image or that of Decimus. He had not seen anything of her since but had vowed that if the opportunity arose, he would kill her without hesitation for her betrayal.

He walked from the duty officer's quarters and into the room where soldiers on standby rested, some were playing dice, others were talking quietly and some slept in double bunks lined against the walls. Those that were up and about wore their white tunics, their armour and weapons laid up near the door. They acknowledged him with a nod or "sir" as he went past. He fastened the chin straps on his helmet and walked out into the warm night air. Leaving the guardroom behind, he went directly to the nearest ladder to climb up onto the ramparts. At the top he felt a slight breeze and twenty paces away was legionary Marcus Pullo, standing looking out into the dark countryside. He heard Varro approach and turned saluting.

"Sir." He said holding his pila straight as a sign of respect to his superior.

"Everything quiet?" He asked of the sentry.

"Like the grave sir, no-one has come in or out since I came on post and it's dead out there as well." Pullo nodded down to the gates and then looked beyond the garrison again.

"That's good legionary Pullo believe me, better to be quiet and boring than to have a war band of hairy arsed barbarians trying to kill us eh?" He said in reply.

"Yes I suppose so sir but I wouldn't mind a bit of excitement once in a while. I've been here six months now and the only Britons I've seen have been polite and courteous. It's hard to believe all the stories we were told in training. Our centurion told us that he had served here since the invasion and had seen human sacrifices, Britons torturing captured soldiers, that they would throw themselves onto our shield walls without a care for their own safety and that they lived on butchered meat and milk. I haven't seen any of that, just the opposite. They may be a little primitive but apart from that, they are no different than us in many ways."

"Well Pullo," Varro said, "I don't know what you were told but I can assure you that things were different than this not too long ago and it could change just like that." He snapped his fingers and went on. "When we first established the fort here Caratacus attacked and gave us a bloody nose. He sank a few vessels just there in the river," he pointed to the water, "they hadn't even been unloaded at the time and we ended up on rations for a while. If the first fort's defences hadn't been so good, they would have breached the walls and slaughtered us all. As it was the entire front line was virtually destroyed by fire." He gazed out across the countryside. "Before that it was even worse, we had to fight for every piece of land, he and others like him are still there, waiting."

Pullo raised an eyebrow, "How many of them were there then sir?" He asked.

Varro screwed up his nose thinking for a second, "That attacked Isca?"

Pullo nodded. "A few thousand," Varro replied, "more than enough to destroy the first century that was sent out against them. The second one didn't fare much better either, they were sent to help the first and had to retreat as they started to take arrows and were then set upon by the bastards that had wiped out the first century."

Pullo looked down to the straight part of the water in the distance." Hard to believe sir really, especially looking at the river now."

Varro smiled thinking back to when he was little more than a recruit. "Don't wish for too much excitement too soon Pullo because you may just get a bit more than you bargained for."

Pullo looked back to his superior. "What's it like though sir?" He cocked his head slightly. "I mean battle, when you have to kill for the first time? Did you just do it without thinking or did you hesitate?"

"It's never easy and you can't hesitate because if you do you're likely to have your head removed or at best a limb. Hesitating is definitely not recommended especially when you're so close that you can smell the stench of the enemy's breath as they scream in your face, someone that is intending to kill you." Varro replied.

"Tullus said that his first kill just wouldn't die." Pullo went on, "He said that he ended up hacking his head off just to make sure of the kill." Pullo said.

"Tullus?" Varro replied. "That sounds Germanic."

"It is," said Pullo, "he's the big German you must know him sir?"

Varro turned and began to walk away, "I don't know every soldier in the Second. He's probably just trying to scare the life out of you, don't think about it." He said.

"Remember, keep your shield tight and up high and your head low, so that you can just see through the gap between the shield and helmet. Thrust and stab out at them with your sword, don't thrash, as you have been taught until they fall, you'll be fine Pullo trust me."

Pullo didn't look convinced, "Thank you sir, I will."

Varro smirked as he continued along the wall thinking about the first man he had killed in Gaul, it hadn't been easy but he wasn't going to tell Pullo that. He could remember every last detail of the encounter, the noise, the smell, the blood, even the man's face as he had suddenly realised that he had been stabbed and was drawing his last breath. Killing was never easy, but a necessary fact of life in the legions sometimes. He checked the other sentries within his area of responsibility and began to make his way back down to the guard house located near the front gate.

"Rider's approaching." He heard Pullo shout from his position above. Varro didn't think much of it and continued on his way. Visitors were always arriving at all hours, merchants, returning patrols even envoys from unknown tribes. The guards at the front would deal with whoever it was. It wasn't unusual for people to come and go at all hours, especially at such a large garrison.

He had just removed his helmet when a soldier knocked on his bunk door. "Yes legionary," he said turning, "what is it?" He asked.

"Sorry to disturb you sir but a group of riders have just arrived at the gate." He reported standing to attention.

"What of it? What's so special about them?" He asked perplexed.

"They're Britons sir, about twenty of them." The soldier replied.

"And?" Varro asked, beginning to feel himself get annoyed by the crumbs of information he was getting. He couldn't keep going in and out every time someone came to the gate. The optio on duty out there was more than capable of dealing with visitors surely?

The soldier saw his frustration. "One of them asked for you sir, by name. She said you would know her."

Varro frowned, "Come on man out with it, who is this mysterious Briton?"

"Brenna sir, she said her name was Brenna and that you would know her." The soldier replied.

Varro felt rocked, dazed, as if the man's words were blows.

Chapter Two

When Dumnoc was absolutely certain that everyone in the villa was asleep, he led his party down the slope on foot very slowly. In the distance at the opposite side of the dwelling he could just make out Drustan's raiding party as they also approached the stone and concrete structure from another direction, small figures moving carefully and silently. Behind both groups walked warriors leading their horses in case a quick escape was required. As he got to the bottom of the sloping rise of the bank and onto level ground he paused, and held his hand up to stop those behind him and listened, nothing moved. It was quiet, peaceful except for the sound of a mild breeze that touched his skin and whispered through the nearby trees. He smiled staring at the villa once more looking for signs of life, but there were none to be seen. He moved again. As he got to within a hundred paces of the structure, where the light walls stood out against the dark night, he could smell smoke from the still burning fires inside, he signalled for the archers to take their places ready to fire. They ran past him slowly and fanned out in a line, ten paces from each other, he was taking no chances. Drustan would be doing the same with his own bowmen at the far side of the complex. He slowly withdrew his long sword from its sheath, looked back at his men and women once more and nodded them onward.

Reaching the wall, he placed a hand against it, feeling its texture, listening a final time for any movement inside. The wall was rough and hard against his skin not smooth as he had expected, he could hear nothing. His warriors stretched along the wall's length silently and waited for his signal. Placing his head against the wall it felt cool, nothing moved inside, he was sure. He waited until he saw that Drustan's warriors were in position as they slowly emerged from the gloom at the corner of the building and stood waiting. Raising his sword, his warriors began to climb the walls helped by each other as they climbed up onto interlinked hands and were pushed upward.

He walked to the gates with Drustan now at his side.

"It can't be this easy." Drustan said quietly.

Dumnoc looked at him through the gloom, clearer now they were close to the almost white wall. "We haven't begun killing yet. I think things are about to change."

Drustan smiled as he looked at the gate and gave it a gentle push, testing its strength. Through a small gap they could see that it was bolted from the inside by means of a wooden bar that ran from each door to the frame on the either side. Suddenly they heard movement and the bar lifted. They stepped back feeling their hearts quicken. The door on the left opened. It was Acheon one of the men who had followed Dumnoc down the slope.

"All is quiet." He whispered carefully putting the squared elongated piece of wood to the side on the grass. Dumnoc walked into the villa's open space where everything looked alien to him. The grass was short and stone paths led round the courtyard with two others dividing the space in the middle making a large cross in the ground. In the centre was a statue of a naked woman, her hands held flowers over her breasts. He turned and waved his warriors inside slowly putting a finger to his lips warning them to stay quiet. When most were in he told a remaining few to wait by the gate.

"Nothing leaves understand, nothing?" He whispered. One of the men nodded acknowledging his order. He turned back to the interior and breathed in listening to the night, knowing that the silence was about to be shattered, an owl hooted somewhere in the distance. He slowly walked to the statue, watched by those now standing by the doorways to the villa and those at the gate, he stood taking in the form of the female statue which was made of some sort of pale stone. It was unlike anything he had ever seen before. He reached out and touched it, it felt smooth, cold. He wondered if her body had been carved and sculptured from a living being or if her form came from one of their gods. Whichever it was it didn't matter now, he raised his sword and with one almighty cleave removed her head completely. The peaceful night was shattered instantly as screaming warriors hacked and kicked their way through the wooden doors of the building.

Claudio Vertuna had gone to bed that night with his wife after telling his little girls a tale about an ogre that lived in the caves outside Rome many centuries before. Their eyes had grown wide as he told them by the glow of a single candle, that the ogre had started to steal sheep as the seven hills of the great city grew, encroaching into his land. The farmers had complained to the Senate, 'how' were they to feed the people and provide wool if this was allowed to continue' they had asked. Men were sent out on horseback to find the ogre but never returned, only their bones were found later, he told his children, the ogre had eaten them.

"What happened next? Please tell us more." His eldest daughter Valeria asked hiding underneath her covers, her sisters cuddled next to her watching their father.

"The champion of the city rode out when the men didn't return. He carried a great lance but when he also failed to return, the city closed its gates and barricaded them all in. They waited for the ogre to come to them." He looked at his daughters, fright over their faces.

"What did the ogre do, did he go to the city?" Valeria asked, her two sisters looking from her to their father.

"After a week the people grew restless. 'We can't stay here bottled up like butterflies in a net' they said, 'we demand that something is done', they said." He took a sip of his wine.

"And so a very brave young man told them that he would go and find this ogre and would free them from their fear." He put his goblet down. "Well as you can imagine the people laughed and howled. 'How will you slay the ogre they asked, you are but a boy. Even our champion didn't return so how do you expect to accomplish such a task' they asked him. Do you know what he said?"

Three low voices answered in unison, "No."

"He said, 'I am Reman descended from Remus who founded this great city and I will kill the demon with this.'

"What?" Valeria asked, "With what, what did he have Papa?"

"The boy held aloft his dagger." He raised his arm copying Reman, the girls looked up as his hand wrapped around the imaginary handle. "The people laughed even more and went home but Reman was true to his word and three days later, he returned to Rome carrying a large head in his hands."

The girls gasped as one and lent forward, eyes like saucers. 'How did he do such a thing?' "The crowds asked as they ran from the gates asking him, cheering his name. At first he wouldn't say until a large crowd had gathered around him. 'Alright, alright,' "he said, 'listen.' "The crowd went quiet as Reman told his tale. He had spent two days walking the northern forests until he came across a huge cave on a hillside. Outside the cave were the bones of men, many men and swords strewn in all directions. He told them that he found the biggest sword and searched the cave for the beast but it was nowhere to be found and so he hid in a tree and waited and waited for it to return." He looked at his daughters. "Well young ladies I think that's enough for one night, time for you to go to sleep I think."

"Don't you dare Father we will not sleep unless you tell us how Reman killed the ogre." Valeria said, her sisters nodding in agreement.

"Very well," he said, "Reman waited until the sun was about to go down and was beginning to fall asleep in the branches of the tree where he had been hiding when he heard something. He sat up and as he peered through the branches, he saw the ogre come into sight dragging a cow behind him. He said he was astonished by the ogre's size as it made the fully grown cow look like a calf. He said that when he realised the ogre was going to walk straight under his hiding place, he moved carefully and waited. When the ogre was directly below him, he put the sword between his legs and pushed himself away from the branch he had been sat on for so long. He said he fell very fast and before he knew it there was a crack and he fell, tumbling. His hands were forced to let go of the sword when it struck the top of the ogres head and he landed on the ground with a thump. He shook his head and opened his eyes, the ogre had let go of the cow and was just standing staring in front of him. Reman said he nearly ran because he knew he had failed and was about to be eaten." He looked at his girls again as they stared up at him, eyes willing him to continue. "And then the ogre fell. Reman scrambled up and just managed to get out of the way before the great fat body landed on the forest floor beside him, shaking the ground. When the dust had settled he saw that the sword was buried deep inside the monster's head. He showed the people where the hole was by pointing to his own head and they all cheered and shouted his name and they all lived happily ever after and that my beautiful daughters' is the story of Reman of Rome and the giant ogre."

"One more Papa please, Papa, just one." They said together, as was their way. "One more story."

"Now that's all for tonight children, time for sleep." He kissed each of them as they frowned on the forehead. "Goodnight, sleep well." He blew out the candle and walked to the open door.

"Night Papa." His girls called as he closed it behind him.

"Goodnight girls, sweet dreams and no nightmares." He quietly went down the corridor extinguishing other candles on wall brackets and got into bed with his wife.

Chapter Three

It took a few seconds for the soldier's words to sink in, but Varro still felt dizzy. "Are you alright sir?" He asked standing looking at his centurion with concern over his face.

"What erm yes, yes I am." He lied. "Of course, where is she now this Brenna?" Varro asked trying to think clearly, trying to clear the fog from his mind.

"They're taking their horses to the stables but the woman Brenna is waiting to speak to you sir." The legionary replied.

Varro's heart pounded so loudly, he thought that it would burst, he was filled with so many emotions all at once but one came to the fore, hatred.

"Thank you, dismissed." Varro said frowning, watching the soldier leave. He felt for the hilt of his sword, grasping it reassuringly.

'Why would she come here of all places?' he thought. His head began to clear, he left the room but his stomach was churning, images of her plunging her blade into Decimus and taking his life ran through his mind as his anger rose. Walking outside the guardroom he saw a soldier walking past, he saluted the centurion. Varro nodded in response not returning the salute, he was too focused on finding Brenna and then he saw her.

"Hello Centurion Varro." She said half smiling. "You can't believe how glad I am that I've found you." Before he could say or do anything in response she continued walking closer.

"I was trapped with the Silures when Decimus and I tried to find the Twentieth Legion." Her face dropped. "All these years I've had to live with them pretending to be Catuvellauni. I didn't know if you'd survived. I remember seeing your columns marching out of the mountains, I thought you'd come back and defeat them but you never returned and I was stuck, I had to pretend to be one of them." Her expression looked sincere enough, the thought flashed through Varro but how can you tell if a snake will strike? She continued, "I got away as soon as I could about six months after the battle but they found me and took me back." She stopped talking and stared at him, eyes pleading for understanding, she appeared genuine.

"What happened to you and Decimus?" He asked. His memory flooded with the image of seeing the head of his friend on a pole and her words of a few years before filled his head as she had spoken of killing Decimus and of having to sleep with him.

"That's what I need to talk to you about." Her eyes filled with tears. "Can we go inside?" She looked at the doorway where he had left the building a few seconds before. He frowned staring into her dark eyes.

"No we can't." He didn't know what to say, he had never seen her look as weak as she did now. Her words of a few years before struck him again like blows to the head. He had got separated from the rest of his group with just Brenna and Decimus. Her brother had died with an arrow strike to the head. He had told Brenna and Decimus to try and work their way north and to find the Twentieth. He had decided to stay and to try and get back to the survivors of the Second Augusta, who were under siege on a mountain peak from Caratacus and thousands of warriors. He had stumbled across a camp fire in the dark where from the safety of trees, he had heard Brenna speak of her betrayal and had seen the head of Decimus, severed from his body and impaled. She had told the men around the fire that she was Catuvellauni and had taken the life of the soldier, a man she had pretended to help.

Varro almost swayed as waves of nausea hit him. "Civilians, even those working with us, are not authorised to go into any official areas unless for a specific task and even then, they must be escorted." His mind was numb. What could she say? He should arrest her and throw her in the garrison jail, kill her where she stood? He didn't.

"I finish my duty at sunrise, I'll find you. Then you can tell me about how my friend died and why you have been missing for so many years." He said turning back towards the door as if she were a stranger. "I trusted you Brenna, as did my men." He paused looking at the ground, "I need to think."

She walked closer reaching out for his hand but he moved away. "I will tell you everything. I know that you probably think I'm a traitor but I'm not I swear it, you have to believe me please, it's the only thing that's kept me alive all these years."

He turned back and stared into her dark tear filled eyes. "If I don't, you will die here today." He walked back into the guardroom leaving her standing there with tears rolling down her face.

The occupants of the villa didn't put up any resistance as the Britons crashed into their home and were quickly overwhelmed within seconds. The slaves were freed, the freedmen were killed, their service to Rome seen as a betrayal. Claudio Vertuna and his family were dragged outside wearing their bed clothes. Vertuna attempted to struggle at one point and suffered a blow to the head from the side of a shield, he collapsed to the ground. His head bled freely, his wife screamed and his children cried as they cowered around him. He was given a choice for him and his wife, die where they stood or be taken north with their children. They all cried and screamed louder. He chose to live and be taken north for an unknown fate. Vertuna's wound was wrapped with cloth and the family's hands bound behind their backs. Dumnoc ordered that the horses be taken from the stable, they would carry the family north with five of his men and the slaves who would go with them. Surprisingly the slaves showed little hatred to their former owners and actually tried to reassure them as they helped them up onto the horses.

"Fire the buildings." Dumnoc ordered looking around at the villa.

Varro left the guardroom at sunrise and looked around for Brenna. At first he didn't see her, but as he walked she moved away from a stable block and slowly came towards him.

"This had better be good." He said, she didn't reply. "We'll go to the stalls, they'll be open but it will be quiet for a while and we can talk." She nodded and followed him.

"Morning Centurion Varro." The fat man wearing a dirty looking apron said as they approached. "And who is this fine looking young lady with you?"

Varro turned and looked at Brenna, "Morning Fiscus," he said, "this is an acquaintance of mine from a few years ago. We used to be good friends."

"Well welcome good friend, do you have a name lady?" Fiscus asked.

"I am Brenna." She replied sheepishly, her head dropping to the ground.

"Well any friend of young Centurion Varro here is a friend of mine, what would you like? It's just warm wine for the time being I'm afraid. I was a little late opening up, it was a late night." Fiscus said rubbing his head and smiling.

"Watered wine will be fine thank you." Varro said.

"Take a seat please. I'll bring your drinks over." He waved a hand at the empty seating area under a large canvas sheet. "As you can see, you have plenty of choice."

Varro guided Brenna through the chairs and tables and took a seat where Fiscus and his ears wouldn't be able to hear their conversation. "Well?" He said.

Brenna took her seat and put her head in her hands and began talking. She told him that after they had split up, she and Decimus had come across a camp fire. She had told him to wait on the track with the horses whilst she went to see who they were and what they were doing. She had thought it strange that they were in what looked to be the middle of nowhere especially when the Romans were under siege on the mountain. They were the males from a large family group, they had explained, who were on their way to join Caratacus but after getting lost they had decided to camp for the night. As darkness fell the sound of battle was carried to them through the valleys, but they knew that could have meant an hour away or a full day, as the sound was carried so far on the wind. "That was when I appeared out of the dark," she continued, "they offered me food and the warmth of their fire. I had intended to slip away as they slept and to find Decimus but then he just appeared from nowhere, I couldn't believe it. Straight away the men knew he was a Roman soldier there was nothing else I could do." She began to sob. Varro stared at her until she went on.

She got herself together and continued. "The men had wanted to torture him before taking his life but I told them that I would deal with it." She tried to dry her eyes. "I got up before the men could and walked quickly to Decimus. I knew we couldn't outrun the men because they had horses and my mind raced because I knew that whatever happened, Decimus would die one way or another. If the men had got to him, he would have been butchered." She sobbed again, tears now rolling freely down her dirty face.

"I walked straight up to him and took his life, as quickly as I possibly could. I killed him Varro and if that means that I have to pay for that with my own life now, then so be it." She said. "We were alone and walked straight into a situation we weren't going to get out of. As it was we would have both died, they would have killed us both and only the gods know what they would have done to me before they sent me from the world. I was a Briton wandering around the mountains in the company of a Roman soldier.

Do you know what that means? Do you know what my people do to such people?" She stared down at the table looking completely lost. "I know what I did was wrong but could see no other choice." She sat sobbing as Fiscus appeared with their drinks.

"Are you alright lady?" He asked.

"Leave us." Varro said harshly without hesitation, it wasn't a request. Fiscus looked at the centurion, nodded and quickly made his way back to the stall.

Brenna waited until Fiscus was back behind his bar before continuing. "Why do you think it's taken me so long to be able to face you? I nearly stayed with them because I was so afraid of how you would react when I told you" She looked up at his face.

"I was there." Varro said.

"What? What do you mean you were there?" She asked confused.

"I heard everything you said." He paused. "I wandered around for a long time and lost my bearings. After what seemed like an age, I saw a campfire and crept through the trees until I was close enough to hear the conversation."

Her mind raced as she thought back to that night, to thoughts she had banished from her mind until now. He saw her thinking, he continued. "Imagine my relief at finding you and then the horror as I heard your words as you described that you had prostituted yourself to me, lied, and lived amongst us." He paused rubbing his head. "I couldn't believe what I was hearing, I felt like everything was a corrupt diseased lie. I wanted to run into the camp and start hacking away at you and those you were with, I nearly did. I was so close to throwing my own life away but then I stopped myself. I looked around the tree and saw the head of Decimus, my friend on a fucking stick Brenna with you and them laughing and joking about how you had killed him. I decided then that I would wait and that if somehow I lived through the hell of that place, I would take vengeance on you and everyone else that stood against us." His eyes were cold. "And here you are, right in front of me."

"If that's how you truly feel then kill me now." She raised her head and turned to the right revealing her neck. "Put an end to this living nightmare I have suffered since that night. If you feel that way, I don't want to live anymore." Tears continued to roll freely down her face though her words were calm. She had accepted whatever fate Varro had decided for her.

"I should report your return to the Legate." He said coldly.

She hesitated and then asked, "Did you tell them what happened, did you tell them that I killed Decimus?"

"I should have, I should have told them everything." He took a large gulp of wine. "But I couldn't," he said. "I was going to, you have no idea, but I couldn't."

She reached out to touch his hand on the table but he withdrew it. A silence fell between them. "Why didn't you tell them?" She finally asked.

He grimaced. "How would it look if I had told them? They would think me a fool, a fool taken in by a woman because she had opened her legs for me." She didn't look hurt by his words, she was too numb. "It wasn't because of some misguided love for you if that's what you're thinking. It was to save my own reputation. They would have destroyed me maybe even had me crucified for being such an utter cunt." He finished his drink. "Fiscus," he shouted, "more wine, no water this time."

"Yes sir and for the lady?" He asked.

"She hasn't touched hers yet." He told him, his eyes still fixed on Brenna.

"So what do you want to do?" She asked.

He shook his head. "How should I know? I thought you had died long ago or were fucking some hairy arsed barbarian bastard, I never thought I'd see you again." He put his head in his hands. "I don't know what to do. Do you have any idea what you were beginning to mean to me? I never thought I'd find someone like you here of all places and yet I did. I've never felt like I did with you, I've never experienced such warmth such…."

"Love?" She asked. He said nothing. "I felt it too." she said. "But I never told you. I told Tevelgus of course and at first he wasn't too happy that I loved a Roman but as he got to know you he came to accept it and that meant so much to me. I even talked of going to see your country and he asked if he could come and visit." She reached out again, this time he didn't pull his hand away." She sobbed. "My brother died fighting for you, not for Rome or the Emperor, but you Varro and your men. That's how much he had come to respect you and he paid for it with his life." She squeezed his hand. "Would I have let that happen if we were really on the side of the enemy? Would we have put ourselves in a position where there was even a chance of that happening? We helped you, we fought side by side. I freed you when you were captured, remember? Are these the actions of a traitor?"

For the first time since he had seen her, his face relaxed and the hard expression evaporated, did she see tears in his eyes now? His fingers caressed hers. "I want to believe you but my head is in a thousand broken pieces. I don't know what to think anymore."

"Are you still thinking of killing me?" She asked her face suddenly neutral.

"I didn't want to kill you Brenna, I never did," he paused, "that's a lie," he said, "of course I did but you know what I mean? What would you have thought if things had been the other way around?" He asked.

She pulled his hand towards her mouth and kissed his fingers. "I would have run into the camp swinging my blade if things had been reversed. If it had been me behind the tree with the head of my brother on a spike and I had heard you say what I had said, I would have killed you first without hesitation."

"So you see my problem?" He asked.

"Well you haven't killed me, yet" she paused, "and that's a good thing isn't it? You could always decide to chop me into little pieces later." She tried to smile.

"Don't make light of this Brenna." He warned her.

"I'm sorry." She said. "Where are your quarters? You must be tired if you have been awake all night."

He looked over to the direction of his barracks. "I wasn't awake all night, I had some sleep. I couldn't sleep now anyway, it's the last thing on my mind."

"We could just rest together then, I need a hot bath. You don't know how much I've craved a proper hot bath instead of a cold stream or small amounts of hot water to wash in from bowls." She smiled and for the first time he returned it.

"We can get a bath but not together." He said. She looked hurt.

"I'll settle for that, for now." She replied.

Dumnoc didn't have to work too hard to find his next target but he did have to wait for things to settle down after his first attack. The Romans surprisingly had not sought retribution but rumours were rife about what had happened to the occupants of the villa and Vertuna's family. All that remained of the building and compound was a burned out husk, within days an auxiliary cohort was sent to demolish it entirely. Perhaps the governor was attempting to keep the matter quiet and had decided that discretion was better than seeking revenge.

Three weeks after the abduction of Vertuna, his wife and children, Dumnoc had begun travelling further south to find another site that would be suitable for attack. The spring days were already getting warmer as he rode past the track to a farm where another villa stood. There were slaves, Britons working in the fields but they didn't raise their heads as he went by. He was aware of the freedmen watching over them, staring at him but he didn't catch their gaze as he didn't want to attract attention.

The building lay in a long sweeping valley where the crops would have shelter from the wind and the householder, one Vanutius Friscus, was said to enjoy working his slaves hard. A local settlement of five roundhouses had been destroyed because they just happened to be on the land that Friscus had chosen to take as his own. Because the Britons had objected, they were driven away, homeless. Friscus didn't have any children but lived with his wife, a skinny beady eyed woman with a large nose and bigger ambitions for her husband to rise up the social ladder.

When Dumnoc was free of the watching eyes, he looked again at the long straight path lined with thin trees leading to the villa. It was larger than his previous target but the layout was virtually the same. He glanced back towards the men and women working in the fields and saw one of the freedmen lash out at a young man with a whip.

"You dumb bastard." He heard the overseer shout, hitting the young man across the face. "Don't you know anything about crops?" He raised the whip again as his victim cowered. "If you put them in the ground like that, we'll have nothing to see for all our hard work, or is that what you intend?"

"Please sir," An older man begged approaching the freedman, "my son has not worked in the fields before, he knows nothing of this." He opened his hands to the ground.

"Get back to your own line," the guard shouted, "or you'll get this across your face as well." He raised the whip again and the father backed away. He looked over at Dumnoc now stationary, he had stopped his horse to watch the incident.

"Be on your way, this doesn't concern you." He shouted. Dumnoc smiled briefly and bowed his head, his eyes cold and nodded. He saw the guard was a thickset rotund man with a long dirty looking grey beard. His brown tunic was drenched with sweat and he had a deep scar running down through his right eyebrow and onto his cheek. Five other freedmen stopped what they were doing, their attention caught by the shouting. He clicked at his horse nudging it gently with his thighs and turned moving away. He heard more shouting behind him as he carried on along the track.

"How wrong you are." He said to himself smiling. "How wrong you are."

Later that night, he watched the villa from the side of the valley now in total darkness. He had made sure that the rest of his people were hidden away over the brow of the rise. Because of the last attack, he had decided to bring fewer warriors this time as he didn't want to risk falling upon a Roman patrol with what would have been a suspicious number of riders. Even then to avoid suspicion, they had slipped away from their settlements after dark and only in two's and three's. He had watched the compound from the same position for the last two nights to make sure of their routine. He didn't want to be caught out knowing that it would mean death for him and his warriors. He was surprised that no guards patrolled the grounds or walls, which he found strange considering the attack further north only a few weeks before. After waiting for a considerable time after the last light was extinguished, he got up and went to where the others waited.

As he led his small war band down the slope of the hill, he waved an arm to Drustan who split off with his seven raiders so they could approach the villa from the other side. As he didn't have the luxury of a lot of people this time, he had decided not to have any archers covering the building. He stopped at the end of the long straight track leading to the large wooden gates and paused to listen and watch in the gloom. There was no movement or discernible noise except for those associated with the night. He walked forward again, his boots crunching on the gravel surface. He moved off to the left and went along the grass at the side.

The walled villa was painted a similar colour to all the others he had seen and stood out against the dark night as they got closer. He turned every now and again to make sure his people were close behind, they were. Getting to the wall, they fanned out along its length then he heard a horse whinny from inside the stable and then a bang. It sounded as if the horse had kicked the door of its stable. He put a finger to his mouth warning the others to be quiet and waited for it to settle down again. Maybe the horse had heard or sensed them moving along the wall. When it was quiet he nodded to the man nearest him, then turned his back to the wall and crouched interlocking his fingers, Drustan stepped up and was pushed upwards onto the top of the wall. He heard a soft padding sound as he landed on the other side. Again he waited in case anyone had been disturbed inside.

After a short time he saw Drustan through the gap in the two gates as he struggled to lift the securing bar. It made a slight grating sound as he lifted it clear from its brackets and the gates opened. He led his warriors inside. His people spread out, covering the doors and windows where Friscus and his wife slept. They were in a room next to the freedmen, so they were close by in case of an emergency, but it wouldn't help them this night. Because he had fewer numbers he had decided previously not to cover the doors where the Britons quarters were, assuming they wouldn't cause them problems.

As war cries split the night and warriors forced their way inside the buildings, axes and swords smashing wood, Dumnoc heard shouting and screaming from inside followed by the sound of clashing swords. Shock and surprise however, had once again ensured that they quickly overpowered all those inside the villa. He discovered that scar face was the one who had tried to put up some resistance but was quickly knocked unconscious and dragged outside, the rest of his men were slaughtered in their beds. The slaves disturbed from their sleep by the attack stumbled outside and congregated together, milling about talking excitedly. Vanutius Friscus and his wife were taken to the middle of the large courtyard where scar face lay on the ground. Friscus, eyes wide looked about in horror physically shaking. His wife stared at their captors, defiance over her features.

"Bring some water from the well." Dumnoc ordered one of his men. He nodded quickly returning with a large wooden bucket that Dumnoc threw over scar face. He coughed and spluttered regaining consciousness, muttering and cursing, looking around.

"You," he turned, "father of the boy." Dumnoc pointed to the man who had come to the aid of his son, he stepped forward. Dumnoc pointed at the bloated and soaked freedman on the ground. "This man struck your son with a whip for no reason, now he can take his revenge."

The father replied, "My son is here but he is only sixteen summers old," he beckoned for him to leave his mother's side, "I don't know if he will want to or if I would want a man's life on his conscience, even if it is the life of an animal like him." The son stepped forward, brutal red lines of dry blood across his face. His father spoke to him quietly and his eyes widened, he rubbed at his face.

"He says he doesn't want this man's life." The father said. Dumnoc looked perplexed, "If he doesn't take action, I will."

The father looked at him his stare hardening, he stepped forward, "I didn't say that I wouldn't, this swine," he said pointing to the man on the ground, "has hurt many of us not just my son and deserves to pay for what he has done but then so does she." He pointed to Vanutius Friscus and the woman beside him. "That creature he calls a wife."

Friscus and his wife clearly couldn't understand what he said as he wasn't speaking Latin, but they could see the venom of his words and knew that the future didn't bode well for them.

"They could have treated us well, with some dignity but because our fate had determined that we were to be their slaves, they treated us like animals." The father continued, "We were fed on fat and gristle, the only bread we ever had was hard and often blue as it rotted." He looked back at Dumnoc. "That scar faced pig even helped himself to the young girls when he chose and raped them all except for the ugly one over there." He nodded to a girl who shrunk away behind her mother, her face covered in a red birth mark, her mouth distorted. "I will take revenge on this animal for all he has done, if I may?"

Dumnoc smiled, "You may." He turned his sword and offered him the hilt, which he accepted. The man on the ground began squealing and crying, begging.

"He," said the freedman, squirming on the stones, pointing to Friscus and his wife, "made us treat them that way." No-one responded. The father of the young man approached the pathetic figure and raised the sword. The freedman covered his head and curled into a ball. The sword swung down and sliced into his arm covering his head almost severing it completely from the rest of the limb, the man wailed, blood gushed out of the wound. Some of those watching turned away. He tried to raise his arm again over his head but the limb hung down at an awkward angle, he screamed as blood dripped freely onto his face. The father scythed down again and the edge of the blade cut deep into his victim's forehead with a wet hard crack. The eyes went wide in shock as his executioner tried to remove the blade, but it was stuck. He pulled on the handle and the man's head was yanked towards him, more blood spilled from the open wound, his arm at an odd angle. The blade was pulled free followed by a gush of dark blood. As he began to gurgle and his eyes rolled into the back of his head, the sword came down again one final time and almost cut his head off completely. The sharp blade cut through his neck severing arteries and spraying blood out onto those who watched, one former slave was sick at the sight of it. The man on the ground fell silent.

The father turned to Dumnoc, now spattered with blood, "Thank you my friend, whoever you are." He held the red stained sword out.

Dumnoc smiled again, "I am a warrior of Caradoc," he said, "Dumnoc is my given name, Dumnoc of the Catuvellauni." He turned. "You have two left." He said pointing to the two Romans. Friscus was now crying freely and had urinated on himself, warm piss evident on his bedclothes. His wife still stood defiant, hatred in her eyes.

"Maybe another would like the honour." The father said turning the sword around and pointing the hilt towards those who were still watching, people he had lived and suffered with in slavery. Most shook their heads, horror on their faces but a woman stepped forward as someone else behind her vomited.

"I will take the wife." She said. She walked forward accepting the handle of the sword. "My baby girl died because she wouldn't feed us properly and when she got ill, because we didn't have enough food, she refused to let me take her to the nearest fort for help."

She walked straight up to the Roman female and swung the large sword with two hands. The tip of the blade struck her on the left temple, slicing through bone and removing an eye. She staggered sideways screaming and fell to the ground grabbing at her head and face. The top of her nose was hanging loose over her mouth where the blade had sliced down through flesh. The former slave now attacked her in a frenzy hacking and stabbing, groaning with effort as she took vengeance for her daughter's death. The wife of Friscus had been reduced to a bloody mass of lacerated flesh and shattered bone in seconds. She was dead.

"Another." The female Briton said panting and staggering towards those who had witnessed her wrath. She held out the sword, her face and arms splattered with blood, a man stepped forward.

"My wife," he said looking at Friscus, "has made sure your whores soul is in the underworld, where she will exist forever in turmoil for what she has done to us." He took a step towards Friscus. "I will take your life now so you can be together in your suffering for all time." He took hold of the sword as Friscus collapsed onto the blood soaked ground crying and wailing. The Briton walked quickly towards him and took one almighty swing with the large blade and cut his head in half from the top down to his neck, he died instantly. Pink blooded grey brain cut neatly in two halves was now visible to those who watched as the sound of vomiting was heard again.

Dumnoc surveyed the scene of shattered and broken bodies before him, "Good but I would have taken a few slices of flesh from him first." He said. Turning he spoke to those standing around the walls.

"You are now all free to go where you wish. Our lands here are occupied but you will find sanctuary with Caradoc in the land of the Silures to the north. You can take the wagons and horses from here," He pointed towards the stable, "or you can try and find your families, it's up to you."

Some of those listening were still sobbing after what they had just witnessed. "If you stay in these lands and the Romans identify you from here, we will not be able to protect you. I cannot afford to let any of my people go with you if you go north so you will have to travel alone. I will give you a few moments to gather your belongings if you have any, then the building will be torched and we will leave."

The father of the young man stepped forward and held out his hand, Dumnoc took his wrist. "Thank you Dumnoc of the Catuvellauni, we will never forget what you have done for us this night. You have given us another chance of life, how can we ever repay you?"

"Payment is neither asked for or required my friend. Now gather your things quickly and leave this place. I recommend you travel north and make haste." Dumnoc replied.

The man tuned and spoke to the former slaves. "You all know me and my family, like you, we have suffered at this place under them," his eyes flicked to the bloodied mass of destroyed corpses. "My family and I will travel north to seek this Caradoc in the lands of the Silures as Dumnoc has said. I know the paths and have been there before as I used to trade with them. You are all welcome to join us if you wish; if not then I bid you a safe journey wherever you go. Think quickly and carefully because the Romans will not like what has happened here this night."

He walked to his wife and son and then they went to find their belongings. Hushed conversations took place amongst all the others, who quickly followed them.

As Dumnoc's warriors lit torches a short time later, the former slaves left the villa on wagons and horses. They had all decided to look for a new life with Caradoc in the mountains. The buildings of the villa were searched one last time and anything of value was taken. The villa was then set on fire and abandoned.

Chapter Four

The sun shone down warming the three men as they slowly approached the harbour on horseback at the end of the estuary. They had travelled for two days riding north taking their time and stopping at settlements along the way. Encouraged by the response of those they had spoken with, they had decided to go further and have a look at the garrison that was being established at what the Romans were calling Deva. It was situated inland along the river where they could establish a reliable supply route. It had all the hallmarks of Isca in the south located on the River Exe, where the Second Augusta were garrisoned. Deva however, was manned by the Twentieth Legion and as the three riders approached the harbour they saw the first signs of their occupation, a flag bearing a boar, the insignia of the Twentieth.

Caradoc, Ardwen and Brennus knew that getting so close to a slumbering beast was always dangerous, but after many conversations and debates about whether it was worth the risk, they had decided it was. They wanted to see for themselves just how far along the enemies defences were, what their disposition was and how the local people were responding to them. Caradoc and Ardwen had asked Brennus to accompany them, not only was he very useful to have around if things went wrong but he was also Ardwen's half-brother on his father's side. Two huge Roman Triremes sat at anchor in the harbour, their large sails fluttering gently in the breeze. Next to them were two supply vessels, one was being unloaded, whilst the other already looked empty.

"They probably came together with one of the Triremes or both escorting them," Caradoc said, "it's a pity we have nothing more than small fishing vessels then we could take the war to them at sea."

"We can still sink them when they get here." Brennus replied. "The problem would be slipping past the guards and getting on-board. The longer we leave it and they establish themselves, the harder it's going to be."

"We'll have a good look round and then decide what we are going to do." Ardwen said. "For the time being we're just three traders looking to see what we can offer our Roman friends and what they can do for us."

As they got to a more established track they watched as the unloading continued on the far side of the river, barrels, sacks, wooden crates and amphorae were lined up in neat rows as they were taken ashore. Carts and wagons waited patiently as the first supplies were loaded on to them before being taken to the newly established garrison, and then others would be distributed around the region. Caradoc and his allies knew how the pattern worked as the Roman plague spread its arms.

On the way north they had passed an enemy fort that had been established on a high rocky outcrop now miles to the south. It lay a few miles inside the border of the Cornovii tribe and over looked the mountains of the Deceangli to the west. It was a natural position for a fort, rising some four hundred feet high maybe five hundred from sea level. The main fortification covered only a small area at the flat top, probably three hundred paces square but it was secured by hundreds, thousands of dark tree trunks that made up its walls. Others lined the slopes on one side as they ran down to lower land in a great wooden arc. It ran for some length on the flat lowland before sweeping back up to the small fort on top of the outcrop. On the far side facing north, was a sheer cliff face where trees still somehow grew out of the steep rocky side. The three men had noted the small garrison located there with interest, aware that it was secluded by some miles from the main garrison fortress at Deva. Bees Stone as it was called, would make an ideal target.

As they got closer to the harbour they saw more evidence that the local people had accepted the occupiers, or at best were living alongside them. Roundhouses ran parallel with the river all the way to the enormous fort. Fortunately few people took any notice of the riders as they walked past and went about their business as if living alongside Romans was a normal way of life. Children ran, chasing each other as skins dried outside some of the houses, men talked discussing their crops or livestock, some nodding in greeting as they went by and door skins were hooked open due to the warmth of the day. It all seemed normal, and that was what Caradoc found most disturbing.

"Let's have a chat with them," he nodded at a group of five men who stood watching them approach, "see what they make of things."

"Greetings strangers," a large surly looking man said stepping forward, "what can we do for you?" He looked back at the men he had been talking with.

Caradoc smiled and brought his horse to a halt a few feet from him. "I am Morcant," he said, "we've travelled here to see what trade can be done if any. We have two hundred head of cattle and the same in sheep at our homelands to the south."

"I am Nynniaw," the serious looking man replied, "I am the elder here and make those decisions for the people. What would you want in return?" Caradoc studied him. He was clearly well fed with a bulbous stomach threatening to burst through his light beige smock. He wore reddish leggings and boots that came up shin high and stopped just before the knees, wrapped around his calves.

Caradoc got down off his horse slowly so as not to pose a threat. The last thing he wanted was a confrontation with these men that would no doubt bring the Romans running, "I was thinking of trading with your guests to be honest, I hear they pay well in gold, is that right?" He pointed at the ships in the harbour.

"The Romans eh?" He smiled. "Well I'm sure they would be interested in so much livestock. They are interested in everything else after all, where have you come from exactly, did you say?"

"We're from the lands of the Dubunni," Ardwen lied getting down off his own horse, Brennus stayed mounted eyeing the man and those stood behind him. "We trade with the Second Augusta there and are looking to expand." Ardwen added.

"Really?" The man said as if unconvinced. "Well I'm sure I could arrange an appointment with one of their officials if you wish. I'm certain they would be more than happy to speak to you but I don't want you stepping on our trade with them. As long as whatever you propose doesn't affect us, I don't see a problem." He turned as if to gauge the thoughts of the men, they nodded their assent. "Obviously there would be a fee for arranging such a deal, a cut of any deal struck." He smiled.

"Of course friend, I'm sure we could come to some arrangement." Caradoc replied knowing that no such deal would ever be struck and wishing he could cut the fat man's throat. "Now is there somewhere we could get some refreshment? It's been a long couple of days."

"Yes, yes follow me." Nynniaw said turning. "You can stable your horses and we'll take you to where you can have your fill of food and brew, as much as you like and all for little expense."

Brennus got down off his horse and they led them to a corralled area where the locals had their own horses. A young man came out of a roundhouse near the gate and Nynniaw arranged for stabling. Caradoc and his men removed their saddles which the young man took inside the roundhouse after which the horses were led into the field. A few of those already there came over to see who the new arrivals were.

"We can arrange for lodging if you wish?" Nynniaw said. "I don't know how long you intend to stay but it may take a while for one of the administrators to come and see you, I can't guarantee it will be today, we have a roundhouse for guests you can use."

"That will be fine, we're in no rush." Caradoc replied. "Besides it will give us time to see how things are here with your guests. I hear they are intending to push into other territories to establish more encampments and roads."

Nynniaw replied, "Yes I suppose they are, they've already taken over the slate quarry to the west and I hear they're digging into the salt mine further south somewhere." He led them further along the track past other thatched houses until they got to an area that was distinctly starting to look different. Men wore togas and had short hair, buildings were made of wood and groups of soldiers marched in sets of eight or more.

"It took some getting used to but the men of the Twentieth Legion aren't bad. We still have problems from time to time but they're showing us different methods of farming and medicine. Things are improving for everyone." Nynniaw said. He took them to a stall further along the street with a broad bench outside. Amphorae vessels were propped up against a corner.

"What will it be gentlemen?" Asked a man from behind the counter, speaking with a strange accent, he was about thirty years of age and obviously Roman. Caradoc studied his face and clothing. He had intelligent eyes and a pleasant demeanour. He wore an almost white coloured toga that was belted at the waist. He wore no blade or dagger.

"I have wine fresh off the boat," The man continued as he held out his hand indicating the amphorae, or if you want something more local, I can arrange that as well?"

Brennus looked at Ardwen and Caradoc, "Wine, not watered I think," The other two nodded agreeing, "Three then."

The man behind the stall put four kiln made cups onto the bench, Caradoc picked one up. Of late he was used to using wooden cups or those made from horn although they had previously had Roman made drinking vessels before the invasion, when the Catuvellauni still traded with them, but that was a few years ago. It was smooth and cold to the touch, he examined it expecting it to be engraved with ornate hunting scenes or something else but it was plain. The stall holder picked up a medium sized amphora and filled their cups, clear golden liquid poured into them. He put the base of the jug into a hole drilled into the bench so they could help themselves.

He saw Caradoc looking at the cups. "They're locally produced." He said. "The clay along the estuary is just the right consistency." If you go further along the river past the garrison you'll see where it's found." He smiled at Caradoc. "If you want anything else, just ask." He smiled again and went into the back of the stall.

"We thought they would treat us badly when they first arrived," Nynniaw said. "Well you hear all sorts of tales don't you? Raping women, killing the men or taking them for slaves but to be honest we haven't experienced anything like that. Yes there are a few that are unhappy with their presence and they want their tribute obviously in the way of crops and slaves, but if they leave us alone I'm happy. I just don't understand why some resist, we can all get along."

"Isn't them being here enough?" Brennus cut in. He looked Nynniaw directly in the eye.

"We don't want trouble here." He said taking a mouth full of wine. "We're content as long as they leave us to get on with life." He looked around. "And generally they do." He wiped his mouth and put his cup down. Turning to Caradoc he said. "I'll see if I can find an administrator and see what can be done about the livestock you want to trade." He stood. "In the meantime please enjoy our hospitality."

He left taking his friends with him. Brennus finished his cup of wine and half whispered. "Did you hear the way he said 'our hospitality' they've accepted the occupiers already, I doubt we'd get much help here if we decided to attack Deva. These sheep would probably fight on their side instead of helping us."

"They aren't like us that's for sure," Caradoc said, "but I wouldn't condemn so quickly though. We were given no choice but to fight. They came looking for us because we wouldn't bow to them and wanted to live independently. These people didn't have the same problems and probably rarely saw anything other than goods or trading by the sound of things." He finished his wine and filled their cups. "We'll speak with this administrator and get a lay of the land and see how things are from their point of view, you never know we might end up the same as these people." He smirked.

Ardwen said. "That will never happen for one thing I doubt they'll ever forgive us for giving the Second Augusta a bloody nose and we wouldn't want to live like this anyway, second to their whims and orders and paying tribute."

"If these people choose to live with them then as far as I'm concerned they are as bad as them and will be treated as such." Brennus said.

"If they ally themselves with them then yes you're right but if they have chosen to live like this, so they are not destroyed then we shouldn't hold that against them." Caradoc said. "We'll see how things are but for the time being our best target is the fort to the south in Cornovii territory, if we can hit that hard it will be a good start. With Dumnoc attacking in the south, it will unbalance them and they won't know where they're safe. A major victory is something we need though like this garrison at Deva. But in the meantime hitting their patrols and villas will have to suffice. Impatience will get us nowhere except dead, patience is an ally and we have to use it well just as they do."

"I understand what you're saying Caradoc." Brennus said, "It just turns my stomach to see our people welcoming them as they have."

"It does mine as well but for the time being we'll enjoy our wine and find out as much as we can. Why don't you go and see if you can find somewhere for us to stay tonight, that house the fat one spoke of?" Caradoc asked Brennus.

"Me?" He asked. "I'd prefer to wait until Nynniaw gets back and taste more of this wine, he said he knows somewhere, he can show us where it is."

"Alright but in the meantime no more talk about what our intentions are, understood?" Caradoc asked.

"Don't worry I don't intend to risk our lives so easily." Brennus answered.

The days of confinement in the garrison had finally passed and Varro was able to ride free to a degree with his men once more. He had come to terms with the death of Decimus as best he could and realised that Brenna had no choice in the matter, if she hadn't taken his life, she would be dead also. He didn't like the circumstances of how it had come about or why but there was nothing he could do about it.

With all their equipment checked, cleaned and polished and any defects replaced, they rode south to liaise with the forts, villas and settlements to make sure everything was in order. With no specific plans to march against the Silures for the time being, they were to consolidate the ground they had already taken, which for small squads like his own could prove equally as dangerous as open warfare, if not more so.

He had already got used to the men who had replaced those who had died when the Second Augusta had made an expedition into the west under Vespasian. The legion of men together with their auxiliaries had been badly mauled and their humiliation was compounded when the survivors were only saved by the intervention of the Twentieth. Vespasian himself had been injured after being hit a by an arrow and had returned to Rome and subsequently retired from the army.

Riding with Varro was Optio Julius Grattius who was from Sicily, the port town of Syracuse on the south east coast. He was considered a veteran who had been in the army for nearly as long as Varro, twelve years. He was from equestrian stock from a prominent family in Sicily but had voluntarily joined the army as a legionary. As well as being an excellent rider he was also a good archer and carried his bow with him wherever he went. The other two members of Varro's part of the *contubernium* eight man squad, were legionaries Balbus and Verus. Leading the remainder was Optio Gaius Marius with legionaries Facilis, Eprius and Maenius. As they were carrying out a routine patrol they didn't plan to split the unit as they would ordinarily if they were scouting ahead of a marching column.

Varro had been ordered to ride south and to check on one villa in particular, it was owned by Vanutius Friscus, who lived there with his wife, a number of freedmen and their slaves working the land and raising crops. The local fort had heard nothing of them for some weeks and had been too busy with their own duties to investigate further. After the attack on another villa in the region where the occupants had disappeared completely, and the freedmen were killed, Varro wouldn't be taking any chances.

It took them the best part of the day to get to the large valley where the farm was located, they hadn't seen anything untoward on the way and the villa looked quiet as they surveyed it from a distance but that in itself was suspicious. If everything had been normal, the workers would be out in the fields but there were none. The usually light coloured walls looked dark and burnt.

"We'll go down as far as the external gate where the long straight path starts towards the villa." Varro said. "Once there Marius, you and your men can wait and the rest of us will go and have a look, understood." The men acknowledged their order as Varro clicked Staro further down the slope. Nothing moved within the buildings of the villa that they all watched as they approached, nor was there any movement in the surrounding countryside. At the gate Optio Marius and his three men stopped whilst the other four continued slowly forward, their horses barely moving.

Varro's eyes scanned the walls of the compound. The main gates he saw were wide open. He could make out something on the ground inside but from where he was, he couldn't identify the shape. Twenty paces from the entrance he stopped and listened but there was nothing to hear except the sound of the country, birds in the distance; the whisper of a slight breeze and the breathing of the horses. Listening again, he heard the sound of flies, lots of flies and knew that was a bad sign. He debated whether or not to dismount and walk the rest of the way but decided against it knowing that if there were hostiles inside, they stood a better chance of getting away if they were mounted. He nudged Staro forward again, pausing at the gate one last time. He could now see a tangle of bodies on the floor and dark stained grass with stones underneath where they lay. Then the smell hit him, pungent, rich and sweet, the smell of rotting flesh. The soldiers quickly removed their neck scarfs and put them over their noses and mouths.

The remains of three people lay inside, hacked to death, two men and a woman. He looked back to make sure Marius and his men were alright, the optio raised his hand. Varro dismounted and led Staro to the stable but it was empty except for hay, presumably put there for the now missing horses. The rest of the men brought their own mounts inside.

"Looks like we've found the illustrious Friscus and his wife and one of their men I'd say looking at those injuries." Grattius said, tying his horse to a wooden fence post.

"Let's go and have a look round, we'll leave the horses here for now, Marius will let us know if something happens." Varro said.

Walking back outside they examined the corpses, they still had their hands tied behind their backs, it was clear they had been executed. Varro pointed to the slaves' quarters and then at Balbus and Verus who went off to check them. He looked at Grattius and nodded for him to follow as he made his way to the charred residential part of the villa.

He put his hand to his nose trying to stop the smell of burnt flesh and whatever else had been inside, before it was set on fire. The window skins were none existent now, presumably they had caught fire as well, and the walls were pitch black and covered in soot. The only thing that was recognisable but had partially melted, was an old iron standing candle frame, it was bent over where it had succumbed to the heat. Varro led the way into what would have been the freedmen's quarters, inside were the skeletal remains of at least six bodies, most of the flesh was gone except for a few meaty bits and black scorched bones remained.

"We'll ride to the nearest fort and report our findings. They can come out and bury the bodies." Varro said. "I don't want us hanging about round here any longer than we have to, we're too few and exposed if whoever did this returns." He walked outside again and into the sunshine where the air was clearer.

"Nothing in the slaves quarters sir, they're empty." Balbus reported.

"I didn't think there would be. I imagine that whoever attacked the villa either took them along or set them free. This is the second attack of this type and I would guess that at least twenty disgruntled Britons were involved." Varro said to his men. "Come on let's get the horses and get out of here."

"Do you think it's locals that are responsible for this sir?" Grattius asked.

"I don't know it's either a few men slipping away at night or some group coming into the area, either way I'd have thought the patrols would have picked them up. We'll go to the fort and let them know what we've found. We're going to have to do something about this that's for sure."

As the daylight was beginning to fade, they sighted the fort, *Statio Deventiasteno* Station at the narrows of Deventia, a few miles to the north. It lay on a slight rise amongst flatter ground and was very small, probably only covering about two acres all told. The land around it had been cleared and it stood out against the forests surrounding it, an unnatural feature. Two soldiers stood guard above the main gate and acknowledged the visitors as they rode towards them two abreast along the worn path. The gates were opened and they went inside where a legionary came to greet them, and to take care of the horses. Varro saw that the fort was of typical century layout containing four small barrack blocks for the men, a stables, the *latera praetorii* in the centre contained the *principa* headquarters block and the officer's quarters in the *praetorium*, adjacent to the barracks was a granary where just outside there was a man sized grind stone and mess facilities. To the rear of the compound was an area set aside for livestock where pigs, chickens and a few sheep lived next to each other in separate pens. The inside of the walls to the exterior, which were originally traditional wooden posts, were re-enforced with thick layers of compacted mud and every twenty feet there were ladders leading to the walkways where the guards patrolled. Over the main gate was a small covered area big enough for four men at a squeeze, where those on duty could shelter from the weather. Four small scorpion torsion catapults were stationed on each corner in the event of attack. They were covered with a wooden roof to provide shelter for their crews that would usually consist of two men on each.

"Centurion Varro!" A voice shouted. He pulled on his reins and caused Staro to stop and leapt down, handing his reins to the soldier.

"Centurion Cammius." Varro said offering his hand. "I didn't know you were in command here, I thought you were still at the garrison."

The two men had known each other for some time but had only met at briefings and in passing. Cammius was a century centurion, infantry born and bred from the fourth cohort and wasn't usually in a position to mix with the cavalry as he spent most of his time with his men.

They shook hands, "No, I've been here for the last month living in the middle of nowhere with the men of my century. It's incredible how much more you find out about each other when you're so close." He smiled. "Too close as far as some are concerned." Cammius smiled, he wore just his white tunic but still had his sword and dagger attached to his belt.

"Vestius," he shouted to a legionary, "make sure you look after the men's horses and then get them some refreshments, I'll be in my office with Centurion Varro here if you want me for anything."

"Sir." Vestius acknowledged.

"Come on, I'll show you where I spend most of my day." He turned and led Varro into his office. It was well lit by three large windows. On the wall behind his desk were large maps showing different sections of Britannia, one showed the country overall, another the region where the Second Augusta were at Isca Dumnoniorum, and the last map showed the area around the fort itself detailing the south east of the country and the land pertinent to the forts area of responsibility.

Cammius sat down and indicated for Varro to take a seat at the opposite side of the desk. Vestius knocked at the door.

"Excuse me sir, your wine."

"Gods balls that was quick Vestius, I hope you've looked after those horses and Varro's men first?" He asked as the legionary handed him a medium sized amphora.

"Tublius is seeing to them sir, he loves em, the horses that is not the men, wants to join the cavalry one day he said. He's already taken the men to get some food at the cook house." Vestius answered bowing slightly and leaving the officers in peace.

Cammius poured himself and Varro a drink into plain brown pot cups. "So what did you find at the villa?"

Varro looked at him with little surprise, Cammius added, "I assumed that was your first port of call as we haven't seen anything of that strange little fella Friscus." He raised his eyebrows. "Is he dead?"

Varro took a drink, "I think he is, there were three corpses in the courtyard, hacked to death and more inside the building itself, but they'd been set on fire so there wasn't much left of them. One of the three outside was female and I assume was the wife of Friscus. There was no sign of the slaves and all the horses and wagons were gone from the stables. So, any of our people are dead and all the slaves have vanished, they could be anywhere by now." He took a sip of wine. "Mm that's the good stuff. I thought you'd be on the vinegar and piss out here on the frontier."

Cammius laughed, "It's not that bad although the thought of being a full day's ride from Isca keeps you alert I can tell you. We're just over sixty five miles from help," he looked at the maps then back at Varro, "but obviously you know that because you rode here." He looked back at the map showing Isca. "If we were manned with a few century's as I should be, we'd be able to cover more ground with patrols but I hear the hairy bastards are up to their games all over the province. It means that places like this won't be up to strength until things quieten down or we get reinforced, which is unlikely to happen for some time."

"So how are you finding it here?" Varro asked and then finished his wine. Cammius indicated for him to help himself and he filled his cup.

"As things go to be honest not too bad, these little fortlet's are quite cosy and as I said, you get to know the men a little better." Cammius began. "We've got another two weeks to push and then we're heading back to Isca, most of the men can't wait. Apart from patrols we're obviously confined to barracks, inside its guard duty, training and not much else. The locals come and have a nosey about but these rural areas have no real system of Government so we're left to our own devices. It's a shame because I'm told there's good fishing to be had at the local river."

"We passed it on the way. Do you have much contact with the auxiliaries at Restormel?" Varro asked.

"Daily as per orders but they're in a smaller place than us would you believe." He pointed to the map. "The forts were put here originally to keep an eye on any movement up and down the peninsula which is all well and good, or it would be if we a had a string of them from coast to coast but of course we haven't yet, early days they say. Constantly the hairy bastards are moving from north to south or vice-versa and we can't tell who they are really, friend or foe, or what they're up to. They could be out hunting legitimately or going off to ambush a patrol or attack a villa. The sooner we take all their weapons away the better it will be except for those allied to us, but can we trust them? Maybe things will change now that Friscus has met a grisly end." He filled his own cup. "Mind you it doesn't surprise me it happened to be honest, word was, he was treating his slaves like shit and threw a load of Britons off the land he took. Ripped their settlement down and booted them off the land with the help of his freedmen. Sounded like a complete arsehole to me. You can't expect to come onto someone else's land and behave like that. Some people have no concept of what they've let themselves in for or who they're dealing with."

"I'm sure the Governor won't be happy. Things had just about settled down around here and within the space of a few days we've lost two villas, the families that ran them and all the slaves that went with them." Varro took another sip of wine.

"I take it you're staying here tonight?" Cammius asked. "There's no point in setting off back now we're already losing the light eh?" He swung his head to the window. "May as well have some food, some more wine and get a good night's sleep, set off first thing." He looked back at Varro. "What do you say?"

"Good idea because tomorrow we'll be heading south before we go back to the garrison anyway, see what the locals have to say about the attacks, nothing I should imagine but the question has to be asked." Varro said taking more wine.

"Vestius." Cammius turned and shouted. The legionary came scuttling in.

"Yes sir." He said.

"Centurion Varro and his men will be staying here for the night. Can you arrange bedding and accommodation for them? We've plenty of room eh?" He said.

"Yes sir." Vestius answered.

"Oh and how about one of those pigs? They are ready for eating aren't they? Bloody things think they own the place anyway and our replacements will be bringing their own stock so we may as well have a feast. Have Cornelius slaughter the fattest one there and tell him to get it roasting on the spit." Cammius ordered.

"Sir." Vestius could be heard answering as he shuffled out again.

"That's very good of you." Varro remarked, "The men will enjoy that."

"Think nothing of it, that's one of the many benefits of being in a place like this you get to choose what and when to eat unlike back at the garrison." He looked around the room, "Has some benefits a place like this see?" He finished his wine. "Come on I'll show you around."

Varro finished his wine and followed Cammius out into the evening sunshine. He saw a thick set legionary leading a fat pig with a carrot into one of the sheds. He assumed that was Cornelius with the night's dinner.

"I'll show you the view from up above the front gate although we're only on a slight rise you'd be surprised at the view." Cammius said proudly. "The engineers did a good job choosing this location." He led the way to the gate and then up a fairly steep ladder banked on the rampart. The two legionaries on duty jumped to attention when they saw him.

"At ease, at ease gentlemen, you'll sprain something leaping up like that." Cammius said laughing. The men smiled and relaxed. "You see what I mean?" He said to Varro pointing out into the countryside.

He was right about the view, they could see for miles in both directions, to the east Varro could make out the coast. "If you look over there," Cammius said pointing, "you see that huge bushy tree sticking up from the rest?" He asked.

Varro adjusted his position. "Well," Cammius said, "that's where our auxiliary friends are, four miles away as the crow flies. They can see the coast like we can," he turned to the sea, "well just anyway. Do you see what I mean about more forts? If we just had three more fortlets, we would see everything that moved down here." He looked around the base, "Mind you that would be doing it properly eh? What do we know we're only soldiers after all?" He smiled. "Come on I'll show you rest of the place."

Later with the unfortunate pig cooked and still roasting, the officers sat at a separate table from the men and dinner began in a room that had been cleared for the occasion. Cammius made a toast to the Second Augusta and Mithras and everyone stood repeating his words. Sixty of the men detached to Statio Deventiasteno were present, the rest were either on the walls or on standby in the small guardroom. They would eat a duty supper later, no doubt consisting of lots of leftover pork. The roasting pig was slowly turned on a large spit by Cornelius as soldiers helped themselves to large pieces of meat using their daggers. Most had served themselves and put fresh vegetables on their plates and were settling down to eat when they were disturbed.

"Sir, sir." Vestius shouted running into the large room.

"What is it Vestius? This had better be good I'm just about to tuck into this food and I'm starving. I haven't eaten since breakfast you know?" He looked back at his plate, his mouth watering.

"The signal torches have been lit at Restormel." Vestius reported.

Varro looked at Cammius. He knew that signal flares were only lit in the case of an emergency. "Fuck it." Cammius said picking up a chunk of pork and stuffing it into his mouth. "Come on Varro let's take a look, it's probably nothing, bloody auxiliaries." The men sat round the tables looked at the centurions expectantly.

"You men stay here for now, if need be I'll call you out, no point in us all going hungry." He got up with Varro following. "Vestius you're with us." The legionary nodded. Outside the smell of burning wood was faint but clearly discernible in the dark night air. The optio of the guard had called out the reserves from the guardroom and most were now standing looking towards Restormel. Cammius and Varro ran towards the nearest ladder.

"All round defensive positions men, eyes open, mouths shut unless you have anything to report." He ordered, "Come on move it and get on those fucking scorpions just in case eh? It could be a diversion remember and if you're all stood with your dicks facing in one direction, the hairy bastards could be scaling the walls opposite." Cammius shouted whilst climbing the ladder with Varro behind him. Scurrying boots were heard elsewhere running to get into an all-round defensive position.

"Now Optio Travelus," Cammius asked reaching the top of the ladder, "what's so important that my dinner has been disturbed, there's some tasty pork on my plate I'll have you know. What are those damned auxiliaries up to?"

He didn't need to get a reply to see what the problem was. Looking out over the now dark countryside, he could see that it wasn't just the signal flares that were alight, the whole fort was ablaze.

"Fucking hades hole." Cammius said as he saw flames rising into the night sky.

"Looks like the entire place is on fire." Varro said.

"The signal flares were lit first, they must have had time to do that before the rest of the place went up sir." Vestius said.

"Well I would say that whoever took care of that miserable shit Friscus is at Restormel right now." He looked at Travelus. "Call them out Optio. I want every man with full kit on the walls as soon as possible, armour, pilums and sharp teeth as well." Cammius said.

"Sir." Trevalus said acknowledging the order and running to the edge of the wall to shout instructions down.

"There's nothing we can do for them I'm afraid." Cammuis said looking at Varro. "You haven't got enough men and I haven't got enough horses for us to make a difference if they're under full scale attack." He looked back at the flames in the distance. "There's a full complement of auxiliaries over there, the same amount of men we have here, only they can help themselves now, the poor bastards." The flames grew and the fire was reflected off the watching faces.

"Even if we went out as a full Century with you in support we could get caught out in the open and cut to pieces." He said to Varro.

"I'm afraid you're right, all we can do now is to wait for sunrise." Varro said confirming his fellow centurion's words. "Mithras, please help them."

Dumnoc had chosen his target carefully and had decided on the smaller fort of the two, Restormel. He had managed to gather one hundred and twenty warriors together for the assault and knew there was a risk of re-enforcements coming from the larger installation only four miles away but the enemy wouldn't know what they faced. He had ultimately thought that although the flames of Restormel would be seen and no doubt their signal indicating that they were being assaulted, he knew the Romans would be wary of venturing out in the dark where they could be ambushed. Nonetheless he had positioned a proportion of his force directly in-between the forts in case the enemy came to the assistance of the Restormel soldiers.

He had waited until the last patrol had returned to Restormel before launching his attack. The fort was small and only a few miles away from the larger installation where full time legionaries were stationed, so he knew re-enforcing this fort in the dark wasn't viable, it was another reason for deciding upon this one first. Another was that it contained auxiliaries, which he hoped wouldn't fight to the death or would perhaps surrender. He had observed the fort for a number of days as he always did when carrying out a reconnaissance of a potential target and at one point had walked straight into a patrol who asked what his business was in the area. He had already prepared for such an eventuality and had produced a rod and line and said he was going fishing. He was from the local settlement and had lived here all his life. The patrol had searched him for weapons and upon not finding anything except for a dagger had allowed him on his way.

It was the same patrol he had watched entering the fort as the gates were closed behind them now. He had seen the signal flares and knew that if they were lit before he could get enough people inside, the chances of reinforcements rose significantly, but he was still willing to take the chance that the full time soldiers wouldn't leave the safety of their walls. Subsequently he had waited until all was quiet except for two soldiers walking the walls, but they were quickly subdued as the first of his warriors had quietly scaled the defences. Here the ground outside wasn't as well cleared and sterile as the land outside the legionaries fort and scrub and wild plants had allowed them to approach on their stomachs, all twenty of them from the opposite side from where the two guards stood talking together. One auxiliary had been dispatched immediately, his throat cut, the other had run and managed to light the signal flare using a torch, he was killed within seconds afterward.

It was too late to stop another small group of warriors from getting inside Restormel and opening the gates. Dark figures quietly scurried forward from the cover of trees and stormed inside. A shout went up in Latin, followed by the clash of swords which was brief. The fighting inside was carried out clinically and those on duty were silenced as they ran from their guardroom but not before alerting those caught sleeping. Those disturbed from their slumber however, didn't have time to get their chainmail on. Most were caught inside the barracks where they could do nothing but eventually barricade themselves in. The wooden buildings containing the men were set on fire and burnt instantly, killing the men inside through smoke inhalation before the flames torched their flesh. The armoury was looted of pilums, swords, shields and bows and three scorpion crossbows were taken. The livestock was quickly herded out of the fort and allowed to roam free. They would be rounded up later if possible. Dumnoc didn't have time to mess about herding them away. He watched as the small exodus of warriors and weapons left the burning fort. He saw one of his lookouts approach from the direction of the other Roman emplacement.

"They were alerted and called to arms but they haven't left. They are just standing watching the flames." He reported.

Dumnoc smiled, "Good," he said, "now let's move on the larger fort."

The majority of the stolen weapons were loaded onto wagons and driven away, they would be buried so they could be used later; some were taken by the warriors who ran towards the next target. Dumnoc urged calm in his people as they jogged through the dark night, the flames of the fort behind them casting shadows everywhere, acrid smoke getting lighter.

The warriors stopped inside the cover of the trees looking up at Station Deventia. From this distance they knew the defenders wouldn't risk wasting their ammunition as they didn't have a clear target. The helmeted silhouettes of the soldiers on the walls stood around stationary, waiting for the attack they must have known was coming.

"Begin the preparations we discussed earlier." Dumnoc ordered to those around him, a group of men ran back further into the trees. "We have as long as it takes so there's no hurry. Their garrison at Isca Dumnoniorium won't even know there's anything wrong until their patrol doesn't return tomorrow and by then it will be too late. Then they'll wait another day before sending more of their legionaries out to find them." He said to no-one in particular. Within a short time he heard the reassuring crack of axes begin as they struck tree trunks in preparation for the next phase of his attack. It was his most ambitious plan so far and knew that if he could destroy both forts, and kill all those within, it would send out a message of hope to the repressed population of Britons not only on the peninsula but across the island as a whole.

Chapter Five

As Caradoc sank into the well filled straw mattress and drifted into a deep sleep, his mind's eye took him away from the present and far away into the past. To happier, safer times, when he still went by the name Caratacus or Cara as his friends and family called him. He felt different in this world, younger, fresh and unburdened by responsibility, almost carefree. At fourteen years of age, when his chores permitted, he was able to roam the tribal lands with his brothers and play, hunt and fish, talk to girls and explore the world around him. Tog and Ad, his brothers, were always close by in those days, as the three boys discovered the land around them and the people who shared it. For the first time in their lives there was no conflict with other tribes. King Cunobelin, their father, had sought treaties with surrounding lands and even strengthened ties with Rome with trade flowing freely to the far off empire in the east.

The three boys had left their roundhouse earlier that day armed with little more than water skins, bows and daggers, intent once more on exploring and hunting. They wore simple short sleeved beige tunics and crisscrossed blue and black coloured leggings, their sandals secured by leather straps wrapped around their lower legs. When they had set out early after breakfast, Cara had noticed for the first time that year, a slight chill on his exposed skin and wondered if they needed more clothing, but the day's sun had soon warmed them, and he felt more comfortable in no time.

His siblings were a little older than him but not by much, although physically he was shorter by half a foot. Ad and Tog were almost men now, they had begun to change, Tog the largest of the three boys had developed muscular arms and facial hair, his voice was deeper, whereas Ad was taller, thinner and wore his fair hair short in the style of the traders from the east. Tog's longer style was more common and drawn together at the back, tied into a pony tail that drifted down between his shoulder blades. Cara often wondered how his brothers were so different from each other, with him sat in the middle, although as personalities went, he was much closer to Tog. He often prayed to the gods that he would be closer to him in strength as well as appearance, but for now no matter what he did his arms remained sinewy. He rubbed at his chin as they rode along wishing to feel bristles but only found the short soft fluff that had started to appear recently, how he wished he were a man.

"Don't worry brother," Ad said guessing his thoughts, "you'll be cursed soon enough with a manly beard and find yourself wishing you weren't believe me."

He frowned but before he could reply Ad continued, "I prefer to have a clean face although," he said cupping his chin, "it hurts sometimes scraping it off every other day." He raised his head and looked around at both brothers as if to emphasise the point. "Father would have to shave every day he says, so he keeps a beard but I doubt I ever will it's so much cleaner like this."

"That's fine, as long as you want to look like a twelve year old girl." Tog said grinning, "Not very, what's the term, warrior-like, though is it?" He smiled at Cara. "Imagine facing an enemy like that, they'd just laugh at you."

Ad smiled, "Well it's a good thing we're all different." He said, "I like a smooth face," he added as he felt his own again, "you wouldn't want a hairy girl would you?" He said to no-one in particular.

"And there was me beginning to think you didn't like girls at all." Tog said as he led them down the track towards the outskirts of the next village. "With the affection you show for the Romans, I thought you might want to marry one of them, men n'all!" He chuckled as he steered his horse along the track.

Ad smiled again, "Oh dear brother, we are in a funny mood today aren't we? We can actually learn a great deal from our friends across the water."

Cara looked at Ad, he was tired of this conversation. Why did everything always come down to this where his elder brother was concerned?

"But they aren't from across the water are they?" Cara asked. "They came from further away to the east, Rome. A great stone city and they slaughtered half of Gaul to get there. Do you really think they'll be happy with that and won't attack us next?"

Ad laughed, "Oh Cara, don't worry about such nonsense. Why would they want to hurt us anyway? We're friends, Father even trades with them, wine, livestock, gold and sometimes slaves. I've even heard that there's talk of warriors joining their legions."

"Ugh," Tog said turning, "where did you hear that? Why would our people want to join them in their wars, we have enough to be getting on with here, surviving is enough and besides that, we need our warriors here."

"Father told me that the barbarians to the north of Gaul were rebelling again and that they'd had to send more legions to the area, they're looking to recruit more auxiliaries from Albion." Ad replied. "Being the sons of a king, we would be officers of course." He looked at his brothers, "Well you two could anyway. I wouldn't want to be a soldier, I'm sure my talents would lie elsewhere."

"Don't you mean Britannia?" Tog said.

"What, erm," Ad hesitated, "well that's just their name for Albion in their language."

"Is it?" Tog replied, "Is it really? Surely such close friends should at least call our land by the name that we call it, the name it has always been known as."

"Why do we always have to argue when it comes to Rome?" Cara cut in, "Anyway Father wouldn't allow it, and he won't let our warriors go and fight for them and we're not going there either, so forget it." Although he was younger than his brothers he had never been afraid to speak his mind, or to tell them what he thought, especially when the subject came to Rome.

Approaching the village they could smell the ever present smoke from fires, children laughing and playing and somewhere in the background, a smith forging metal as he struck molten chunks together to form whatever he was creating.

"Hello Cara." A pretty blonde haired girl walked towards them. She was slender at the waist and wore a cheeky grin as she reached up for his reins, "I thought I'd see you again."

Her name was Mott, although everyone knew her as Mo. They had met at a birthday celebration when her father, who was a local Chieftain, had brought her along to their major settlement.

"What have you brought me?" She asked smiling and reddening slightly. He couldn't help glancing at her sensual shape, the top of her breasts were visible from above, but he tried to keep his eyes fixed on hers. They were dark brown almost black and not for the first time he felt himself lost to them.

He frowned, "My brother Ad of course." He said quickly looking to his brother for support. "He's of the age now to take a wife and I told him all about you after the celebrations."

Now Mo frowned, "But I only have eyes for you." She blushed and dropped her gaze and let her hand graze his thigh palm first. "Anyway I want a warrior to warm my bed not a bare faced boy."

Tog laughed, "See Ad! I tried to tell you but you wouldn't listen. There are many benefits to a manly appearance." Ad looked at Mo in disdain.

"Are you staying long?" Mo asked Cara.

"We're just passing through." He replied, "On our way to do some fishing, maybe a little hunting."

She frowned again, "Without a rod and line?"

"We're going to make them when we get there." He lied, "we have sinew for a line and will find good sticks for rods. "Why, what are you doing?" He asked trying to change the subject.

"Come and see my new baby goat." She raised her dark eyebrows pleadingly. "He's only a few weeks old and very friendly and cute."

"We don't have time for such things young woman." Ad remarked as he rode past a stationary Cara.

"Young? I'm sixteen summers I'll have you know, bare faced one. You look about six with your baby bottom smooth face." She looked back at Cara. "Come on please, please, please," she begged, "it won't take long."

He looked at his two brothers, "I'll catch you up this won't take long."

Tog smirked looking at Mo, "I'm sure it wouldn't." Being older and more experienced with females, he had already had his share of them. Cara blushed slightly.

"We'll wait for you at the smith's," Ad said, "just don't be too long." Caradoc smiled at Mo as she again took his reins and led him through the village.

"You'll love Edbutt," she said, "you'll see." As she led him away people saw who she was with and nodded respectfully, he smiled in return. At first he had found it strange when he began to realise that he was different to most boys as he was the son of the king, but usually forgot about it and went about his business of being a lad. Such things could wait, although he often wished he were just like other boys, anonymous.

She led him to her roundhouse where there was a small animal enclosure at the rear, he heard Edbutt before he saw him as a loud bleating started as Mo climbed the fence. There before him staring up at them was a small fawn coloured goat shouting, 'Mmmmnh mhhh mhhh.'

"Oh Edbutt stop all the racket!" Mo said, "You know father has said you'll be for the pot if you keep this up."

Edbutt ran over to Mo as she knelt down, his tail furiously wagging, "Mmmmnh." He cried excitedly, even more despite the warning. "He accepts me as his Mother now." Mo said as Cara frowned then raised his eyebrows as the little goat nuzzled up to his 'mother'. He was slightly larger than a small dog and was almost white except for a darker stripe running along his back and he had a dark face, tiny horns stuck out from the top of his head. He pushed himself into Mo's legs as he began to calm down.

"I had no idea goats were like this." Cara said. "I've had dogs who behave like it but never a goat."

"That's because people keep goats for milk and meat not pets but they're very friendly when you get to know them." She said patting his neck and rubbing his soft hair as he lifted his head enjoying the attention. "Smell him." She said.

"What?" Cara's head bobbed backwards. "Smell your goat?"

"Yes," she replied raising an eyebrow. "He's very fresh," she leaned back, "go on try him." He climbed the gate still unsure about sniffing the young animal but he went ahead and screwed his face up as he leaned forward. Edbutt turned shaking his head. "Is he going to....!" Before he could say another word the little animal rose up on his hind legs and butted Cara's knee. He grabbed the green woollen neckerchief around the goat's neck and pulled him away.

"Ah he likes you." Mo said clasping her hands together in glee.

"Likes me? He just tried to butt me out of the way." Cara replied.

"No that's just his way of saying hello." She said stroking the goat's head. "You just like him don't you?" Mo asked the little goat as he made more noise, his tail wagging vigorously. Cara smiled as he suddenly realised how taken he was with Mo.

"What?" She asked smiling and showing her straight, almost white teeth.

Cara reddened, "Nothing, nothing." He said, "He's just cute, for a goat I mean."

She stood up smiling, "See I told you." She took his hand, "Come on."

"What ... where are we going?" He asked, almost being pulled along.

"I want to show you something else." She said as she began to climb out of the pen. He let go of her hand and followed as Edbutt tried to as well but stopped short and started bleating again at the fence. Cara followed Mo hand in hand into a small thatched room attached to her family roundhouse, it was quite dim inside but a roof vent at the top allowed for some light.

"What exactly is it you want to show me?" He asked as he widened his eyes to try and adjust to the dark, Mo turned.

"Mmm, well not show you exactly." She smiled and drew him closer, and he noticed that she smelt clean, better than Edbutt he thought anyway. Her eyes grew larger as their noses touched and then their lips, as she kissed him gently, soft and warm, he let himself become absorbed in the moment. He moved his body closer still to hers as she closed her eyes, wrapping his arms around the curvature of her waist at the back as he felt slightly dizzy with strange sensations running through his body. In that moment nothing else mattered, he wanted to lose himself, and then he did. His head spinning, he almost felt as if he was falling. He had never kissed a girl before and as suddenly as the thought entered his head it was gone, as he felt her hands at the back of his head, gently caressing him as her warm tongue pushed inside his mouth and he was lost completely.

"Where have you been?" Ad asked as Cara rounded the corner and walked into the shade of the smith's area. "We nearly went without you." He added to emphasise the point.

Cara blushed and replied, "I wasn't that long. Anyway I was just helping Mo with her goat." He said dropping his eyes to the ground.

"Is that what she calls it?" Ad replied laughing to himself, "strange name for her virginity." He added. "Come on we need to get going."

Cara reddened again, "It wasn't like that, we kissed that's all," he untied his horse from where the reins had been secured to a wicker fence and jumped up. "I'm ready, let's go."

"Kissed?" Ad asked, "Is that all?"

"Leave him alone." Tog said, "Well done Caratacus," he added using his full name, "I was beginning to worry you preferred boys, a bit like that one." He said nodding towards Ad.

"Very humorous, I wonder sometimes if I'm actually a brother of you two." He said, "Now come on before the day is over."

"So do we, so do we." Tog whispered to himself. The three brothers walked their horses away from the smiths. Cara looked back and saw Mo standing with Edbutt on a lead of some description, she was waving. His heart pounded in his chest as thoughts of their kiss returned.

"Ah true love." Ad said as he saw the glance. "I hope that you don't go all soft on us now that you're going to take her as a wife."

"I suggest you be quiet brother or I'll give you something else to talk about." Tog said, defending the younger of the boys. "Now let's concentrate on what we're supposed to be doing. Are we going fishing as we planned to do, or are we going hunting?"

"I don't care." Cara replied. "Let's just see where the path takes us."

After a while, the boys found themselves entering a wooded area not far from Mo's village. There were paths leading off in different directions where the locals had travelled through the area over the years. Tog who was leading the three as usual, pulled his horse up and motioned for the others to stop by raising his hand. They sat listening for a few moments and heard branches breaking some distance away.

"It must be a deer." Tog said straining his eyes and ears as the sound went away from them. "Come on." He pushed forward as his horse moved on along the path which wound along in the same direction and adjusted his bow on his back. The boys followed the sound through the trees where shards of sunlight were slicing through the branches above them, foliage at the side of the path brushing against their exposed lower legs. Suddenly the sound of the running animal ahead of them stopped, Tog pulled up listening again. The peace was followed by the sound of something to the left, far off, something else moving through the undergrowth.

"Wolf?" Ad asked. Silence followed.

"Come on." Tog urged moving forward again as the hunted creature ahead bolted from its hiding place. The boys picked up speed recognising that their prey was making a concerted effort to flee from whatever was tracking it.

"What if it's a wolf after it?" Ad shouted above the sound of hooves and whipping branches as they raced along. "We could get into trouble."

"If it's a wolf, it will turn and run when it sees us." Tog shouted back spitting a leaf from his mouth. "Ugh," he scraped his tongue with his fingers, "they don't attack people anyway. It's an old woman's tale."

"What if it's a pack?" Ad shouted.

"Shut up and ride." Tog replied steering his mount along the winding track in the direction of the panicking animal. Ad frowned and lowered himself towards his horse's neck to avoid branches and cursed to himself as Cara smiled behind him. The chase went on for some time as the three boys travelled further into the woodland, until once again Tog pulled up to get his bearings and to listen. It was virtually impossible to follow anything whilst you yourself were crashing along a path even as well-worn as this one had proven to be. The sound of the horse's heavy breathing, their hooves and the occasional branch to the face, always ensured losing whatever you were chasing unless you stopped to listen.

Tog calmed his own breathing and leaned forward cocking his head, his muscular arms shone with a film of sweat. He was the biggest of the three brothers in breadth by some way. Again they heard the sound of whatever was tracking the animal ahead moving slowly now, stalking not rushing. It wasn't another animal.

"It's probably exhausted." Cara whispered and whatever's hunting it is closing in for the kill."

"Come on." Tog said as he slid from his horse and tied his reins to a branch. "We'll go on foot from here." The other two dismounted and secured their own horses. One by one they pulled their bows to the front and reached for an arrow. The woods were quiet now as they moved forward crouching low, trying to mingle with the bushes and undergrowth, where possible Tog led them along the path using the track to avoid noise. He turned pressing a finger to his lips urging the other two to be quiet.

"Just ahead," he pointed, "the woodland dips down into a small valley, the deer is down there, it's gone to ground again but whatever is following it, is over there." He pointed to the left where branches concealed their view. "Come on and be quiet."

Cara and Ad followed crouching as low as possible. Tog held his bow in his left hand as he brushed leaves and branches away with his right whilst moving forward. The place was quiet now except for birdsong nearby and the occasional rustle of leaves in the trees above. As they traversed into the valley below, the canopy above made it cooler and slightly darker which made the hairs stand out on Cara's arms. Tog raised his bow arm indicating that he had seen something. Cara peered through the greenery and could just make out a white furry tail almost hidden, a few feet in front of them. Then he saw an arrow sticking out of the rump of the wounded deer, and deep red blood, where it had trickled down the wounded animal's side.

"It's not a wolf that's after it but a hunting party." He whispered looking at Tog who was staring at the wound. The deer tried to stand but slumped down, tired and exhausted after the chase that had brought it to this place. "Tog, what are we going to do?" Cara asked.

"These are our lands." Ad said, "There won't be a problem, we can do as we like." Without waiting for a reply, he strode forward unsheathing his dagger and sank it into the stricken deer's throat. Dark red blood shot out squirting over his hand and arm. The stricken deer let out a high pitched yelp but quickly slumped and died.

"What are you doing brother?" Tog asked. "You have taken someone else's kill." As he said it they all heard branches breaking and the sound of running feet coming towards them.

"It's too late now." Cara said standing up from a crouch just as the hunting party emerged from the bushes. His hand automatically grabbed for the handle of his bone carved dagger, Tog armed himself with his bow, an arrow ready to fire and Ad did the same.

"What is this?" It was a girl, about the same age as themselves. "That," she said trying to stop panting and pointed, "is our kill. We have been stalking that deer for most of the day." She was tall, as tall as Tog, athletic looking, and had long dark black hair. She wore some sort of animal skin leggings and a short sleeved woollen top that showed her sleek muscular tanned brown skin. Her dark eyes stared at the three boys taking each of them in, one at a time. In seconds she was joined by four males, all of comparative age. The largest of which stepped forward and saw the dead deer. He was dressed in a similar fashion to the female and Cara thought he saw a resemblance, were they brother and sister he wondered? They were joined by three others.

"Move away or there will be trouble between us." The large male at the front said.

"Now we don't need to argue," Ad replied, "there's more than enough for all of us, he stepped forward loosening the string on his bow and let the arrow un-cock.

"Take one more step and you're arguing days will be over boy." The male said and stepped forward knife in hand, raising it slightly.

"You're outnumbered and you're trying to steal our kill," the girl added, "I really do hope that you see sense and withdraw or my brother here," she touched his shoulder, "will see to it that you end up like our prey," she looked directly at Cara, "and you wouldn't want that to happen would you?" She half smiled and he suddenly noticed how beautiful she was.

"That's enough Brenna," the largest of the boys said turning to his sister, "maybe the scrawny one is right."

"Tevelgus," the girl said stepping around her brother, "we've chased that animal from our own land, it's ours by right." Her face was full of determination and anger despite the long exhausting chase.

"So you are intruding onto our lands in order to take our food?" Ad said as he looked at his brothers for support, "A grave mistake on your part I would say." He looked back at Brenna. "You are to go back now and leave this beast, you are the ones intruding and trying to steal from us it would seem." Cara saw the half grin on his face, an expression that had always annoyed him when they got into arguments. It was an awful sneer that never failed to make him feel uncomfortable.

"We are still five to your three." The female said.

"I don't think you're helping Brenna." Her brother said. "Anyway he's right, we shouldn't have strayed this far, and it's only a deer, there are plenty more."

"He said we could share." She said staring at Tevelgus.

"Ah, that was before we found out that you had crossed the border." Ad said. "You have broken the pact between our two people and you could start a war with this intrusion." She laughed.

"Let them have it." Cara said.

"What? Have you lost your sense little brother?" Ad said anger building.

"It's a deer for the god's peace." Tog said, "Cara is right let them have it, they earned it."

Ad couldn't contain his rage any further and strode quickly back to the corpse. He threw his bow to the ground and took out his dagger. "I will not allow these thieves to come onto our land, shame us and take what is rightfully ours." He then plunged the blade into the carcass and began to cut away at a hind limb.

Tog frowning, looked at Cara, he raised his hands and nodded at Ad as they both walked towards their brother and grabbed an arm each.

"Come Ad, it is but one deer, the woods and forests are full of them. We will find our own." Tog said as he applied pressure to the arm he had grabbed.

"Take your hands off me." Ad demanded. Tog however ignored his older brother and pulled him up and away from the carcass. As Ad struggled to get free, Cara let go of his grip and his flailing brother spun round and fell to the ground. He landed roughly, face first and quickly jumped up to confront Tog. Although Ad was the elder of the three boys, he stared at his brother prepared to fight, fists raised.

"I warn you now Ad, you may be my brother but you will regret this, I won't allow you to do it and if you attack me, I will respond." Tog said.

The girl Brenna spoke, "Adminius?" She looked at him as he stood scowling, breathing heavily. "You are the one to be crowned King, the heir to the Catuvellauni lands?"

"What do you know of me, of us thief?" Ad asked. "Well?"

She moved forward slowly, "More than you will ever know." she said. She approached Ad and raised her hand to his face, he pulled back.

"I won't hurt you." She assured him, "Come." He hesitated and then stood his ground as she reached over and touched the left side of his face with her palm. She looked into his eyes, as her own seemed to glaze over as her head rocked forward slightly.

"It is you." She whispered.

Ad looked from her to the others in her group, "What is she talking about? How does she know me?"

Tevelgus answered, "She is a Shaman."

"A what?" Tog asked.

Tevelgus walked to his sister and placed a hand on her shoulder, she was still staring at the Catuvellauni.

"A Shaman, well she will be soon anyway." He looked at Adminius, "She can talk to the spirit world, to our ancestors, to the world beyond where we are."

Ad pulled back breaking the physical contact from Brenna who then jerked her head whipping backwards as if she had been struck to the face.

"It's true." She said, beginning to pale.

"What's true? What is this nonsense? What are you talking about?" Ad demanded. "Spirits, ancestors, another world, I think you need to take your sister home, she's lost her mind. A Shaman?" He laughed, "I think she needs one."

Brenna looked from Ad to his two brothers, "Traitor." She whispered. It was barely audible. Ad frowned but before he could say anything she continued. "You are not like your brothers. You want power, to take from others, to dominate, you care nothing for others. Your soul is black." She stepped away. "Come, she said looking to each of her group, "leave the deer, it's theirs, I want nothing from this place."

"Wait, what did you see?" Cara asked.

"It's lies brother, she saw nothing, twisted words and lies nothing more, she's mad. You yourself know I'm not as she says." Ad said but Cara was still looking at the girl. He had recognised the words, the description she had used for his older brother. Although strange it was oddly accurate when spoken aloud. There were times when Adminius behaved totally different than he and Tog and he did have a cruel, vicious streak. How did this girl know these things? His mind churned, was it possible that she could communicate as her brother described?

"Why did you call my brother a traitor? He is to become King when our father passes to the next world, why would he be a traitor, to who?" Cara asked.

Brenna turned her dark eyes to him. "You weren't meant to hear. I can't see that but it is true, it will happen. He will betray you, your brother and your people." She turned, "Come we must go." She said to Tevelgus.

"Lies and madness," Ad said. "She knows nothing of us, of me and I would never betray you or our people, you know that."

Brenna stopped and turned and focused her eyes on Cara, "Don't trust him. Whatever you do, do not trust this one," She pointed, "no matter what he says or does, or where you go, the time will come when he will care nothing for you or yours. He will betray everything for his own gain. Nothing means anything to him except what he can get for himself. You Caratacus of the Catuvellauni," this time she pointed at him, "are the only one who can stop him." He felt a chill rush through his body, he shivered and knew what she was saying was true. Brenna nodded her head, turned and vanished into the thick undergrowth.

"Tog, go and get the horses, we're not dragging this through the woods, Cara give me some help to get this out onto the path." Ad said as he stooped down to look at the deer. A few seconds passed and neither brother had moved.

"Come on let's move, we can't stay here all day." His brothers did as he'd asked with concerned expressions on their faces. From that moment, nothing would ever be the same between them.

Chapter Six

Caradoc woke with a start, sitting up suddenly and breathing heavily, cold sweat on his brow and chest, his pillow damp, it had been a dream, but it had been so real. He remembered back to the day when the girl had told him of the treachery of Adminius, why had it now come to him in his sleep? All those years ago, he had been warned, and although he had felt that what she had said was true, he had ignored her warning, how was this possible? He pushed himself off the bed, his naked skin felt cold due to the sheen of perspiration and reached for the ladle in the pail of water beside the bed. He poured some into a wooden cup and drank. He thought back again to that day, when his world began to change and nothing would be the same again with his older brother. Another incident returned to his thoughts and he wondered why he had now begun to think of these things again. His brother was a traitor and he had paid for his betrayal with his life, a life he had taken not long after the death of Tog.

Adminius had slowly grown distant after that day and sought companionship from others, while he and Tog had stayed together, growing older. It was three years later when reports began to come in that Adminius and his new found friends were crossing into other tribal lands. He had also started to drift away from their close-knit family as well and although it was clear that the King was unhappy about his behaviour, he never discussed it with his other sons. Cunobelin had worked tirelessly to ensure a peaceful existence after years of inter-tribal conflict between the Catuvellauni and surrounding lands. Trade had slowly prospered and treaties were agreed, even marriages took place and there was a melding of the people. More traders soon began to arrive from across the water to the east, and for the first time in memory his people could concentrate on their daily chores without a threat from outside.

One day, during the start of winter, he had seen an emissary arrive from a neighbouring tribe. The rider had dismounted from his horse and had been quickly ushered in for an audience with his Father. He had sat listening outside, leaning against the wall and watching leaves as they fell from nearby trees, trying to overhear the conversation. He had heard his Father raising his voice and the name Adminius was mentioned again and again. Soon after, the rider had departed looking flushed and had left the settlement quickly.

"Find my sons." He had heard his Father shout from within the great hall where he received guests. Startled he turned quickly and began to walk away then he realised he had nothing to be guilty of. Before the warrior who had been ordered to find him and Tog could say a word, he pre-empted his request.

"I heard my Father. You will find Togodumnus gelding the colts in the lower pasture." He had told the guard as he went inside.

His father was a large man, both in height and breadth and had been a great warrior in years gone by. The seasons however, had begun to take their toll and his hair and beard were flecked with grey, he walked awkwardly, limping slightly from an injury caused whilst falling from a horse, but he still had the bearing and power of a man not to be reckoned with.

"Ah Caratacus there you are, where is your brother?" The King asked his voice booming in the large room. He had fixed him with a stare that made him feel slightly un-comfortable. He wasn't used to seeing his Father angry, as he clearly was now. He wore a large silver torc around his neck that overlapped his brown tunic, matching leggings and dark leather boots.

"Tog is with the foals Father. I told Werewik where to find him." He replied referring to the warrior he had spoken with.

"Mm yes of course he is, with all these other things to deal with," he waved an arm at things unseen, "I often forget about the gelding." He answered. Seeing the look on his son's face he continued, "Best to get it done now with the onset of winter, less flies you see, always remember that, otherwise the dirty little bastards can cause you all sorts of problems, disease and the like."

"Yes Father of course." He stood waiting for Cunobelin to go on.

"Where's your older brother, that rancid little turd Adminius?" The king asked, he had a way with language.

Caratacus hesitated, he knew that both of his parents were aware of the distance that had developed between their sons but they had never spoken of it openly.

"I think he left a few days ago, hunting I believe with his friends," Caratacus replied.

"Where? Where did he go hunting, do you know?" The King asked.

"South but I don't know where exactly, he hardly ever talks to Tog and I anymore, he's more interested in his friends." Caratacus said.

"Mm really." The King replied pushing himself off his chair with a sigh. "Maybe I should have Togodumnus geld that little prick as well eh?" Caratacus grimaced, although he knew his Father was joking, the gelding of men had been known to happen. Rapists or those who interfered with the young, both male and female were known to be treated this way.

"What's happened? What has he done Father?" Caratacus asked as his Father poured some wine into a large wooden flask and took a mouthful. He walked to the table and poured himself some. "Roman?" He asked.

"Yes it is, nice eh? I must admit those skirt wearers know how to make a nice drop, we must try to make our own." His Father said as he stalked around the room. "Wait until Tog gets here and I'll tell you what that weasel turd has been doing now. Gods, why can't he be like you and your brother?"

Caratacus looked away peering into his wine, he took a sip. "The Romans' warm theirs and water it down, they say."

Cunobelin tipped his flask draining the contents into his mouth, he poured another. "Mm, so I hear. Something to do with avoiding drinking the water pure, that's often full of things to make you ill, or maybe it's because their strange bodies can't take it." He laughed. "Ah Togodumnus, good." He said as Caradoc's brother entered the room, he was breathing heavily having run from the pasture.

"What is it Father, trouble?" Tog asked.

"You could say that," he said, "take a seat both of you." They did as they were told sitting on a smooth wooden bench against the wall. "I want you to go and find your brother."

"I've still got colts to geld Father. They have to be done now because they're starting to cause problems with each other and the females." Tog said.

"That can be done by others, you don't have to do everything yourself, I'll find someone else to do that, there are plenty who know how."

The young horses, those aged between twelve to eighteen months were at an age where they were now challenging each other and were getting dangerous. Fighting between dominant males could become a serious problem and so they were gelded before animals were injured or killed.

"What's our brother done now?" Tog asked.

"They say he's been taking liberties, drinking, whoring, taking property, fucking girls who don't want his maggot inside them, getting into fights with that band of bastards he rides with, you know the ones." He sat down. "It's no way to behave, at least on the lands of others with their folk. If he were here, inside our territory, I could settle the matter quietly but he's bringing shame on us and I won't have it." He took another drink, "I especially won't have it when he's doing it outside the tribe on Regni land, the stupid, reckless fool."

The Regni were the tribe to the south who lived along the coastline. Problems with them could mean a restriction on trade from over the sea and that couldn't be allowed to happen.

"I want you to go and find him and bring him back as soon as you can." The King ordered.

"What if he refuses? Tog asked.

The King leaned forward, "You tell him that I sent you and that if he refuses I will come for him and if that happens he'll be glad to have just his balls removed." He stared at both sons sat before him. "I'm running out of patience with Adminius, ever since he met those Romans all those years ago, he has been a problem. He must think that because he's first in line that no matter what he does, he'll become king when I'm dead, well it doesn't always happen that way. He needs to change and change quickly, he needs to earn respect, not have contempt and hatred from those around him. How old is he now?"

"He's twenty years Father, one year older than me." Tog said.

"Yes, yes that's right, three older than you Caratacus and you're more reliable as a son." Tog and Cara had never heard their Father say anything like this about Adminius before but he was clearly very unhappy and angry.

"Take some of the men with you, and bring that despicable little runt back here and if he refuses, use force and if that fails, tell him his life won't be worth living if I have to come looking for him."

They left their brooding Father alone, "It's not worth leaving now." Tog said looking up at the sky, "It'll be dark soon but we can get things ready for tomorrow and find some suitable riders to come with us. We'll leave at first light in the morning, try and get a good night's sleep I think we'll need it."

***

They set off the next day after a hot breakfast of pork and vegetable broth that their Father had insisted upon. Riding with twenty seasoned warriors of the King's personal guard, they headed south at a steady trot. The weather was turning now, with grey skies overhead and leaves falling from the trees all around them. The men were wrapped up against the cold wearing heavy cloaks and long animal skin boots. Caratacus cursed silently to himself as he felt the breeze wash through his outer layers.

Tog saw his discomfort, "Don't worry little brother we'll be back in a few days."

Cara looked over to him riding at his side at the head of their small group, "That may be but if it wasn't for that fool Adminius, we wouldn't be riding out at all in this weather." He replied guiding his horse with his upper legs. "I can't understand why he has to cause so many problems. I couldn't sleep properly thinking about it last night. He has everything he could need or want and he's going to inherit all that Father owns in time, yet he shames him all the time, why do you think that is?"

Tog pursed his lips, "I really don't know, but he's always been the odd one out of all of us. He's always gone his own way it must be in his nature or something. I've never heard Father so angry before, he's never spoken of this with me but it seems his patience has been exhausted this time. If our brother had done these things that he's accused of in our territory, it wouldn't be that bad, bad enough I'll grant you, but recompense could have been offered. Shaming us in front of the Regni is a different matter altogether, it makes us all look like fools and makes it seem as if Adminius is above the rule of anyone including Father. He has to be brought in line and quickly."

Caratacus shook his head, "What do you think he'll do when he sees we've been sent to get him?"

"I'm sure I don't know but if he refuses to comply with our Father's wishes, he'll make him wish he was never born." Tog replied.

"I heard him talking to the men before we set out," he indicated to those riding behind them with a nod of his head, "he told them to make sure we return with Adminius and those he has with him or not to return at all."

Tog smiled, "Father is just angry, he'll come back with us don't worry about that, even if he has no wish to do so, we'll make him. If he resists, those with him will be cut down and we'll strap him to a horse if we have to."

"And what of later, when he becomes king? How will he treat his kin then, us I mean?" Caratacus asked as a gust of wind blew his long hair into his face. "Curse this weather."

"We shall worry about that when the time comes but I hope it's not for many years. Our king has a while before he passes," he looked at Caratacus smiling, "I hope anyway, so our good brother won't take his place for many years. Maybe by then he'll behave in a manner more fitting to rule the land. Mother told me that some take longer to mature but that she thought he was actually getting worse not better, if we were all the same, life would be a little drab though eh?"

"He cannot become king as he is. Everything Father has worked so hard for would be ruined." Caratacus looked at Tog, real anger in his eyes.

"I agree and together we will make sure that doesn't happen believe me, he must change or we will have little choice. I have no wish to take Father's place but I will not see Adminius take his seat unless things change and change for the better."

"Are you saying we kill him?" Caratacus asked. "Kill our own brother?"

"We would have no choice as things are. Can you imagine him as king as he is? He already takes women because of his position, thinking he has a right because of his family; he shames us all. He's disruptive to those around him as if he enjoys their pain, just look at his attitude to the Romans? He does it to hurt Father I'm certain, dressing like them, cutting his hair like them, always talking of Rome and how we should be more like them. If he became king what would he do concerning Rome? Hand over lands, become one of them totally, a puppet ruler on behalf of their empire? No, he has to change not just for our people but for us as well Cara, I won't live like that."

"Nor I brother but how has it come to this?" Caratacus asked.

"I don't think the how is what matters anymore, it's what we do about it that counts." Tog answered.

"Remember that girl a few years ago, when we were out hunting and I had just met Mo? She warned us about him even then, that must have been three summers ago now." Caratacus said. In the intervening years his relationship with Mott had grown and they had become very close.

"The girl with dark eyes, yes I remember, her brother had said she was to become a Shaman. Even she, who didn't know him, recognised the deceit inside." He shook his head, "I thought she was a mad woman at the time, how wrong I was."

***

That night they camped by the side of a river in a shallow ravine. It afforded them some shelter from the wind that hadn't let up all day. A fire pit was dug a few feet deep to keep the draft away and some of their group went hunting before they settled down for the night. For supper they shared wild boar roasted over the flames before wrapping themselves in thick woollen blankets and trying to get some sleep.

When they awoke early the next morning, the wind seemed to have blown itself out but it was still cold, at least it was dry. After packing their belongings, they set out again heading further south and around midday crossed the border between their lands and those of the Regni. There was no immediate difference to their surroundings but a short time later they came across a group of armed riders, clearly Regni from their clothing.

Tog raised an arm halting his men, "Greetings Regni warriors, I am Togodumnus, son of Cunobelin King of the Catuvellauni, we come in search of a party led by my brother Adminius. Your own king sent a messenger north, saying that there have been problems, we come to return him."

A man at the head of their band, clearly their leader spoke, "We seek him ourselves. He and his men have behaved like animals since they crossed onto our land. We were told they were last seen nearby heading towards the next settlement." He pointed along a track away to the left. "Our people here are farmers with few goods or things of value, yet they steal and take anything they choose, they use our women and behave almost as if there were war between us."

Caratacus saw the Regni were well armed, they carried bows as well as swords, shields and some had spears.

"We can find him together." Tog suggested. "He has brought shame upon our people and my Father wants him to pay for the insult he has shown you by behaving like this."

"I am Colgan." their leader said, "We are tasked with dealing with this Adminius and his men. We do not need your help." He began to turn his horse.

"Colgan," Tog shouted, "I know my brother is a fool and has broken the treaty between our two peoples but if you take matters into your own hands, the situation will become worse." He raised an eyebrow emphasising his words. The Catuvellauni were a much larger tribe than the Regni, he didn't need to explain the consequences of what hostile action against Adminius would cost.

Colgan looked around at the faces of those with him and then answered reluctantly, "Very well, we will go together, but I want anything that he and his men have taken. It will be returned to those he has stolen from, this is not a request, do you understand?"

Caratacus felt the tension rise and knew that in the blink of an eye, men could be dying.

"Very well, agreed." Tog said, "But no harm is to come to him, our Father and king will determine his punishment."

"Agreed." Colgan said, "But if they draw arms, we will defend ourselves."

"If they draw their weapons, we will deal with them. You and your men can stay behind us. If we are attacked, you will see us deal with them. My brother may be a fool but he has never been a fighter......or a good one at least."

Colgan nodded his agreement and the Regni fell in behind the Catuvellauni riders heading in the direction that he had indicated.

A short time later, they heard screaming and kicked their horses into a gallop. Caratacus kept pace with Tog as they approached the village where smoke was rising but not from fires within the roundhouse, they saw, instead that its roof was ablaze. As they rounded a corner, he saw a line of people standing against an animal pen being guarded by young Catuvellauni warriors. Adminius ripped the dress of a young girl exposing her breasts.

"STOP." Tog shouted pulling his horse up. "Stop this now."

Adminius turned, clearly shocked, "Brother! What are you doing here?"

Tog jumped from his horse and walked quickly to Adminius, who began to move backwards but not far enough to avoid the back handed strike from his younger sibling. His head jerked backwards with the force of the blow, one of Adminius' companions moved as if to attack Tog but Cara leapt from his horse knocking him to the ground.

"How dare you strike me!" Adminius shouted, blood dripping from the side of his mouth. The youth on the ground underneath Caratacus struggled trying to get up.

"Stay down." Cara warned him as Adminius' companions approached in a threatening manner. Tog drew his blade, a sharp dagger and put it to his older brother's throat.

"Our Father wants you home, now! We have been told to bring you back," He looked around at those beginning to surround him, his own men dismounting to protect him. "He didn't say anything about bringing your friends home," he lied, "Maybe Colgan here, could find a use for them."

The youth under Caratacus struggled again and managed to un-sheath a knife he had hidden in a boot. Caratacus grabbed his wrist and slammed the hand holding the blade into the ground. He shuffled his body up, placing his knees against his opponent's throat. The boy gurgled struggling for breath, red faced.

"I appreciate your loyalty to my brother but believe me, if you struggle anymore, I will kill you where you lie." Caratacus said determination in his stare.

"Leave it Smydion." Adminius said to the boy underneath his brother, "my Father will hear of this insult."

Tog moved closer to Adminius, "And what of this insult brother?" He looked to the girl with the ripped clothing, now covering her breasts, "You cross the border and treat these people like this? You risk war, after all that our Father has done to ensure peace?" He grabbed Adminius by the throat, his strong fingers gripping the flesh and tightening. Adminius gasped.

"You are a disgrace to the Catuvellauni and if you weren't my brother, you would die right here like the dog you are." Adminius couldn't respond, Tog nodded at one of his men who came forward, as he threw Adminius to the side, he began choking immediately struggling for breath.

"Bind them all." Tog instructed. "The King will deal with them when we return. He looked at the youth still underneath Caratacus. "One word from you and you won't live to see your homeland again, understand?" The stricken friend of Adminius could just nod his understanding.

With Adminius and his group bound, Tog turned to Colgan. "My brother won't disturb you or your people again. I will take him north where my Father will deal with him and his unruly friends."

Colgan looked at him with suspicion, "And how will I know there will be justice? You could ride back and nothing would be done." He looked at Adminius," This one your brother, is their leader but the others were as bad, what do I tell my chieftain…..that your word is good?"

Tog stared at the Regni warrior and knew if the situation were reversed, it would be unlikely he would let a band of riders just ride away. He looked at the group who had trespassed onto this land, their heads bowed except for Adminius.

"Choose one." He said to Colgan. Adminius struggled but was held firm by one of Tog's men.

"What do you think you're doing?" Adminius demanded but Tog didn't answer. Colgan pointed at the young man who had grappled with Caratacus on the ground.

"This one," he said, "I choose him." Colgan said pointing at Smydion, who lifted his head, concern growing on his face.

"What are you going to do?" Smydion asked beginning to struggle with the bindings holding his hands together, as he was shoved forward away from the others.

"Take him there," Tog said, "where your people can see."

Colgan grabbed him by the shoulder and marched him into the centre of those gathered all around. He stopped and looked at Tog, "Well?" He asked.

"You want a guarantee of justice?" Tog said striding toward Smydion. "On your knees." He commanded as he pushed him down to the floor.

"Stop now, stop what you are doing." Adminius shouted. Tog turned to his brother.

"You are responsible for this." He pointed at Smydion and then took out his dagger. He walked behind him as he began to scream but it was too late, the cry was cut off as Tog sliced into Smydion's throat and ripped his blade through his flesh from ear to ear. Colgan jumped backwards trying to avoid the gush of fluid but his legs were instantly covered. Blood shot out of the open wound spraying the soil dark red as the gash widened, white flesh stark against the awful image. Smydion's eyes rolled backward into his head, he tried to speak, to say something but no words came out. His body began to jerk unnaturally, then spasm uncontrollably. Blood continued to spurt hitting the ground like heavy rain until it slowed. Tog pushed him forward and he landed with a wet thump onto his own life's blood now pooled on the floor, he was dead.

Colgan looked up at Tog, shock over his face.

"Do you require further guarantees?" Tog asked the Regni. He turned and pointed at the others, hands bound behind their backs now standing trembling. "Choose another." He said, "Any except for my brother."

Colgan backed away, "No, that was enough, I believe you, and I don't want any more bloodshed." He turned to his men, "Come." He ordered as he jumped onto his horse, "King Cunobelin will deal with the rest of these savages."

Tog ensured that Smydion was buried in a ditch on the outskirts of the settlement before they left and headed north. They rode slowly through the night crossing the border before the sun rose and headed home.

***

Cunobelin stared at Adminius, his eyes boring into his very soul as he stood in front of his reckless band. They had been taken directly to the hall the King used for large gatherings, a place normally reserved for official meetings, celebrations and festive occasions. The King stood up from his large wooden chair and walked towards his errant son, Adminius couldn't look him in the eye.

"So tell me," he said his deep voice calm and deliberate, "what shall I do with you?" He walked closer. "Rape, theft, brutality and worse, you did it inside Regni lands, you crossed the border like some uncivilised barbarian. What were you thinking?"

"Father I…" He spluttered.

"SHUT UP," Cunobelin ordered his voice booming, Adminius lowered his head. "It was not a question for you to answer boy."

"Tog killed Smydion." He whispered.

"I told you to shut up!" The King shouted. "Your brother here," he pointed to Tog, "probably prevented a war between us and the Regni or at least stopped them from taking retribution on our own people." He turned back to Adminius. "He did the right thing, you," he said leaning into him, "are lucky that I didn't come to get you or the rest of your little war band here would be buried along with the other one." The King moved away and looked at the others. "Talking of which," he said, "get them out of my sight. If they ever come to my attention again I'll have the flesh torn from their bodies and what remains fed to the pigs. The only thing that's saving that from happening now is that you were following this fool." He stared at Adminius again. "Now take them away." The others were escorted out of the hall leaving the King with his three sons, Cunobelin returned to his chair.

"How can I ever trust you again?" He asked. "My oldest son and heir behaving in such a way, is this how you will rule when I'm dead? You would bring war to the tribes after all we've done to ensure peace, a good way of life." Adminius didn't answer. "I must have done something wrong with you," the King continued, "why can't you be more like your brothers?" He raised his head looking at the high roof. "Gods I'm just glad your Mother isn't alive to see how you have turned out, a vile, treacherous sliver of weasel dung that would ruin everything we've worked for over the years." He stared at his son who stood head down. "Look at me when I'm talking to you!" He shouted. "At least demonstrate some real kind of courage." Adminius looked up his face red.

"So tell me, why did you do it?" The King asked of his son. Cara and Tog looked from one to the other.

"We should take their land." He replied almost whispering.

"What?" His Father asked.

"We should take their land Father." He found his voice. "Are we not the stronger, the larger, most dominant tribe?" He looked at his brothers. "We aren't all farmers, glad to work the land, rely on others to allow trade. The Regni control the coast where the goods come from Rome and Gaul. They could hold us to ransom, stop the imports, how would we live then?"

"What, what are you saying, can you hear yourself?" The King asked. "We have lived in peace with our neighbours for many years. They have never tried to stop the traders, messengers or anything else. We freely take goods to the coast to board the ships bound for Rome and elsewhere across the water, why would the Regni suddenly stop that? If they did, we would then do something about it but have they? Do they obstruct the flow of goods going either way? Is there something my son is aware of that I am not?"

"The Romans wouldn't allow this." Adminius said. "They wouldn't let a lesser people dictate their commerce, their trade, who was allowed to barter with them, to reach their lands. They would crush them, so the problem didn't exist."

"We are not Romans Adminius, you are not Roman. For generations the different peoples of Albion fought and killed each other for land and where did it get them? I'll tell you, nowhere, except for the borders we now see between us. Even they had to stop the fighting, the killing and slaughter eventually. In the end there was peace, no cross border attacks, no more wars and bloodshed and trade grew, peaceful co-existence, we've changed, we live side by side now and it is better this way. We no longer have to look to defend ourselves, trying to sleep at night wondering if we're going to be attacked. You have never had to live like that, and for that you should be thankful, not go on about the mighty Roman way of life. Do you really believe they would let us live like we do if they came to Albion?"

"It is weak." Adminius said. "And they aren't as you say, you have never been there, how would you know?"

"How would I know? Did I not send you to Rome to study when you were younger?"

"Yes you did Father and I'm grateful, more so than you'll ever know but we can't carry on living like this. One day they'll cross the channel with their legions and what will they find? They'll find divided people with no unity, tribes that, as big as they are, are not one people." Adminius said. "I've always said that we should be more like them and this is our chance but we have to be bigger, stronger and if we take the Regni lands and do with them as we please, the empire will respect us more so than they do now."

The King sat shaking his head, "Where has this nonsense come from? Why now do you of all people decide that this should happen? There is no threat from Rome, why would they send their soldiers to Albion, they already trade with us."

"Did we not send warriors to Gaul to fight against them?" Adminius asked.

"That was years ago. What relevance does that have to us now, today?" The king asked.

"Did Albion send warriors to fight against Rome in Gaul?" Adminius asked again, without waiting for a reply he continued, "The answer Father is yes and once the Gaul's were defeated, the legions came to Albion."

"And they were defeated." The King said. "They were thrown back into the sea, twice they came and twice they lost, their great General, victor of Gaul, Caesar himself."

"But Albion was not divided then as it is now, don't you see? If we are stronger, they are more likely to be our allies, friends rather than our enemies." Adminius said. "All we have to do is defeat the likes of the Regni and the lands all the way to the coast are ours. No longer would we have to rely on their goodwill, we would rule most of the south the most important part of the land as far as the empire is concerned. We can give them that step to the rest of the island."

"What are you saying, give them our land? Why would we do this? Do you realise that what you're saying isn't real, there is no threat from Rome, there are no legions waiting to board ships and go to war, we are at peace with them." The King repeated his frustration growing.

"No Father, the last thing I'm saying is that we should give them our lands but we can prevent them from trying to take them. Here let me show you." Adminius said. Cunobelin bit his lip and nodded his permission as Adminius plucked a spear from the wall and began drawing in the earth.

"This is Rome," he said sketching a long piece of land with a foot at the bottom, "here is Gaul, Germania and Hispania." He drew a rough map of the known world. "Now years and years ago, the influence of the empire was here," he indicated a line on the map, "but today," he drew another, "it is here." The drawing showed that the Roman Empire had come to their door and that only the channel and the Regni lands now separated them. For the first time that day the King was silent. He sat staring at the floor, at the rough map drawn by his son.

After the conversation with Adminius that day, Cunobelin became sullen and withdrawn. He had ordered that his unruly son be confined to their own borders and was not to be in the company of more than five of his friends or companions again. Still, the years passed and the events of the infringement into Regni territory were forgotten and life went on peacefully. There were no disputes with other tribes, reparations were made to the Regni King and his people and trading grew with Rome. The Catuevellauni even began minting their own coins, a lesson learned from traders and instead of bartering, many people then traded coins for goods.

In time, the restrictions on Adminius were all but forgotten as crops, herding, trading and the very chore of existing continued, life could be difficult enough as it was without keeping an eye on him. Cunobelin even began to let him meet with outsiders and to cross the border once more as the years took their toll and he began to age.

Things had never been the same between the brothers after that day years before. Adminius never forgave Tog for the death of his friend Smydion and Caratacus had just happened to be there, so he was equally blamed for undermining him. As the influence of Adminius grew, the warning signs were there for all to see except for the King, who had taken to his bed and could no longer govern effectively and so left the running of the land to his sons.

And so it was a few years later that another dispute occurred once more concerning the Regni when it was claimed that a herd of cattle had been stolen from a settlement in Catuevellauni territory and driven south. Adminius seized the opportunity to ride across the border with two hundred warriors and raised three settlements to the ground, killing those who had lived there and leaving nothing in his wake. He had returned home telling every one of his triumph and began making plans to conquer the Regni completely. Togodumnus and Caratacus were appalled by this and informed their king who was equally angered by his oldest son's further betrayal.

Subsequently, Adminius was once again brought before his Father and King in the large hall, with his other sons present. As his eldest son tried to argue and give reasons for the attack, Cunobelin sat listening with tired eyes. When his heir was finished Cunobelin spoke.

"I have been too ill of late to keep a close watch on you as I promised I would, just a few years ago and you have betrayed me for the last time. Maybe you saw me getting frailer and reasoned that you could do as you pleased as you have once more, but I am not too old to see the evil in you." Adminius tried to speak but his Father raised a hand silencing him.

"I am told that you have slaughtered nearly a hundred people of the Regni and they are now gathering warriors as I speak to retaliate." He took a sip from a large wooden mug. "They intend to ride north and take vengeance for your actions, no doubt intending to do what you did to their people to ours and I cannot allow that." He looked at each son in turn.

"Why you could never be like your brothers, is beyond my ability to understand, you have always been so. How many times I have lain in my bed worrying about how you would behave if I died and you became king, I could not say. The nightmares you have given me I couldn't count, you are like a shadow to my thoughts and a dark cloud waiting to hover over these rich lands." He drank again his voice getting faint.

"In many ways you have made my decision for me, so I thank you for that. You have given me no choice in coming to the conclusion I have reached, that I had to reach for the future of our tribe and for those who live by our sides. If you were any other man you would be dead already, but as much as it hurts me to say it you are still my son and so shall live."

Adminius saw some hope and his expression began to lighten but his Father continued, "Togodumnus is now my heir and will become the next leader of the people being the next son in my line. You Adminius will finally have your way and you can go live amongst your Roman friends as you will be banished from Albion. When I have finished speaking, you will be escorted from this place and will be taken to the coast where, if the Regni don't kill you, you will be taken to Gaul never to return."

Adminius was white with shock at his Father's words and started to tremble, everything that he had ever wanted, everything that he was going to have, had just been removed and there wasn't anything he could do to retrieve it.

"You can't do this." He shouted, "I am to become King, me….not him." He said pointing to Togodumnus who looked as shocked as he. "I did what anyone would do. I was merely protecting our people because you couldn't." He shouted.

"Take him south and round up his close friends, they are to be banished also, I don't want them here, poisoning others with their words." The King ordered not looking at anyone except his soon to be exiled kin. "I will mourn you Adminius as you are no longer my son, this you have brought upon yourself, now go. Leave this place while you are still able." The King struggled to his feet as Adminius continued to shout trying desperately to change his Father's mind but it was to no avail. As the king slowly walked towards the door at the rear of the hall, Adminius tried to run towards him but was stopped by Togodumnus and Caratacus. He tried to resist, screaming and shouting at his Father but they were too strong and held him firm. As the King left without looking back, Adminius began to sob as he realised his life with his family was over.

Togodumnus immediately sent a messenger south trying desperately to avoid the blood bath that would surely come if the Regni weren't told of Cunobelin's decision to exile his son. He gathered as many warriors as he could for the journey, he and Caratacus would themselves escort Adminius to the port where a vessel would carry him across the channel.

Content that the rebel who had taken so many lives was to be sent across the water, the Regni king allowed safe passage for the Catuvellauni party as they journeyed to the Roman merchant vessel that stood at anchor unloading goods. Also exiled but at a time of their own choosing, would be the warriors who had followed Adminius and carried out the atrocities.

Negotiations were made with the captain of the ship, who agreed to take Adminius east when he saw the Regni tribesmen waiting nearby, ensuring that the deal was done. He didn't want to become embroiled in an internal dispute involving angry Britons who it seemed were ready to kill each other.

"Despite all the differences between us brother, I'm sorry it has come to this." Togodumnus said. "I never wanted to inherit Father's title, I hope you know that?"

Adminius looked at both his siblings, tears in his eyes, "I know that Tog and I swear to you that I was only doing what I thought was right." He looked at Caratacus, "Well little brother this is goodbye, look after him won't you?" He said looking at Tog who was standing to one side. "I will miss you both, please tell Father that I'm truly sorry for any hurt I've caused."

Caratacus let the tears roll freely down his face as he hugged his brother, "Goodbye Adminius, take care. One day I'm sure we'll see each other again."

Adminius leant back, "Be certain of that." He straightened looking at Togodumnus once more serious. "One day I shall return."

Chapter Seven

Varro had watched in horror as the flames had grown higher in the distance at Restormel, bright red and orange licking upwards against the dark sky, the fires danced above the fort as it burnt. He and those around him knew there was little hope for the men in the small buildings inside, what they didn't realise was that they would be next.

"Stay alert men, fire at will once you have a clear view of any targets, aim for the centre of their bodies or at massed groups, and make your shots count." Cammius ordered looking around the walls. The command was specifically for the scorpion crews manning the large cross bows at each corner, underneath their covered towers. Other legionaries lined the walls wearing full armour and watched as dark silhouetted figures approached through the woods, but then stopped still under the cover of the trees, not entering the killing ground of the sterile area all around the fort. Roman archers *sagittarius* stood, every third man and lowered their bows their arrows still knocked and watched the ground outside.

"What are they waiting for?" A legionary asked nearby grasping his pilum, before anyone could answer the sound of chopping broke the eerie night.

"I would guess that they're either fashioning some sort of ram or trying to build some siege equipment of some kind, maybe they're learning eh? Whichever it is, it looks like they've changed their tactics from just running around and screaming like banshees, so it could be a long night." Cammius said. "They must know we'll slaughter them once they step out from under the trees, shame really." He added almost lazily. "Don't worry lads, we'll have them lying dead and fertilising the plants before long, they won't get in here." The expressions on the men's faces showed they weren't convinced.

He turned to Varro his expression changing from one of mild humour to serious concern and asked quietly, "How long before you're missed?"

Varro looked at him, his face full of anguish, "If we don't return to the garrison by this time tomorrow night, and it looks like that might be a distinct possibility, the earliest we can expect to see some sort of relief is the night after probably. It's a full day's ride from Isca remember, but any search party would come here first." He hesitated, "Well that's where I'd head for anyway."

"Bollocks, that's what I was thinking." Cammius said looking around at the soldiers looking to him for reassurance. "Don't worry lads we can hold them off indefinitely here if need be and by the time someone comes looking to see what's going on, we'll have destroyed every last stinking one of them."

The faces staring back at him said they didn't share his belief. A lot of his men had known the auxiliaries at Restormel, they had been detached to the south at the same time and had met with them every day to share information and resources, jokes and laughter.

"I said it didn't I?" Cammius remarked to Varro almost muttering. "I knew it. Those bloody stylus pushers haven't got a clue. We should have had at least a full cohort down here, a squadron of cavalry and onagers." He looked back to the flames, "The bastards wouldn't have dared attack then."

Varro replied, "We're going to face them sooner or later I suppose but to be honest I'd have preferred it to be on open ground with a legion behind me, never mind a cohort. They had the element of surprise with Restormel, they don't have that now and we've got better defences, better trained and equipped men." He looked over the wall and down into the ditch. "We'll slaughter them if they try and climb up here or anywhere else along the defences." He turned again to Cammius. "Have you known them to attack like this before?"

"Not this lot no, there's a first time for everything though I suppose." He turned and faced inside the fort. "Vestius, Vestius." He shouted. "Where are you man?" The legionary appeared from the shadows.

"Yes sir." He shouted back.

"Go and cut some strips off that pig and bring them up here on plates." He shouted. "May as well not go hungry while we wait eh Varro, it'll perk the men up a bit and take their minds off things for a while." He said to his fellow centurion who looked at him surprised at his calmness.

"What?" Cammius enquired. "You can fight hungry, or fight with a belly with some strength giving food inside you, I know which I prefer." He looked about him, "Don't eat if you don't want to lads but I would if I were you. And it'll make the hairies jealous eh, the dirty bastards?" He laughed to himself as he patrolled up and down the wall.

As the night wore on and the tension within the fort grew, the sound of chopping from the nearby woods was replaced by other sounds, sawing and banging. Cammius had ordered that water be drawn from the well in case of fire and twenty full buckets littered the small area below. He had also sent half his force to get some rest if they could whilst the other of half of the century manned the walls and waited. Just before dawn one of the sentries saw movement in the trees.

"Sir," he shouted, "directly in front of my position." The legionary pointed into the still dark woods. "Something's coming this way."

Varro felt the hairs stand up on the back of his neck, not because of the coming fight but because of the legionaries words, 'something's coming this way.' He knew it was Britons but the words hadn't helped the already nervous soldiers manning the defences. He strained his eyes looking into the woods, leaning forward in an effort to try and work out what it was that was coming towards them.

"I've got movement to the north as well sir!" Shouted another soldier, he was on the opposite side of the fort.

"Here too!" Reported another, "Directly in front of my position!" Shouted a legionary to the left.

"What the fuck is going on?" They're coming from all around us." Cammius said turning to Varro.

"Well at least we'll see what they've been up to soon enough then." Varro said.

Cammius turned inward and shouted. "Stand to. Stand to." One of the men struck the triangular alarm bell and the sound of running boots reverberated around the lower level of the fort as men ran putting on their helmets, it was quickly followed by the noise of them climbing up the ladders. Within seconds they were all in place puffing for breath, looking out over the walls. The sound now coming from the woods was that of plants and small trees snapping. Large dark shapes moved towards them until they got to the edge of the tree line but they were still obscured in the poor light.

"I still can't make out what the fuckers are up to, can you?" Cammius asked.

Again Varro strained his eyes, "I think they've made covers, wooden shields." Varro said.

"Standby!" Cammius shouted as archers knocked their arrows and the scorpion crews prepared to unleash volleys of bolts into the attackers, those with pilums stood ready with their arms back, left feet slightly forward and then everything stopped. Soldiers looked out into the gloom but nothing moved. Varro squinted into the dark but could only make out large black clumps in the foliage, and then it started. From somewhere outside a horn blew, and from all directions, the Britons advanced on the fort under the cover of layers of wood hammered and roped together.

"The fuckers must have used the kit from Restormel." Cammius said. He turned to the defenders and shouted, "If you can't get a clear view go for the feet and legs."

Immediately arrows began to thump into the wooden shields held above and in front of the attackers and as soon as they were within javelin range, pilums began banging and thumping into the wood, sinking deep, but none of the Britons fell.

"Fire arrows." Cammius shouted as his archers began to light their arrows from the braziers on the wall. Within seconds the lit sleek missiles joined the others that were being fired, but still the Britons advanced eerily silent.

"Keep it up lads, the bastards will start to drop soon enough." Cammius ordered. He grabbed a light javelin from a stack leaning against a corner and hurled it at the nearest flat shield. The covers the attackers were carrying were now all like large hedgehogs as they got closer, large spikes quivering with the movement of the men below.

"The ditch will slow them down." Varro shouted. Before the wall, the Britons would have to negotiate an eight foot ditch that was six feet wide all around the perimeter of the fort. The only place there wasn't a ditch was just in front of the gate where two hedgehogs now approached. Elsewhere the hedgehogs were closing the distance to the ditch.

"The caltrops will sort some of them out." Cammius said but his face turned to horror when the attackers detached outer layers from their shields and slid them into the ditch, some on fire. Now they had fresh shields, the caltrops were covered and the ditches virtually ineffective except for their depth. Slowly the Britons entered the ditches under cover and got to within feet of the walls. Men leant over the defences and hurled javelins downward sighing with effort, they sunk deep into the wood but still had no discernible effect. Suddenly men to the left and right of Cammius and Varro began to fall, struck by arrows fired from the treeline.

"Cover!" Cammius ordered as soldiers brought up their shields or dropped down behind the spiked wood that made up the top of the walls. Varro crouched down next to Cammius as arrows continued to smash into the defences, shards of wood and splinters beginning to fly through the air where some of the missiles hit the top.

"We can't stay under cover." He shouted to Cammius over the sound of the raining arrows. "We have to see what they're doing and where."

"And just what do you suggest at the moment? If we put our heads up they'll take them off." He replied to Varro hunched down.

"And if we stay down here, they'll be over the wall in no time." Varro said just as a loud banging started that shook the forts timbered front.

"They must have a battering ram of some sort and are going for the gates." Varro said. "I'll take my men and cover it." He said to Cammius, stooping and making his way to the ladder. "To me." He shouted as the figures of his men scuttled to the ladders nearest them.

"Cornelius where the fuck are you?" Shouted Cammius.

"Here sir." An uncomfortable voice replied from somewhere on the length of wall adjacent to his own position.

"Take ten men and help Centurion Varro man the gate. We can't let those blue nosed bastards inside. If we do we're done for."

"Sir." Cornelius replied and then began shouting men's names as he descended a ladder.

"Keep it up lads. These fuckers are not, I repeat not going to take this fort. Do you hear me?" Cammius shouted.

"Sir." A chorus of voices acknowledged his order as others continued to hurl javelins, their archers now firing into the trees to try and keep the enemy bowmen at bay.

"Now get up and take some lives." He ordered the others.

Varro skidded to a halt just before the two gates as another thump hit the other side, they bowed inwards dust flying up and he caught sight of the attackers through the gaps in the wood.

"Get some of those pilums over there on the double." He shouted pointing to another stack of javelins that had been propped up against a corner of the barracks. A soldier passed him one and he waited for the next strike on the gate. With a tremendous bang the gates bowed inward again. He thrust the javelin through the gap and heard a scream of pain as the wood came together again trapping the pilum. There was only about a ten foot space on the inside of the entrance to the fort and five soldiers now waited there for the next strike against the gate.

Repeatedly the Britons rammed the entrance again and again, they were stabbed with pilums through the gaps when the wood bowed threatening to break.

"Sir we can't hold them like this forever." Grattius said.

Varro desperately looked round the interior of the fort. "Take two men and get the wagon from the stable. I saw it when we first arrived and anything else you think is useful, we'll barricade the gate." He said to Grattius.

"Breech." A voice shouted from up above on the wooden ramparts. "Breech." The voice repeated.

Varro glanced up and saw that fights were breaking out above all over the walls as the Britons leapt inside. Somehow they had managed to get into the fort.

"Stay here." He told the men with him. "And make sure this gate is secure."

Those with him looked up at the fighting. "Don't look at that lot, concentrate on what you have to do here or we're all fucked." He turned and ran to the nearest ladder, climbing up he saw Cammius directing the battle.

"How did they get in?" Varro shouted from behind him.

"It looks like they've stuck javelins into the walls and climbed up them, not bad for a load of barbarians eh, clever bastards aren't they?" Cammius looked round the walls once more. "Shields," He bellowed, "use your shields, get behind them and push the fuckers back over the walls."

Warriors continued to climb over the sharpened wooden stakes that made up the top of the fort's defences. The legionaries now had no alternative but to fight behind their shields in one's and two's. Varro saw one soldier thrust forward striking an attacker with his shield boss; the rounded metal struck the man squarely in the middle of his face. Quickly the soldier pulled back the shield and punched it forward viciously catching him again. Varro saw the damage the boss had done to the man's face when the shield was withdrawn and readied to strike again; his face was a crushed bloody mess. The second shield punch rendered him senseless and he fell to the ground and then off the platform and into the interior of the fort, where he was stabbed with a gladius by one of the legionaries below.

Other soldiers were now crouched behind their own shields with their legs braced punching them forward and thrusting with their swords like pistons. The centurion saw one who got his timing wrong as the tip of a long sword blade cut deep into his face just above the nose, blood gushed from the wound and the legionary fell back screaming in agony and shock. For an instant Varro saw his own death. Was he really to be slaughtered in a minor skirmish at a place no-one would remember in the future? The image of his hacked and stripped body propelled him into action. He picked up a scutum and charged forward at the nearest Briton punching out and then thrusting with his spatha. Battle rage took over as he thrashed, ducked and killed mercilessly.

He was suddenly calm as the rage continued and then took over. He was aware of his body moving, his sword cutting, stabbing and slashing, his shield being propelled half an arm's length out and returned in an instant to cover his width, this was battle. As he moved the horse hair plume on his helmet waved and bobbed as he relished the moment, in, out, parry, slice. He was faintly aware of screams around him, of cries of pain and shouts of anguish, it was close as if somewhere on another level, he continued his work, he felt more alive than he had for a long time.

Another Briton hurdled over the wall and landed setting his eyes on him, he carried a double bladed war axe, he snarled and advanced. Varro pursed his lips vaguely aware that this new opponent was muscular and athletic looking, a real test. He set his feet, legs slightly apart, left foot facing his foe first, shield close, body crouched, sword ready. The Briton launched himself into the air slamming down with his axe. It hammered into the shield splitting the metal skirting. Varro had a chance to stab him but as he thrust forwards the warrior twisted ripping the blade free and the point of his Spatha hit air.

His enemy grinned showing brown teeth, his eyes white. The centurion backed up giving himself space but he bumped into a legionary fighting another intruder facing the other way. He crouched lower not daring to turn as the Briton ran at him again. He feinted as if to leap into the air but then ducked low and swiped the weapon at Varro's feet. He dropped the shield until he heard it strike the ground but the blow of the axe was so great it knocked the scutum inward, causing Varro to lunge forward. The warrior punched up with an elbow, it struck the side of his face guard, making him unsteady on his feet, dizzy, his ears ringing but he smiled. That incensed the Briton who brought his axe up for another enormous blow and then he froze and jerked forward, once, twice, a third time and then fell face down. Varro saw three arrows embedded into his back, he looked over and saw an archer wave quickly and then draw another missile ready to launch it elsewhere. He'd been lucky, battle rage or not.

The mayhem seemed to go on for an eternity, in reality it was probably only mere minutes, but the defenders slowly began to win the fight for control. Dumnoc's warriors were thinning out on the walkways and those that remained were surrounded by the Romans and killed or pushed back over the walls.

"That's it lads," shouted Cammius in the thick of the fighting, "now contain the bastards and make sure they don't get up again."

As the soldiers began hurling javelins and firing arrows at those still trying to climb the defences, the Britons launched another volley of arrows of their own from the woods, but this time the Romans ignored them seemingly impervious. They weren't however and many were wounded taking sharp iron barbs into their exposed flesh. Projectiles deflected off armour and flew at every angle as the desperate resistance continued. Varro was suddenly aware of white hot pain in his left shoulder, looking down he saw an arrow had struck him and forced its way through his chainmail. Automatically he grabbed the shaft and pulled it free shrieking in agony as he did so. He threw the arrow over the side of the wall and looked down at the gate on the interior. The wagon was now upside down and pilums had been thrust into the ground behind it to stop it from moving, soldiers stood around crouched and watching the entrance for the next attack.

"Concentrate on the gates." Cammius ordered. Legionaries ran to the position above and rained javelins down. The large shield the Britons had fashioned to cover their heads was now falling apart and pilums were penetrating the wood easily. A horn blew from the woods and those around the perimeter started to retreat. A hail of missiles followed them wounding a few who fell away from their huddles crying in pain, they were instantly targeted and fell silent. One group under their makeshift shield abandoned it as it started to fall apart and ran. The men of Statio Deventia cheered as the enemy fell back into the undergrowth of the trees to no doubt regroup and lick their wounds.

"Excellent, excellent lads well done, told you we'd stop the bastards." Cammius shouted, turning he saw wounded and dead all around him. "Right let's make one of the barracks into an infirmary. Get these men down out of harm's way and get them treated and if any of them," He pointed to a prone Briton, "are still wriggling, give them some iron and hurl them over the side." He looked down into the interior at the gate. "Get those defences re-enforced with anything you can find, they'll be back at some point, I'd wager a thousand denarii on it and make sure a raging bull couldn't breach it."

Later as the sun rose high up into the sky, clouds began to appear and the next few hours were taken up removing the dead, who for the time being were placed at the rear of the fort. The wounded were carefully helped off the ramparts and taken to the infirmary. Those who could walk went by themselves or with each other if they needed help. The cost of the attack was high, eleven dead, five more were likely to die and nearly thirty wounded, some of whom were capable of fighting on, others who would require specialist treatment something the medics couldn't give them. They were kept comfortable, injured limbs and torsos were bandaged and those that were suspected of being broken or fractured were put into splints.

Varro climbed down and removed his helmet. Wincing he tried to remove his chainmail but found it impossible with his wounded shoulder.

"Let me help sir!" Shouted a legionary running over to help him get his chainmail off as Varro almost fell over grimacing in pain.

Varro bent forward and the soldier pulled his armour over his head, it slammed to the dusty ground. He pushed his blood stained tunic off his shoulder and saw that he'd been lucky. The arrow had penetrated his skin but not too deeply, a small neat hole at the entry point was covered in blood and it hurt like hell.

"Better get that seen to sir, you don't want it getting infected. Looks like it's just a flesh wound though, you should be okay in a few days." He pointed to the infirmary. "Get it bandaged and padded when the medics have finished with the badly injured." He removed Varro's neck scarf and rolled it into a ball. "Hold this on it for the time being, get the blood stopped eh?"

Grattius came running over, "Bastards got you did they sir?"

Varro smiled in gratitude at the legionary who had helped him. "Thank you." He turned to Grattius, "Is anyone else injured, our men I mean?" He asked.

"Came through without a scratch sir, the lot of us, 'cept for you of course, lucky eh?" Grattius replied.

"Good, that's good." He raised his arm testing the pain and movement.

"Better to rest it for a bit eh? Take it easy sir?" Grattius said. He looked over to the temporary infirmary where a line of walking wounded was already beginning to form." Get yourself in there sir." He walked over to the line. "Right you bastards there's a wounded centurion here, make way."

"It's alright Grattius." Varro said. "I'll take my place in the queue. Go and check the men and see if Cammius needs any help will you."

"If you're sure sir, I could stay here with you if you like?" He replied.

"No go and find Cammius," Varro said, "I'll be fine. He needs you more than me at the moment, do whatever he asks."

"Burial detail." Varro heard an optio shout at the rear of the fort near the corpses of the fallen legionaries.

"Sir." Grattius acknowledged and ran back to the nearest ladder. Varro slumped against the wall more through sudden exhaustion than the pain of his wound and waited to be treated.

As the morning turned to afternoon, more clouds gathered over the small fort and rain began to fall, light at first but as the hours wore on it got heavier. Sporadic arrows were launched from the woods, keeping the sentries heads low and reminding the defenders of the situation, the enemy was still there.

"At least they won't be able to torch the walls eh, not with this lot falling?" Cammius said to Varro looking up at the sky. "So if you're correct, if we can survive tonight, we should expect to see a relief force sometime tomorrow night?"

"I should think so." Varro replied. "Its standard procedure if a patrol hasn't been heard from, they'll come I'm sure."

"Good, good, how's the shoulder?" Cammius asked.

Varro looked down at the padded wound. "It's not too bad, arms a bit stiff." He stretched his left shoulder up. "I'll be okay. At least it wasn't my right one so I can still hold a sword."

"No shield though eh, so that means if the bastards get in again, you're no good to me." Cammius said looking at his shoulder, where a small amount of blood had seeped through the white bandage. "Hopefully we'll be able to hold them off anyway without your help. They must have taken just as many casualties as us if not more." He looked at his cup on the table. "More I'd say because there must be about twenty of them lying dead outside as well." He looked at Varro, "It all depends on how many of them there are out there I suppose and how strong a desire they have to take this place. We've done better than those poor sods at Restormel that's for sure." He took a glug of water from his cup. "Ugh water, still at least its fresh, got to keep a clear head though. Good job we've got the well or we'd be in trouble. So what do you think our friends out there will try next?" He asked Varro.

"I don't know," he replied, "maybe they'll realise that it's a nut they can't crack and just disappear. One thing's certain though, as soon as I'm out of here I'll be doing my best to track them down."

"Maybe it would be better if they attacked again." Cammius said. "They can throw themselves at the walls all they like and we'll keep stopping them, we'll kill more of them than they do of us and they'll give in eventually."

"Yes but if they have hundreds out there it won't matter to them because they'll keep whittling us down until there's no-one left to fight." Varro replied.

"Mm good point, do they view life so recklessly?" Cammius asked.

"It's not about life so much as honour. They see us as occupiers who are repressing their people and taking their land, they'll do anything they can to stop that." Varro said.

Cammius frowned. "I know a little about them through a few I know." Varro went on but not willing to say who it was he knew or why. "They believe we betrayed them after years of peace between the Empire and Britannia, years of trade and relative prosperity. They see us as thieves, liars and betrayers and those out there will either get what they want or die trying."

"Really?" Cammius replied. "Well I don't know about any of that, but what I do know is that they've chosen the wrong soldier to fuck with this time and I'll do everything I can and so will my men to ensure they don't take this fort."

"And so will I, and my men obviously. I'm just telling you what I've been told. I'm sure we would do the same if they were on our soil." Varro took some water.

"Yes I suppose you're right," Cammius replied, "but we're just soldiers and it doesn't pay to get too close to the enemy or our so called allies for that matter. Too much thinking will get you killed, that's why I try and avoid it." He laughed. "Bollocks to it, a little wine won't hurt hey?" He said reaching for the amphora nearby.

The tension had dropped somewhat around the fort, since the savage fight to repel the attackers. It was always the same during a battle and the men settled into a routine of checking weapons and stocking up on others where they would be needed most. With the rain still falling, the chance of fire damage was all but gone for the time being, but the buckets remained in place just in case, Cammius was taking every precaution he could. Sounds could be heard from the forest as the Britons made their own preparations for another assault as sentries watched from the walls avoiding the occasional arrow fired in their direction.

"I doubt they'll come again whilst it's light, once its dark maybe, if they've got any sense anyway. They'll know they haven't all that much time before someone comes looking for my patrol and then they'll be gone." Varro said.

"The best result would be for them to try again tonight, lose a lot of their people and then for the survivors to get caught by some of our cavalry before they can slip away. They'd be cut to pieces." Cammius replied.

"Their leader doesn't seem naïve, certainly not from the way that first attack went anyway, I even saw some of them wearing helmets and mail that they'd taken from Restormel." Varro said.

"Yes I saw that as well, quite disturbing, good job they don't know how to form testudos isn't it? They'd have had more success with one of them than lurking under that wood they nailed together." He grinned, "I don't suppose anyone survived at Restormel. What do you think the chances are?" Cammius asked.

"I'd have thought that if any did survive the initial assault, they wouldn't have lived for much longer afterwards, better to have died straight away than be taken alive." Varro replied finishing his wine. He stood up, "That's enough for me I want a clear head, I'm going to check on my men."

The rest of the day passed fairly quietly, only one legionary was slightly injured through an arrow shot into the fort, it struck his shield and glanced off opening the flesh at the top of his nose. The rain continued to fall, and the ground in the interior of the fort started to turn to mud where there weren't any wooden walkways, as men walked to their posts, everything was either wet or damp. As the sun started to fall, Cammius doubled the guard on the walls whilst others tried to sleep. Fires could be seen through the trees, more fires than they expected to see, clearly, the enemy still had large numbers willing to fight. The Roman defenders knew an attack was imminent but the question was, when it would come. A few hours after dark had enveloped the entire region, the sentries began to see movement in the trees, shadowy figures dragging equipment towards the edge of the tree line. Cammius and Varro had gone to have a look expecting an attack to start but it didn't come and so they waited, hour after hour and still the rain fell.

"I'd have got fed up by now and gone home. You have to admire them I suppose." Cammius remarked standing next to his fellow centurion. "They must be as wet as us? Surely they know they won't penetrate our walls again?"

Varro didn't know if his words were a question or a statement, and he certainly didn't know if it was correct, he didn't reply, just continued to stare out into the wilds. The scorpion crews waited like everyone else, piles of javelins were propped in corners or lay end up in the iron rings designed to hold them for such an eventuality. Archers walked along the walls glistening with water, carrying their bows, whilst legionaries stood holding their pilums, watching the woods.

"I did think about asking you and your men to make a run for it this morning. At least if you'd got through we'd know that support was on its way to deal with these barbarian bastards." Cammius said.

"I was waiting for you to ask and as the commander here, you could have ordered us to make the attempt. The trouble with that would be the gates would have been open for us to get out on horseback, and you'd have been weak until you managed to secure them properly again. Even if we'd managed to get away from here, we could have been ambushed further away and you wouldn't have known a thing about it." Varro said.

"How many of them do you think are out there, hundreds, thousands?" Cammius asked.

Varro turned to look at him, rain falling from his helmet, "Have you considered that this may be an uprising and as we sit here Isca is under siege as well?"

Cammius grinned sarcastically, "You can't be serious, a full rebellion all over the country, is that what you mean?"

Varro shook his head to get rid of some of the water on his red plume and rain splattered over Cammius. "Sorry." He said. "Yes a full scale rebellion, we don't know what we're dealing with. I thought you had considered the idea of us breaking out and had discounted it for that same reason."

Cammius wiped his face, "I hadn't thought about it, Mars help us if you're right though." He lent forward watching the rain running off his plume, "All the more reason to hold fast then eh?" He stood up. "You haven't mentioned this to any of the men have you?"

"No, it's the last thing they need running through their heads. What I have told them is that by this time tomorrow night a full cohort will be here and will be cutting them," he nodded outside, "to ribbons." Rain fell from his helmet again.

With thick cloud cover and rain still pouring, the Britons attacked again. They had constructed larger wooden shields and walked slowly towards the forts walls. Scorpion bolts, arrows and javelins thundered into their covers, once more having little or no effect.

Chapter Eight

At Deva, Caradoc, Ardwen and Brennus had waited at the wine stall all evening until it had eventually closed but no Roman official had come to see them. Nynniaw had returned to find the three still sat outside with two large amphorae's unopened and had passed on the Quaestor's apologies. He was a very busy man but would make efforts to see them the next day they were told.

"What is a Quaestor?" Ardwen asked. "Sounds like something we'd find in our fishing nets."

Nynniaw looked surprised. "You don't have a Quaestor in Isca? They are very important administrators that work directly for the Governor, surely if you sell livestock to the army, you must have come across one of them?"

Caradoc realising that Ardwen may have overstepped the line by demonstrating his lack of knowledge said, "We don't speak with them, we're farmers not administrators, all business transactions are carried out by the elders, they oversee all trade with the Romans."

"Mm," Nynniaw said, "well they spend their days with their heads buried in scrolls dealing with all manner of things, receipts and the disbursement of money. When they're not doing that they maintain all official records and oversee contracts. As well as that they look after all the equipment for the legion they are responsible to and the pay of their soldiers. As you can imagine its very time consuming but Batius has assured me he will find time tomorrow to see you." He looked from man to man. "I'll go and check with him first thing and come and find you."

"Well it looks like we'll be staying for a couple of days then." Ardwen said, "May as well enjoy some more wine." He smiled opening another amphora and poured more wine.

"It's late and time for me to turn in. My wife will be wondering where I've been all day." Nynniaw said. "Are you staying here all night or do you want me to show you where you can sleep tonight? If I were you I'd have a clear head for tomorrow's meeting with Batius."

"That would be good of you, thank you." Caradoc replied. He turned to Ardwen and Brennus, "I'll go with Nynniaw if you two want to stay here for a while?"

Ardwen picked up the amphorae and passed the other to Brennus. "May as well come along, there's nothing else to see anyway except patrols of Romans wandering around."

Nynniaw showed them to a roundhouse that was empty except for a fire place and four beds. "Take your pick," he said waving at the beds, "we use this house for relatives when they visit. It's basic as you can see but I'm sure you won't mind that."

Caradoc walked to one of the straw filled beds whilst Brennus lit the fire. "This will be fine," he said, "after travelling I could sleep for a week in a thorn bush, thank you again Nynniaw, we'll see you in the morning."

"Goodnight." Nynniaw said and pulled the door skin shut as he left.

"What do you think?" Ardwen asked Caradoc collapsing onto the bed with his amphora. Dust blew up as he landed.

"We'll see what tomorrow brings. I'm sure this Batius will want to see us in the fort, it'll give us a good opportunity to have a look around eh?" Caradoc replied. "Haven't you had enough of that?" He asked looking at the cup in Ardwen's hand.

"I'll have this one and then get my head down, you too Brennus, I don't want you with a sore head tomorrow." Ardwen said. "Do you want one more?" He looked over to Caradoc but he was already snoring.

The next morning they were still asleep when Nynniaw arrived. "Good morning gentlemen." He said pulling the door skin aside to reveal a sunny morning.

"Ugh the light," Ardwen complained rolling over. "Shut the door before you blind me."

"I've spoken to Batius," Nynniaw went on ignoring Ardwen's complaint, "and he'll see you in a couple of hours," He tied the door skin open, "at his office. I trust that is acceptable?" He looked round at the prone figures. "He's a very busy man remember?"

"Yes that's fine." Caradoc replied. Do you know where we can get some food?" He asked.

"Yes," Nynniaw said, "if you walk past the wine stall where you were last night, further along the road is a place that sells everything you could want for breakfast, although it's mid-morning now." He smiled. "They're open all day though, have you coin?"

"Yes thank you." Caradoc replied rolling up onto his knees. "We'll meet you there later."

"Very well, don't go missing now or Batius won't be happy." Nynniaw said leaving the roundhouse with the door skin tied open.

"Ugh my head feels like a herd of cattle have stampeded through it." Ardwen said moaning.

Caradoc stood up and stretched, "Maybe that last cup of wine was off eh?" He picked up the amphora lying beside Ardwen and turned it upside down, it was empty as was the one Brennus had taken to bed. "Or maybe it was the quantity you drank?"

"Why are you two shouting?" Brennus rolled over to face them.

Caradoc laughed, "You two need to curb your drinking if you can't handle it." He pulled the rough blanket off Ardwen. "I feel fine but I didn't guzzle as much as you pair." He looked at the groaning men. "Come on up, we've got work to do." He said. Brennus and Ardwen moaned again.

A few hours later refreshed somewhat after breakfast at the stall Nynniaw had recommended, they waited for him to re-appear. They didn't have to wait long as he met them with a smiling face, "Are you ready? I was afraid you'd still be in bed, I'm glad to see you made it."

"We're ready, lead on." Caradoc said.

Nynniaw took them further along the track where already, the garrison walls were visible, tall and imposing. Banners bearing the symbols of the Twentieth legion fluttered gently on the breeze, a wild boar below three spears.

"How do you find them?" Caradoc said looking at the huge gates as they came into view.

Nynniaw smiled. "It was strange at first, we didn't know what to expect but we're used to them now, trade is good and they're fair if we treat them the same and of course we do, you don't want to get on the wrong side of these boys. I know they've taken some of the young men from the region but not from the garrison area itself, taken them to train as auxiliaries in Gaul with promises of money. A lot wanted to volunteer until they found out they'd be leaving Britannia, then they weren't so keen but most went willingly nonetheless, better that than be made to go I suppose. Apparently they take men from the Provinces and they serve elsewhere in the empire, never where they've come from for some reason."

"In case they mutiny maybe?" Caradoc replied looking at the wide river that ran adjacent to the fort. "Imagine training a few hundred or worse a few thousand men in your ways of fighting, equipping them; and then they turn on you? They wouldn't want to risk that."

"Yes, yes I suppose you're right." Nynniaw said as they walked into the shadow of the garrison wall. "Here we are," he said, "I'll talk to the guards, wait here." He walked forward as a soldier came out from the open gate, leaving another where he was. Nynniaw spoke to him and then turned waving, "Come on gentlemen, we don't want to keep Quaestor Batius waiting."

"Wouldn't want that would we?" Ardwen said under his breath.

Caradoc looked at the size of the structure, it was enormous. "It has to be over three hundred paces wide, maybe more."

"Oh yes and this is the narrower part of the garrison, it's twice as long along the other sides, enormous it is." Nynniaw said ushering them forward as they walked through the large open gates of Deva. Caradoc almost felt as if he was being swallowed by some huge stone animal. Inside there were people dressed in Roman robes and soldiers in uniform everywhere they looked.

"The gate we just walked through is called the Porta Praetoria," Nynniaw said demonstrating with his arms, as they walked further into the belly of the beast. "This road we're on now is called the Via Praetoria and it leads all the way down to the Principia, which is the building you see directly in front of you, it's where we'll find Batius in the garrison headquarters. That's the building that was first built and determined the way the rest of the garrison was built on, fascinating isn't it?" He said smiling, almost as if he had constructed the buildings all around them. "These Romans certainly know how to construct things eh? Now to your left is the hospital and to the right a granary, which is obviously where we bring the wheat from the fields. Beyond those buildings on each side are barracks where the soldiers live, they call them centuriae. They build them near every gate of which there are four in case of emergencies. Would you believe there are still tribes resisting them, how backward eh? Fighting a people who can accomplish this sort of thing is just stupid if you ask me."

Brennus said, "There is a settlement in the south built by Britons that is constructed along similar designs, it has straight roads and the houses are built along lines. None are high like these though."

"Really," Nynniaw said. "I wouldn't have thought it possible because we've certainly never had anything like it up here." He replied. "Come along now," he said seeing the three men staring in wonder at the high buildings all around them. "We don't want to miss our appointment, we were lucky to get this one after someone dropped out, come along now."

He led them further along the road describing a huge building to the left where the occupants bathed called the thermae. "Oh yes that is very popular, I'll show you inside when we've seen the Quaestor if you like, you'll be amazed. They have different rooms, one where you exercise to work up a sweat and then hot, warm and cold baths where they go to relax after a hard day's work. It's where some of our people work for them as well scraping their skin and making sure things run smoothly."

"Slaves you mean?" Ardwen said.

"Well I suppose you could call them that but they have meals provided for them and accommodation, some of their masters even give them gifts and take them to their villas in the summer if they have them. In the winter they are warm did you know they even have heating under the ground?"

The three men looked at him in surprise, "What do you mean warmth from under the ground?" Caradoc asked.

"Yes, yes it's true. They have perfected a system where before they construct the actual buildings, they dig out what they call foundations in the earth, large holes for the place to stand on. Inside the foundations they put in these square blocks that the heat runs through, hypocausts they call them, amazing things. They make the walls hollow as well sometimes so that the heat flows along these hypocausts and rises into the walls so in the winter you have warm feet and don't have to have a fire burning all day and night inside."

The three men looked at him quizzically as they continued along the road.

"Oh yes," Nynniaw continued, "we can learn a great deal from them, just look around, magnificent isn't it and all built around the curve of the river so there's plenty of fresh water and the waste gets washed away. Very clever indeed I must say."

"You sound as though you admire them and that they've improved everyone's lives." Brennus said.

"Well I suppose I do if I'm being honest." Nynniaw replied.

"I'll wager those working as slaves don't have the same view on life." Caradoc said.

"Mm maybe," Nynniaw replied and went on, "now on the right we have the tribunorum, this row is where all the tribunes' live and directly in front of us is our location, my good men. Now when we get inside I will speak with the Quaestor's secretary and when he's ready he'll call us forward, in the meantime we will be given seats where we'll wait." He looked them up and down. "You'll have to do as you are I suppose."

The three men looked at each other again and Caradoc could see that Brennus was getting agitated by Nynniaw's attitude. He looked at Brennus glaring, imploring him to calm down. They entered an unguarded door and walked along a well-lit corridor thanks to lots of windows along the external wall. Caradoc took a mental note of the windows realising that they were just too small for a grown man to climb through. He led them up a set of stairs and into a large room where a man sat behind a desk.

"Good day to you secretary Pulmos." Nynniaw said in an ingratiating manner.

Pulmos looked up almost dismissively, "Ah Nynniaw, these must be the men from the south you told me about take a seat, the Quaestor will be with you presently." He said and returned to his scrolls. They waited for some time until a door to the right finally opened and two middle aged men appeared, both wearing togas.

"Thank you Quaestor," one of the men said. "I will ensure that business is sorted out properly."

"See that you do, I don't intend to have this conversation again Aprilus." The bigger of the two men said. Aprilus nodded and made for the exit rubbing his hands nervously.

"Ah Nynniaw," the Quaestor said turning, "here again I see and you have brought the livestock merchants with you, good, please come in." He said ushering them in to his office with a wave of his hand.

Nynniaw hurriedly got up, followed more slowly by Caradoc, Ardwen and Brennus. The Quaestor took his seat behind his large desk, there were none for visitors.

"Now to business," he said, "forgive my abruptness gentlemen but you have caught me at a very busy time. If I didn't have to go round wiping other men's arseholes, my life would be a lot easier." He looked up at the men with Nynniaw.

"So, two hundred head of cattle and the same in sheep, is that correct?" He asked looking at no-one in particular.

"Yes it is." Caradoc replied. "We trade with the Second Augusta usually but they have more than enough stock for the rest of the year. One of the soldiers down at Isca said that you may be interested." The Quaestor was already looking down at the table reading one of his many scrolls.

"Good," he said without looking up. "And how would this affect your trade Nynniaw and the locals, would your people be happy for these gentlemen to provide us with meat?"

"As long as it doesn't adversely affect our own trade then we have no objections sir. To be honest it will mean more food for our people because as you know, some went hungry last winter and we had so few livestock left." Nynniaw was going to add, after you took all our livestock but thought better of it.

"Very good that's settled then." He looked up from the table. "If you can get them up here and in one piece and they're all healthy obviously," he paused, "I'll take them off your hands for a good price."

"What's a good price?" Ardwen asked.

The Quaestor looked at him as if he were something foul on the sole of his boot, "A good price will depend on the quality of the animals." He stood and walked to the door. "Now if that is all gentlemen, I'm very busy and have got an awful lot of appointments to get through today."

As they were ushered out of the office another group were waiting to see him as if to emphasise his point.

"Thank you for your time Quaestor." Nynniaw said bowing. They left the secretary's office and descended the stairs. "Well I think that went very well don't you?" he asked them without giving them a chance to answer. "Once I've taken my money for arranging your deal, you'll still be in pocket don't you worry."

"Brennus grabbed his shoulder and spun him round, he almost fell down the steps. "What are you talking about?" He glared at Nynniaw. "You didn't mention anything about us paying you money."

"Nynniaw tried to lean away from the angry Silurian. "You can't expect me to set up a deal for you like this and not get paid. I've given you my time, my experience, knowledge, accommodation and of course an invaluable appointment with the Quaestor, these things don't come free you know."

"It's alright Brennus," Caradoc said, "We'll pay Nynniaw for his trouble, don't worry about it. Besides if it weren't for him we wouldn't have got to see the inside of this magnificent garrison would we?"

Brennus blushed suddenly remembering that the entire visit was a ruse. "Oh yes, well if you say so." He shoved Nynniaw and let the matter go. He took them back to the settlement straight away having either forgotten about taking them to see the baths, or was unhappy that Brennus had manhandled him.

"Well my friends," he said, "that all went very well indeed. Now don't forget when you return with your livestock to send a rider forward to find me first and I'll arrange for somewhere for them to graze."

"And how much will that cost?" Ardwen asked smirking.

"Oh nothing, nothing," he said, "Well I'll add it to my costs eh?" He smiled like someone Ardwen wanted to punch.

"Thank you for everything." Caradoc said, "We'll be seeing you soon." He grasped Nynniaw's wrist. "You have been more help than you'll ever know."

The three warriors retrieved their mounts and headed south.

As soon as they were clear of listening ears Caradoc said, "That was convincing, you two being upset at that Roman churl taking our money."

Ardwen smiled, "I forgot for a moment it was all make believe. Still he won't doubt our word now eh?"

"You should have let me cut his tongue from his head." Brennus said. "Then he wouldn't be able to stick it up the Quaestor's arse ever again."

The three men laughed and kicked their horses into a gallop.

"Stand to." Cammius ordered as men ran from the barracks through puddles and mud to climb wet ladders. Night had fallen completely now but fires could be seen burning in the woods, where the enemy had concentrated their force. Cammius had ordered his men to construct torch posts that now lined the fort's walls and despite the rain, animal fat kept them alight, scutums covered others from a few feet above. The flames from the torches allowed partial visibility below where an eerie half-light existed and seemed to feed on the fort's defences like a fiery tide. Arrows were launched from every side towards the defenders, some fell, most were lucky and a few saw arrows glance off their helmets or shields.

"Jupiter's balls," Cammius shouted hurling a heavy spear down into a wooden cover that was nearing the walls, it penetrated with a satisfying thud. "Where did this lot appear from? There are twice as many of them than there were before."

No-one answered as men fired and hurled projectiles at the covered warriors, every now and again one would fall out from cover, injured with a javelin or with an arrow in a leg or foot. They didn't live long.

"They'll find it a lot harder to climb this time thanks to all the rain." Varro shouted as he threw another spear, it landed square in the shin of an attacker who screamed and fell unseen under the cover he had been holding.

"Hold," Cammius shouted, "cease fire. Wait for them to try and climb up, we need to conserve what we've got." He picked up another pilum. "Wait until you're certain of a target." He shouted as the soldiers drew closer to the edge, as more arrows were sent their way, hitting an unfortunate few and missing others. Cammius watched from behind his shield as one arrow careened off the side of his helmet and ricocheted into the fort somewhere behind him, landing unseen.

"Wait for it lads, hold." He shouted, as he saw his men's faces eager to return fire, to launch a volley of their own.

"Now, loose!" He screamed, as deadly hails of javelins were hurled from above onto the now unshielded Britons who were desperately trying to scale the walls. Shrieks of pain and anguish met their ears as the enemy fell back to the ground. One landed on the top of the large wooden shield he had used previously to get close, a pila piercing his shoulder. He tried to rise as an archer fired an arrow into his screaming face, embedding itself between the nose and upper lip. He fell back again and was finally silenced as a scorpion bolt entered his head from the side as it bent at an unnatural angle. The corpse fell from the wood and into the mud and blood that was now the surface the Britons were fighting against, as well as the defenders. Another attacker was speared by a javelin that hit him on the right cheek the sharp weapon sank deep, exited his neck at the rear and embedded itself into his back. He fell, eyes wide in shock.

Varro stopped throwing javelins for a second as he saw what he knew could only be a shield covering the battering ram approaching the gates.

"Ram," he shouted, "They're going for the gates."

Cammius saw the danger, "Archers and scorpion crews, concentrate your fire on the ram, take their legs out." He ordered, his voice cracking through all the shouting. Scorpion bolts and arrows quickly disabled the oncoming ramming crew as their legs were hit. The large shield buckled and fell to the ground at the front with Britons trying to take cover behind. More missiles smashed into the wood as javelins joined them. The men at the rear suddenly dropped the shelter and turned for the cover of the trees, arrows followed them as some fell wounded into the sanctuary of the darkness.

The Roman defenders made short work of those still trying to climb the walls, those that weren't wounded or killed before they reached the top, were stabbed as they tried to enter the fort and fell away. Soon a horn blast ordered their retreat and those on the ground withdrew. The injured lying prone and unable to move were left where they lay until archers put them out of their misery.

"Hold your fire." Cammius ordered turning to Varro, both men were soaked and panting for breath after their exertions. "That should keep them away for a while." He looked around the defences. "Right men let's get the injured to the infirmary."

Varro said, "That just might be their last attack, they'd be fools to try again."

"Never underestimate the enemy." Cammius said as he lifted a legionary under his armpits and helped carry him to a ladder. "The trouble with barbarians is they don't know when they're beaten."

"Come on," Varro said, "Let's get him down," looking at the injured soldier who was unconscious, "and get out of these clothes."

Dumnoc had watched as his people ran back into the trees as bowmen covered their retreat. One, a young man suddenly fell forwards dropping his sword. As he landed Dumnoc saw that an arrow had hit him right in the middle of the back of his head, he died instantly.

"Get back out of range." He shouted as others ran past him, "Get to the fires where the druids are, they will help those who are hurt." He waved at them as two others dragged another beyond him by the arms, his legs trailing in the mud. The injured man looked terrified as he tried to scream at a scorpion bolt that had punctured his chest from the rear, blood poured from his wound but he couldn't form any words.

Dumnoc felt fury and anger at what he had witnessed, at what he had asked these people to do, at their suffering. He had lost count of those dead or dying and wanted nothing more than to leave this place. The Romans had built their fort well and he now realised that this was a mistake. They had revelled in their victory over Restormel and should have slipped quietly away but buoyed by the destruction of the smaller fort, they had gone a step too far. He looked up at the burning torches where legionaries stalked the walls and ground his teeth in frustration. Soon re-enforcements would come looking for the patrol he had seen riding in through their gates, knowing they were not a resident troop, it would only be a matter of time before others came searching for them. He was running out of time and had suffered too many casualties, turning he followed his retreating warriors further into the woods.

"Make sure the men stay alert, they shouldn't need any reminding after what they've been through, but I don't want to take any chances." Cammius said instructing an optio. "We must have nearly broken their backs but you never know and get the last of the pila up there on the walls."

"Yes sir right away." The optio saluted, turned and left the room at a trot.

"Help me out of this will you?" Cammius asked Varro, struggling with his armour. The two officers helped each other out of their armoured shells and quickly removed their damp tunics. Cammius placed his segmented armour over a standing wooden cross designed for the purpose, as Varro draped his chainmail over the back of a chair. They looked at each other wearing just their breeches and boots and laughed.

"These can come off as well." Cammius said as he undid the tie holding his trousers up and whipped them off. He hurled them into a corner where they landed with a wet thump.

"Vestius." He shouted.

"Yes sir?" The ever present Vestius answered running into the room, he halted suddenly seeing his commander virtually naked.

"Find me a towel and a fresh pair of breeches and the same for Centurion Varro here before we freeze our bollocks off and get that fire lit man." He said indicating the dead ash in the grate.

"Certainly sir, right away." He replied and left quicker than he had arrived.

"How's your shoulder?" Cammius asked looking at Varro's wound.

"It doesn't feel that bad at the moment but I'm sure it will stiffen up again soon, I didn't even have time to think about it during the attack." Varro replied.

"Good, that's good." Cammius said easing himself into a chair. "Sit, sit please."

"I need to take these off." Varro said undoing his breeches and removing them. Cammius picked up an amphora.

"I think we've deserved this Centurion." He said, grinning as he leaned forward pouring the golden liquid into two cups on the table, as he felt water drip out of his boots. "These two can come off as well." He removed his boots and hurled them towards his tunic.

"Damn these barbarians, couldn't they wait for more civilised weather conditions before launching an attack?" He emptied the cup in one go and poured another. "I can't see them coming back tonight after the hiding we've just given them. Their dead are everywhere out there and it's going to take a day to clear them all up. Varro removed his boots and sat down picking up his cup, he too drained the contents without stopping just as Vestius reappeared carrying fresh breeches and tunics.

"I'll be back with the wood in a moment sir." He said realising the two centurions were now completely naked.

"Good man." Cammius said and then took another drink, he looked over at Varro. "I'll bet you didn't think you'd be in a position like this when you rode down here eh?" He asked smiling.

"Bollock naked?" he grinned, "With another centurion in the middle of the night, or being under siege inside this fort?" He replied pulling on his fresh breeches.

"Either, well both, I suppose is as unpredictable as the other I would say." Cammius said.

"You're correct on both counts, we all thought we'd have a nice quiet ride down here and go back without witnessing anything, how wrong you can be?" Varro replied.

Cammius topped up their cups. "So what's it like being in the explorates? I should imagine you and your men are used to seeing your fair share of action."

Varro frowned, "Most people just think we're regular cavalry or maybe messengers until they see we're not auxiliaries, in answer to your question though, it's good I enjoy it. I've always ridden and when the opportunity came to join the equites legionis and do something different than shouting at soldiers, I jumped at the chance. After nearly ten years I looked to do something different and found it. Things can get a bit hairy sometimes, especially when we're in the middle of nowhere with no support, but I wouldn't change it for the world," he hesitated, "well almost anyway." He took some more wine.

"Why, what do you mean?" Cammius asked.

Varro hesitated, "My entire troop got wiped out a few years ago, I was the only one to survive and if I had been with them, I wouldn't be here tonight."

"What happened?" Cammius asked.

"We found ourselves surrounded by Caratacus or Caradoc, whatever he's calling himself these days. We got ambushed and took refuge on this bloody great mountain well most of the survivors did anyway." He said pausing.

"I heard about that, it was not long after we invaded wasn't it?" Cammius asked. Without waiting for a reply he continued. "I was still in Germania at the time training recruits." He returned to the subject, "The good old Twentieth came and pulled you out didn't they?"

Varro stared at the table thinking back to the night he had spent alone on the hill watching the men of the Second Augusta fight for their lives. "Yes that's the incident. Even the General took an arrow, not our finest moment."

"Leading from the front though eh?" Cammius smiled. "He's a good man Vespasian and a brilliant leader." He emptied his cup and poured another, he saw Varro watching him. "Don't worry I couldn't get drunk even if I tried after tonight's events."

Vestius returned carrying wood for the fire, which he placed in the grate and on two iron burners that were free standing in the office. Within minutes the two centurions could feel the warmth from the flames.

"Argh that's better eh, luxury compared to before." Cammius said standing holding his fresh pants near a burner to warm them. "Shame we don't have a hypocaust under the floor isn't it?"

Varro laughed, "Somehow I don't think the army cares that much for its soldiers in places like this." He sat back and felt the wine and warmth begin to relax him. "So you don't think they'll come again tonight, the Britons?" He asked.

"I think we've seen the last of them until at least dawn, they'll be out there in the rain trying to plug wounds and burning their dead if they can. It wouldn't surprise me if they've vanished tomorrow." He looked up at Varro and saw that he was falling asleep. He smiled and emptied his cup.

Chapter Nine

Their reconnaissance of Deva complete, Caradoc, Ardwen and Brennus left the newly established garrison town and began to ride slowly south. They had decided to go via the relatively small hilltop fort at Bees Stone to the south-east approximately fifteen miles away. It was far enough from the major garrison not to arouse suspicion as long as they weren't found to be paying too much attention to it and the surrounding land. If they were recognised their plan was to claim ignorance about the Quaestor's duties, they were merely traders seeking to sell their livestock to the men of the legions wherever they found them. The small fortification was easily identifiable from a distance, as it sat on a crag that rose up from the relatively flat plain of the surrounding countryside, nearly four hundred feet high. The fort's walls gave a breath-taking view of the territories to the west, lands that were held by allies of Caradoc, the Ordovices and further to the north, the Deceangli. These lands were hostile to the men of the legions and the sight of the dark mountains in the distance covered in trees did nothing to encourage them to explore the interior.

The brief lowland between the fort and the mountains was a no-man's land, where few ventured except for those who lived there in small settlements of roundhouses. Inevitably they were allies of the indigenous population and were a good source of information for the war bands looking for intelligence about the occupiers to the east, but they tried to live in peace with the invaders. The site of the fort had been in use by the local peoples for centuries and had been a natural location for a hill fort for those in the area that was until the Romans had arrived and taken it from them. The crag loomed large as they approached and from this side the three men had a clear view of the sheer sandstone cliff that led to the summit. On the opposite side, a gentle slope led to the top, but here it was a natural defence that would be accessible to only those brave enough to scale a dangerous vertical wall.

"That would be the best way in." Caradoc said looking up at the cliff face. "They have a few walls on the other side but here, only at the top. We could be at the wall and inside before they knew we were even near and if we went in under the cover of darkness, they wouldn't know they were being attacked until it was too late."

"It's a good plan and one that I want to be involved in." Brennus said. "My sword thirsts for Roman blood and it will drink well from their streams until I make them rivers." He smiled as he spoke.

Ardwen smiled as well, "Do you think you can haul your big bulk up that cliff face Brennus? We wouldn't want your carcass falling and crashing into the trees, it would alert them to our presence and no doubt take about twenty of us with it."

Brennus turned smiling once more, "Don't worry about me, I'll be fine and I'll also be up there before you with your little girl's arms and spindly legs, you must have forgotten our time as young boys climbing in the mountains, I'd be resting at the top whilst you were still pulling your scrawny body up tree roots and crevices. Here," he said looking at the crag, "my blade will be gorging itself deeply from their veins while you are still struggling up the sandstone and tree roots."

Caradoc turned from the crag and looked over as the two men remembered their time as youngsters, when all they had to worry about was raids from other tribes. The attacks however were aimed at livestock not people in the main and there were enough cattle, sheep and pigs for it to be a rare event. The forests were rich with wildlife as well, where dangerous boars were to be avoided unless hunters had a keen eye and were experienced bowmen and hunted in groups with spearmen. Wolves were also to be found wandering in packs but were rarely seen during the daylight hours, unlike the boars they would rarely attack a human being unless cornered, injured or provoked.

As they continued along the track to the base of the fort, they came across a small settlement, it was a cluster of about ten roundhouses where dogs barked and children ran out to greet the riders as they approached.

"Food sirs?" One grubby boy asked his face streaked with dry mud. "We have new food brought to use by the Romans, would you like to try some?"

The three men exchanged glances. "What food do you speak of boy?" asked Ardwen.

"We have fresh apples sir, not sour like our crab apples, they're sweet and tasty. There are also grapes, mulberries and cherries, very nice and sweet as well, come try them my mother has some to sell." He pointed over to one house in particular.

"How did your mother come by these foreign things boy?" asked Brennus.

"She is friends with one of their soldier's sir," his face lit up with pride, "he visits when he has time and gives us food to try. He's also given us vegetables, we've even started to grow our own now and they're all tasty and make our food much better."

"What does your mother do in return for these gifts?" Ardwen asked.

"Nothing sir," he said looking confused, "he just gives them to us, he wants to be our friend, that's all." The boy said grinning honestly.

"We'll take a look." Caradoc said, "thank you." He looked at the small settlement and then back to the boy, "what's your name lad?"

"Elus sir, my name is Elus." The boy said beaming. He turned and ran with the others towards the settlement that was surrounded by a low wicker fence.

Out of earshot of the boy Brennus frowned. "The whore's probably spreading her legs for the entire legion and getting apples in return," Brennus said.

"They're probably just doing what they can to survive my friend, that's all." Caradoc said as they got closer, he saw the boy leading a woman by the hand that he assumed was his mother. She wore a green plaid shawl around her neck that looked to be made from wool and a dress down to her knees made of the same material. She was attractive and in the mid-twenties, perhaps reasons for the generosity of the newcomers.

"I welcome you in peace," She said looking up at the men and smiling a warm greeting, "Would you like some refreshment for your journey?" Five men appeared from the houses behind her carrying swords and axes.

"Are your men as friendly as you?" Caradoc asked watching the men behind her standing like guards. "We are unarmed and are travelling south back to our homes at Isca after trading with the garrison at Deva." He was surprised at how easily he lied. Maybe he had convinced himself he was actually a trader who wanted to live side by side with the Romans in a different reality.

"Trading you say?" Asked one of the men walking forward but drawing level with the mother, he was as tall as Brennus but a little more well-fed as his stomach testified and not as muscular as the broad Silurian.

"Trading yes, we have livestock they are interested in buying, what is it to you?" Caradoc asked.

"We don't want any trouble here." he replied. "If that's all you're interested in, you are welcome, please tether your horses here and take a drink with us." He indicated to the wicker fence and turned walking away, followed by the others. The three Britons dismounted and tied their horses up.

Elus had suddenly become shy and was standing peering from behind his mother. "I am Deorwynn, Elus' mother, welcome to our home."

Her brown hair was long and ran to the middle of her back where it was tied into a tail; here there was also a carved bone pin. Caradoc saw she wore Roman style leather shoes on her feet.

"Thank you," said Caradoc, "we can spare a little time for your hospitality. Your son tells us you have food provided by the Romans?"

She half turned blushing slightly and frowning at her child, "Well we did have quite a lot but most of it has already been eaten, you are welcome to try what we have left if you like?" She said. "Wait here and I'll get some." She turned and went into a roundhouse and returned a few seconds later carrying a tray with different coloured items on it.

"What are those things?" Ardwen asked pointing to a pile of red balls.

She smiled, "Try them they are tasty," she put the tray down on a table, "these red ones are called cherries." She picked one up and handed it to Ardwen, he frowned as he took it between two fingers.

"It feels strange," he looked at Caradoc and Brennus, "like I would imagine an eye to feel if it were outside the head." He grinned and quickly threw the cherry into his mouth, his eyes widened as he bit down onto it.

"Mm," he managed pulling a strange face, "it's full of some sort of tasty juice like a large berry," he grimaced smiling, "quite nice though, try one."

Deorwynn laughed as the three men tried her fruit and Elus lost his shyness as he saw them relax.

"Elus bring four chairs out." She said.

"You have chairs as well?" Brennus asked.

"Of course," she replied smiling once more, "what do you think we are barbarians?" She laughed, the men frowned.

Brennus raised an eyebrow, his features turning dark but before he could respond Deorwynn said, "They are very useful both inside and out but better out here when I have more supplies. With them I don't have to stand all day and set the food up on the table by the track with chairs for anyone who wants to rest and have some refreshment. The soldiers from the fort stop by as well sometimes when they are out on patrol." She pointed up at the fortified wooden structure looming over them from the high crag.

"And what do they give you in return?" Ardwen asked.

"These," she said her hand going into a small purse attached to her belted dress. "They're tiny but we can use them to buy other things at Deva when we travel there, which isn't often but when we do go, I can buy goods." She turned, "Like my hair pin, look, it has a snakes head at one end and a tail at the other." She smiled proudly.

The men leaned forward looking at the pin. "Why would you want a snake pin of all things?" Brennus asked.

"The Romans don't look upon them as evil as we do, to them they are a sign of life and of medicine, don't ask me why but they are." She picked up an amphora and filled three wooden cups. "Here try some wine."

"We don't have Roman coins to pay for it." Caradoc said.

"Don't worry, you can have it for nothing this time but when you come back to trade, you can buy some goods from me and pay me then." She said smiling once more.

The men drank the wine in one.

"Have you been to the fort?" Caradoc asked looking up at the crag.

"Of course many times," she began, "before the Romans came it was an old hill fort, our ancestors lived there, I was brought up on its slope." She pointed. "It's around the other side you can't see it properly from here. The Romans identified it as a good location for their own fort so they threw us off, it's one of the reasons they give us food now to try and make up for it."

"Does it make up for it?" Brennus asked his gaze suddenly serious.

"Well at first….." Deorwynn began to say before she was interrupted.

"No it doesn't" The man said who had first approached them when they had arrived. He had apparently been eavesdropping from the cover of the nearest roundhouse. "Our ancestors lived there as Deorwynn said for many generations but they came and forced us to live down here."

"Oh be quiet," Deorwynn said, her face reddening once more, "you know it's not too bad here and we're out of that dreadful wind in the winter." She turned to the big man. "How many times have we talked about this? We can't do anything about it and things are so much better now in so many ways, we have better food and have access to their doctors and medicine and fine wine, we never had those things before."

"I'm just saying that's all." The man said and turned once more lifting the door skin he went back inside.

"It seems not everyone around here is happy now the Romans have come." Ardwen said.

"The men are unhappy when they remember the old ways but they are still free to hunt and roam the lowlands as they were before." She said. "They're not happy unless they're grumbling about something. I think they feel unmanned by their presence but it's senseless complaining," she looked up to the fort, "they are here and there's nothing we can do about it, we just have to get on with our lives as best we can." She looked at the three men, "Will you take another drink?" She asked.

"Thank you but no," Caradoc said, "we have to be going, we've a long way to travel." He smiled at Deorwynn. "Thank you for your hospitality, do you think your man could show us the best route south?"

She laughed, "Oh he's not my man, that daft oath, Elus' father died three years ago, he's my brother." She went inside and then came out with him following her looking rather sheepish. "Show these men the best way south Elud, it will give you something to do and stop you moaning." He didn't look happy but nodded and went to get his horse.

Two days later as the daylight was fading, Caradoc looked upon the fort once more, but this time he had three hundred warriors with him. They were still some distance away but the prominent crag stood out clearly across the lowland, to the left was a long tree lined ridge rising about two hundred feet, it would provide ample cover for their approach. Elud had agreed to once more help show them the best route to take only on this occasion it was in order to attack the Roman fort at Bees Stone. He had virtually volunteered his services a few days before when it became clear he hated the occupiers as much as Caradoc and his men, telling them that he would do anything to help clear them from their land. There was no doubting his venom as he spoke of their ways and how they had taken over parts of their land and limited their lives. When the warriors had confided their intentions to him, he had said that he and his friends would want to take part in the attack even if it meant moving afterward and leaving his sister behind. He had been told not to say anything of their intent because if word reached the Romans, they would be slaughtered to a man. Elud had reluctantly agreed but had begged to go with them after the assault on what had been his home. Caradoc had agreed saying that he could always use brave men to fight the oppressors.

As darkness began to quickly fall and it became difficult to make out the ridge and the crag beyond, Caradoc raised his arm and signalled his warriors forward, they would use the thick woods as cover and find Elud at the base of the ridge where he had agreed to meet them, saying his sister would be told he was out hunting. Brennus had argued that it wasn't wise to trust the Cornovii, the local people, but he had eventually succumbed. They had agreed that in the unlikely event that they were being led into a trap, they would fight their way clear and disperse back into the mountains to the west as quickly as possible. They knew that the Romans would be hesitant to pursue them, knowing that they could be easily led into an ambush themselves in hostile territory. Caradoc and Ardwen had ensured that they only took only their very best warriors with them, men that they could trust and who would fight their way clear if need be.

Silently, except for the sound of their horses hooves padding on the pine needle covered ground and their breathing, they slowly made their way towards the ridge where their mounts would be left to await their return. Caradoc wondered briefly how many horses would return led by others, rider-less, but he quickly dismissed the idea, now was not the time for hesitation. He knew that Dumnoc was taking the fight to the enemy in the south and had already led two successful raids on villas, now it was his turn to lead by example.

Varro had been wrong about the Britons vanishing the next day and as dawn broke, pale drawn faces stared out at them from the trees across the clearing. The rain had stopped but the ground was covered in mud all around the sieged fort and littered with already decomposing and bloated corpses that were starting to smell.

"Here we go again," Cammius said quietly to Varro, "don't they ever give up?"

He didn't wait for a reply before going on and shouting across the walls. "Choose your targets carefully men and only fire when you are certain of hitting them, this will be their last chance because reinforcements will arrive today and they'll all cover the ground tomorrow, dead and putrid like their friends out there." His words were met with nervous smiles, clearly the men weren't reassured.

As they watched, one man stepped forward out of the trees, he raised his arms showing that he was unarmed but bowmen and the scorpion crews trained their weapons on him regardless.

"Hold." Cammius ordered raising his right arm. He turned to Varro. "Mm I wonder what he wants." He asked.

Varro replied, "Maybe he's going to ask if he can surrender." He smiled, "or most likely, ask, for our surrender."

"Well if he is, he won't get it but what he will get though is an arrow through his head for his trouble." Cammius replied frowning out over the bodies between them and the Britons. He looked quickly to the interior of the fort, "and we haven't got enough space for their surrender anyway." He said smirking.

"Romans," the warrior shouted in heavily accented Latin, "we go now and leave you to this place. We know that your leaders will send help and after many days of fighting we are in no position to face fresh soldiers. We have taken many injured in our number, but we have also bled your men and the other fort is destroyed and its men all dead." He pointed off in the direction of Restormel. "Know this......" he paused, "we will return to this place. We will not let you rest until we have sent you back to the sea. This is our land, our soil where our ancestors were born, you do not belong here and we will fight to the last man or woman, wherever we find you."

The pale faces began to vanish into the foliage until there was only one left, the man who had shouted. He bowed slightly as if in respect and then turned and disappeared into the trees.

Cammius turned to Varro, "Quite eloquent for a barbarian eh?" He said. "Dumb bastard!"

Varro continued to stare outward, "We should wait until we're certain they are gone. It could be a trick." He said.

"Yes I suppose you're right, tricky these Britons eh?" he turned to address his men. "Right, all those who were due to be stood down, go and get some rest, those others are to stay on duty until relieved." He began to walk towards the nearest ladder. "Come on Varro let's get some breakfast and then we'll decide the way ahead eh, I wonder if there's any pork left over?"

By mid-morning there had still been no movement outside the walls of the fort or in the woods beyond, it was quiet except for the carrion fighting and squawking over the corpses below. Cammius and Varro had climbed the ladder three times since the appearance of the chieftain, but had not seen or heard anything that would indicate the Britons were still there, they were sure they had gone. The two centurions had decided upon a plan, rather than waiting for fresh troops to arrive, a squad of twenty four men including Varro's Equites Legionis would venture outside, all had been briefed that at the first sign of trouble they were to retreat to the safety of the fort immediately. The remaining legionaries were stood to and manned the walls and gate, ready to respond if required at a moment's notice. Varro's men had been given legionary scutums that would afford them better protection in case of attack, and they would form a testudo with the other regular troops and withdraw under cover from the defences.

The twenty four men were in six rows of four as the gates creaked open for the first time in days. They all wore full armour, chainmail in the case of Varro's men, segmented armour, for the regular infantry. The first task was to reconnoitre the immediate perimeter where the dead lay up to the edge of the woods, if the area was all clear, they were to look for any signs of the enemy where their camp had been, but were ordered not to enter the woods immediately. It was all to be done in slow time, they couldn't risk any more casualties and they certainly couldn't risk any of the Britons getting beyond their own perimeter.

Varro was to lead the reconnaissance patrol and stood in the front rank with his eyes searching the mud and corpse strewn ground in front of him beyond the gates. He raised the pila he had been given for the task and indicated for the patrol to move forward, shields raised, every soldier was carrying a javelin. Once the last man had exited the gates, they were slowly closed behind them but were not secured in case they needed to retreat quickly. Varro stopped and listened for any sign of movement, his ears scanning in all directions but there was nothing. He turned and looked up above the fort's gates and saw Cammius standing ready, he shrugged down at Varro.

The centurion turned away and said quietly to the men who had volunteered to go with him. "Remember at the first sign of trouble, we're to double back to the gates, shields up and they'll be opened for us, so get inside as quickly as you can. The men on the walls will take care of anyone coming after us, just don't look back."

Mutters met him in reply as eager eyes roamed the ground that had become a cemetery like wasteland outside the fort.

"Advance." Varro ordered quietly as he slowly moved forward lowering his javelin level with the ground. Taking single steps, progress was slow as the small column of legionaries moved away from the gate, a few men gagged quietly at the stench of the swollen and bloated corpses.

"Get your scarves round your mouths and noses if you can't stand the stench." He said ordering the men to halt while scarves were pulled up around their faces, including his own.

"Advance." He ordered again and moved forward. It took some time for them to satisfy themselves that the Britons weren't nearby, except for the dead. Varro halted the men again and called Grattius forward.

"We'll go and have a look from the edge of the trees. The men can wait here while we do it." Varro said.

"Oh good I was hoping you would suggest that." Grattius replied sarcastically grinning at his centurion. Varro didn't reply and told the rest of the men to remain where they were but if he and Grattius were attacked they were to make their own way back to the safety of the fort.

"It gets better." Grattius responded.

"Tip of the spear, remember my friend." Varro said winking and began walking forward with Grattius close behind. Reaching the foliage before the wood, Varro stopped again and listened for any sign of the enemy. He turned to Grattius who shrugged.

"Nothing." He said.

Varro looked back to the walls of the fort where Cammius shook his head and indicated that there was still no movement beyond his position. Varro turned and peered into the undergrowth, another dead body lay on its stomach just inside the bushes with a scorpion bolt buried up to the feathers of its shaft in the centre of the back.

"What can you see?" Grattius whispered moving from foot to foot nervously.

"Nothing except another dead Briton, I can't see anything else, the trees and bushes are too thick." He whispered back without turning still looking into the shadowed cover.

"Good now let's get back inside." Grattius said.

Varro stuck his javelin into the undergrowth and examined the corpse prodding it. He saw that blood had risen to the top surface of the skin in a spotted pattern on the naked back and he knew that it indicated it had been there for a while.

"Come on let's go back, there's nothing else to see and we aren't going to achieve anything stumbling about out here." He said. They turned and got the troops back to the safety of the gates that were quickly closed and barricaded once they were inside.

As the sun started to fall, a full cohort came along the track cutting through the woods, the men on the ramparts cheered and the gates were quickly opened allowing them inside where conditions were slowly getting worse, especially with the seriously injured. With four hundred men in addition to those still fit to fight, it meant the injured could be evacuated to Isca and patrols could be sent out to scout the countryside for the Britons, it also meant that the ravaged auxiliary fort Restormel could be restored and the dead buried. The corpses outside the small legionary fort were piled up and burned, the smell was awful but it was something that had to be done as quickly as possible in order to prevent disease. That night for the first time in many, most of the resident occupants got a good night's sleep as the men of the cohort volunteered to mount the guard around their defences.

The next morning mounted troops set off in three different directions; Varro had chosen to take his men to Restormel to see the damage for himself. The tracks and woods were eerily quiet on the way and once in a while they came across a dead Briton abandoned by those who had decided to leave so quickly. As they got to the clear ground before the wooden walls of the fort, the devastation was apparent for all to see. A large hole now existed along the front approximately fifty paces from the actual gate, where now only smashed wood and charred remains stood at odd angles. The auxiliaries must have been attacked in the same manner as they had been only here the Britons had succeeded in getting beyond the defences properly. The heads of some of the defenders were impaled on the wooden stakes on the top of the walls, they're eyes already gone, more than likely eaten by crows or other carrion.

"It doesn't look like they stood a chance." Grattius remarked looking at the damage."

"This isn't going to be pleasant but someone has to do it, come on." Varro said clicking Staro forward. He stopped again a few yards short of the entrance when the smell hit him.

"Scarves." He shouted as they all lifted the material over their faces and mouths. He got down off Staro. "Grattius, leave your horse with Balbus, let's have a look inside first."

Grattius got down off his mount looking none too pleased and handed the reins to the legionary, he resisted the urge to say something to his commander knowing it wasn't a good idea in front of the men. Varro led the way inside where he was surprised to see a few wooden buildings still standing, the shells at least, he could see the roof had collapsed through the now none-existent doors. He held the material of his scarf against his mouth and nose as the smell threatened to penetrate the cloth.

"Gods it stinks in here." He commented mumbling and moving forward. Inside the shell of one of the old barrack blocks they found the majority of the men who had been forced to retreat there. Charred, blackened bodies lay, some now skeletal through the heat of the fire, others with limbs missing burned away by the intense heat. Open jawed skulls, teeth still white lay amongst ashes with white bones, their mouths open wide in terror as they had been when they died.

"The poor bastards didn't stand a chance once they were in here." Grattius said looking around.

"It was either that or face capture and torture, I suppose." Varro replied, "Personally I don't know which would have been worse."

Every step they took, they had to pick their boots up high to avoid spraying dust clouds of ash and were careful putting them back to the surface. It was impossible to account for all the men who had once manned Restormel. Outside and along the defence's walls that were still intact, they found more headless corpses than those that were still in one piece. Clearly the fight for the small fort had been savage and the defenders had eventually lost, there was however, evidence of dead Britons outside and a few inside, so the attackers hadn't had it all their own way.

"This could have been us quite easily." Varro said. "At least we were warned when they were attacked here, I doubt we'd have been so fortunate if they'd come to us first with the element of surprise."

"What are we going to do about the dead sir?" Grattius asked.

"We'll do our best for them, we would want the same, there's no point in waiting for a burial party to get here from Isca, it will be tomorrow by the earliest." He looked around at the devastation, "They sent a scout back as soon as the cohort got here so there will be a few hundred more troops with us tomorrow. We'll let Cammius know what we've found after having a look round the outlying area and we'll do what we can, even if it's just to get them all in one place."

They checked around what was left of the rest of the small outpost and found virtually nothing of any worth, it had been stripped bare by the raiders and picked clean save for ruined weapons, they had taken the livestock, pay chest, weapons, armour and horses and were now probably miles away. Varro and his men searched the countryside nearby but found nothing in the mud except for a few more dead, who had now become victims to the local wildlife who had taken chunks of flesh from them.

It took a few days for the dead Britons to be burned, and burial in a mass grave for the soldiers who had fallen. More reinforcements arrived from Isca and soon the injured were evacuated safely there and reports were presented to the Governor. The entire fort at Restormel was knocked down and taken apart and rebuilt with larger, stronger defences and manned by legionaries not auxiliaries. Two full centuries now manned both forts as plans were drawn up to build others in line with the suggestions by Cammius. The Britons had come close to destroying two reasonably well fortified and defended positions and it couldn't be allowed to happen again, and every step was taken to ensure it didn't. Ten days after the cessation of hostilities Varro, together with Cammius and his men, slowly made their journey north and back towards Isca. Fresh troops watched them leave from the defences as the small convoy of men, horses and wagons departed, some wishing they were going with them.

Chapter Ten

The fort standing on top of the crag looked peaceful, almost tranquil as Caradoc looked out at it from the highest point of the ridge a few hundred yards away. He and his men had been led into position by Elud a few hours before just as night was falling, but now a virtual blackness coated the ground, although the small garrisoned fort was still visible against a grey cloudy background. This was the nearest point they could reach without the risk of being discovered, and he now watched as warriors passed by him and made their way to the left of the enormous mound and onto the sandstone cliff face. It was a risk because if any of the men were seen by the guards patrolling the walls, the raid would be over even before it started and they would find themselves retreating to the west. Caradoc could just make out a fluttering flag above a tower but so far had not seen any sentries who he knew must be there watching the low ground.

"Are we ready then?" Ardwen asked gripping the hilt of his sword, his teeth white against the dark night and the mud he had smeared across his pale flesh.

Caradoc looked from him back to the defended position once more. "Well I think if they were going to be alerted, they would have been already, come on let's go." He said moving slowly and down the ridgeline following the direction of the men who had gone before them.

Covering the lowland had taken a lot of time as they had moved very slowly so as not to make any noise and they had arrived undisturbed by watching eyes. The majority of the force were gathered at the base of the steep climb, now under the cover of trees and were sat quietly whispering when Caradoc, Ardwen and Brennus arrived.

Caradoc nodded a greeting to those nearest him and walked straight to the sheer cliff face where he checked his sword and looked for a suitable spot to begin his ascent. Looking up he could make out various thin trees and roots which would make for a relative easy climb, or so he hoped.

Elud tapped him on the shoulder, leaned forward and whispered into his ear, "It's like this all the way to the top. The only time it will be really difficult will be when you reach the walls of the fort, because there is only about a foot or two in-between the edge and the actual building, apart from that you won't have a problem."

"Thank you." Caradoc said heaving himself up off the ground. "Remember if you choose to come with us, your life here is at an end. Even if the Romans don't suspect you of any involvement, your life will never be the same again."

Elud tapped his sword handle. "Wouldn't miss this for anything, I'll be coming with you after and they can keep their grapes and cherries." He grinned and moved back out of the way as others grabbed tree roots and pulled their bodies up.

The climb upward although made relatively easy by strong roots and small trees was still quite long and testing. As Caradoc pulled himself up over the edge he was joined by Brennus as he stood there smiling and enjoying the view. A few seconds later Ardwen huffed as his hands sought out purchase but Brennus grabbed them and hauled him clear. His face showed he wasn't happy at being beaten up the cliff face by the larger man but he couldn't or didn't dare say anything to express it further, it would have to wait. There was quite a strong breeze from the open plain below coming from the direction of the mountains to the west, but fortunately it wasn't strong enough to cause them any danger for the time being. Caradoc standing with his back to the log wall looked out over the trees below and the low ground they had covered, where he could just about make out the last of his men slowly moving across the shadows below. He had to concentrate his eyes to be able to see them but he knew where to look, no trumpets had sounded and no alarms had been raised so he assumed they had made it so far undetected.

He removed his dagger and turned to face the wall, where the Romans had packed the spaces in-between the wood with mud and clay. He placed the point of the blade against one large log just above knee level and pushed against it with his entire body weight, the sharp tip sank in about an inch. He covered the hilt with a small padded piece of cloth and hammered it home with the palm of his hand until he was satisfied it was deep enough. Brennus then did the same with another dagger placing it about a foot higher than Caradoc's but a foot over to the left. He leant against it and sank it as deep as the first knife without the need to bang it home, smiling he turned to

Ardwen. Ardwen looked at him eyebrows raised as if to say 'anything you can do' and then tried to do the same above Caradoc's dagger but couldn't get the blade in far enough, Brennus moved him out of the way and pushed it home. The same thing was occurring all over the wall and the warriors slowly built temporary steps up towards the top of the wood, the noise of the wind covering the sounds of light banging to secure the blades.

Brennus was the first to test the daggered steps as he gingerly stepped onto the first that he, Caradoc, Ardwen, and others had forced into the wood. With the blades horizontal to the small shelf and buried deep into the wood, they took his weight. He hauled himself up and paused as he looked over the wall, without turning he waved a hand upward indicating for others to begin their next short climb. Caradoc went next in his group and slowly made his final ascent up and over the wall and crouched on the far side straining his eyes searching for guards. Torches were burning on the far side where a cover of sorts stood over a gate. It was where the flag flew that he had seen earlier, where he thought he could make out two helmeted figures inside. Either the Romans were over confident or they didn't believe their safety was in doubt, after all what fools would attempt to gain access to their fort by climbing a sheer cliff face. Ardwen joined the two crouched figures.

"What have we got then boys?" He asked whispering.

Brennus replied in a hushed tone, "Well when we first got here there were six sentries on this wall but Caradoc and I have taken care of them." He beamed jokingly, "Good of you to join us by the way."

Ardwen grimaced, "Very funny I'm sure, we'll see who gets the most blood flowing in a while." He looked into the fort taking in the barracks and other buildings constructed of wood. "Don't be surprised if it's me, if there are eighty of them in here as we think, my blade will have at least ten just you wait and see."

"If we can get the two guards over there in the tower before they can raise the alarm, the attack is nearly over, well the hard part anyway." Caradoc said nodding to the two figures. "If we can kill them before the others are alerted our people should be safe."

"Take it as done." Brennus said making his way forward crouching.

Ardwen looked at Cardoc, "The cheeky bastard." He said, "Those two don't count, looks like they're asleep anyway."

The Britons began to take up places on the walls so they could drop into the fort. Caradoc watched as Brennus got closer, he couldn't believe that he was still undetected but he watched as two swift strikes of a flashing blade quietly took the lives of the two sentries, and then men all around him began to drop to the ground inside the fort. They had discussed what they thought could be every eventuality the day before and warriors now moved silently to cover every doorway of every building.

Caradoc jumped down and gave the signal for the men to take torches from the iron holders that stood around the camp and were attached to walls bent out at angles away from wood. Others he pointed towards and then indicated where they should stand with their bows ready, others knelt in front of them, swords at the ready. The archers would release their arrows and then the men with swords would go about their deadly work. He looked around one final time, his men were everywhere and the Romans he hoped wouldn't even know what had hit them.

They were standing in a large, almost oval defensive position with numerous structures built uniformly within. A large gate was at the far side, no doubt leading out onto the slope that was also enclosed by walls running down the gradual slope on either side to the lowland below. They had seen other buildings out there but this was the heart of the small fortress where the majority of legionaries would be. The ancillary structures and any occupiers would be dealt with after the first target.

Brennus returned to Caradoc's side, "They were sleeping and will go to their gods without knowing what carried them there, can you believe it?" He said quietly.

"Sleeping men don't count." Ardwen said gripping his sword, Brennus just grinned and raised two fingers.

Caradoc stepped in front of his line of warriors and said quietly, "I want that building over there torched," He pointed to the structure. "Once it's ablaze, those inside may start shouting and wake the others, be ready."

His instruction was conveyed to the men standing by the building, it was a barrack block, long and narrow. Flaming torches were thrown onto the roof, quickly followed by others, the breeze wafted the flames and soon the tell-tale crackle of fire could be heard on the thatched surface. Within moments the roof was burning and dark smoke billowed into the air this way and that, the wind took it high so it didn't obstruct the attacker's vision. They waited some moving from foot to foot holding their weapons tight, anticipating the response from those inside, they didn't have to wait long.

The first sign that the occupiers were aware that something was wrong came in the form of coughing from inside, then the door opened to the barrack block. A man stumbled out clearly struggling for breath and holding his hands over his nose and mouth, he was wearing only a tunic and more came after him, barging into his back. Before they could shout a warning or get any words out, arrows were launched from the waiting Britons, they slammed home into their targets after zipping through the air at speed, hitting the Romans in their chests and stomachs in the main. The occupants' eyes went wide in confusion as they began to fall, landing on each other as more tried to get out of the burning building as panic set in.

Those still inside were quickly obstructed by the dead and wounded piling up outside the door and couldn't get out as arrows continued to rain into them. A voice rang out from inside shouting and obviously trying to alert the other occupants of the fort but his cries were quickly snuffed out as smoke took hold of his senses. Whether it was his shouts or the sound of the crackling fire, Caradoc and his men didn't know but moments later they were aware of movement from the other structures.

"Fire the other buildings, now." Caradoc pointed to the building where Romans were obviously beginning to stir. The Britons did as they were ordered as more thatched roofs were set on fire, the pattern of attack followed that of the first building and the occupants were cut down before they were barely aware they were under attack. Caradoc's warriors stood almost impassively launching their missiles into the struggling men as they fought to get away from the smoke filled barracks. The attack quickly turned into a rout as the previously sleeping Romans struggled to get outside, but without armour or weapons and shocked by what was occurring and disorientated, they stood little chance as they were slaughtered to a man. Those still alive but wounded were quickly despatched.

Caradoc waited and watched as his warriors went about their business, he hadn't even drawn his sword. Ardwen and Brennus were gutting and killing those who had fallen as if it were a race and once in a while looked up to see where the other was. He saw that the smoke was now being carried upward and up into the dark night sky away from the top of the crag, he looked to the gate almost expecting to see reinforcements from the rest of the small garrison but there were none. When he and his war party were satisfied that they had completed the first part of the attack, he ordered that every remaining building was searched. The task was completed quickly and without incident as the remaining structures were empty workshops or granaries.

"Once we've secured the rest of the fort, we'll take what we can and slip back into the hills." Caradoc said to Ardwen looking west. "First we've got to clear the area beyond the gate." He looked towards the large wooden doors. "Whatever we find out there I want the same tactics used understood?" They nodded. "We've lost no-one so far except for one man who got too close to the flames." He referred to an over eager warrior who tried stabbing through a window and paid a heavy price for his actions.

Brennus and Ardwen acknowledged the instruction as the three men walked towards the barred gates, their warriors behind them. "Before we go through I want you to speak to the men and tell them to be careful, I don't want our retreat to the west slowed by anyone injured through being careless if we can help it."

Caradoc reached the gates and peered through the gaps in the large wooden poles, the ground beyond dropped away beyond quite sharply but on the lower ground he could just make out buildings and a few tents. He took hold of one side of the large wooden square cut bar that secured the gate, as Brennus put his arms underneath the opposite side. They heaved the wood upward and it came loose easily. They carried the bar and placed it on the grass at the side of the entrance, as Ardwen cracked open the wood and peered outside.

"I can't see any movement." He reported whispering as Caradoc joined him. "There are more buildings down there than we could see from outside."

"As long as we keep our discipline we shouldn't have too many problems." Caradoc said looking down the slope. "This is what we'll do." He looked back to Brennus and Ardwen. "I want you to take a third of the men each, Brennus, you to the right, Ardwen to the left, I'll take the centre. We'll go down the slope slowly and in a line walking, no running and no shouting understood?"

They both nodded that they understood their instructions. "Once we get to the buildings we'll deal with them as we find them and then move lower, taking them one at a time unless things change. I don't know that using the same method will work down there as the structures are too spread out. I want each force to have an equal number of archers to cover those who go to the buildings, now go and brief your men before we move."

The attacks on the lower ground went according to plan and the Britons took few casualties, none dead, eleven injured but not fatally, the Roman count was far worse and twenty three legionaries were taken prisoner, the rest were killed as they tried to fight against overwhelming odds. With the Beeston fort secure and no sign of enemy reinforcements, Caradoc ordered that the crag was to be stripped of anything they could use, weapons, food, horses, grain and wagons, the remaining buildings were destroyed by fire.

As dawn began to brush away the night, the Britons were beyond the ridgeline they had used as cover to approach the fort and were moving into the safety of the west. Smoke still rose into the sky behind them and although they were tired and exhausted, they were in good spirits after their victory over the fort on the crag at Beeston.

After returning to the garrison at Isca Dumnoniorum, Varro and his men were given a few days to recover after their ordeal in the region to the south. The *primus pilus,* senior centurion had decreed that all those who had survived the attacks, were to be given a few days off to recoup their energy, eat well and exercise. So it was a surprise that after only two days Centurion Pilo, the aforementioned senior centurion, came to see Varro in his quarters.

"Weren't sleeping were you lad?" Pilo said walking in unannounced, Varro opened his eyes. He had been in the middle of a dream, more of a nightmare, and was in his mind, back on the walls of Statio Deventiasteno fighting for his life next to Cammius at the small legionary fort. He was covered in a fine sheen of sweat and quickly swung his legs off the bed, threw his sheets to one side and stood to attention, naked.

"Sir." He acknowledged.

"At ease lad, at ease, take it easy." Pilo said placing his vine cane under his arm, his badge of office. Varro sat back down again, a fine dust exploded into the air from his straw filled mattress, rubbing his eyes and covering his modesty, he looked up at Pilo. He was a typical senior centurion, thick set, muscular and had more scars than a Nubian snake wrestler. His grey hair was thinning on top but was cut short, so short that he almost looked bald. He wasn't a man to mess around with as his reputation confirmed, and was known to be firm but fair.

"Sorry sir, me and the boys were training all day yesterday and then had a few jars of wine last night, I wasn't drunk though." He added quickly, "I must have gone out like a light, can't even remember getting back. Still catching up after the siege I suppose." He looked up at Pilo who raised an eyebrow.

"I'm not surprised after what you and your lads and of course Cammius' lot went through down there, I'm not surprised at all Centurion, you deserved a rest." He replied. Varro noted the words *deserved a rest.*

"So how would you like something to ease you back into the real world, get the blood flowing a bit now you're all recovered eh?" Pilo asked.

"The sooner the better," Varro replied lying, in truth he could have done with more time to relax and recuperate, "what have you got in mind sir?"

Pilo removed his helmet and took a seat next to the bed, "A few of the troops from the third cohort got into an altercation last night, specifically it was between the second and third centuries in one of the bars. Daft bastards decided to beat the living daylights out of each other which in itself wouldn't have been too bad but," he paused looking at Varro, "unfortunately one young Legionary called Frontus died of stab wounds. Seems like he was wounded a number of times to the stomach and chest, he was dead as a roast doormouse before the medicus could treat his wounds." He paused again looking at his helmet plume as he rotated his head ware in his large hands. "Mind you I don't think it would have made a scrap of difference looking at the holes in him, one was so deep it punctured the skin of his back."

Varro frowned confused, "Where do I come in sir?"

"The provosts are away, or I should say all those that are worth a shit are anyway, some escort duty or something or other, the legate didn't give me the details." Varro felt his heart sink but Pilo went on, "So I thought it would be a nice easy duty for you and your optio to get back into the swing of things, you know, question those who were in the bar, find out who started it and more specifically who used their dagger to kill poor Frontus. What do you think?"

Varro tried to hide his anger, "Certainly sir, when do we start?"

Pilo smiled, "That's the spirit eh lad? I've got the barman from the Boar, that's the bar where it happened, waiting for you as we speak." The senior centurion stood smiling, "I'd do it myself but I've got enough to be getting on with, I'll be glad when we're out in the field again personally. Let me know if you need anything, you know where to find me. Be assured the legate and I are right behind you and whoever was responsible will receive the sternest punishment." He bent over and patted Varro's shoulder, "Keep an eye on that wound and all, this shouldn't be too rigorous anyway, so it'll give you time to heal properly." Without another word he left the room. Varro collapsed back onto the bed with his eyes closed, heart sinking and feeling awful, he grimaced as the injury was pulled taught. He had been involved in enquiries within legionaries before and had never enjoyed the experience, the provosts weren't the most popular of personnel and those standing in for them were regarded with even less respect. No soldiers, especially those on active service, appreciated being questioned and hostility towards the provosts was common place.

"Wonderful." He said. As he dragged himself off the bed he saw that his wound was starting to seep blood again. He quickly splashed water over his face and swilled his upper body from a water bowl and got dressed.

"You have got to be fucking joking sir, surely to gods, acting fucking provosts? What the fucks that all about then? Doesn't that fat cunt Pilo know we've just spent days fighting for our fucking lives and defending the fucking empire down at that fucking shit hole Deventiasteno?" Optio Grattius was even less impressed than Varro with their new duty. Varro had bumped into him walking towards the baths with a towel draped over his shoulder, wearing just his loin cloth.

"Let's make sure we don't use all those fucks up before we get started eh Optio?" Varro said.

"Sorry sir." Grattius said. "Well I can tell you this for fuck all, I ain't fucking happy and if any of those turd burgling bastards from the Third think they're going to fuck us about they've got another fucking thing coming, mark my fucking words." Grattius almost roared. "I'll stick my blade up their fucking holes for 'em if they start to mess us about."

"Yes thank you Grattius, I think I've fucking got that. Now go and get into uniform, we've got the barman to see at the Boar." Varro said.

Grattius' face lit up, "The Boar eh, maybe things won't be too bad after all."

A short time later, Varro knocked on the thick wooden door that was the entrance to the drinking den known as the Boar. A picture of a rampaging wild pig adorned the wall outside, there was no reply. Varro moved closer and rattled the door with his fist.

"Centurion Varro and Optio Grattius, open the door." He shouted. They heard movement inside.

"He's probably just pulling his cock out of the wench that works in 'ere I should imagine sir and we've disturbed 'em, mid poke." Grattius said grinning.

"Let me do the talking Optio, see where the land lies eh." Varro said.

"In the fucking mortuary ain't it sir? Dead as gutted pork?" Grattius looked at his commander who wasn't grinning. "Sorry sir."

Just then they heard the sound of a latch turning and the door creaked open, a fat red blemished face peered out at them. "Don't open until the evening, you'll have to come back then." The door closed again.

Varro hit the wooden frame making the entire door shake. "Open the door now. We're here to investigate the murder last night." He turned to Grattius his frustration rising.

"Want me to throw a few fucks in now then sir? It may help open this bastard's ears up a bit?" Grattius said.

"I'll let you know when Grattius." Varro replied his anger rising now as well as his frustration. The door opened again and the man could be seen in all his glory, he was about five foot tall, round and naked from the waist up, a putrid stench wafted out at the two soldiers. Varro saw that he had a wart the size of a man's thumb in the middle of his chin, it was dark brown and far too big.

"Well, why didn't you say that the first time then?" He said, "Come in then, although I don't know what I can tell you if I'm honest." He ushered them inside hobbling and it took a few seconds for their eyes to adjust to the gloom. The place stunk of stale ale and wine, a female looked up from cleaning a table with a grubby cloth as they entered and blushed. She was tall and attractive and quickly finished what she was doing, adjusted the upper part of her dress making sure her breasts were visible and walked to the back of the bar and left via another door.

"What did I tell you?" Grattius whispered as they were led to the serving area that consisted of a rough plank lying on top of barrels. "I'll wager he was giving her a good seeing too." Varro didn't reply but gave his optio a look of disgust.

"Servius Verius Pubess at your service sirs," the barman said taking his place behind the plank bar, "although like I said, I don't think I can tell you much, everything seemed to happen so fast." He looked from one soldier to the other. "Well if you lot weren't trained so well maybe I could have done something, but a man in my condition ain't fit enough to grapple with fit young fighters." He jumped up onto a large stool. "So what can I tell you?" He leant forward on to the plank. "Want a drink before we start?" He asked.

"Yes." Grattius replied.

"No." Varro countered. "We want clear heads for this but thank you." He glared at Grattius who looked away glancing around the area. Turning back to the man with the wart, Varro said. "Just tell me what happened last night, what time you opened up, who came in, who were they with, did you recognise anyone and what was it that started the trouble?" He took out a wax tablet and a stylus to take down any pertinent details.

Pubess thought for a second scratching at his wart, "Usual time, legionaries from the third cohort, second and third centuries." He looked up at the ceiling, "don't know their names except for an optio like you." He said looking at Grattius.

"I wasn't here last night." He said.

"No it wasn't you - like you, same uniform I mean, an optio. He was sat over there at that table." He pointed and then climbed off the stool and came round to the front of the plank. "Here." He touched a table. "He was sat here and the lad that was injured," he paused, "sorry killed, was sat here." He pointed to a table nearby.

"The optio was sat at that table when Legionary Frontus was stabbed?" Varro asked. Pubess and his wart resumed their perch behind the plank.

"Yes I'm sure." He looked back into the room. "Certain actually because this optio dragged one of his lads out of the melee, that was when I first saw the blood. All cleared up now of course, I like to keep a clean bar you know."

He poured himself a jar of wine from an amphora and took a drink.

"Blood?" Varro asked. "Was this when the lad was stabbed or could it have come from someone else?"

Pubess thought for a moment, "Couldn't tell you but if you find that optio, he'll tell you I'm sure. He dragged his lad out who was kicking and screaming, covered in blood he was, all down his white tunic, that's how I saw it so easily even in this place. The lights terrible, I've asked Centurion Pilo if he can do something about it but he says it's my responsibility as I'm the proprietor or something like." He took another drink. "Anyway, then all hades kicked off and the others were knocking lumps out of each other, even Attia got out of the way and came behind here." He indicated behind the plank.

"Attia. Who's that?" Grattius asked eager to get involved. Varro gave him a look.

"She's me wife, you saw her when you came in." He turned and shouted and began scratching at his groin. "Attia come in here will you?"

Varro and Grattius exchanged looks and the optio held out his hand indicating the difference in height between Pubess and his wife, shaking his head.

"Yes Servius what can I do for you and these fine young men?" She appeared smiling and stood by her husband's side, chest thrust forward.

"Centurion Varro," Varro said introducing them, "and Optio Grattius." He waved a hand at Grattius. "We're here looking into the circumstances of the incident last night when one of our legionaries was stabbed. Is there anything you can tell us?"

She blushed again, "I think you would be better off talking to Optio Anicius."

"And he's the optio that dragged the lad out is he?" Grattius asked,

Varro looked at him but he was focused on Attia, primarily her chest. Varro made some notes.

"Yes but don't ask me what the other one's name is, I couldn't tell you, young lads hold no interest for me." She said reddening again. Varro looked at Pubess.

"We offer a variety of services sirs." He said looking at his wife with a cheery grin, Varro didn't ask.

"Well thank you for your time this morning." Varro said, "If we need anything else, we'll be back to speak with you." They stood up.

"We'll look forward to it." Attia said smiling.

"Come on Optio." Varro said, the two men headed towards the door.

"Fuck me did you hear that?" Grattius asked, "The dwarf's wife is up for a shag. I didn't know the Boar provided those sorts of services did you?"

"I haven't been in there before and if I can help it I won't be going in there again. These people are all the same Grattius, they'd rut a dead pig if they could." Varro said placing his helmet on his head.

"Well I ain't too fussy sir, I'll be back here later." He put his own helmet on, "Mind you, half the legion has probably been through it never mind Pube or whatever his name is. Did you see the size of that fucking wart? What's she doing with that short arsed bastard anyway? Can you imagine him giving her one?" Grattius laughed as the two men walked into the fresh air outside. "I told you that was what he was up to when we first got here."

Varro ignored him and didn't reply but led Grattius towards the direction of the cohort's barracks. Entering the blocks, Grattius removed his helmet. "Put it back on," Varro ordered, "we're not here making a social call." Grattius did as he was instructed. They walked into a large room filled with bunk beds along each side of the wall. Legionaries were sat around polishing their equipment. Varro approached one soldier.

"Centurion Varro," he announced, "I'm looking for Optio Anicius." There was no reply.

"On your fucking feet now legionary." Varro shouted, even Grattius was startled and jumped, everyone else in the room stopped what they were doing. The soldier in question stood up sharply and came to attention dropping his armour. He stared straight ahead not looking at Varro.

The centurion leaned into his face. "What's your name soldier?"

"Legionary Abudius sir." The man replied, Varro saw that he had bruising under his right eye.

"Where's your Optio?" Varro asked.

"Pilum training sir." He replied.

"That wasn't too difficult was it?" Varro said.

"Were any of you cunnies in the Boar last night when a soldier was stabbed to death? Grattius asked. Blank faces stared back at him. "I'll take that as a no shall I?" He walked into the centre of the room. "Mark my words if we have to come back here after finding out that any of you were present, the Centurion here won't be happy and neither will I." Various faces reddened and averted their eyes from the optio's glare. The two officers turned and walked towards the exit, Varro could feel eyes on his back.

"Ignorant fuckers, I'll be having words with Anicius about his men's attitude." Grattius said as they left the building.

"Let's just concentrate on the task in hand for now shall we eh?" Varro said. "Let's go and have a look at this dead trooper before we speak with Anicius."

In the cool of the mortuary, laid out on a marble slab, was a body covered in a shroud, the smell was like a butchers shop, only worse. The Greek looking attendant removed the sheet. "He was dead when he arrived, last night sir," he said, "all we could do was clean him up a bit." The man was tall and thin with a large hooked nose; he stood to one side holding the sheet that was marked with blood. On the slab was the body of a young man, his stomach and chest had multiple dark wounds where blood had coagulated, Varro counted, nine wounds in all.

"He was hit hard," the attendant said reaching out and taking hold of the corpse's shoulder and hip. He rolled the body onto its side, it stayed firm with rigour as if frozen. Varro and Grattius could see that one wound had perforated the skin of the dead man's back near the spine.

"We've got his records here if you want to see them sir?" The thin man asked placing the body down and picking up some rolled up scrolls from a bench. He shuffled the paper, "Legionary Frontus, aged twenty years, joined the legion," he squinted at the details, "six months ago from recruit training in Germania."

"Was anything brought in with him?" Varro asked.

"Just his clothes," he turned and went to a bench and picked up a blood stained tunic and a pair of sandals. "That's all he had with him, oh and his belt and loin cloth, they are covered in blood as well, you can see them if you like but I don't think they will tell you anything." He held the tunic up but it didn't fall freely as dark blood stains covered the majority of the material sticking it together, he pulled the base and crisp dried blood cracked as it was pulled free. Only the shoulder areas were clear of staining. "If you ask me he didn't stand a chance, such a waste of a young life."

"Thank you for your time," Varro said. "Please keep these items available, we may need them later." The attendant nodded as the two men left.

"Jupiter's bollocks it stinks in there." Grattius said as they got out into the fresh air.

"Not pleasant is it?" Varro said. "Right, it sounds as if Optio Anicius has a few questions to answer, let's go and find him." He led the way to the area set aside for pilum training, where dozens of men were either throwing their javelins at large straw targets or waiting to get onto the range. An optio was directing the practice.

"Optio Anicius?" Varro asked.

The large man turned, he was equal in height to Grattius and just as muscular, he frowned as Varro and Grattius stood staring at him.

"Sir?" He looked directly into the eyes of Varro; bright blue determined eyes stared defiantly back at the centurion.

"I need to speak to you now Optio, your training here is finished for the day, have your senior man either take over or escort the rest of them to the barracks."

Anicius hesitated for a moment. "Problem Optio?" Varro asked.

"No sir, I'll sort the boys out and be right with you." He said.

"Might have to be a bit hard on this fucker sir," Grattius said, "looked like he was gonna punch you then."

"I'm sure you would have saved me." Varro replied.

"Fucking right sir, I'd have had him on the floor in no time, no worries there." The optio replied. Varro smiled. With the legionaries marching back to their barracks, Anicius returned to the edge of the training area. "All done sir, what's all this about then?" He asked.

"We'll discuss that in the guardroom Optio Anicius." Varro said, "Follow me." He turned and Anicius fell in line between the centurion and Grattius.

Inside the relative cool of the provost's office in the guardroom, Varro removed his helmet and indicated for Anicius to take a seat. The centurion sat opposite him with Grattius standing behind, despite another seat being available. Varro got straight to the point.

"You were in the Boar last night when an incident occurred and were seen dragging one of your men out of the chaos, why?" Varro asked leaning forward and placing his arms on the table. The optio looked as if he had been slapped in the face.

"I didn't want my lads caught up in a load of trouble, so decided to get out of there. You know what they're like once they get too much wine inside them."

Varro stared straight into Ancius' blue eyes. "So neither you nor the Legionary you dragged outside were involved in the trouble?"

Anicius stared back, "No like I said, I just wanted to get out of there. Once trouble kicks off in places like that we're better off out of it."

"What's the name of the man you took away?" Grattius asked cutting in, Varro looked down at the table.

"Abudius," he replied, "his name is Abudius, good lad one of the best I've got, reliable if you know what I mean."

"That's the man we spoke to in the barracks," Varro said turning to look at Grattius for confirmation.

"Yes," Grattius said, "insolent little shit. If he's your best I'd hate to have to rely on your others. He was lucky not to get knocked onto his arse, insubordinate little bastard." Anicius stared up at his fellow optio. "Got something to add?" Grattius said in a challenging manner.

"My lads don't appreciate outside interference Optio, you should know that." He looked at Grattius with disdain. "Then again, you can't really call yourself a soldier can you, being an investigator," he looked at Varro, "no disrespect to you sir obviously."

"We're not investigators Optio Anicius, far from it we're regulars just like you. We were just unfortunate to get this duty on behalf of the Primus Pilus." He said, surprising the optio with the mention of the senior centurion's name. He continued, "The civilians that work in the bar have said that your man Abudius was heavily involved in the fight with the dead legionary and that was why you pulled him away and got out of there."

"Who said that then, that fat fucker with the wart on his face or his whore of a wife?"

"Regulars in there then are you?" Varro asked.

"Not much else to do is there after training all day, it's either go for a few drinks or sit playing with your cock at night. I know which I prefer." He glared at Grattius.

"I get someone else to play with my tackle son, not one of my lads if you know what I mean." Grattius said an evil grin on his face.

Anicius stood quickly, knocking the chair over behind him. "Say that again and I'll rip your tackle off."

An almighty crack stopped the two optio's in their tracks as Varro brought his vine cane down on the table. "YOU," he shouted pointing at

Anicius, "sit fucking down and YOU," he turned to Grattius, "go and get us some water."

Grattius frowned, coming to attention, "Yes sir." He gave Anicius a look of anger before storming out of the office.

"Now Optio Anicius let me tell you how this is going to work. I'm going to ask you some questions and you will answer, truthfully. If you do not and I find out later that you have lied to me, I have the authority of the senior centurion to take any action I feel necessary to get to the bottom of this." He let his words sink in before leaning forward. "Now, there's a dead legionary in the morgue, one of your men is responsible. I couldn't give a shit whether it's your best man or your worst, or if it is the boy that takes it up the arse for you, but what I do care about is getting his name and I want that name before Optio Grattius returns, am I clear?"

Anicius dropped his eyes from the centurion sat in front of him. "Abudius." He said. "It was Abudius that stabbed him." He looked up.

"Why?" Varro asked.

"Something about that whore Attia, I don't really know, wasn't interested. I saw the stupid bastard draw his blade and start stabbing." He paused, sitting back in his chair. "I think they were arguing about her, I don't know if they were both shagging her or what, I just saw what happened and got him out of there as quickly as I could. You'd have done the same if it had been one of your lads."

"Why didn't you arrest him?" Varro asked.

"Couldn't sir he's one of my lads, you know how it is."

"Right thank you Optio Anicius, you will accompany me and Optio Grattius to your barracks where Abudius will be arrested and then brought here." He stood up. "I expect your full co-operation, you are in enough shit already, and I don't fancy your chances once Centurion Pilo hears what's gone on. Do you understand?"

"Totally sir." He replied. As Grattius returned to the room carrying a jar and three cups, Varro said. "Leave them there Optio." pointing to the table, "we're going to arrest Legionary Abudius.

Chapter Eleven

A few miles to the north-west, the majority of men from two centuries of troops sweated and toiled as they worked to dig the foundations of a new fort. Due to hostile action by Caradoc and his men, the place had become a virtual no go area for soldiers as patrols been attacked and convoys destroyed. It had been decided therefore, that a series of forts and fort-lets would be the best way of controlling the ground as the Roman war machine moved further west.

Legionary Valerius knew the dangers all too well, as he had been besieged with the Second Augusta in the Silurian mountains a few years before during an ill-fated attempt to destroy the enemy on their own ground. Now as he looked towards those same mountains, shrouded with mist, the thoughts of those few days returned to him and he tried to block them out. As he looked at the forbidding mountains again, he had taken cover with a small contingent of archers, keeping a look out for the enemy as the engineers supervised the construction of the new fort on the flat ground below.

The site had been chosen as it provided a clear line of sight for the surrounding countryside and the first unobstructed view of the hills and valleys, with the mountains behind where Caradoc was thought to be carrying out his raids from. The sound of digging and men talking was a welcome distraction from the drizzle that was falling finely and soaking everything. A line of carts loaded with stone blocks, wooden poles, rope and tools was beyond the men waiting to be used as the digging continued. It was always the same it seemed wherever they went, dig first, dig second and then dig some more. Dig until you had a position from where you could defend yourselves and the rest would work itself out.

They had set out at first light arriving at the chosen position a little before midday and had eaten a brief meal before work began in earnest. The plan was to dig out the ditches and foundations first in the large square block where the installation would be sited. As a section of men dug the ditches that would provide the first line of defence around the fort, another began to shovel the disturbed earth up into packed ramparts that would form part of the wall, whilst others began to move the stone blocks into place. It was a tried and tested format for such constructions and like most it would be virtually identical to others they had built, this cut down on construction time which was vitally important in hostile areas.

Patrols had been sent out and continually scoured the land primarily towards the west looking for any sign of trouble, and a small contingent of auxiliary cavalry patrolled further out to provide a covering screen so the men could work, assured that they were relatively safe.

By mid-afternoon the drizzle had stopped, the legionaries had received a second break sometime before and were back at work. The site had already been transformed, the ramparts nearly completed, the outer ditch finished and all the stonework had been moved into place for the interior buildings; barracks, a granary, a smithy and stable area. As with all such places, space was limited inside but it wasn't being built for comfort.

Valerius looked at the sky and estimated that the building should be secure well before dark. It had been decided by the Tribune, Tribune Celvius who was leading the Roman force, that both centuries would reside in the fort that night. It wasn't worth taking the risk of a lone century marching back to Isca, so in the morning whilst one manned the new construction, the other would return. During the following days a fresh century would relieve the existing men and would remain in position for a calendar month, carrying out patrols and keeping an eye on the locals. This system of constructing forts and moving further into hostile territory would continue until Caradoc was either forced to fight or moved north, his only route of escape.

As Valerius took a swig from his water skin, washing down a hard tack biscuit from his pack, he heard a slight rumble. At first he thought that it was thunder as the clouds had begun to clear and spots of blue sky had appeared above, he didn't know why but it was common for that to occur when there was a mixture of the two. He turned his head listening but the thunder continued, getting louder. He frowned and removed his helmet and walked clear of the trees looking in the direction of the sound but could see nothing, although the sound was still getting louder.

Other archers followed him and he noticed that the legionaries had stopped working on the fort. Then the noise seemed to come from all around them echoing from the surrounding natural rises of the rolling countryside. He replaced his helmet and made his way back to the small copse of trees where he had spent most of the day just as he heard the tribune shout, "Cover, to arms men, form up."

Valerius looked to the south and saw what Celvius had seen. Appearing over a rise in the land, was a line of spears as they moved up and down clearly being held by mounted warriors. He reached for an arrow from his quiver as did the other archers.

"Stand to." Valerius shouted, "Enemy approaching from the south." His legionaries rushed to their kit lying nearby and hurriedly began to put it on, helping each other. Those who had been standing guard rushed to the tribune and formed up inside the partially constructed fort. The centurion who had accompanied them began rattling out orders and pointing to various positions where troops ran to. The rumble of the hooves got louder and within seconds the heads of woad covered warriors rode into view at the gallop.

"Gods Valerius," shouted the archer nearest to him, "we can't stay here we're too isolated." With that, he ran from the trees and raced towards the fort, Valerius backed up into the copse knowing he wouldn't make it to cover before the riders were on them. Another archer and then another broke cover and ran clear of the trees heading towards the construction area. Then he heard the shouts of the Britons as they cried their war cries, some now wielding large swords around their heads, he crouched low and then saw more riders approaching from the east, more enemy.

As he lay down flat on his stomach, he removed his helmet knowing that its shine might attract the warriors. The men that had run from the trees were now halfway to the fort, some turning and stumbling, the centurion was bellowing words from the rampart but he couldn't make them out. The other archers still in the trees looked to Valerius for instructions panic on their faces, as he was the most senior amongst them. He shook his head and indicated for them to take cover and to move away from the edge of the tree line, he knew there were too few of them to be effective.

The Britons quickly reached the running archers as they were hacked and ridden down, one turned, threw his bow to the ground and held his hands aloft trying to surrender. He was slashed at by a charging warrior with a huge blue steel long sword, the fingers of his right hand flew up into the air and then another horseman chopped down with his own blade and it sliced into his helmet, he fell in a heap to the ground.

The attackers continued galloping on as fast as their mounts would carry them but slowed as they approached the ditches at the sides of the fort. The centurion led his men up onto the ramparts hurling a javelin at one rider who was impaled and fell from his horse; he was trampled by other horses. More legionaries threw their javelins and other riders fell, but the wave of attackers was too much, as they swarmed the small building from all sides and then began to leap the ditches, their mounts struggling up the sides.

Britons jumped from their horses as the defending soldiers massed on the top of the ramparts, some with shields, others without, some cowering behind their scutums, other stabbing wildly with their pilum's. Valerius saw the plume of the tribune behind that of the centurion's converse horse hair moving rapidly as he fought for his life and that of his men as more warriors leapt from their mounts before the ditches and joined the attack.

A horn sounded from the west, clear and distinct over the sound of fighting and Valerius recognised it as Roman, the auxiliaries he thought, they must have heard the battle and were returning from the position where the tribune had deemed them most vulnerable, the west. He saw that some of the attackers had heard the horn and had turned their mounts to face them on the instructions of one of the warriors who was shouting orders and pointing. A body of warriors turned their horses as more did the same from other sides of the attack. They blended together like water forming and charged at the returning cavalry who were now in clear view. The auxiliaries under the command of their Decurion drew closer together as they formed a wedge. They had seen the threat and were clearly intent on punching through their lines. Three hundred paces from the battle raging at the fort, the two opposing sides clashed, horses fell, men were thrown to the ground and the auxiliaries were surrounded in seconds, their momentum stopped, as swords collided and blood was spilt. So enveloped were the cavalry that some attackers broke off their onslaught on them and started back to the first fight.

The ramparts of the fort were now covered with Britons as those closest to the defenders fought like demons, hacking, slashing and screaming at their enemy determined to take their lives. The Roman legionaries fought on, those who didn't have their shields had disappeared from view, no doubt dead and trampled underfoot by the hordes swarming up the slope. Valerius saw the centurion's plume jolt backwards as he too vanished from sight, quickly followed by the tribune as the Britons took the top of the rampart and began hacking at the men below.

The battle became a slaughter and Valerius knew he could do nothing about it, although he recognised that he that had made the right decision, he still felt shame as he backed further into the trees. As he did, he was aware of the mounted Britons who had ridden out to meet the auxiliaries, now riding back to the engulfed position where the survivors still fought on. In moments it was all but over and through thick bushes he watched as about ten soldiers were dragged over the raised embankment, they must have been the only ones still alive and were thrown down into the ditch where they had previously been digging.

"What are we going to do?" Valerius jumped, he hadn't even heard the other soldier crawl towards him.

"Just what do you think we should do?" He asked. "They're dead, there's nothing to be done except lie here and hope they don't see us." He replied anger flaring in his eyes. "Or we'll be next."

They looked out as severed heads and limbs were thrown from the ramparts to great cheers from the warriors surrounding the construction site, some put on helmets taken from the dead legionaries, others carried swords and armour as they danced about celebrating their victory. The survivors were dragged out of the ditch and lined up, some bloodied looking terrified, others defiant. The leader of the Britons pointed at them shouting something that Valerius couldn't understand, the other Britons laughed.

"Please don't kill them." He said to no-one but himself and then thought that it was probably better to die here than to be taken prisoner and made the play thing of these barbarians. He watched on as the chieftain argued with those around him as he gestured to the mountains to the west, he assumed they were debating what to do with their prizes. A short time later, the soldiers were stripped down to their tunics and tied together, with ropes around their necks, Roman ropes, and were led away.

Some of the Britons began collecting the equipment together that the soldiers had been using, and put it into the carts, no doubt to be carried off west as well as the prisoners. Some of them then began digging away at the compacted mud of the ramparts, ruining the work done previously, as more dead bodies were dragged free of the structure. They were stripped bare and left lying face down in the mud.

Caradoc and his warriors had spent a few days relaxing beyond the western border after the successful raid on the fort at Beeston. As promised, Elud had joined the other Britons and had been more than happy to arrange for the distribution of Roman prisoners throughout the territory. The victory over the enemy hill fort was greeted with joy by the tribes and the standing of Caradoc was elevated to new heights when the prisoners were given to the local chieftains to be used as slaves. Elud had shown no signs of regret in leaving his sister and was settling into his new way of life well. Casualties had been low in comparison to the occupiers and had demonstrated to those who were dubious of the Catuvellauni's leadership credentials, that he was the right man to lead them against Rome.

So far from the enemy, life was almost normal as people went about their daily business of growing crops, looking after their livestock, bringing children up, hunting and fishing, but there was always a dark cloud on the horizon and Caradoc knew it would never go away until the occupiers were either destroyed or were forced to leave Albion. He had heard news via messenger of the successful annihilation of another fort in the south by Dumnoc and his warriors, and of the siege of the other garrison but they had come at a cost, many lives had been lost as Dumnoc had battled the occupants of the second fort. However, he had reconciled himself that losses were to be expected against such a force who, lived for war, unlike his people.

More prisoners had also been brought in after two full centuries had been wiped out together with their cavalry support whilst trying to construct a new fort by an Ordovices war band, who were themselves now fully committed to the war. Although things were going well, he knew these were small victories compared to the enormous task that faced him.

Today however, that was put to one side as he, Ardwen and Brennus and a few others were to go out hunting wild boar in the valleys shaded by the mountains. They had set off early on horseback at first light and were now some distance from the settlement they were currently occupying in the heart of the west. He had decided that to stay in one place was too dangerous, so he and his closest family and friends moved around regularly to avoid the enemy discovering their location. With allies in all the tribal regions now, they were accepted by all the tribes who had allied themselves with the Catuvellauni leader.

The day was bright but the first chill of autumn was in the air as they reached a large forest said by Ardwen to be rich in boar. They had brought a pack of hunting dogs with them, who were now panting heavily, tails wagging and eager to chase the quarry they somehow knew, they would be after that day.

"We can start here if you like?" Ardwen said. "The forest isn't too thick and we can manoeuvre well enough. I've started here or hereabouts before and have been fairly successful. It depends on what you want to do, let the dogs lead or take them into the forest and let them flush the boar out, make them come towards us."

Brennus laughed, "Whichever it is, I'll get more than you today so it doesn't really matter."

"We'll see." Ardwen got down off his horse. "The thing with hunting boar is that they are clever little beasts and," he looked up at Brennus, "you're not." Now he laughed.

"Have you two always been like this?" Caradoc asked.

"Like what, oh I see, me being better than Brennus you mean, of course. He tries, well sort of, but ever since he was small, if you can believe he ever was, he's been just that, a trier. He was still being weaned by his mother when he was fifteen summers gone."

Brennus got down off his horse, "And after those fifteen summers I was suckling on your mother's breasts, enjoyed it and all she did." He laughed again.

"Alright you two let's start from here then shall we." Caradoc said changing the subject. "Who's going to run with the dogs?"

Ardwen raised his arm, "I will, they're afraid of that oaf anyway," he said looking at Brennus, "he'd only lead them into trouble." He untied the rope from the back of the saddle they had been secured to.

"Right then if someone would like to take my horse," he handed the reins to one of the others in the hunting party, "I'll be off." He looked down at the dogs whose excitement was building. "Come on then my beauties." He said and walked to the edge of the forest.

"Be careful and don't get too far ahead." Caradoc warned.

"I know, I've been doing this since I could walk." He replied and disappeared into the undergrowth.

"We'll give him a while to get ahead and then follow. It'll probably take the dogs a while to pick up a scent anyway." Caradoc said. As soon as he'd finished the sentence, the dogs bayed indicating that they'd picked up a scent.

"That was quick." Brennus said.

"I told you I was good!" Ardwen could be heard shouting from somewhere in the forest. The rest of the hunting party crashed into the trees on his trail. It wasn't difficult to follow him thanks to the barking of the dogs and Ardwen shouting at them to slow down every now and again. He was no doubt getting pulled along by the dogs on the rope he'd attached himself with. Caradoc had learned a long time ago, back in his own territory that there was only one place to be when hunting boar and that was on a horse. They were quicker than a running man and could not only sense danger from animals such as boars but they could avoid them when they turned as well. He also knew that Ardwen would be getting scratched to pieces as he was dragged through the foliage. He led the rest of the party deeper into the forest as the dogs yapped and barked at their quarry, leaning low on his mount to avoid branches.

"This way." He shouted as he guided his horse onto a thin path running along the forest floor where he could build up speed.

"We're gaining on him," Brennus shouted, "but I think he's over there, that way." He nodded to the right.

"This path runs level and we can go faster using it." Caradoc shouted in reply kicking at his horse for more speed. An excruciating yelp broke through the canopy of the trees just then. It could mean only one thing. Within moments the rest of them had caught up with Ardwen who was crouched over one of the dogs. The others were straining against the rope trying to continue the chase.

"What happened?" Brennus asked.

"It turned and went for the dogs," he said, "hurled this one into the air. It looks bad the tusks must have got him."

Caradoc jumped down from his horse. The dog was lying on its side panting heavily, it didn't raise its head but he saw its eyes turn as he approached. Blood was pulsing out of two large gashes in its chest. The other dogs were nearly pulling Ardwen over in their excitement to continue the chase, seemingly unaware of the other dog's injuries. Caradoc knelt down by the injured animal's head where he put a reassuring hand.

"There boy take it easy." He said as the dog whimpered. "He won't last long he's losing too much blood." Caradoc said to Ardwen.

"I know but I'm not leaving him to die on his own. That was the biggest boar I've ever seen," he looked down at his wounded hound, "nearly as big as Raider here." Ardwen replied.

Brennus grabbed the rope holding the other dogs back. "I'll go and track it while you stay here with him." He said looking at the stricken hunting dog. Ardwen didn't argue, he just let the rope go. Brennus crashed off into the bushes dragged by the wailing hounds.

The injured dog's breathing slowed, his big black eyes looked round one final time, flickered and then he was gone. Caradoc saw that Ardwen had tears in his eyes but he quickly turned away trying to hide his face.

"I've had them all from pups," he said, "they were in the same litter, but he was the best. Never knew when to back down, I always told him to choose his fights." He said.

Caradoc stood, "Come on let's make sure his death wasn't in vain." He ran after Brennus. Ardwen patted his dog on the head one last time, "I'll be back for you boy," his voice cracked. "I won't leave you here." He wiped his eyes, stood and ran after Caradoc.

It took a while for the dogs to gain on the boar after the injury to Raider and the chase went on for some time, but now Caradoc could see the large hairy dark brown back of the animal as it careened through the bushes and undergrowth. Brennus and the dogs had been overtaken and were falling back with the huntsman gasping for breath, his job done.

"It's mine!" Ardwen shouted as he crashed past Caradoc on his horse.

"Be careful." Caradoc shouted back as the tail of Ardwen's horse disappeared into the leafy bushes. He kicked at his mount once more trying to pick up extra speed as branches whipped at his face, arms and legs. He clung onto his horse praying he didn't fall off, he knew a boar could do as much damage to a man as it could to a dog, especially if you were unfortunate to face one on the ground. A memory flashed into his mind of a childhood friend who was attacked by a large rogue boar in his homeland, the boy was lucky to survive and had carried the scars to manhood. He quickly dismissed the image from his mind and concentrated on the task in hand as he heard Ardwen shout.

Breaking into a clearing Caradoc saw that he was now one horse length behind Ardwen but couldn't quite believe what he saw next. His cousin climbed up onto the back of his horse and hurled himself forward and off the animal's rump. Time seemed to slow briefly as Ardwen screamed bringing his spear down with both hands towards the charging boar. He landed with a thump and a flurry of dust, Caradoc heard an inhuman scream and quickly pulled on his reins desperately trying to stop his galloping horse. Before it was stationary he cocked his head over his mounts head, leapt out of the saddle and to the side, landed and rolled, the momentum allowing him to get straight back to his feet. He turned quickly towards Ardwen who was stabbing down furiously with his weapon repeatedly, blood spraying up from the mortally wounded boar who still screeched. As he approached Ardwen, he saw the boar's legs twitching frantically as it squealed again trying to get up but it was to no avail, Ardwen continued stabbing until there was no sound and the animal moved no more. Panting for breath, Ardwen collapsed over the dead creature, he was covered in sweat and blood as his chest heaved for air.

"I think you got him." Caradoc said just as Brennus fell out of the foliage behind them, dogs straining to get to the carcass.

"Well done......!" Was all Brennus managed before his legs gave way and he fell flat on his face exhausted. Later with Raider buried and a leg of the boar roasting over a fire, the men recounted the hunt.

"You could have killed yourself leaping from your horse like that." Caradoc said to Ardwen.

"He wasn't going to get away after killing Raider. I'd have given my own life as long as I took his." He replied with a distraught expression on his face, turning the leg over on a spit.

"At least he died doing something he loved." Brennus added. "He was a good dog." He turned patting the others who had dragged him through the forest, they were now tied to a tree and were sat salivating at the smell coming from the cooking meat, drool dripping from their panting mouths. "These are good hunters as well. I thought they were going to drag me straight into a tree trunk at one stage today, they were that keen to get to it." Brennus added.

Ardwen didn't respond, he just sat there staring at the flames and watching fat drip from his victim. Caradoc threw a drinking skin towards him, it landed near his feet.

"Take a glug of that my friend, it's not water." Ardwen reached out and took the skin and drank heartily. The hunting party ate their fill as did the dogs and they camped out overnight, before heading home the next day.

Miles to the south Dumnoc had identified his next target, despite the dead and injured after the attacks of the two Roman forts, his determination to do as much damage to the enemy had not diminished. He had returned to his adopted settlement where he worked as a tanner, telling the man he worked for that he had been home as his mother had suddenly taken ill. For a few days he had kept his head down and got back into the routine of working for a fellow Briton who provided leather and hides for the local area including the Romans. Dumnoc had questioned his motives for working with the occupiers but the man had simply said that he had to support his family. It angered him that a man who had survived quite easily before the invasion was now lying about having to trade with the Romans, Dumnoc vowed to ensure that his family would lose their provider if things didn't change. After the destruction, loss of life and theft of land he had witnessed, nothing less would do, as far as he was concerned if his fellow Britons weren't part of the solution, they were part of the problem.

Ten days after returning to work for Bricius he had been given a day off and had gone out on his horse. A few miles to the south and clear of any settlements, he had come across a team of Roman engineers who were carrying out the initial work in order for a road to be constructed. It was a small party of about fifteen soldiers who were using strange tools and planting markers into the ground after ensuring the new road would be in a straight line. They used thin wooden pieces of wood that were joined together in a frame from which weights hung on rope, these weights were aligned with others further forward on other frames and then the markers were staked into the turf. Miles to the rear other engineers were doing the hard work of digging and bringing gravel and stone forward. Dumnoc knew that the advance party were vulnerable and planned to hit them with a war band of twenty five, which should be more than enough especially if they could use the element of surprise and were far enough away from any support. He would have to limit himself to such tactics until such times as his numbers grew from reinforcements sent by Caradoc.

He was surprised that these engineers weren't guarded by legionaries considering the attacks of late. They were either becoming over confident or were too stretched to provide covering patrols, he suspected. During the morning he had ridden by them counting their numbers and making sure there weren't any sentries hidden nearby, and had done the same thing, later in the afternoon. It was as he suspected, they were alone and isolated.

Returning to Bricius during the evening, he helped with some work and then turned in, getting an early night before the raid on the engineering party. He planned to sneak away from the settlement a few hours before dawn and meet up with his war band at a pre-arranged place a few miles short of their target's location. He dressed quickly and quietly slipped out of the roundhouse he occupied and rode to get his weapons. Feeling a sense of excitement and fear he recovered his sword, spear and shield from where he kept them hidden by three large oak trees and then met up with the others. After a brief discussion with them about how he wanted the attack to proceed, they set off looking for the engineering party.

When he suspected they were close, they began walking their horses, leading them by their reins. He knew the soldiers wouldn't be far from the last place he had seen them and would have travelled directly in one straight line as they had a tendency to construct their roads. Sure enough over the next rise, he saw their tents in the rolling countryside below, three of them, there were two men on guard standing off to one side.

He indicated for the others to stop where they were below the height of the hill so they wouldn't be seen and pointed at two of the older warriors, telling them to follow him. He crouched down and went forward dropping to his knees and then crawled along slowly on his stomach, the two others following.

"We'll have to take the sentries first." He whispered looking across the plain. Despite the darkness, the tents were visible as there were lamps glowing inside and one was a short distance from the two guards.

"It would be too dangerous to get any closer, we'd be seen and they would raise the alarm." Dumnoc said thinking aloud. "Some of the men have bows with them, you," he said addressing one of the men, "Crawl back and bring four bowmen with you, I've got an idea." The man did as he was told, returning a short time later with the archers.

"I want two of you to take the man on the right and the other two to shoot the one on the left but not until I give the word, you are to stay here with me." He turned again to the man who had brought the archers, "Now go back and get the others, I want you to encircle them but from a safe distance as best you can. Once the arrows fly, we'll move in but not before, do you understand?"

He nodded, Dumnoc said, "Once you have them in position give the signal and we'll take the sentries down, then the rest of us will move in and deal with the others, clear?" He nodded again and moved off. Dumnoc lay there waiting for what seemed like an age with the four bowmen who had spread out slightly giving themselves space for when the order came to fire at the guards. Just as he got so frustrated that he was about to go and find out what was going on, he heard the hoot of an owl, the signal that the rest of the war band were in position.

"On your feet," He said to the archers, "Remember to fire together or as close as you can and don't miss." He turned back to the guards and waited, listening to a slight breeze. The Roman sentries were about one hundred and twenty paces from their position, easily within range of the arrows. The bowmen waited for the breeze to settle and then loosed their missiles, there was a faint twang as their drawstrings relaxed and within no time they were lost in the dark. The archers loaded more arrows but they weren't required as one of the soldiers dropped to the ground instantly, within seconds dark figures appeared from all around and descended on the tents. The second guard was seen clutching at his face and staggering towards the nearest tent, but he was brought down by a warrior who jumped on him from behind.

Dumnoc rose and ran seeing the Briton who had felled the legionary thrashing downward with his axe, the noise of the contact on his armour was quite loud but then he saw him roll him over and begin to pound his face with the bladed weapon. Dumnoc was certain that the sound would wake the other soldiers but knew that if it had it was too late as they had reached the tents.

He stopped short by a few feet, quickly looking at the warrior who had leapt onto the guard and could see his face splattered with blood, another sliced the throat of the other prone man who had two arrows in his face. The three tents were completely surrounded. Dumnoc walked over to the lamp the sentries had near them and picked it up, walking back towards the tents, he threw it at the one in the middle. It landed on the side of the slanting roof, at first nothing happened, and then the oil began to run down the sides of the goat skin surface, the flame caught and it burnt. From within the structure the other soldiers quickly began to stir and then he heard the others in the two tents on either side were waking up.

The legionaries were allowed to exit the tents, fear on their faces as they realised what was happening. One tried to speak but was struck on the side of the head by the shaft of a spear, the sound was loud as it thumped against his skull and he fell to the ground moaning and grasping at where he had been hit. They were lined up on their knees terrified, the battered man dragged up, they looked at Dumnoc who stood in front of the others. He stared back at them and then knelt down and picked up some dirt. Standing again, he rubbed the soil between his fingers allowing some of it to fall, staring at the captured men.

"You come to our lands, kill and enslave our people, take our gold, silver, remove our cattle, sheep and goats and you build your roads." He said speaking in Latin, looking at their markers. "What shall we do with you?" He asked.

One of the men replied, "Let us go please, we're just soldiers, we were sent here to put the markers out for the engineers that's all. We're not involved in the fighting and we haven't even drawn our swords since we've been in Britannia."

Dumnoc struck him hard across the forehead and he toppled over landing on his side groaning, "Our land is called Albion not Britannia Roman." The man got back on his knees. "It matters little to me or these warriors you see before you whether you have drawn blood on our people or not. The roads you help to build move your soldiers through our lands so to us you are all the same." He looked at the other legionaries on their knees. "How much mercy did you show the Catuvellauni when you first came to our shores? How many tribal kings have taken your gold with promises of land, treaties?" He paused. "Albion was a friend of Rome for many years, we traded peacefully and your Emperor betrayed that trust by sending men like you to kill us, to steal our land and enslave our people."

"Please." The legionary begged, the others looked at him expressionless, "We don't want to hurt you, we were told to come here. We don't have a choice when we're ordered by our officers. We'll leave, just please let us go I beg you, we're engineers, we just build things."

"And what if you are told to return? You will do as you are asked, you just said that, you are a soldier, you have no choice." Dumnoc said. He turned to the assembled warriors stood watching, they stared expectantly at him waiting to be told to execute the prisoners.

"Remove their right hands," He instructed, "that way they won't come again."

Some of the legionaries screamed and tried to fight or escape but they were quickly overpowered. Others were simply too shocked by what was about to happen to them and awaited their fate in silence. As Dumnoc turned and began to walk away, the screams intensified, he suspected that even the quieter ones were now voicing their pain.

Chapter Twelve

"This is bollocks sir." He looked at the centurion, "and I mean that with no respect whatsoever by the way," Grattius remarked frowning as they neared the stone barrack block via the parade ground with Optio Ancius. It was just before dawn and the sun was showing signs of another day as streaks of light began to appear above.

"Orders are orders Grattius," Varro replied, "anyway we can't have soldiers going about stabbing each other, there won't be any left to face the Britons." He smiled.

"I still think it's a job that could have waited for someone else to do or even the primus pilus. It could start all sorts of problems this between the centuries." Grattius muttered.

"Sir if you wouldn't mind." Ancius interjected and stopped walking, Varro turned pausing.

"What is it Optio?" He asked curtly becoming frustrated with Grattius' complaining.

"Well sir, Legionary Abudius is one of my men, it might be better if I went in first, you know, friendly face. Might help if you know what I mean?"

Varro considered his suggestion, "Mm you're probably right, we'll be right behind you, no funny business, understand?" He turned to Grattius, "And no more moaning from you."

"Of course sir wouldn't dream of it." Ancius said, "Anyway he's not got anywhere to go and I'm not risking my record for the likes of him, no. He's got what's coming, can't be helped." Ancius replied as they continued walking. The main door to the block was closed and creaked as they entered. Lines of double bunks were situated along either side of a narrow walkway down the middle of the block, the room smelt of stale clothes, sweaty bodies and wind of the human variety. Armour was piled up in-between the bunks against the wall. Optio Ancius removed a lit oil lamp from near the door frame. "Hope I don't set off all the gas in here." He said venturing further into the room.

"He's down here sir," He pointed, "lower stall." He said indicating with his head, they followed the optio between the bunks in the dim light. A sleeping legionary rolled over and let out a loud brace of farts, another murmured an insult in his sleep.

"Oh charming." Grattius whispered.

"Here he is sir." Optio Ancius said faintly, pointing out the sleeping form of Legionary Abudius. He leant forward and shook him by the shoulder. He grunted and turned to face him but didn't open his eyes.

"Abudius wake up." Ancius said talking normally.

"Mother." Abudius replied." Grattius smirked.

"I'll mother you in a moment if you don't wake up." Ancius said.

"Optio," he said, trying to open his eyes, "is it morning already, what are you doing here?"

Ancius shook him again, "On your feet lad, there's a centurion here to see you."

Abudius squinted and then opened his eyes fully and took in the sight of the two officers with Ancius, a resigned look of recognition dawning on his face.

"Bollocks." He muttered and swung his legs out of the bed. He went to get his equipment but Grattius blocked his route.

"Tunica and caliga only," he told him, tunic and boots, "You won't need anything else where you're going."

The young soldier looked to his optio for an explanation, "They know you killed that lad the other night son, I'm sorry but there's no more I can do for you. It'll be for the Legate to decide and then the Governor probably."

"It was an accident, he came at me. I didn't mean to kill him." He said anxiety over his face. "What will they do to me?" He said collecting his tunic off the ground and pulling it over his head.

"As your Optio just said soldier, it's not a matter for him or for that matter, us either. We're here to escort you to the stockade, now get your boots on." Varro said as Abudius sat on his bunk tying his leather laces up.

"I'm fucked aren't I sir?" He looked up at Varro, tears in his eyes.

"It's not up to us Legionary Abudius, are you ready?" He asked. They led the legionary out of the barrack block, just as a trumpet somewhere outside on the rampart sounded the dawn call and the others began to stir. They escorted the prisoner over to the guardhouse where the stockade was situated. A note was recorded on the log of his admittance by Varro and for the crime of which he was suspected, murder of a fellow soldier.

"Right in you go." Grattius said opening the thick wooden door of the small cell. Abudius looked inside and saw a small thin cot at ground level, a bucket and a high window that at least let some light in. He turned to his optio and said, "Sorry," as the door was shut behind him.

"Stupid bastard!" Grattius said as the three officers returned to the duty centurion's bunk, while Varro gave a further explanation to the night staff.

"I wouldn't like to be in his boots." The centurion of the watch said after hearing the report, "The last one accused of murdering another legionnaire was executed in front of his entire century, ruined morale for months."

"Bad business all round," Varro said, "and for what, some dirty whore by the sound of things?" He turned to the two optios, "Right now that's out the way perhaps we can get on with our own duties."

Two days later, Varro and Grattius were summoned by the Governor of Roman forces in Britannia to give their assessment and knowledge of the incident that had led to the death of a legionary in their garrison, or so they thought. Optio Grattius wasn't happy at the prospect.

"I knew this wouldn't end with that little bastard getting locked up and now look." He gestured with a flailing arm as they rode slowly east, "all the way to Londinium to see none other than Aulus Plautius, gods above and below, nothing good will come of this, you mark my words." He said muttering away to himself.

"He's a good man," Varro said chewing on a piece of salted beef and patting his horse Staro, "I met him not long after the initial landings. He probably just wants a report first hand. After all he's to decide whether Abudius lives or dies. It can't be an easy decision even for him."

"Mm maybe so but that doesn't make it any easier, I'd rather be heading in the other direction if you know what I mean." Grattius said taking in the countryside around them. "Been to Londinium before then?"

"No, first time. I've heard it's grown significantly though since the Governor moved from Camoludunum a few years ago." Varro replied. "It's said to be so big there's no wall around it, not that it's in any danger they say, being so far east away from the conflict."

In time they began to see unnatural objects on the horizon and as they got closer, they saw that there were huts and roundhouses in settlements, plumes of smoke rose to the heavens. The once solid tracks became mud paths the closer they got and the stench of the outlying districts grew as the roundhouses were replaced by more wooden huts and then small brick buildings came into view. They walked their horses parallel with the river Temasis *Thames,* said to be one of the longest stretches of water on the island, it had got its name, meaning dark, due to its dirty content. It never ran clear.

Soon they saw more troops heading west, centuries marching along in their columns, fresh faces, with new uniforms, moving along neatly, accompanied by the odd bellow from a frustrated centurion or optio keeping them in line. Before dark they took a room rented above a tavern near the centre of the city. It wasn't the best of places but provided them with a warm meal and stabling for their horses.

They arose early the next morning and made their way to the Governor's headquarters. After having their identities confirmed by an overzealous guard at the main archway leading to the building, they were allowed access. After waiting some considerable time in an outer office, they were called forward by a clerk.

"The Governor will see you now," he announced," Waving them forward, "Come, come, he hasn't got all day you know, he has a Province to run." He said as the two soldiers rose from their seats and exchanged angry glances with each other.

"Prick." Grattius whispered as they approached the large door. The clerk swung it open as if he were performing on a stage and smiled at the two officers as they walked past.

"Cunt." Grattius said loud enough for him to hear, the clerk screwed up his face as if he had just smelt something foul and stared at the optio.

"Ah Centurion Varro," Aulus Plautius said rising from his chair, "it's been a long time, welcome, welcome." He walked forward and grasped Varro's hand, "it's always nice to see proper soldiers again," he looked at the clerk, "dismissed."

"May I present Optio Grattius sir?" Varro replied turning, Grattius snapped to attention.

"Pleased to meet you Optio." Plautius said to Grattius taking his hand and shaking it thoroughly, "Please gentlemen take a seat." He said, indicating to the two chairs by his desk. The room was decorated with frescoes on the walls, where there weren't campaign maps showing the locations of various legions, roads, roads under construction, forts and garrisons. Tables at the side of the room were covered with scrolls and writing tablets, clearly the Governor was fully occupied Varro thought.

Plautius took a seat, "So before we get down to business, can I offer you a drink?"

"No thank you sir, we're fine." Varro answered. Although he respected the General, he still felt rather uneasy in his presence and wanted to be out of there as quickly as possible.

"Very well centurion, very well." He said smiling. "I should imagine that you think you're here to discuss that nasty business back in Isca?" He asked, "Well you're not, the Legate will take care of that nonsense, I'm sure he'll make the right decision and whatever that is I'll support him fully."

Varro and Grattius exchanged looks of surprise.

"I've asked you here today because I wanted to speak to you personally and the less people that are aware of this, the better." He stood again and walked to one of the larger campaign maps draped over the wall. "This is where we are at the moment." He picked up a long stick and indicated the areas detailing the positions of the legions progress in the west. "It's taken us a long time to get this far, far longer than was ever envisaged when we first came to Britannia, too long in other words." He looked back at the two soldiers. "In simple terms we're at something of a stalemate, this Caratacus has buried himself like a Syrian tick on a dog's arse and so far we haven't been able to dig him out. It's also given him the opportunity to make punitive raids across the border moving south," he pointed to the south westerly part of the island, "Where his war bands have destroyed forts and villas," he pointed to the central belt of operations, "and into the heart of the country, where he's doing the same and even attacking columns and engineers." He placed the stick down and returned to his seat, poured himself some water from a jug and continued.

"We could be stuck like this for years gentlemen, unless we do something. We've tried to tempt him out to face us in open battle but he's learnt well from his mistakes of just a few years ago and won't move. We've even tried taking the fight to him," he looked at Varro, "which you know all too well with the Second Augusta and even that didn't turn out very well." He paused, "So now we have him virtually encircled, that's if you can call it that, as he rules over the entire west of the island in the far west, the trouble is, it's a vast area and one that won't be conquered easily even by combining legions from different angles of attack." He looked at the map again. "Even then, how many men will we lose over that terrain; mountains, hills and valleys, not to mention swamps and bogs? I tell you gentlemen it's another disaster waiting to happen and I don't want to be remembered like Varus, my legions butchered, my eagles, and my standards taken, forced to take my own life and beheaded and disgraced for the world to see."

Varro looked from Grattius to the General, "What do you propose then sir and how can we help you?"

Plautius took his eyes off the maps and looked at the scrolls in front of him on the desk. It's a problem that's kept me awake for far too many nights but I now have two solutions, or at least I believe I have. The first of which involves you two, which I will go into in a moment. The alternative involves a co-ordinated intrusion into their territory from the south, north, east and even the west, involving the navy carrying men and equipment to the far shore." He got to his feet again and walked towards the door, opening it, he shouted out to the clerk, "Bring them in Osterius." He ordered as Varro heard the clerk's chair scrape as he stood up.

"I've got a bad feeling about this sir." Grattius whispered but before Varro could respond his attention was drawn to the clerk who had re-entered the room. He felt waves of emotion flow through his very being as stood behind him, was Brenna.

It was nearing dawn by the time Valerius and the small group of survivors saw Isca on the horizon. They were hungry, tired and fearful of how their commander would react when he was told that the rest of the engineering party, escorting legionaries and cavalry had been destroyed. Not only that but the centuries' standards had also been taken, some said it was better to die defending the standards than allow them to fall into the enemies hands. Valerius wasn't too sure about that, all that mattered now was getting behind the garrison walls to safety.

As they got to within a hundred paces of the rampart, a guard shouted down at them and called for the on duty centurion. The legionary on sentry duty asked for the password but they didn't know it as it had been changed in their absence.

"We were with the fort building party that went out two days ago." Valerius shouted up.

"No password, no entry." The guard shouted down as Valerius saw the plume of a centurion appear above the brick defences and question the sentry.

"Approach the gate and be recognised." The centurion shouted down. Valerius and the eight others waited by the huge gate until it creaked open.

They were quickly identified and taken inside and escorted to the guardroom.

"We've had patrols out looking for survivors for days," the centurion said, "they found the site of the massacre and knew from the body count there were legionaries missing." He looked at their ragged kit. "You can all get some sleep for a few hours and make your reports later after you've had some food." He pointed to the duty bunks that had all been vacated by the night watch as the sun was about to come up.

"We couldn't do anything sir, they killed them and took the standards." Valerius said.

"You can't change what happened soldier, get some sleep. I'm sure there will be time for questions and answers later." He turned to the others. "That goes for the rest of you, get your heads down."

As the sun came up over the mountains, Caradoc left his roundhouse with a blanket wrapped around his shoulders and stretched, it was quiet. A mild frost coated the ground and glistening silver shards were everywhere, winter was coming.

"You're up early," Mott said behind him, holding up the heavy door skin, "can't sleep?" She asked.

"I slept well enough," he replied, "they're never far from my thoughts." He said nodding to the east. She knew he meant the Romans but didn't want to talk about it again, it wouldn't change anything.

"Come back inside, it's cold out here she said," smiling, "I'll warm you up."

He returned her smile, "I'll be back in a moment." She watched him walk gingerly, bare footed across the frosted ground. Letting the door flap drop she turned and felt the warmth of the fire warm her again and got under the fur skins of their bed. She stared at the fire thinking about their fate and how they had come to this place, and of days long before when they were safe from harm before the invaders had come. As her eyes closed and sleep took her once more, her mind felt the warmth of a summer day on her face and she was lost to the past.

After she had first introduced Cara to Edbutt and she had kissed him for the first time, her life changed. Gone was the boring dullness of everyday, as her thoughts focused on the King's son, she felt a warm sensation now in everything she did, people she saw and wherever she went, was it love? She had heard people talk of it, but was it supposed to be all consuming, absorbing? It was as if a glow had entered her very being and although she had always been a happy person, she now felt complete, what had that boy done to her?

It wasn't anything to do with his status that was certain. In fact she preferred that he wasn't the heir to the land, she wanted a private life. His older brother would be king and if anything were to happen to him, Tog would replace him as heir and everything would be fine, they could have a life together. But wasn't she getting ahead of herself? Something told her she wasn't and that one day Cara would be her husband.

He had returned to her later that day with a tale about what had happened after he and his two brothers had left. A girl who he had described quite vividly, called Brenna had given him and Tog a warning about Adminius. She herself had felt uneasy around the older brother, it was a feeling that she could never fully explain, but this girl had forewarned them of his treachery. Cara had been concerned about the warning and had taken it seriously, Adminius had always been different he had told her, had always been the odd one out and had eventually been banished by his father.

"Mo........." She heard his voice, it was distant.

"Are you asleep again?" He asked, clearer now, she was back in the present and opened her eyes.

"I was dreaming." She said.

He threw his cloak down, "Something nice I hope?" He asked.

She looked at his upper torso and smiled, his broad shoulders and defined muscular arms were covered in swirling patterns. She had started the tattoos herself not long after that day when they had spoken about Adminius. Mo had been surprised that he had said she could do them. He had no idea that she could draw or tattoo, but he had placed his trust in her from the start of their relationship and had removed his top, inviting her to begin.

"What are you so happy about?" He asked.

"I was just thinking back to that day when I began your woad tattoos and you jumped when the first wooden needle pierced your skin." She smiled and he sat down beside her on the bed, she touched his shoulder following the curving patterns.

"They help define you husband, why did you let me do them that day?" She looked into his eyes.

"I don't know, I trusted you," He kissed her neck, "and I also knew that if you had messed them up and made me look a fool, I would have got them covered up." She hit him playfully.

"Things were so different back then." She said. "The biggest thing we had to worry about was the minor disputes with other tribes, the harvest and our livestock." She looked down. "But now I feel like there's a dark cloud on the horizon constantly threatening to destroy us, we've been forced from our lands, have witnessed our people killed, our animals slaughtered, what have we done to deserve this burden?"

He kissed her again, this time on the mouth, "We have done nothing, nothing except live our lives but the great cloud gets closer every day. We are hurting it though, halting their progress, making them think, we were stupid to face them as we did but we learnt and now they bleed as much as we do."

"But can we hold them back? Keep them out of the mountains?" She asked as her hand stroked lower, he smiled.

"We will do everything we can, everything that I can to try and stop this, even ways that don't include our people or even theirs dying." He let his hand fall inside the fur cover she was under and cupped her breast, feeling her nipple harden against his palm.

"And what does that mean?" She asked smiling and pushing her tongue gently into his mouth as her hand traced the back of his neck, his lower head bristly from a sharp knife.

"Time will tell wife, you just have to trust me now." He said lying down beside her and pushing himself closer to her warm body.

"Oh you're still cold from being outside." She said as she hooked a leg over his cold waist and drew him closer still.

Valerius and the other survivors were stood to attention awaiting the decision of the Legate as to their fate. If they were found guilty of cowardice, they would surely be executed, if the Legate believed their version of events, he may be inclined to be more lenient, what that could result in were a whole array of things.

"So having read your reports," The Legate said, looking up from the wax tablets and examining the men stood before him, "You were isolated and were too few to have any realistic effect on the enemy once they had swarmed the engineering position and had begun to slaughter them." He paused, was that a question or a statement? Valerius decided not to say anything not knowing whether the pause was meant to be just that or if the Legate wanted a reply.

"The enemy," He continued looking at a tablet again, "were upon you even before those who were building the fort could form up and come to arms. The construction area was enveloped from all sides and even the returning cavalry were hopelessly outnumbered, they were stopped from reaching the post and were destroyed a short distance away."

He looked up again, Valerius swallowed, the cavalry had given their lives trying to get to the engineers and the legionaries charged with guarding them. They on the other hand had not.

"So you men, seeing this from your position, a vantage point that gave a clear view of the building under construction and one that was easily within range of your weapons," he looked down again and Valerius knew he was referring to his tablet, "decided that instead of engaging the enemy and aiding your fellow soldiers, you would push back further into the copse as the battle was doomed and hope not to be seen. You planned to remain there until the centuries were dead along with the engineers and then hoped to return to Isca from where you could serve Rome again." He looked up again his eyes boring into Valerius.

"Erm yes sir, we knew we were too few to affect the outcome and our deaths would do nothing to serve the empire. It was my decision, well I suggested it sir, and the others agreed. It was the only sensible option to me at the time." Valerius said. "Survive and return to Isca." He added.

The Legate opened a scroll on the desk. Valerius recognised it as a century legionary record. "I see that you have faced the enemy before and with distinction Legionary Valerius. On the documented record," the Legate continued opening the scroll, "you fought in a situation not too dissimilar from the one you faced a few days ago and yet you lived to fight another day."

"We were surrounded on all sides sir, deep inside Silurian territory but I was not isolated on that occasion, it was very different from this incident, there, there was hope, a few days ago there was no chance of defeating a much larger force on open ground." Valerius said realising that he sounded desperate now and knew that he had nothing to lose. The Legate was closing in for the kill. He looked up at the assembled group.

"Having read all your reports and having seen the site for myself, I am ready to make my decision." Valerius swallowed again and felt his legs begin to tremble. Was this how his life was to end after serving his legion? Accused of cowardice in the face of the enemy, was he truly a coward for making the only sensible and practical decision at the time? No, he didn't believe he was but another man, this man could easily decide that he and those stood with him were.

"I could easily have you executed and perhaps I should as an example." Here it comes, Valerius thought. "But I won't….." He couldn't believe it. Did he just say they would live? Valerius felt dizzy, the Legate continued, "You will be absorbed into the existing centuries, I don't need to lose more men especially needlessly. Be warned though the Primus Pilus will be told to watch you men very carefully, step out of line even with the smallest infraction, and I will expect him to come down on you so hard that you will wish you had never been discharged from your father." He stood. "We face a barbaric and dangerous enemy here in Britannia, one that we can't hope to defeat unless we are all working together for the same cause." He walked around the table to where the legionaries stood to attention.

"Perhaps we need more centuries available in the forward positions, clearly almost two hundred wasn't enough the other day and we underestimated the strength of the enemy, it won't happen again rest assured." He turned, "Primus Pilus."

"Sir." The senior centurion acknowledged stepping forward.

"March them out and have them put into different centuries, Valerius however, I want in the first century, the rest all within the first cohorts, two will have to go together but I don't see that as a problem." Valerius swallowed again. So they were to live but he would now serve in the first cohort of the lead century which meant that in any given battle formation, he would be at the front, the first to face the enemy. A cohort generally consisted of around four hundred and eighty men made up from six centuries each with eighty legionaries to a century. Valerius knew that the odds of him surviving the campaign in Britannia had just been greatly reduced.

Varro stared at Brenna in disbelief as she entered the room accompanied by another female, another Briton by the looks of her clothing he assumed. The other was slightly taller, with blonde hair, attractive but with a hard pinched face, she stared at the centurion and muttered something to her companion who acknowledged her with a nod. Varro felt rocked to his very core, what was she up to and what was she doing here?

Plautius motioned the Britons forward, "Come, come," he turned to Varro, "Centurion Varro, may I introduce Brenna? She's one of the many leaders of the different people here in Britannia."

For a moment he didn't reply, he looked at her petite frame with mixed emotions, he hadn't had any contact with her for some weeks.

"Yes sir I know Brenna quite well sir, in fact she saved my life a few years ago.

The Governor beamed, "Oh good, good, that will make things so much easier." He said smiling and indicating for the two women to sit down. "If only all the Britons were like her eh? We'd have a settled Province by now if they were that's for sure." He moved back to his seat and sat down, "So tell me Centurion, how was it that this young lady came to save your life?" He stared at Varro.

"Well sir, my men and I were captured not long into the campaign, days after we'd landed actually" He thought back, his mind trying to avoid the images of his friend tied to the tree next to him. "I already knew Brenna and her brother Tevelgus and fortunately she came across us as we were being tortured, demanded we were released and managed to persuade the Britons holding us that she had something even worse in mind."

"Well, well," Plautius said, "fortunate indeed." He turned to Brenna. "Oh forgive me, where are my manners, excuse me a moment." He stood and quickly walked to the door, opening it he shouted, "Osterius."

"Yes sir?" The clerk replied from somewhere outside the office.

"Can you bring the refreshments in now?"

"Sir." The clerk acknowledged.

Grattius exchanged a mischievous look with Varro.

Plautius returned to his chair and continued, "And I understand this woman is a cousin Brenna and I believe I'm right in thinking that she's a Silurian?"

Brenna looked at the two soldiers to see if there was a reaction, there wasn't but Varro felt Grattius stiffen, "Yes," she replied, "her name is Lita and her knowledge of the territory will be invaluable."

"Territory?" Varro asked but at that moment the clerk returned carrying a large tray with their refreshments. Plautius raised a finger to his mouth. Clearly he didn't want word getting out as to the reason for this meeting.

"There we are sir, if there's anything else." Osterius said placing the tray on one of the many tables.

"That's all for now." The Governor said as he watched his clerk leave and close the door behind him. "Please, help yourselves." He said, moving towards the table himself. He picked up a cake and bit into it, "Try these they're very good, oat and berries of some description." He held a plate out to the two females who each picked up a cake. "Please gentlemen." He said, forcing the centurion and optio to their feet.

"Now this is to go no further than this office." Grattius looked confused, "The conversation we're about to have Optio." He added.

"Right, yes certainly sir, I wouldn't dream of mentioning it to anyone."

Plautius looked at the large map detailing the area to the west where Caratacus was thought to be operating from. "Now," he picked up a smooth thin stick and pointed, "I think, well it's my firm belief that during times of conflict such as this, that we should make every effort to reduce the loss of lives on all sides." He pointed to the garrison at Deva and then lower; to the one at Isca. "We have Caratacus and his forces virtually surrounded but this area here," he pointed again to the land in-between, "is vast with valley and mountains that would make any assault extremely difficult. If we do decide to go in with force, I'll make use of the navy but that would mean taking resources from elsewhere, resources that we can ill afford for the foreseeable future."

"So your plan sir?" Varro asked.

"Brenna's plan actually Centurion." He looked at the cakes, "Mm I think one of these next." He said choosing another, "Come on help yourselves, or they go to waste or worse, that grubby little clerk will eat them."

Varro turned to Brenna, "Would you care to explain?"

"It's quite simple," she said, "I want to minimise the loss of life as well. I may be seen as a traitor by some but there's a chance we can end this war before things get worse."

The Governor interjected, "I've already got raids further south, villas have been destroyed, even forts have been attacked, one manned by auxiliaries was completely annihilated, every man killed. Now they're even venturing into the mid lands," he pointed his stick again, "an engineering detachment with two centuries and a squadron of cavalry was wiped out here. So you see, Caratacus is getting bolder and all attempts so far to draw him out have failed. If we could get him into open battle, we could finish this but he's not willing to risk his warriors."

"He learnt well and quickly." Varro said.

"He also now has Silurian warriors and those of the Deceangli, the Ordovices and the Demetae ready to fight for him." Lita said, "And my people tell me that there are at least five thousand Catuvellauni survivors with him, all ready to lay down their lives if your legions step into their territory."

"Which makes this mission even more important?" Plautius said, "If this fails, we could lose thousands of lives on both sides and it could go on for a long time to come, years maybe."

"And so the plan sir?" Varro asked fully aware of the dangers of not doing anything.

Brenna answered, "We go and talk to Caratacus."

Varro looked from her to the Governor, "We just ride into hostile territory and ask to speak to Caratacus, a man who has fought us for years, seen members of his family die, has been displaced from his own land?" He looked back to Brenna, "Well I'm glad you cleared that up."

"I realise that it's dangerous Centurion and I know that I'm asking you and Optio Grattius to risk your lives but we have to take this opportunity, it cannot be ignored." Plautius said.

"How many men will I be taking?" Varro asked.

"One, you and the Optio here," Plautius said, "to take anymore would risk provoking them and of course these two ladies." Lita looked slightly aggravated by his words but he continued, "A small group has far more chance of slipping inside the mountains and making contact with his chieftains. Lita assures me that they are as tired of this conflict as we are so we can't afford to miss this chance, it could bring an end to all our troubles here in Britannia."

Chapter Thirteen

As Grattius threw his sword on the bed of their rented room later that evening, he wasn't a happy man, "This will be the death of us you know?" He said to Varro who was unclasping his own weapon. "Even if by some miracle we can make it as far as the mountains, they'll strip our flesh and feed us to the crows and Caratacus will eat what's left." He stared at his centurion, fury in his eyes, "I'd rather eat shit straight from a pig's arse than be involved in this madness."

Varro slumped onto his own bed, "And what would you have me do? Tell the Governor of the Roman Province of Britannia we're not going?"

Grattius growled, "Better that than to be made into hats by the Silures warriors, gods above and below and all around, of all the things to be volunteered for, this is just madness." He unclipped the harness on his belt holding his dagger and hurled it into the corner of the room. "I may as well take that and start carving away right now," he looked at his thigh, "here this is probably a good place to start, plenty of meat."

Varro smiled, "The gods haven't been kind to us today my friend, but what can we do apart from accept our lot?"

"It's not today I'm worried about, it's being surrounded by thousands of hairy bastards in the future that worries me." Grattius replied. "Is it too late to transfer back to the infantry do you think?" He asked with a sarcastic grimace on his face.

"Come on, let's get tidied up and enjoy our last night in a civilised place, I'm paying." Varro answered, removing his chainmail and walking to the water bowl on a table by the small window. "We'll have some hot food and a few gallons of wine, perhaps it will help to take away the pain."

They found a table downstairs in a corner and ordered a hot stew with plenty of wine to help wash it down. The place was just starting to fill up with traders, legionaries and a few locals, a large fire was roaring away nearby keeping the place warm.

"So do you think there's any chance, any chance at all that Brenna and her friend will get us through this in one piece?" Grattius asked his centurion.

Varro took a swig of his wine, it was a little sour and one eye blinked shut as he swallowed, "Hardly the good stuff is it?" He said and shivered. "I don't know and to be honest I don't even know how much I trust her anymore after what happened." He took another mouthful and pulled a face. "Don't have much choice."

"First sign of anything that even remotely makes me believe she's going to remove my head and I'll skewer her and her friend." Grattius said taking a drink, "Mm not bad." Varro frowned as his optio tipped his cup back and emptied its contents in one. "Not the worst drop of juice I've had." He said and then let out a loud belch which prompted someone on the next table to turn around with a look on their face of utter disgust. "Oh and you don't get wind I suppose?" Grattius said staring at the man who was clearly a civilian, "Here, have this one as well." He added as he leant forward and belched even louder. "Mind your own business," He said, "or there'll be trouble." The civilian turned away, muttering to his companions.

"Here," Grattius said, "that's an idea." He leaned towards Varro, "We could beat the living life out of a few civilians and get locked up for a bit, that would put a stop to this stupid business eh? He poured another drink. "A few months in the stockade would be preferable to that don't you think?"

"Mm I'm sure it would and what else would we get, busted back to legionary and sent into the mountains anyway, probably in the front ranks," Varro replied trying some more wine, "no thank you, I'll take my chances with Brenna first. I'm not throwing my career away anyway and it would be cowardice."

"Who's to know? Would you tell anyone?" He looked at Varro, "Thought not."

"Bringing the army into disrepute, beating up civilians, the Legate would do to us what Caratacus is likely to do," he took a drink, "this gets better," his eye only shut a little this time. "We have to just accept what we've been ordered to do and get on with it my friend and besides, just think of all the tales we'll be able to tell afterwards."

"What with no bollocks, my head on a pole, arms and legs removed and eaten by goats, oh yes I'll look forward to that." Grattius said an ironic look on his face.

At that moment a girl came over carrying a large tray with two big steaming bowls on it and four bread loaves. The two soldiers moved their wine cups and flasks out of the way and she put them down.

"Will there be anything else?" She asked in good Latin.

"How about you later?" Grattius said.

"If you want whores, you go down the road and round the corner, third building on the left." She said, "I'm here because my father owns this place not to get pox from the likes of you and your riddled maggot."

"Ugh charming," Grattius said dishing out two of the small loaves to Varro, "at least we know where to go later eh?"

"Erm I don't think so, not me anyway," Varro said, "I'm going to get this inside me," he nodded at the stew, "attempt to drink some more of this until the shock of today begins to fade and my vision blurs and then I'm going to get some sleep. We don't know when we'll get another chance."

Grattius ripped one of his loaves apart, dunked it into his stew and said, "Even more reason to wet your whistle, might never get the chance again after tonight." He plunged the stew soaked bread into his mouth, "Mm good," he said, as he took two chews and swallowed, "probably won't have a whistle to wet in a few days anyway."

Varro was woken up early the next morning just as daylight began to light up the room through the wooden shutters covering the window. At first he didn't know where he was, then he realised he'd drunk far too much the night before and turned over intending to go back to sleep, and then he heard Grattius straining. He opened his eyes to find a naked optio sat on a pot against the wall.

"Oh good! What a sight first thing." He muttered and closed his eyes again.

"You should have come last night, you missed out there. Really classy some of those girls were, knew what they were doing n'all, if you get my meaning...." Grattius said as his words were cut off by a large blast of wind.

Varro buried his face in the pillow, "Why me?" but it didn't stop the sound, akin to thunder, from preventing him from going back to sleep again, not that Grattius would stop talking.

"Should've asked the Governor to let us grow our hair and beards for a few weeks, you know, help us blend in with the stinkies." He said.

Varro spoke into his pillow, "I think you'll do just fine as you are."

After a breakfast of bread and cheese, they went to the stable where they had arranged to meet up with Brenna and Lita, the two women were already there.

"Rough night gentlemen?" Brenna asked.

"For some more than others." Varro replied walking to Staro and patting his neck. "Hello boy," he said, "I hope they've been looking after you?" Staro's big dark eyes looked at him as he nudged his chest.

"You'll need a change of clothing." Lita said.

"What?" Grattius replied rubbing his head.

"Unless of course you don't want to even make it over the border, it's up to you but I would advise a change of clothing, something more local."

"She's right," Varro said, "we'll get a change of clothing at Isca before we make the final leg of the journey."

"Mm," Grattius muttered, "and final it'll probably be." He said as he lifted his saddle cloth. "Are you sure it's not too late to go back to the infantry?"

Varro smiled, "Quite sure Optio Grattius, now let's get out of here before I change my mind."

It took a while to prepare the horses for travel, Brenna and Lita had indigenous animals, they were slightly shorter and stockier than the Roman mounts but were known to be hardy. As the first rays of sunshine began to burn away the slight frost on the ground they set off, heading west.

Caradoc examined the shield he held and turned it over, it was rectangular in shape, virtually as large as a Roman shield and bowed inwards slightly at the edges. It was lined with brass and in the centre on the side that would face the enemy, was a large bulbous shield boss, he smiled.

"How much protection do they offer?" He asked of the carpenter and smithy, both had helped create them. Behind the two was a cart laden with other examples.

"They can stop stabs and blows and prevent arrows, their javelins too for a time." He said. "The problem will be making more, I can't produce them quickly, I have to find the right wood, bind it, the metal smith," he pointed to the man next to him with a dirty face, "here has to create the edging or they'll just splinter and be worthless."

Ardwen walked over to the cart and examined the pile of shields and picked one up. He drew his sword and placed the shield on the ground, "Let's see shall we?" He said and struck the boss with a mighty blow sending sparks flying into the air. The tip of the sword slid to the wood in the same movement and embedded itself. "Mm impressive but how are they after a few blows, in a real battle?"

"We'll see shall we?" Caradoc said pulling his sword free of its scabbard and hefting the shield he held.

"Oh right, like that is it?" Ardwen frowned and then smiled. "Come on then mighty King of the Catuvellauni, let's see what they can do shall we?"

The two warriors crouched and approached each other, "I don't want you holding back." Caradoc said, "This is to be a proper test."

Without answering Ardwen rushed forward screaming and brought his weapon to bear in an overhead arc, Caradoc just had time to raise his shield properly as his opponent brought his sword down wildly. The blade bit into the edging made of bronze as Caradoc moved to the left and pulled his shield away, there was slight damage but nothing more.

"My turn." He said not giving Ardwen any more notice as a flurry of blows struck the Silurian's shield forcing him backward. Caradoc's long sword pounded against the wood repeatedly, the weapon becoming a blur, fast blows striking again and again as splinters of wood flew all around but the shield held. Ardwen jinked to the right and brought his weapon up.

"Now mine." He said, stabbing with one hand whilst peeping out from behind the shield and advancing, the point struck Caradoc's defensive barrier again and again but still it held. Caradoc moved forward, bending low and punched out, he could feel the impact of his cousin's sword as he struck the point of the sword, metal against metal as blade struck boss, again Ardwen was forced backward.

"Our swords are heavy to be held with one hand like this." He said peering over his shield, "Now I know why those Roman bastards use those children's weapons they carry." He laughed as Caradoc lunged again, his entire weight behind the blow as he knocked Ardwen to the ground.

"Enough, enough," he said, "for now anyway." And got to his feet, both men examined the shields. They were slightly battered but had held up considerably well.

"I want you to begin making more right away." Caradoc said breathing harder than he had before, "I will send you young men who you will teach, old men too, who are too old to fight. Our warriors are brave but they stand no chance against an army trained to fight behind shields like these. If it means cutting down an entire forest then so be it, we have to have better protection." He turned to Ardwen. "We also need to train the men and women to fight with them, sword in one hand and a shield in the other. With the winter coming we'll have a few months to prepare, they'll be tucked up behind their walls until spring at the earliest, so we have time to organise."

He said nodding in an easterly direction. "I want the better warriors trained first and then they can train the others, not the play fighting they're used to, and we need more archers and slingers." Ardwen looked pleased with his plans, "We can do this cousin, I'm certain of it."

"And who will we find to train them?" Ardwen asked.

"We have soldiers as prisoners still, the ones we took off the mountains when the mighty Second Augusta came, they will help us or die." Caradoc said.

"That's if the druids haven't sacrificed them all." Ardwen replied.

"They haven't," he paused and stared at Ardwen, "I told them to stop when I heard what they were doing the stupid fools, there are over a hundred of them still alive on Mona and more are captured every day."

Ardwen stared at his cousin but Caradoc continued before he could say anything. "They are too valuable to just slaughter, these men aren't just soldiers. They can build things, create things, they can make tools and they can train our people. We let them live, we feed them and make sure they're looked after and they will help us."

Ardwen didn't look happy. "Shields and training it is then but a lot of the men won't be happy cowering behind shields you know, it's not our way." He said.

"And would they be happier left to rot or thrown into the ground dead at the hands of the legions?" He looked from Ardwen to the carpenter and smith, "Many lives depend on your crafting skills, make them quickly but make them well. While you teach others and make more you can show riders what trees you want and they can look for them so you two aren't wasting your time scouring the woods and forests." He looked back to Ardwen and then addressed them again. "I cannot tell you how important this is, but know it will be as vital as the crops we grow, the animals we raise and the air we breathe. You must give this task everything you have, do you understand?"

Both men nodded.

"I want to know straight away if you encounter any problems," he thought for a moment, "if you can't get the right wood or the stone for smelting or if someone isn't working properly and doing as you say, if you need charcoal, whatever it is, you come to me or better, send a messenger so you can keep working. Is that clear?"

The men nodded again.

"Good, then be about your task and good luck." Caradoc said dismissing the craftsmen. He turned to Ardwen, "Send a messenger to Mona and tell them that I want all the prisoners sent here."

"They won't be too pleased about that." Ardwen replied.

"Then ask them which of them will stop the Romans when they come across the mountains again in spring. Who of them will fight and kill the invaders? They will have to co-operate or they may as well just throw themselves into the sea and be done with it. We are fighting for our very survival and if the druids don't do as I ask, then I shall visit them and wipe them from the face of the earth myself." Caradoc said angrily.

"We can't say that," Ardwen replied, "they may not have been as important to you where you come from Caradoc, but to speak in such a way would only bring destruction on all we are trying to do."

"How?" Caradoc asked, "How will they bring destruction to us?" He raised his sword, "With these? I don't think so. Will they call their gods from the underworld or the heavens to strike me down?" He smiled, "It's a chance I'm willing to take because if they don't do as I ask, we're all doomed anyway." He replaced his sword and began to walk away, "Get it done Ardwen. I want those soldiers back here within three days."

Grattius and Varro led the way west with Brenna and Lita slightly behind them, "I suppose I've got the blonde one then?" The optio asked, "Seeing as you're in love with Raven hair."

"What?" Varro asked turning his head.

"Blondie, I said, I suppose I'm left with the blond one."

Varro turned around and looked at Lita, "What makes you think she'll be interested?"

Grattius looked hurt, "Ugh," he almost choked out, "stands to reason doesn't it."

The centurion looked confused, Grattius continued, "She's helping us, must be a reason which more than likely means she wants a bit of Roman steel inside her."

Varro scowled, "I don't think the two necessarily go together but you can always give it a try if you like, just don't come running to me if she turns feral on you."

Grattius glanced backwards at Lita and smiled, she returned a glare, "Mm maybe you're right." He said, "So what about you and the beautiful Brenna then? She's a bit small for me mind you. I prefer 'em a bit taller, you know longer legs."

"That's good to know, I'll bear that in mind once we're in the mountains and leave the longer legged ones to you, they'll catch you quicker." Varro said.

"Oh, you had to do it didn't you? Now you've reminded me of where we're going." He closed an eye and looked up trying to find the sun through the grey cloud. "It might be my last chance to get close to a woman then."

I wouldn't say that," Varro replied, "if we get captured and tortured, they'll get close to you alright."

Grattius contorted his face, "I don't mean like that." He looked up again, "Anyway we'd better start looking for somewhere to camp for the night before we lose the light."

Varro looked around, "Mm well at least you're right about that." He said, "The next good place we find will do, sheltered and covered if possible."

They rode on slowly for a while along the track they'd been following until they came to a small outpost where messengers exchanged horses and rested for the night. It was manned by an optio and three soldiers but there was no space available, the optio suggested that they could use the tents at the rear of the small building or the stable. The stables were full of horses and smelt quite badly, so they went and had a look at the tents. They were packed with dry goods, barrels, spare equipment, saddles and bridles but there was enough space in both to lie down, just, as long as you didn't mind being cosy.

"Gods breath, that does it." Grattius said, "Lita and I will take this one," he said pointing, "and you and Brenna can share the other." He turned to the others smiling, eyebrows raised. Lita's expression was that of utter rage.

"If you think I'm going to lie with you, you stinking excuse of a man, you've got another thing coming, I'd rather mate with a dog." She spat.

"Mm," he murmured turning to look at Varro, "Looks like you and I are stuck with each other then, Centurion."

"So it would seem." Varro replied, "Come on let's get the horses settled and get some food sorted out. There's bound to be rations inside the post, maybe some relatively fresh wine as well, not that vinegar we had in Londinium."

"Fussy for a soldier aren't you Centurion?" Grattius said.

"Not really Optio," he said emphasising the others rank, I just have a discerning taste." Varro caught Brenna's eye as he said it and saw what he thought was a faint smile cross her lips.

"Will they have baths?" She asked.

"Doubtful, very doubtful," Varro said, "Although they could have a tub or something to squeeze into if you're lucky."

"Anything would do, just to get the dirt off from the ride today." She said. It was the first time she had spoken since they had left earlier that day, the first time she had spoken to him anyway and somehow it made him feel better.

"Come on then let's get sorted out." Grattius said leaving the tent, "horses first as always."

Optio Vidus, the outpost's temporary commander turned out to be a veteran from Hispania. He was around thirty years of age and had spent most of his adult life in the army, twelve years. The same height as Varro with a slightly darker complexion, the only other noticeable difference was the almost white grey hair around his ears. Varro looked around the small interior of the outpost and spoke to Vidus.

"Thank you for the hospitality, we'd have spent a night under the stars if we hadn't found you." He said. In reality the outpost was little more than a stone hut, albeit a large one. Inside there was space for five cots, three for those stationed there and two for soldiers, predominantly messengers passing through, they were currently occupied by sleeping men. With nine people inside there was virtually no room to move around, to one side in a corner there were two tables with small tools around them.

"We're just about to start the evening meal if you'd like to join us?" Vidus asked, "It won't be much but here," he waved at a legionary preparing food, "is a very good cook and we get fresh rations every three days, so there's plenty to go around."

Varro smiled, "That would be most welcome, thank you," Varro said pointing at the stools, "We'll take a seat over here out of the way."

"Please help yourselves." Vidus said, "Who are the females, Britons I presume?" He asked.

Brenna and Lita turned but Varro answered before they could say anything, "Yes allies, they've worked closely with us for a while now, a number of years." He lied in Lita's case, "and can speak our language very well." He warned just in case the optio said something derogatory.

Vidus motioned towards the stools, "Well you're all welcome, please take a seat while Helco works some magic."

They did as they were asked and whilst they chatted quietly about their mission Vidus brought some wine over as the smell of freshly cooked bread wafted around the room. Vidus saw their faces light up.

"We may be in the middle of nowhere but there's always a place for fresh bread." All legionaries were well versed in bread making and it had become an essential ingredient of their daily food intake, often supplementing their rations. "We only have a small oven but it can make a few little loaves at a time." Vidus remarked as Helco chopped some onions whilst humming and then threw some vegetables into a pot. "It won't be long." He took a stool and sat down next to Varro. "So where are you headed?" He asked.

"Back to Isca." Varro lied, "We're taking Brenna and Lita there as they know the lay of the land. They're going to be helping the scouts as we prepare to move west when the campaigning season begins again." He took a sip of his wine, "Mm that's better than the last drop I had back in Londinium."

Grattius gave him a frown, "I'll just check on the horses quickly." He said standing up and draining his cup and walking to the door, "That smells good my friend." He added to Helco nodding at the bubbling pot, the legionary smiled and sprinkled some herbs into the food he was preparing, "I'm starving." He was heard saying as he closed the door.

Soon after Grattius returned, they were joined by the messengers who had been woken up for their supper and they enjoyed the meal prepared by Helco. They talked of their experiences in Britannia both good and bad and even Lita lightened up and joined in the conversation. They talked of their fears and expectations and compared some of the island to northern Gaul, which Brenna and Lita found intriguing, having never been there. Afterwards Varro's group thanked the outpost's men once more for their hospitality and made their way outside.

"Just going for a piss," Grattius said disappearing into the dark as Lita went directly to the tent she was to share with Brenna that evening. Varro smiled at her and turned to their tent.

"Wait," Brenna said to the centurion. "Is everything alright between us?" She asked.

He smiled, "Of course," he said, knowing it wasn't actually the truth, "we're fine."

"I hope so," she moved closer looking around to make sure nobody was watching and took his hand, "I wish I was sleeping with you tonight, I miss you."

He felt a warm rush glide through his body and his heart quicken, he looked down at her as she raised herself up onto her toes, her dark eyes getting closer and kissed him tenderly on the lips. He responded in kind feeling her warm soft lips against his own as he felt her tongue flick into his mouth.

"Right, now that's out of the way, it's time for some sleep," Grattius disturbed the moment and they quickly moved apart, "pissed like a stallion then." He said seeing Brenna and Varro, he pointed, "No farting and snoring tonight either Centurion, I need a good night's sleep."

Varro pursed his lips and glowered at the optio as he walked past them, threw the tent flap aside and vanished from sight.

"What do you mean they said no?" Caradoc asked the messenger who had returned from Mona.

"They said you can't have the survivors, they're to be sacrificed, all of them." The man said. He was dirty from his ride and clearly fearful of relaying the message he had been told to give.

Caradoc turned to Ardwen, "Saddle the horses and gather as many men as you can quickly."

"What do you intend to do cousin?" Ardwen asked.

Caradoc began walking towards where the horses were, "It's time the druids were told that they can't just kill when they like, who they like and for whatever reason they like." Caradoc replied. "Those Romans can help us, their knowledge is essential, surely they can see that?"

"They want the favour of the gods Caradoc it's always been this way." Ardwen said.

Caradoc stopped, "And just where have the gods got us so far, remind me? Surrounded on all sides, pinned in from the north, east and the south, that's where Ardwen. Will they suddenly find favour in us if they kill all those men and sweep all the legions into the sea? I don't think they will, now do as I ask."

Ardwen watched Caradoc walk away and turned to the messenger, "Very well cousin but I don't think this is a good idea. Get some rest." He said to the man who had brought the reply as he ran off to gather some warriors.

It took the best part of the rest of the day to get to the channel between the mainland and Mona and night time was approaching as the fifty riders slid from their mounts.

"We'll cross at first light." Caradoc said looking at the small boats on the shoreline. He could see light from fires on the large island as a cold breeze hit his face.

"Do you think this will achieve anything?" Ardwen asked. "They don't take kindly to being told what to do."

Caradoc removed a rug from his horse as it began to chew the grass at its feet and tied the reins to a branch. "Do you suppose I care what they think? Those men that 'we' captured can help us and if that means them living then I'm certain they will co-operate, surely that is more important than sacrificing them for nothing."

Ardwen tied his own horse up as the warriors with them made their own preparations for an uncomfortable night on the water's edge. "I'll support you whatever they say Caradoc, but I don't know if this is a good idea," he turned and looked at Mona, "that place is very strange, sacred they say. They won't take kindly to us turning up like this and that's before you even say a word."

Caradoc knelt down and unfurled his blanket, "I'll bear that in mind." He said and got down, covered himself and said no more.

In the morning he was woken by rain hitting his face, he pulled the blanket up over him and turned over, he lay there for a while thinking about the day ahead.

"Come on then," He heard Ardwen say, "let's get this over with."

He rolled and sat up, "Get the men in the boats." He said, a dark look on his face. It took a while to get all fifty warriors onto Mona, and they were greeted by a druid who mumbled something about this being an intrusion. After an argument about Caradoc and his men carrying weapons, which the druid lost, they marched inland. By midmorning they came to the first settlements as shocked faces met them. Ardwen guided them to the edge of what he called the Sacred Groves where a large group of druids were waiting for them. News of their arrival, it seemed, had gone before them, a druid dressed in a dark garb stepped forward.

"What is the meaning of this intrusion?" He asked his head partially covered with a hood. Caradoc looked at the man whom he estimated to be easily sixty plus years of age. His robe was full length obscuring his feet. He held his hands together at the front.

"I sent a messenger to get the Roman prisoners, you refused." Caradoc said his voice harsh, he knew that the tribes revered these men and that he should ordinarily show them some respect, but he had decided to take a hard line with them.

"Those that still live, are to die," the druid said, "you cannot change this, to do so would anger the gods." He added opening his hands and putting them to the side of his body as if he were conversing with something unseen.

"Those men can help us against their legions, I want them released," he stepped forward, "now."

The druid smiled, "I'm afraid that's quite impossible Caradoc." The smile turned to a sneer, "Come, I will show you."

Caradoc didn't know what he meant and followed the druid as he turned with the others but kept his distance, his men behind him. Just as the rain stopped falling and the sun appeared through the clouds, they came to a small dip in the path they had been following, beyond he could make out the tops of trees.

"Not far now." The druid said wearing the same sneer on his face. They entered the wood with silver trees and light branches and continued walking until a clearing came into view. Caradoc could see what appeared to be lined tree stumps ahead.

"All will become clear." The druid said.

Entering the clearing Caradoc saw that there was a huge circle of neatly cut tree stumps with a stone block at the centre. The wood had outer and inner layers, too many to count, some were taller than others and then he saw that there were bodies slumped at the base of most.

"As you can see we have splayed the invaders and most are already dead, those that are not will soon be so. The others, well most were burnt to death as is our custom but splaying is like their habit of nailing a man to a cross."

Caradoc didn't want to know the answer to the question of what this meant but as he got closer, he saw for himself. The druids had cut into the prisoners along the back of their hands, up their arms and had peeled the flesh back to the shoulders. The men had then been tied by their own flesh to the wood facing outward, nails embedded into the dying skin to secure them. He felt bile rise in his mouth as his face contorted in disgust at the sight before him.

"It works quite well," the druid continued, "the pain they endure is like nothing on earth and sometimes they survive for days." He pointed, "This one for example." He walked closer to a corpse his head slumped forward, skin white, strips of flesh tied to the rear, congealed blood formed around his mouth. "Lasted three whole days before he went, quite unusual but he was a very strong individual." He looked at Caradoc and pushed back his hood, "So you see King Caradoc," the sneer returned, "it is not possible for you to have them, they are all dead, to a man. Those who weren't executed straight away were splayed after your messenger left."

Later, when he had tried to explain his reaction to the druid earlier to

Ardwen, all he could say was that it was like being taken over by something. Without thinking he had removed his dagger from the belt at his side and thrust it upward into the druids lower chin, piercing the skin instantly and driving the blade up into his skull through tongue and brain. He had stood there with blood pouring onto his arm and turned to the other druids now standing in shock all around them, pivoting with the dead man's eyes staring at him he shouted.

"You will all, all of you to a man share his fate and worse," he spat out, "if I find that you have done this or anything like it again." He raised his arm and then hurled the dead man to the ground, other druids backed away as the body bounced and rolled.

"He was our leader, our high priest." One man stepped forward, Caradoc recognised him.

"I know you. We met soon after the Romans landed." He said.

"Yes we did and I warned you of what was to come." The druid said.

"You didn't see this did you?" Caradoc asked, anger flaring as he looked at the dead attached to trees all around them. "We are fighting for our very survival and this," he waved at the corpses struggling to find the words, "this will not help. No more." He pointed the blood soaked blade at the hooded faces. "The Romans will be the last of your concerns if I hear this has happened again." He wiped the blade on his cloak, its sharp edge easily slicing through the thick woollen material.

"From this day forward if there are any prisoners brought here, even one, I want to know about it. If I'm not told but find out, I will return with hundreds of warriors and cover the ground with your bloodied and tortured corpses and leave you for the birds to eat. Do you understand?" He said clenching his teeth as he walked towards the druids, who hurriedly nodded their understanding.

Chapter Fourteen

After an uncomfortable but dry night, Varro and his companions packed their kit and bid their farewells to Vidus, Helco and the other soldier at the outpost. The messengers had already left before first light, heading to their own destinations. The day was cold and overcast but the rain threatening to fall held off and they continued their journey. As a light drizzle started, Isca came into view on the horizon as the travellers hunched down trying to prevent the wet from seeping down their necks. Approaching the large garrison's gate, one of four, rain fell freely off Varro's helmet.

"I'll be glad to get into a hot bath," he said, "my feet are numb."

"I second that." Grattius replied and then shouted up to the guard above who, straining through the now heavy rain, recognised them and shouted for the doors to open. They cantered in and headed directly for the stables where a legionary happily took their horses.

"Right let's get out of these wet clothes." Varro said, "Then I'll go and see the Legate and tell him about the task we've been set, I'm sure he'll be overjoyed." A group of eight legionaries marched by outside followed by another, two tent parties glistening in the rain.

"Grattius, you can go and see the quartermaster and see what he can give us, anything local, clothes, boots, carrying bags, you know what we need, but get these two some accommodation first and not in the barracks with the men, we'll never see them again." He smiled at Brenna and Lita. "I'll come and find you later." He headed off towards his own accommodation as Grattius and the two females spoke briefly.

"Well ladies, looks like you're mine for the time being, come on I know just the place for you." They looked at him with worried expressions, "Don't worry it's nothing awful although it is at the back of the stables, not attached," he added, "and it has heating and baths, even a roof. It's used for visiting dignitaries," the women looked at him confused, "important people, like you." He smiled and waved an arm indicating the way, "Come on, the sooner we get out of these clothes the better, and no I don't mean in that way." He led the way to the building where they were to be accommodated.

After Varro had taken off his soaked clothes inside his warm room and dried off, he changed into a fresh tunic and draped a cloak over his shoulders, checked his appearance in the long brass mirror against the wall and went to see the Legate. All the permanent buildings were now served by the hypocaust under floor heating system so he felt the chill again as soon as he went outside. He knew that the information was to be kept to a minimum regarding the plan to speak with Caratacus, but clearly the Legate was one person who had to know the details. As it turned out, the Primus Pilus was discussing plans with the legion's commander when he entered the *Principia* headquarters well lit room. He was vaguely aware of the unit's symbols on the walls, Capricornus the horned goat, Pegasus the winged horse and Mars, god of War, son of Jupiter and Juno. Varro handed over the scrolls given to him by Aulus Plautius and was promised every assistance he required, he acknowledged their words with a salute but felt dizzy, not at all like himself. As he left the building he shuddered, feeling the cold as if it had entered his bones, he pulled the cloak around his shoulders and sneezed. He walked quickly back to his room and threw the now wet cloak down over a chair and picked up a thick blanket, he wrapped it around himself and then fell onto the bed and was asleep in moments.

"I can't believe you killed him." Ardwen said to Caradoc once they had mounted their horses and were heading back travelling east.

"Can't you?" He shouted over the noise of the clattering hooves on the path. "We aren't animals but even an animal wouldn't do that to another. I don't have a problem killing the enemy but those men didn't deserve to die like that Ardwen. Nobody deserves a death like that."

"They do the same to us," He shouted back, "when they nail our people to trees and crosses."

Caradoc pulled on the reins of his horse and stopped, "We're not going to argue over this cousin and I don't care what they do, we are not like them. They," he pointed in the direction of Mona, "will not behave like them nor will we, war is one thing, barbarity of that kind is something else altogether."

Ardwen frowned clearly not understanding his cousins reasoning.

"Imagine yourself in the same position as those men, stripped of your flesh," Caradoc said, "in agony, seeing it happen to others, those around you, men you had lived with, fought with." He spat. "That is no way for a warrior to behave, take arms, cleave heads and kill but do it in battle where there is honour, man against man or woman for that." He reached out and grabbed Ardwen's wrist. "We are better than that vile diseased creature back there or do you think me wrong?"

Ardwen was surprised by the question, "I didn't think of it in that way," he placed a hand over Caradoc's, "but you're right, it is no way for any man to die or any creature for that."

Caradoc turned his horse and addressed the warriors that had accompanied him, whose very presence had assured his safety on Mona after the death of the high priest, "I did not go there intending to kill a druid on their sacred island, but I will not allow that sort of torture to prevail as long as I lead you as a people. Do not think of me as weak for I am not, but if you cannot abide by what I say as an entire people, then I will re-consider leading you against the threat we face." His horse whinnied. "If you kill a man in battle, take his eyes, cut out his heart, rip the flesh off his face, then do it as men not as cowards who lurk waiting for those to be sacrificed later." The horse spun round sensing the tension. "That is all I ask, I understand your hatred of Rome and all it stands for believe me, I have seen what they are capable of but that," he pointed again to Mona, "is no way for anyone to behave and I will not accept it from any of you."

He examined the faces of the men listening to him expecting to see anger or resentment at his words but there was none. "I will do my best to help protect you, all of you, and your families and expect your loyalty in return, that is all I ask of each and every one of you." He paused, "When we get back later, I want you all to tell those who are close to you exactly what happened today, leave nothing out. Tell it as it happened so everyone is clear, do you all hear me?" Heads nodded their understanding. "We have to be united against the legions of Rome, each and every one of us or we're doomed to failure. Those men who have made those so called sacrifices to our gods have done nothing to help us in that aim, in fact they have merely done us harm. I would have persuaded those soldiers to help us but that is no longer possible because those fools did what they did. Do you all hear me and understand what I'm saying and why I'm saying it?" He asked. They did. "Come then, let's get back and out of this weather." He said and led them west.

Later that night in the warmth of the roundhouse he shared with Mott, he discussed the day's events and watched as she screwed up her face in disgust as he explained what he had seen on Mona. He told her of the speech he had made to the men and what he had told them he expected of them, she smiled approvingly at his words.

"Husband I would expect nothing less from you and if they don't agree," she caressed his face, "we'll know soon enough and we'll take our people and leave, but I don't think that will happen. The Silures, Ordovices, Deceangli and Demetae have sworn their allegiance to you. They are proud and know that you will do whatever you can to ensure their survival." She kissed him.

"Do you believe that, even though I killed one of their druid leaders?" He asked now doubting himself.

She kissed him again and led him to their fur covered bed, "Yes husband I do." She said and pulled him into bed.

Varro woke up three days later. He was barely aware of the time in-between from wrapping himself in a blanket and falling onto his bed, until he tried to open his eyes again. Blurred images flashed through his mind, fits of coughing, cold sweats and an almost drunken sensation, where was he? His eyes were still heavy as he struggled to open them, sensing someone was near. He felt something against his flesh and then realised he was naked but he didn't remember undressing. He shook his head slowly and heard a slight rustle as his dark hair brushed the pillow.

"Ah you're awake." A voice said, slightly husky, he searched his memory, it was familiar, he tried to concentrate but the pain in his head prevented it. A wet cloth was applied to his forehead.

"You've been out cold for days, three in fact." The voice said, "We were worried you might never recover at one point when you became delirious and started shouting and trying to fight us."

"What, what are you talking about?" He managed through a croaky voice.

"It's me Varro, Brenna. I've been here since Grattius found you when you didn't come to our room that night. He came looking for you and found you thrashing around, wrapped in a blanket, we've been so worried."

He raised his head a little, it pounded somewhere at the back. "What happened?" He felt her sit on the side of the bed.

"The medicus thinks it was a fever brought on by the cold and rain, I'm so glad you're alright now." She touched his left shoulder. He focused his eyes and her blurred face became more defined, then clear, her own dark eyes compassionately staring down at him. He saw she was wearing a short sleeved tunic, her light brown thighs exposed. Automatically, without thinking, he placed the palm of his hand there. Her skin was smooth to the touch.

"You've been here all along?" He said trying to sit up.

"Stay still," she said and poured some water, "here, drink this." She held the cup to his mouth and he took a few sips. Then he suddenly tried to sit up quickly.

"The mission," he said eyes wide, "we're not supposed to be here." She pushed him back, "Don't worry, it's been delayed until you're fit to travel." He lay back closing his eyes.

"Grattius wanted to go without you, but the Legate wouldn't allow it and I didn't feel happy with just him and Lita for company." She looked at the window at the dark clouds above, "It's probably a good thing you got ill here or we'd have been stuck outside in the middle of nowhere, no shelter, you could have died."

"Grattius would have strapped me to Staro and brought me back." He opened and closed his eyes blinking, "I feel like I've drank the legion's entire wine cache, my head." He brushed a hand through his thick black hair.

"Lie still and relax, in a few days you'll be fine." She rubbed his stomach. "You need to rest and recuperate. You know you men suffer worse from these things than women." She smiled and looked down seeing the physical reaction to her touch, "See, you're beginning to feel better already." Her hand moved lower and the door opened.

"Ah awake at last." Grattius said bursting into the room. Brenna pulled her hand back quickly. "We were beginning to think you'd sleep through the entire winter." He looked down at Varro, "So, feeling better then? You've had Brenna looking after you for three days solid. She hasn't left your side except to wash, even slept in that chair." He looked at the large framed wooden two seat chair against the wall. They both stared at him, "What?" He raised his eyebrows. "Oh right I see," he smirked, "feeling a lot better then?" He walked back to the door, "Well don't overdo it, you'll need all your energy once we get moving." He grabbed the door handle, "I'll be back later."

Hearing the door closed firmly, Brenna smiled, "Now where were we?" Her hand moved back to his stomach and then went lower.

Four days later, Varro and his small party were ready to move out.

Their horses were packed as were two mules that carried rations, clothes, blankets, bowls and food. The day was overcast, a grey sky overhead threatened rain but it was relatively mild as the clouds moved slowly above. Varro and Grattius were dressed in local garb and carried long swords, they knew the disguise might work form a distance but if anyone got close, they'd see their short hair and become suspicious.

"Juno's cunt!" Grattius said looking down at his clothing and then up at Varro, "We look like a right pair of barbarian ball breaking bastards dressed like this, I just thank the gods my poor old mother isn't here to see this, she'd slice me a new hole in my arse that's for sure." He said pulling at the thick woollen jacket he'd been given, "And will you look at these fucking pants!" He bent forward and examined the chequered trousers the quarter master had supplied him with, they were a dull yellow with light brown lines criss-crossing them, "I don't know about a trip east, how about a fool in the circus?"

Varro smiled coughing, he still hadn't fully recovered from his virus, "Ah we'll be fine and at least our legs won't get cold eh?" He looked down at his long trousers that matched those that Grattius was wearing.

"I'm glad our type of clothing is to your liking." Lita said as she appeared in the stable with Brenna closely behind her.

"Yes, most attractive you both look," Brenna added, "I don't know if the females along the way will be able to resist you, it may take us some time to reach our destination." She went to her horse and threw the saddle up onto its back.

"Very funny I'm sure, you two could join the act on stage. We could make a fortune between us, the two Roman fools and the barbarians with blades." Grattius said securing his own saddle. "How I ever got myself into this mess I'll never know."

It took a few moments for them all to be happy with the way things were packed onto the mules and to sort out what they were carrying, weapons primarily, before they led the mounts out of the wooden framed building.

"Off somewhere nice then Centurion?" One of the young legionaries asked who looked after the horses and mules.

"Never you mind, you nosey little bastard." Grattius said climbing onto the mounting bench located outside and jumping up onto his horse. "You just go and groom some of those animals in there and mind your own business." The trooper who couldn't have been more than twenty years of age looked hurt.

"No need for that Grattius, the lad was only asking." Varro said.

"Really, didn't you see the smirk on the little fucker's face? Bloody laughing stock we are and this will be the last they see of us, dressed like bloody blue nosed hairies before we vanish for evermore." He rocked forward in his Celtic saddle and got his horse moving. "My bloody balls won't last that long though anyway not riding on this thing." He grabbed between his legs and re-arranged himself, "Ah that's a bit better." He moved about in the saddle, it was a lot smaller than the Roman style he was used to, "Bruised balls, dressed like a savage and off deep into enemy territory wonderful, just wonderful."

"I hope you're not going to complain all the way there are you?" Brenna asked but Grattius didn't answer, he just gave her an angry look as she fell into line behind him.

"Take a good look at civilisation for the last time," Grattius said as they headed slowly towards the main gate, their two mules at the rear attached by ropes, "goodbye, farewell." He said to various pedestrians as they walked by. "We'll see you in the next life, enjoy yours here won't you?" He was met by frowns, the occasional grimace and a few smiles. Varro took the space behind Brenna and watched as her body moved with the motion of the horse and wished that they were anywhere else other than where they found themselves.

"Once we're out on the track, I want Brenna and Lita up front so that they can do the talking if we come across any Britons, we're not going to get very far if the locals see there's two Romans dressed as them on the move."

"I wouldn't worry," Grattius said, "they'll probably be too busy pissing themselves laughing when they get a good look at us to care about where we're going."

And so the tone for the first leg of their mission was set with Grattius complaining bitterly about his saddle, horse, sword and clothes, until the first of the mountains came into view on the horizon and then he became quiet. Brenna led the four of them around the estuary and crossed the river where the horses were comfortable in the fast running water. They camped overnight with the mountains now a thumbs width high in the distance, the view against the darkening grey sky even more foreboding.

"We'll get a good night's sleep and set out at first light," Varro said untying his blanket roll as Grattius set about lighting a fire, "I'll take first watch after we've had some food, no need to take any chances."

Their supper was eaten in silence until Grattius asked Varro and Brenna about their last experience in the mountains. The conversation didn't improve much after they had told their stories from their own perspectives. Varro had found himself alone, isolated and cut off from his men and Brenna had found herself at the camp of the enemy, where she had been forced to kill Decimus. She explained that had she not killed him, she would have shared his fate and although it had been an awful thing to do, she had found herself with no choice, "It was him or both of us." She had said.

"I'm stunned," Grattius had remarked and had even stopped stuffing food into his mouth for a while, "and we're going there?"

Varro winced as the image returned to him, the shock, disgust and brutality of that moment ingrained into his very soul. How many nights had he lost sleep over what had happened that night, he didn't know. He had wanted to run out from behind cover, sword in hand, it didn't matter if he survived, he just wanted to avenge his fellow soldier and friend but something had held him back. Time had taught him a valuable lesson, things weren't always as they seemed, but that didn't take the bitterness he felt in his heart away every time his memories brought it back.

A light drizzle woke them in the morning. Grattius was already busy packing his blanket roll and tying it onto his mounts rump. "Ah good morning fellow travellers," he said, "a great day awaits us." He said gesturing upward at the falling rain.

Nobody felt like eating, so within the time it took the rest of them to pack their things away, they were heading slowly west again. Before long they could all feel that the gradient of the surface they were travelling on had changed and although they weren't at the foot of the mountains, the valleys lay before them. The wind had picked up and the rain was now horizontal at times and lashed into them in waves with the wind.

"I didn't appreciate how much I'd actually be enjoying this," Grattius shouted through the neckerchief he'd pulled up around his mouth, "but it's so good that I think that I'm going to soil myself."

Lita rode her horse closer to him, "Shut up you fool, anyone nearby will hear your big mouth."

He turned to Varro, "I do believe she's actually warming to me you know." Lita shot out an arm and struck Grattius' shoulder. "See," he said, "it could be love soon." She pulled her horse away and caught up to Brenna at the front. Eventually they found a shale path and followed it up as it wound its way higher and higher.

"How much further?" Grattius asked.

"Until we're where exactly?" Varro answered, "You'll see when we get to the top of this valley it's not as simple as that." Grattius screwed up his features and pulled the neckerchief higher. Sure enough when they got to the summit, out there in the wind and rain was the shadow of another valley in the distance.

"Marvellous." Varro heard Grattius mutter under his breath, "Bloody marvellous."

Caradoc was just settling down for an evening meal with Mott when a scout reported to his roundhouse.

"Are you certain they came from Isca?" He asked of the man who was standing before him soaked wet through to the skin.

"I followed them all the way and skirted around them at midday and came straight here. There can be no doubt, they left the Roman Garrison yesterday, four riders two women, Britons I'd say and two men, both Roman but dressed like us. They wear our clothes but they ride like them, I'm sure of it."

Caradoc smiled, "Go and find my cousin straight away." He stood and reached out for the scout's hand, "You have done well my friend," He shook the hand firmly, "Go and get yourself dry and warm."

Varro woke with a start. He shook his head and opened his eyes and immediately felt cold and wet, he began to shiver. He peered out from underneath his blanket and saw Brenna's form next to him, the fire was black. It must have gone out some hours before soaked through by the rain.

"Ugh," he groaned sitting up, "does it ever stop raining here?" He asked no-one in particular.

"It helps the grass grow, which in turn feeds the sheep, the sheep feed us." Lita said standing and shaking the water from her own blanket.

"I think I'm soaked right through to the scrotum." Grattius said, "And no I don't mean the thing carrying coins."

"But the contents are just as useless around here anyway so I wouldn't worry." Lita said smiling.

"Give me a chance to show you and you'll change your mind." Grattius said as Lita's usual frown re-appeared.

"I'd rather sleep with that mule." She said pointing to the animal grazing away quite happily on the lush grass nearby, rain bouncing off its back.

Grattius got up, "One day my girl, I'll show you what you've been missing."

Brenna came down from the high ground where she had been keeping watch for the last few hours, "Are you ready to go?" She asked the sodden group.

"Ready as ever." Varro replied tying his wet bedroll up and then sneezed.

"I hope you're not getting ill again?" Lita asked, "If you go down with that virus out here we're done for."

"Don't worry it was a sneeze nothing more, it doesn't mean I'm getting ill again." He said.

"It's not too late to turn back if you think you're going to go down with that virus again, you were out of it for days last time." Brenna said, concerned, "We need you at your best."

He climbed onto his horse, "I'll be fine I'm sure." He said and sneezed again.

They travelled slowly further into the valleys and before midmorning, they were consumed by huge green hills with steep falls at the side of paths, carpets of forests below where masses of pine trees awaited them, silver streaks of river snaking their way along the forest floors.

"How much further?" Grattius asked from behind the hood now covering his face.

"If you ask that one more time, I swear I'll kick you off your horse and into the valley below." Lita said.

"Ha, I think I'm a little damp for foreplay at the moment Lita but thank you for the offer, maybe later eh?"

She ignored him and continued riding, just as the patter of rain hitting them stopped and a shard of sunlight fought its way through the cloud. Varro shuddered, head down and looking pale.

"I think we need to warm up," She said, "perhaps stop for a while and build a fire." She was looking at Varro who was riding with his head down, his dark hair slick with rain water.

"Don't worry about me if that's what you're thinking." He coughed, "I'll be fine." His words said one thing, his body said another.

"Maybe I should ride on and look for some shelter? Lita suggested, "There are settlements in the next valley, I remember them from when I lived here as a little girl." She looked at Brenna and Grattius for a response, "I could get help. We need to get him inside as soon as possible, he needs shelter, warmth."

Brenna looked around becoming more concerned, "Go," she pointed further along the track they had been following, "stay on the path, the last thing we want is to get separated. We'll keep going and if we get to a fork in the road, we'll wait for you."

Lita nodded, turned her horse and galloped off, splashing water. "Come on," Brenna said leading the two men, "we have to keep going."

As they got lower, winding their way down the path they were following, the canopy of trees above shaded them from what little sunlight there was, Varro was visibly trembling now.

"We should stop and get him into some dry clothes." Grattius said looking about, "I'm going no further." He stopped his horse, jumped down and secured the reins to the branch of a tree.

"I was going to suggest the same." Brenna said as she got down off her own mount, "Over here." She said peering through the branches, "We'll leave the horses there so Lita sees them when she gets back. I think there's a cave or something here." She said crouching down and walking through the undergrowth. "Well more of a shallow scrape out of the side of the hill but it will do," she said from inside the trees, "it'll give us some shelter though, so bring him through."

Grattius reached up and grabbed Varro who was slumped over his horse shivering uncontrollably and pulled him to the side, "Come on, it's a good job you centurions have us optio's to look after you isn't it?" He said dragging Varro off the horse by his shoulders, he didn't even respond to the quip and his legs fell to the ground heavy and lifeless. Grattius threaded his arms under Varro's armpits and dragged him to where Brenna was beginning to gather some dry sticks together.

"I don't know how much wood we can find that hasn't been soaked." She said piling up the twigs she had found. Grattius gently laid Varro down and went back to the mules, returning a few moments later with an enormous leather sack.

"Right let's get his clothes off quickly and get him into something dry, once that's done we'll worry about the fire." Grattius said to Brenna as they both helped undress the centurion who was now either heavily asleep or unconscious, they weren't sure which.

"Should we wake him?" Brenna asked pulling off the heavy tunic he was wearing. Grattius held Varro's head up and looked at his face, "I don't know what to do for the best," he said, "let him sleep." He looked at Brenna. "It's supposed to help isn't it?"

They stripped him down completely and then wrapped him in dry thick woollen blankets and began preparing to light the fire. Not long after the small flames began to warm them, they heard Lita's voice calling for them.

"Over here Lita, follow the path we've cleared from the horses." Brenna shouted.

"I will," she called back. "I'm not alone though." Grattius and Brenna exchanged nervous glances. The optio reached for his sword.

"I don't think that's a good idea." Brenna said to which he grimaced.

"And why not, what if they're hostile?" He asked.

She looked round, "Remember where we are and there are three of us, what would you hope to achieve?" He frowned and moved his hand away from his hilt clearly not happy about the situation.

Legionary Valerius was acclimatising to his new cohort in the century and although the men in his tent party had been briefed as to how he had come to join their ranks, they were quite understanding and welcoming. He had expected a hard time but these men had quickly accepted him as one, of their own but he had been questioned nonetheless.

"So you had no choice then?" Pollo, a seasoned veteran had asked looking around at the others when he had first been introduced to them. "I'd have done the same, no point in dying for nothing eh?" The other six sat on their cots had agreed nodding. "Imagine if you and your friends had starting launching arrows at the hairies, you wouldn't be sat here now that's for sure would you?" He took a bite from a biscuit. "No you did the right thing friend believe me. It's all well and good these brave bastards sat behind the lines slurping on fresh wine and buggering slaves every day, to start spouting all that bile about duty and honour but you tell me, when was the last time they saw any action eh? The last time they drew their swords in anger it was probably a wooden one in training. They can all tell heroic tales of duty and honour and how they'd lose their lives defending a lost cause or chasing after a standard, but in reality they've never done a day's soldiering in their miserable lives." He took another bite and chewed.

"Anyway," he continued, "it's not so bad being in the first cohort it's all about looking out for each other, covering each other's backs, you do that and you'll be fine. Step out of line and you'll have a problem, believe me and you'll soon know about it and it's not as if you're a recruit is it?"

"Six years in." Valerius said. "I've been here from the start. I was stuck in the mountains with Vespasian deep inside Silures territory for days, surrounded by thousands of the bastards, killed my share of them."

Pollo smiled, "There you go, nothing to worry about then." He finished his biscuit. "In reality you're probably better off being with us up at the front of any large engagement, know why?"

He shook his head.

"What deranged lunatic is going to attack a square of centuries head on?" He asked, "We're at the front for a reason, we know what we're doing and anyone that attacks us is going to come head first into a huge row of pointy teeth and get introduced to this." He pulled his gladius from its scabbard. "The hairies have learnt their lessons by now and it's costs them plenty of lives. No, I'd rather be at the front than be in a century at the side, open to flanking you see, that's where the threat will be. We'll be covered off, tucked up, shields raised, swords out, heads down. You'll be alright with us and with the amount of training we do, it'll all come back to you soon enough now they've taken your bow away, don't you worry."

That was how his first night went as they sat around discussing previous encounters with the enemy, how they'd performed, personal stories, the few that had been killed and more that had been injured. Rumours of the next big push into the east Pollo had said were just speculation, Rome could wait and so would the Silures although the incursions into Roman held territory were disturbing, they were to be expected. He had assured him that he had joined them at the best time, campaigning season was over for the winter and the winters in Britannia could be long, so he had time to settle in and get to know how they worked.

They shared wine and joked, played dice and spoke of home, each man telling Valerius in turn where they grew up, how long they had been in the army and of their families back home. He quickly came to like Pollo, who it turned out had been recommended for promotion to Optio, but he had turned it down twice preferring to 'keep his feet on the ground' he had said. He had been in the legion twelve years and had fought in Germania and had lost many friends but had gained a lot more, he assured him he would see 'him right' and he was true to his word.

Within the garrison during the winter, there was little else to do except train, build, create and train some more. Their training consisted of simulated battle formations using training swords where centuries would face each other, advance in their squares, shields locked, men braced against each other, locked together, front and back by way of harnesses at the rear of each legionary. Optios and centurions would shout and scream orders as the two sides clashed and fought for supremacy, often for bragging rights later. Bruises and black eyes were often common place and even the occasional broken bone from over exuberant participants, but these were hazards of the training.

Changing lines was practised over and over again as it was the most vulnerable time to be facing the enemy in a legionary square but the men on the front line couldn't stay there indefinitely. After a period of time whilst fighting, usually decided upon by the centurion, and dependent on the circumstances, the front row would retreat and be replaced by the second row coming forward. The former front line would retreat to the rear where they could recover, have injuries dealt with or fall out of line completely if their injuries warranted it and so the tactic would continue.

Training such as this was absolutely essential for the individual to become a part of the unit and for the unit to work as one, like one huge machine knocking down their enemies before them. Likewise and equally essential was the testudo training, which a lot of legionaries actually preferred especially when they were the ones attacking their comrades in the defensive formation. Some centuries became so proficient in it that they were able to hold off two and in some cases, three other centuries while encased in the tortoise formation. Although primarily used for defensive purposes, there were times when it was also used to get a body of men into position in situations such as sieges or to advance whilst coming under attack from archers or slingers.

Practise at pilum throwing in squares was equally important, rotating the men, using the light javelin or heavy spear dependent on the situation, but there were also the more mundane duties such as guarding and kit cleaning, marching in unison, kit pole carrying, switching step from the military pace to the full pace. The military pace was used for tight formations such as preparing to face the enemy, whereas the full pace was used for marching long distances and would be used for the inevitable days marching from point A to point B. Out of the campaigning season, the centuries would also keep fit by running, although this was for physical conditioning, as charging into a fight was strenuously discouraged.

Other units trained within their specialisations, as Onager and Scorpion crews practised with their weapons on the training ranges as did the archers with their bows. So as the weeks went by, Valerius settled into the routine of training with his new comrades. He prepared himself as best as he could by getting to know those around him for the inevitable day when the Garrison's gates opened once more and they marched out to face the enemy.

Chapter Fifteen

Varro was covered in a fine sheen of sweat by the time Lita reached them. Brenna and Grattius looked up as she came forward through the undergrowth followed by a group of strangers, it was clear they were locals. They were dressed in heavy hooded skins, lean faces peering at the prone figure of Varro.

"I told them about our friend and they say we can go to their village, it's not far from here," She knelt down and felt Varro's brow, "he can get shelter and warmth there and be properly looked after, he can't stay here."

The newcomers came forward and studied the centurion lying prone on the ground, wrapped in blankets and then looked at Grattius. In unison they frowned because although Grattius was dressed in a similar fashion to them, his hair was cut short, instantly the atmosphere changed.

"Romani?" One of the males said, Brenna stood up.

"We're here to find Caratacus," she said turning to the optio, Grattius looked furious, clearly thinking that she was about to reveal the nature of why they were there, he was right. "This man," she went on pointing at Varro, "and his companion here, have a very important message for Caratacus. It is of the greatest importance that we find him but this one is too ill to travel." She knelt down again and touched the sleeping centurion's brow. "He has a fever," Varro murmured something but it was unintelligible, "see." She showed her palm and it was covered in sweat. "They are not here to hurt you," she looked at their suspicious faces, "they are here to try and help, to stop the trouble between your people and those of Rome."

The man who had spoken stepped forward, hand inside his fur, he spoke to Lita in his tongue, her language, but Brenna didn't understand although she heard the word Roman or Romani mentioned a few times as the man looked from Lita to Varro and occasionally to Grattius. The others behind him listened intently, while the optio fidgeted, eyes fixed on the man's covered hand. At one point the conversation got heated and it was clear that Lita was arguing their case, why they had brought Romans to their land. The Silures' head cocked to one side taking in the information repeatedly and then he would ask questions and look back at the others who had come with him. Eventually he seemed satisfied by the answers given.

Lita spoke to Brenna and Grattius, "He says we are lucky that we found him, if I'd gone to the next settlement, we would all be dead by now as they hate the Romans there. He said his family are tired of the fighting, young men going away, some not returning, he wants an end to the war but does not know how Caradoc will react. He does not go by the name Caratacus anymore because it is too Roman, he said. He has agreed to take us in while Varro is ill and in the meantime will send one of his sons to find their leader. He says that we must do everything he asks or we'll find ourselves in grave danger along with his family and he won't risk that."

"Tell him he has my thanks and that we'll do everything he tells us to do, we aren't here to cause trouble to him or his family." Brenna said. Lita spoke to him again and although he looked far from happy about the situation, he nodded his agreement. He then spoke to the males behind him, who could have been his sons Grattius thought. They then stepped forward and lifted Varro up and began carrying him the way they had come. He was carried to the waiting horses and draped onto one face down. Grattius nodded at them and was allowed to climb up onto the horse. He would ride him to wherever they were going. He felt hopeless and silently cursed the gods for finding himself in this situation.

They rode slowly for a while, the Britons on their own mounts, heads covered against the rain. After a while they began to follow a winding stream and in time came to a group of roundhouses nestled on a bend near the water's edge. The man, clearly the leader of the group or possibly their father, spoke to Lita who told Brenna that this was their home. She smiled in response but the man just looked at her and raised his eyebrows, a determined look in his eye.

"Don't worry, we are here to help." She said. Lita translated her words but he just turned and rode on.

After a heated discussion with a woman the visitors decided must be the wife of the leader, Varro was taken from the horse and into the nearest house. Inside it was warm, in the centre was a fire with an A frame, a large pot hanging from it. Towards one side of the large room there were beds raised off the ground on relatively well carved wooden foundations, there was a wooden frame near them where bows hung, a few swords and cooking pots on the floor. On a rudimentary table there were clothes and on another vegetables; carrots, onions, lentils and barley. The man spoke and Lita translated his words.

"He says we are welcome to stay here," she raised her hands to the roof where there was a hole allowing the smoke to escape, "he has another roundhouse next to this one where his son lives," she looked at a young man of about twenty summers, "he says if our being here helps to stop his son from fighting, the hardship of a few days will be worthwhile." He spoke again.

"He says that they have medicine that will help the soldier, herbs, they will prepare some and bring them here. In the meantime we," She looked at Grattius, "are all to stay here. We are not to go outside, to do so could be dangerous. Whilst we are his guests we are to abide with his wishes and rules at all times."

"We got that already thank you." Grattius said taking off his soaking over garment. The Briton came forward and took it from him and walked to the tables, he leant down and picked up a few poles from behind and quickly put them together, Grattius smiled, "A clothes frame, who'd have thought it?"

The Briton laid the garment over the frame and dragged it towards the fire and gestured for the females to remove their clothes. He spoke to Lita.

"He says we can use these clothes on the table, or the blankets while our own dry." Lita said. The man then turned and left the roundhouse talking to Lita as he did so. "He'll bring the medicine once it's been prepared."

"Well I for one am desperate to get out of these clothes, I don't know about you two?" Grattius said removing layers of clothing and placing them on the wooden frame the Briton had erected. Brenna and Lita exchanged looks and began to undress, "That's right ladies, get them off or you'll be next just like the centurion here." He stripped down to his loin cloth and looked around, "Ugh even these are soaked, ah well." He said and whipped them off, placing them with the other wet clothes. He then walked straight to the fire and began rubbing his hands. Brenna and Lita smiled at each other admiring his white bottom.

"Enjoying the view I hope ladies?" He asked without turning, "Don't worry I'm sure we'll all get to know each other quite intimately, all living in here together, no need for shyness eh?"

The women stripped down, dropped their wet garments and quickly fetched blankets from the table where the other clothes were located and wrapped them around themselves before placing the wet clothes on the frame to dry.

"Don't get your hopes up Optio Grattius and don't expect anything else to be raised either." Brenna said joining him by the fire and looking down at his groin, Lita smiled approvingly.

"So where do I take a piss?" Grattius asked, "Surely you people don't do your business in your homes?"

"Of course we don't." Lita replied, "There will be a place nearby, if it was the summer you would have already found it or your nose would have, be thankful its winter."

"I don't know how they'll react if we go wandering off." Brenna put in, "You heard what he said about others seeing us."

Grattius picked up a blanket off the table and wrapped it around himself and then looked at the clothing the Briton had referred to and bent forward to sniff it, "Smells fresh enough I suppose."

"We aren't quite as barbaric as you imagined then?" Lita asked.

Grattius pursed his lips and looked around the interior of the roundhouse, "No, not really." Lita frowned, he continued, "I'm not being insulting but we moved on from living in huts a long time ago that's all, I didn't mean to offend you, again."

"Don't worry we're not so easily offended." Brenna said smiling. She turned and looked at Varro who was still asleep. "I hope he'll be alright, I knew it was stupid for him to leave the Garrison so soon after being ill."

Grattius walked to his friend and knelt down, "He's tough, he'll be fine, just needs some rest to get it out of his system."

At that moment the Briton returned with a wizened old woman, they were both carrying pots, the male spoke to Lita.

"He's brought some food for us and the old woman has some herbs, he says she's a healer." Lita translated as she watched the woman go to Varro and usher Grattius away with a wave of her hand, as she muttered something totally unintelligible. She touched his brow and then put a hand inside the blankets feeling his torso. She turned and spoke to the male.

"She says he has the fever chill and will need to be kept warm for a few days and drink plenty of the brew she'll make." Lita said as the old woman went back to the pot she had left on the table and began grinding its contents.

"What's in it?" Grattius asked.

Lita asked her but she shook her head, "She says she can't tell you, the ingredients are for healers not for outsiders."

"Mm okay," he said, "can you ask your man here where we are to perform our bodily functions."

Lita spoke to the man who turned and left the roundhouse, he returned a short while later with a large bucket that he placed near the door skin.

"You have got to be kidding me." Grattius said, "I'm not taking a…..well you know what I mean, in front of you two, it's not right."

"We'll put something up to hide your modesty, don't worry." Brenna said, "How do you think we feel?"

Grattius muttered to himself clearly unhappy and then walked to the bed next to Varro's and sat down, "Ah well, may as well make myself comfortable I suppose." He looked at the old man, "So what did he bring in his pot?"

Brenna looked inside, "The ingredients for a chicken stew by the looks of it." She smiled at their host, "Thank you." He nodded and left.

Once the old woman had finished grinding her herbs she spoke to Lita and told her how to prepare the potion that they were to feed to Varro, she then looked at them all in turn, smiled briefly and left the roundhouse.

"I'll sort a cover out for the, you know what." Lita said as she made preparations to hang a cover from the slanting roof near the door. Brenna put the stew pot into the iron frame above the fire and began stirring the contents with a wooden ladle. She looked over at Grattius who was now lying down flat on his back with his hands over his eyes.

"Don't worry we won't be here too long Optio, in a few days as soon as he's well enough, we'll be on our way." Brenna said.

"We have to make sure he's actually recovered this time though, there's no point in us leaving to find Caradoc and him collapsing again." Lita said. "Does he always get this ill?" She asked Grattius.

"I've never known him to be ill before, not like this anyway." He said, "Coughs and colds you know, the usual but never to be knocked off his feet. He's as fit as any of them in the legion and stronger than most, must've just got this one bad I suppose."

"I'll see if I can get some of this inside him." Lita said staring into the pot of ground herbs. She poured some water in and began heating it over the fire and removed it just as it started to bubble.

"Smells like cow shit that stuff." Grattius remarked now covering his nose. "I prefer the smell of the stew."

"I'm sure it will help," Lita said, "healers usually know what they're doing with such things." She placed the pot on a low table. "I'll let it cool down and then try and wake him."

"Don't you think you should just let him sleep?" Grattius asked, there was silence, no reply. He removed his hands from his face. "What?" He asked, "I'm just saying that while he's asleep, shouldn't we let him be, it's supposed to be the body's way of healing itself after all."

"She said we need to get him to drink some of this as soon as possible, even if it means waking him." Lita said, "So that's what we'll do."

Grattius looked over, "Alright," he sat up, "come on then I'll hold him up, better cool it down with some cold water though first hadn't you?"

"The hotter the better she said, it's not bubbled completely so it should be alright now. Come on then lift him up." Lita replied.

Between the three of them they managed to prop Varro up, he looked pale and his skin was clammy, cold, although he still had sweat on his brow. He tried to open his eyes aware that they were doing something but then closed them again.

"Come on Varro you need to help us to help you." Brenna said pushing the damp hair from his forehead. Lita poured some of the green fluid into a wooden cup and placed the edge near his lips under his nose, it wrinkled.

"Told you it smelt like shit didn't I? Even he thinks it does and he's asleep." Grattius said propping his centurion up, "Come on wakey wakey, just for a moment." Grattius said as bleary eyes opened a little. "That's it now open your mouth and take a sip, its medicine and it'll help to make you feel better."

His lips parted a little and Lita tipped the cup but as soon as he tasted its contents his head shot back and he screwed his face up and began coughing.

"I hope they're not trying to poison him." Grattius said.

"Don't be so stupid, if they'd wanted us dead, we would be already." Brenna said.

"Mm I suppose," Grattius replied, "right come on then Centurion, let's have you."

With a lot of patience and repeated attempts and despite Varro's condition and his obvious disgust at the contents of the cup, they eventually got him to drink it all. Lita put the pot containing the rest of the brew on the table.

"We'll give him some more before we go to sleep." She said.

Brenna finished cooking the chicken stew and then found them some wooden bowls near the frame holding the bows and they ate their meal in relative comfort in a warm roundhouse.

Grattius stirred in his sleep, he was enjoying a dream, or so he thought. His mind's eye showed him wrapped in warm furs, on a relatively comfortable bed inside the roundhouse where they had sought refuge. To the side of him were the forms of two sleeping females and beyond them, slept Varro. He drifted through images, all of them lit by the flickering light of the fire, occasionally a slight crackle broke the near silence and then he felt movement. Felt, or dreamt, he wasn't sure but he knew it wasn't threatening as the fur blanket was pulled aside covering his body. He felt warm, almost hot flesh against his own and hands touched his thighs, moving upward. The sensation felt real but he was always having vivid dreams.

"Shhhh...." He heard and rolled his head and began to open his eyes. It was darker than his imagination had made the interior of the house and almost immediately he smelt smoke from the fire. He focused and saw the shape of a female body and watched as she wrapped the fur blanket around her shoulders and lifted herself over his legs and almost squatted on his groin.

"Don't speak," Lita said, her hands moving over his swelling manhood, "We don't want to wake them." Her head darted to the still sleeping bodies of Brenna and Varro as Grattius began to struggle.

"What the....." He managed before she clamped a hand over his mouth.

"I said be quiet," She leant forward, eyes wide, "or I'll go back to my own bed."

He stopped struggling and allowed himself to fall back onto the bed, a half smile on his face, "Not a word or a gasp or even a sigh, understand?" Lita said as she lowered herself onto him, he nodded his understanding.

A bang from somewhere suddenly woke Grattius and he sat up. He looked around, Lita was back in her bed, had he dreamed last night's events he wondered? He could see dawn's light through the side of the door skin and lay down again.

Bang. A voice shouted something from outside but it was in a language he didn't understand, it sounded like the same as Lita and the old man had spoken the day before. She sat up as did Brenna.

"They want us outside." Lita said, "And they know your Roman."

Grattius swept his legs over the side of the bed, "Of course they know, are they stupid?" He walked to the door and peered through the small gap between the frame and the door skin. Looking outside he could see a group of some ten Britons, some on foot, or sat on horses, most carried flaming torches. All of them had their attention focused on the roundhouse. They were armed with swords and axes.

"Shit," he said, "it must be the bastards from that place nearby." He turned back and saw Lita and Brenna quickly dressing, throwing their clothes on "The others must have told them we were here."

The voice shouted again, "He says come out now or we'll set the place on fire." Lita said securing a belt. "We don't know that, maybe we were seen with them."

"Throw me that tunic." Grattius said to Brenna.

"What are you going to do?" She asked.

"We can't stay in here, we'll burn." He replied, "I'll go out and talk to them, give you time to get away." He pointed to the rear of the house, "Cut your way out."

"And what of Varro?" Brenna asked, "I'm not leaving him."

"And how are you supposed to talk to them, you can't understand a word they're saying?" Lita asked.

"Mm didn't think of that." He replied as he quickly threw the tunic on.

"We go out together or not at all." Brenna said walking towards the door, "How many are there?"

Grattius peered through the gap again, "At least ten that I can see, maybe more elsewhere."

"Come on, we face this together." Brenna said and swung the door skin aside, the other two followed. She squinted as she walked into the pale light as the flames of the torches were bright. The man, the shouter, spoke again from his horse, the look of disdain evident for all to see.

"He says we are to die, you first," Lita said looking at Grattius, "and then Brenna and I after they have raped us for bringing you to their land."

"Fuck me. I haven't even eaten breakfast yet." Grattius replied looking round and smirking at the two women.

"This is no time for humour Roman, they mean to kill us." Lita said.

The leader of the group, who had been shouting, got down from his horse and pulled a huge sword from his scabbard, the others crept forward, he spoke again, spitting out the words.

"And just as I thought things were improving after last night." Grattius said turning to Lita, Brenna frowned. The Briton got closer and hefted the sword above his head and quickly approached Grattius and then the world changed.

***

Valerius was woken that morning by the dawn trumpet call, he opened his eyes and sat up in bed and felt for his boots on the cold floor.

"Who in hades was doing all that snoring last night?" He said rubbing his face and yawning, "It kept waking me up, three times it happened. If it hadn't been so cold I'd have got up and given them a kick"

"It was Pollo again, same as usual, he's always doing it. We could use him instead of the trumpet to wake us all up in the morning." Vescus said throwing his blankets aside, "Eventually you'll get used to it like the rest of us and after a few months it won't bother you anymore."

Valerius raised his eyebrows, "After a few months, I'll be dead from exhaustion if I don't get any decent sleep. Can't we do something, peg his nose? Cut it off?"

"It's the wine," Vescus said, "if he has wine, he snores and last night he had wine."

Pollo stumbled out of bed on the other side of the room, "Ah morning." He said searching for his boots, "I thought I heard the morning horn." He fumbled about and picked up a few things from a small table at the side of his bed and walked towards the door that led to the latrines, "Sleep well?" He asked Valerius as he walked by, who just shook his head in response.

After the morning ritual of the latrines where they sat talking about the day ahead and then cleaning themselves, they dressed and prepared for the new day and ate some breakfast. Valerius pulled his boots up around his shins they were essentially made from one piece of leather with hobnails on the sole. He wrapped the leather thongs around his leg and tied them off securing his boots in place. Picking up his *cingulum* a small metal apron, he placed it round his waist, belt like, and secured it in place. It was an essential piece of armour that covered a legionary's groin, a place no soldier would want to be stabbed. Hefting his *lorica segmentata,* segmented armour, up off the ground where it had spent the night, he placed it over his shoulders and fastened the buckles at the front. Then he pulled down on his tunic as the fabric had a tendency to overlap underneath and become uncomfortable.

"What are we doing today, anyone know?" He asked as those around him put their own uniforms on.

"I heard it was a forced march, out and back, twelve miles each way." Vescus said.

"Rampart building I heard." Another voice shouted from somewhere at the back of the barrack block, "Practising for when we start campaigning again in the spring."

"Fuck me how many times do we have to do the same thing?" Pollo said, "I'll have blisters on the end of my cock if this carries on. It's actually easier in spring because we're out there doing it."

"The newer lads need the practise I suppose." Valerius said. A couple of the younger faces reddened and looked away.

"Practise," Pollo said, "my wrinkly sack," he turned and spoke to one of the new lads, "how many marches did you do during your basic training?"

"Lost count Pollo," he replied looking up, "towards the end we were out every day virtually, quick marching n'all, full kit too."

"And how many marching camps did you build?" Pollo asked.

"Put it this way, if we went out, we built," he scratched his head, "no idea to be honest, must've been over thirty I say."

"Do you see what I mean?" Pollo said, "I wonder how many miles we will have marched and how many camps we'll have built by the time our service is up?" He looked at the faces staring back at him, "Hundreds I'd say." He sat back down on his mattress, "Maybe I'll just stay in bed today instead, could do with a day off." Valerius smiled as the door to their barracks was flung open.

"Right you shower of shit," it was Optio Crispus, he was standing in the doorway looking as pristine as ever, the white plume on his helmet shaking as he shouted, "outside. Stop blathering and playing with each other's cocks and get yourselves outside, double time." The men scrambled for pieces of kit and headed towards the door.

"Forgotten something have we?" He shouted, faces reddening, they stopped, some skidding to a halt. "Entrenching tools, axes, spades...." He paused, "In fact bring it all, you idle lot." He looked around at the men now picking up extra pieces of kit, "I think you'll need them unless of course you want to use your dicks to dig up soil," he looked at Pollo adding, "and no Legionary Pollo, that wasn't an excuse for you to tell us about that shrivelled up maggot you call a cock and how you've used it to build garrisons before." His beady eyes stared through Pollo, "Come on, outside the lot of you, we're going to show the second cohort how we're not only quicker but can build better, bigger ramparts." His eyes flashed from soldier to soldier, "Love it don't you, you bastards?" He smiled, "I almost wish I was a mere mortal again and could dig with you but someone's got to show you how to do it eh Pollo?"

"Yes Optio although I think that most of us know by now." He said.

Crispus feinted being surprised, "Well thank you General Gaius Julius Fucking Caesar," he pursed his lips together, "Tell you what Pollo, why don't you spend the day playing with yourself in that fart filled, greasy bed of yours and we'll go out and hammer the second eh?"

"Tha……." Pollo began.

"Get your stinking carcass outside onto that parade square right now Pollo and the rest of you." He walked further into the room. "Move it, come on quickly or you'll find my boot wedged so far up your tight little arseholes, you won't be able to shit for weeks." The men of the first cohort ran past the optio and out into the morning drizzle, equipment clanging and banging against each other. Crispus followed quickly behind.

"Behold," he said raising his arms to the heavens, "what a glorious day for digging. Come on, form up quickly."

As they formed their lines the legionaries of the second cohort were being screamed at by their equally cheerful optio a few feet away, it was going to be a long hard day.

Just as it was beginning to get dark and the light was starting to fade, the palisades that the men of the first and second cohorts had built were non-existent. All their hard efforts were now reduced to compacted mud where they had destroyed their work on the orders of their optios. As was befitting of their status, the first cohort had completed their rampart before the men of the second and had been the first to reduce it to rubble and then to put the soil back into the earth afterwards, Crispus was a happy man. The soldiers of the first and second cohorts stood breathing heavily, saturated in sweat and covered in mud.

"Well done men," Crispus shouted addressing both sections, "especially the first cohort." He lowered his voice slightly, "Now I know that this can become mind numbingly boring and tedious, but we do it for a reason." He examined the sweating faces before him, "If we're out there in the field and have had a nice long walk through the rolling hills and enemy territory, we need to be able to build a marching camp and build it very quickly in order for you to rest your pretty heads. This will enable you to rise the next day, weary I know, but you'll still be alive and then you'll be able to butcher the enemy, so there is a good reason for this." The men stood almost to attention were beginning to sway. "Now when I give the order to dismiss, you are to return to your barracks, clean your kit, wash yourselves in the bathhouse and the wines on me and my fellow optio here." For the first time that day the first and second cohorts smiled in unison. "And no fucking fighting because if we get called out to sort you lot out, I'll make you all sorry. Any men caught fighting will have their balls burnt on a brazier in the morning. Do you understand?"

After a few chuckles there was a chorus of, "Yes Optio Crispus." It boomed around the parade square.

"Right good lads now get out of my sight the lot of you, first and second cohorts, dismissed."

They fell out and wearily headed towards their adjoining barrack blocks, bits of mud still falling from shovels, axes and spades. Behind them the parade ground was level again, the soil compacted flat. It was a routine that would go on for months and tomorrow it would be the turn of another two cohorts to construct a rampart from the earth, at least the soil wouldn't be hard as it had been for the first and second.

Before Grattius was aware of what was occurring, it had happened, and all he had time to do was flinch and flinch again. One second he had been standing waiting for the sword to fall, not believing that his life was to end on some stupid errand, killed by an uneducated barbarian pig and then the cracks began.

He watched transfixed, unsure what was happening at first as he heard a crack and the eyes of the Briton with the sword held high, rolled into the back of his head. He began to fall, straight down as the first impact was followed by others, crack, crack. Before he hit the ground, Grattius saw there were four arrows buried deep into his back. Looking up he saw that his comrades shared his fate as they too were felled by arrows ripping into their flesh. Heads and bodies were pierced by sharp barbs and in mere moments it was over, the threat was gone. Grattius scoured the trees but saw nothing, he turned back to Brenna and Lita who were obviously as surprised as he was by their escape from death but silence surrounded them. He strained his ears listening but all he could hear was the falling rain.

"Who are you? What do you want?" He shouted searching the trees around the houses, nothing moved except the wet leaves then a voice called out.

"You are fortunate that we got here when we did Roman, or you and your women would be dead by now." A heavily accented voice shouted from somewhere beyond the leaves and bushes.

"Who are you?" Grattius shouted backing up slightly.

"His women?" Brenna whispered. "I'll carve a steak from that man's flesh."

The leaves parted, "I am Caradoc"

A tall Briton walked forward through the low branches. Grattius stared at him as others appeared holding bows. The Briton was not as he had imagined him, he was bald, his head glistening in the rain and handsome, a well-defined strong jaw, visible cheek bones and a muscular frame under his clothing. He wore a dark red hooded cloak over black furs.

"The elder's son found me and told me that you were here, we travelled through the night and it looks like it's a good thing we did." He looked around at the bodies, one man was still alive and moaned, "Some tale about preventing a war, some plan you have come to tell me about."

A man with him stepped forward and thrust his sword into the injured man's neck. He squirmed and gurgled, pinned to the ground.

"Finish him Ardwen, quickly." Caradoc commanded. Ardwen pulled his large sword free and hacked down at the stricken man's neck. One blow was enough to kill him but not enough to remove the head completely.

"Sinew and bone," Caradoc said, "It's surprising how difficult it is to remove a man's head."

Ardwen arched down again and the head rolled free, dead eyes staring at nothing from the mud, "Yes, but if you keep trying," He said smiling, "You can achieve anything."

Chapter Sixteen

"Centurion Varro I presume?" Caradoc stepped forward.

"Ugh, erm no...." Grattius stuttered turning and pointing at the roundhouse, "He's inside, ill."

"No he's not." Grattius turned fully and saw Varro leaning against the door frame to the roundhouse. He was pale and wrapped in a blanket, Brenna ran towards him.

"Get inside now you stupid man or you'll catch your death." She reached out and grabbed him by the shoulders, Caradoc smiled.

"Listen to her Centurion. Women know what's best for us, even if we don't sometimes. Get inside and get well, our talk can wait." He spoke to Ardwen, "I'll leave some men here to make sure there isn't a re-occurrence of this." He looked down at the dead Britons, "I don't want to have to murder more of my own people." Looking up at Grattius he added, "I may need them to kill Romans, some day." He was about to reply when Lita nudged him.

"Don't say a word." She whispered, her elbow was sharp in his back.

"What is your name Roman?" Caradoc asked.

"Grattius, Optio Grattius." He said almost adding the word sir and coming to attention. Caradoc studied him and walked closer, he pushed the hood off his head. It was almost shiny in the morning murk and rain.

"Stand easy soldier, I wouldn't want you to sprain yourself." Caradoc said.

"You speak our language well." Grattius said.

"My brother was educated in Rome, he taught me well."

"Where is your brother now, in the mountains with you?" Grattius asked.

Caradoc smiled, "My brother? My real brother is dead, killed by

Romans like you after the battle of the two rivers. He died well though, a warrior's death." He paused. "It broke my heart to see him wounded so badly, his chest punctured in so many places." He looked down but kept talking. "What matters is that he died defending his people, his land, he died with honour." He looked back up and directly into Grattius' eyes, "The other one, my eldest brother died by my own hand, his name was Adminius and he was a traitor. He betrayed everything we stand for and deserved a coward's death after declaring his loyalty to Rome."

He stared at Grattius now, dark eyes unblinking. "I must leave, bring your friend when he is well enough to travel, this one knows where to come." He gestured towards the elder's son. "Don't worry Roman, I will guarantee your safety for the duration of these talks, you and those with you will not be harmed, you have my word on this." Caradoc moved quickly to his horse and jumped up, "Thirty warriors will stay in this area, if you need anything speak to them."

Varro coughed as Brenna wrapped the blankets around him back inside the roundhouse, "You should have stayed in bed, it was stupid to go to the door in your condition."

"I couldn't ignore our host could I?" He said and coughed again, he lay down. "So that's the great Caradoc? He's not what I expected."

"And what did you expect of a man who has united the western tribes?" Lita asked, "Don't say a barbarian? I'll be disappointed."

"I don't know exactly, he seems like a man who may listen to reason that's all." He said wiping his mouth with a cloth. Brenna got him a cup of water.

"Drink." She said offering him the cup. "You need to drink as much as possible remember?"

"As long as it's not got any more of that dung in it or whatever it was that old crone brought me." He replied taking a sip.

"Made you well didn't it?" Grattius asked, "Or nearly, it appears to be helping anyway. I'd rather eat my own shit than be as ill as you were." Varro smiled.

"I'm glad our situation hasn't dampened your wit, my friend." Varro said and drained the cup. "I was out of it for a while," he looked around, "where are we exactly?"

"Lita found the elder from this village and a small party of hunters after you collapsed, we brought you to their dwelling." Brenna said, "His son went to find Caradoc and got back just in time."

"He was very good looking don't you think?" Lita said smiling.

"Caradoc?" Varro asked, "I suppose so but not my type really, Brenna pushed his shoulder laughing.

"Yes he was." She added.

"If you've all finished your, 'oh how wonderful was the rebel king' conversation, we'd better go and find some food for later." Grattius said.

"We still shouldn't go wandering about out there, even if we're being guarded." Lita said, "I'll go and ask the elder's son and see what he suggests, it's better to be safe."

A few days later Varro was well enough to travel and the four packed up their things and thanked the elder and his family for their hospitality. It turned out that Caradoc had left his cousin Ardwen with the group of warriors to make sure they were safe and he provided them with an escort to where Caradoc was located. The rain had finally stopped falling during the night and glorious sunshine shone overhead for their journey through the mountains. Although it was still cold when they were in the shade, the sun warmed their exposed skin when they were out in the open. Through valleys and across rivers they trekked virtually in silence with Ardwen leading the way, his men following behind. Varro and Grattius exchanged uncomfortable glances every now and again as they got deeper inside enemy territory, each step taking them further and further away from safety despite the assurances they'd been given.

"There's no going back now." Grattius said quietly.

"It's got to be done, not that we had any choice in the matter anyway." Varro replied.

"Caradoc is a man of his word," Ardwen said, "if he says that you'll be fine and are not to be harmed, then that's exactly what will happen. We keep our promises," he said, "this isn't Rome."

The two soldiers didn't reply and Varro saw Lita smile as they rode on. Eventually they rode adjacent to an enormous ravine and Ardwen pointed, "That's where we're going."

The others in the group looked up and saw tiny plumes of smoke rising up into the azure sky, some distance away on a mountain top.

"I would have had us blindfolded for the journey." Grattius said.

"Maybe they don't care that we know where they are." Varro replied.

"You're right Centurion Varro, we are not hiding here. This is free land, our land and even if you were to go back and tell your leaders where we are, there are many thousands of spears and swords between here and them to stop them." Ardwen said. "Remember you face us now and the Catuvellauni, those that you didn't destroy when you first arrived anyway. No tribes within these lands will bow down to your emperor Claudius as they did in the east."

It was a sobering thought as they slowly made their way upward and the smoke rising into the air multiplied from the mountain fortress where Caradoc waited. Long before they arrived at his location, they started to come across smaller settlements. Ardwen named the people along the way, the names of tribes that Varro and Grattius hadn't heard of. Faces stared at the small party as they rode on, clearly word had already reached them of their arrival. Some stared in hatred at the two short haired men dressed like them, whilst others looked on with curiosity, the two women were ignored.

Eventually they crossed one final river and joined a well-worn path and the ground levelled out, the horses stopped working so hard and the panorama opened up before them. Huge grass covered ramparts hid the settlement inside, beyond the first was another and then another. The tiny figures of people could be seen on top of them, watching as the riders approached.

"Why do I feel like throwing up?" Grattius said to Varro under his breath.

"Tip of the spear my friend," Varro replied, "tip of the spear."

"Just behave normally if you can manage it." Lita said kicking her horse forward level with Ardwen. She spoke in their tongue.

"What did you say?" Varro asked. Lita turned her horse around and faced the two men, "I told him that it was nice to be home."

"What? You said what?" Grattius asked.

"You heard me; this is my home, where do you think I came from?" She said her face neutral. "Some swamp or some hut somewhere?" She asked. Grattius pulled up.

"Wait a moment," he struggled to control his horse who could feel the sudden tension, "you mean to tell me that you knew all along where to find Caradoc? You double crossing bitch." He spat the last words out.

"Hold on Grattius you misunderstand." Brenna said, "We made no secret of the fact that Lita is from here, that she's Silurian."

"That's right Grattius, if I had known he was here then this is where I would have brought you. Do you believe him stupid enough to stay in one place?" Lita said. "With your legions waiting to pounce?" Her horse spun round. "This is but one mountain fort, there are many as there are many tribes in these lands, I didn't betray you, you fool."

"Alright let's just calm down and get inside shall we?" Varro said, "your talking is beginning to give me a headache."

They rode through a gap in the ramparts and followed Ardwen as he led them along the track and upward, coiling around the perimeter of the huge mountain fort. In time they rounded a corner between high grassed banks and came out into an opening, the interior of the fort, it was huge. Smoke billowed upward into the air from hundreds of roundhouses, there were ploughed fields, animal pens containing, horses, cows, pigs and chickens. The clanging of a blacksmiths hammer, no, two hammers could be heard somewhere in the distance. Off to the left they had an archery range where men and women alike practised with bows, firing arrows at least three hundred feet into large straw filled targets. Beyond the bow range there were lines of warriors holding square shields and walking into each other, thrusting through the gaps with wooden swords, Varro and Grattius exchanged more worrying looks as they went deeper into the city-like fortress.

"And there are more of these?" Varro asked Lita.

"Yes there are a few," She replied, "though not all are as large as this."

"Come," Ardwen said, angling off to the left, "we'll stable the horses and go and see Caradoc."

A short time later Ardwen led them to a large wooden building, tall straight timbers made up the walls, between each was packed hard crammed mud, Varro thought that it resembled the concrete they themselves used. A high roof angled into a V at the top where there was a large carved wooden effigy of a ram charging.

"What does that signify?" Varro asked.

"The charging ram? It's said and thought that's where Caraodoc's name originated from, many generations ago. It is now the symbol of our combined people although the Deceangli, Gangani, Ordovices, Cornovii, Demetae and my own Silures retain their own unique patterns. These your legions have not faced in battle yet," he smiled, "maybe that won't happen if your talks are a success."

He led them to two large doors, there were no guards controlling entry, on opening them Varro and the others saw into the interior, it seemed bigger on the inside. Large square windows allowed good lighting inside and there were two large fires in the middle of the floor located at either end, providing heat and banners of various tribes displayed on the walls. Thick wood tables lay in-between the fires and at the far end was Caradoc sitting talking to other Britons. Caradoc rose and approached the new arrivals.

"You made it," he said extending a hand to Ardwen and to each of the guests in turn, "I trust your journey was uneventful and that you are feel better Centurion Varro?" Varro took his hand. It was a firm, strong greeting.

"Welcome to all of you, please," he extended his hand to the waiting tribesmen, "let me introduce you to the kings who lead our allies and tribal chieftains." Although the two soldiers didn't receive such a warm welcome from the others, they merely nodded a greeting; there was no open hostility toward them. "Take a seat and I will arrange some refreshments." They were shown to a table nearest the one seating the waiting Britons, while drink and food were brought in for them. Caradoc took his place at the head of the other table.

"Please eat, drink you must be thirsty from your journey." He lifted a large jug and poured a dark fluid into an ornately carved cup and took a drink. "We can discuss your General's proposal afterward." He smiled, lifted his cup and raised it in the direction of his guests. "Welcome."

The meal was eaten in virtual silence on Varro's table while the Britons and Caradoc laughed and joked, speaking in a language that was unfamiliar to the Romans.

"It seems our hosts are very relaxed." Grattius pointed out.

"They have every right to be," Varro said, "they are a long way from the reach of Plautius and even if he decided to march on them in spring, it would take a long time to fight their way here, weeks, months, maybe even years. It would appear that they have amassed quite an army of many thousands to face us and there is the terrain to consider." Varro took in their surroundings and looked at the banners on the walls bearing different animal insignia, Ravens, Wolves, Bears, Horses and Boar and some he didn't recognise. Gold and silver ornaments were displayed on small tables along the walls, vases, jewelled cups and plates, weapons and shields adorned the walls between the banners. The warriors sitting with Caradoc wore their hair long, some tied up at the back. Nearly all had torques around their necks and arms, as did the King. Most had blue swirling tattoos curling around their thick biceps and at least three had them, extended to their faces, making them look fierce and extremely primitive. Young women brought more food and ale, Varro and his guests were offered wine, Roman wine that Varro avoided wanting to keep his wits sharp, although Grattius indulged remarking that the wine was good.

"Where do you think they got that from?" Varro asked of the wine.

"It's probably from the raids they have been making into Roman territory." Lita said with a contented look on her face, "What?" She asked seeing the expressions on the men's faces. "You must know about the raids surely? It's well known that Caradoc has war parties deep inside your lines. I've been told they've even destroyed a number of forts and villas that your people built to enslave the local populations."

Varro bit his tongue not wanting to make a scene in front of the assembled Britons but Grattius couldn't resist saying something.

"I think you'll find that most of those families that were murdered were treating the slaves they had very well." He said.

"And I think that YOU will find Optio Grattius, that all of those people were free people before your armies arrived and that the land they worked, used to be theirs." Lita replied stabbing a knife into a chunk of meat and carving it as Grattius imagined her doing to his chest, at that moment, if she were able.

"And that," Brenna began, "is just one of the obstacles that you're going to encounter when you begin talking to Caradoc. The self-appointed Roman Governor of Albion…sorry, Britannia," she corrected herself, "may have come up with some ideas to try and pacify him but there has already been a lot of blood spilt. The Roman army is not here at the invitation of our people and even if, as you claim it was in some circumstances, the behaviour demonstrated so far has been less than friendly to say the least." She finished her drink, "What exactly does he propose in his message?" She filled her cup again, "Will he allow Caradoc to rule the west without Roman overseers? I can't imagine that he would agree to anything less and I cannot see that he would agree to pay any tribute or taxes, so just what does Plautius propose to make us all one big happy family?"

Varro looked at her angrily, "Look Brenna I'm just here to relay the message that's all. I took no part in creating its content, as I've said before I'm a soldier just like him." He pointed at Grattius who was back to eating large chunks of meat off the end of a knife, "We do as we're told and when we're told. Sometimes we like what we do and sometimes we don't but, we have no choice, that's all there is to it. I will reveal the contents of the scrolls to Caradoc at a time of his choosing and when he's ready to sit and listen." He looked at the Britons on the other table, "I don't think that this would be a good place to discuss such things in the present company but I'll leave that to the King to decide."

Lita leaned forward, "So you know what the scrolls say?" She asked.

"I just said that I wasn't prepared to discuss it now but I wouldn't have come all this way not knowing what I was carrying. Any number of things could have happened to the scrolls, so I felt it best that I and Grattius for that matter knew what they contained."

"So Caradoc isn't going to be happy about their content?" She asked.

"I didn't say that and there's no point in continuing this conversation because you, just like everyone else, will have to wait to hear what is written on them, they are for Caradoc."

At that moment a door at the rear of the hall opened and a group of large hunting dogs, accompanied by young men entered. The dogs ran inside, noses twitching at the smell of the cooked meat.

"Here." Caradoc shouted and every dog stopped in its tracks, turned and went to his side, there were at least ten that Varro could count. They were taller than the dogs he was used too, the dogs the legions used to herd their cattle, sinewy but clearly powerful. Caradoc looked over to their table.

"Do you like dogs?" He asked of no-one in particular.

"We use them to herd our animals on campaign but they're shorter, stockier than those." Grattius said, he got up and approached them, all but one were now lying down. The dog that wasn't was sat erect and watched Grattius' every move as he got closer. The animal growled and showed its white teeth, lips curling.

"Careful Optio Grattius," Caradoc warned, "he can be very protective." This dog was male and had grey and black flecked fur, its face wolf like. Its black eyes stared at the Roman as he went down on one knee.

"Hello boy." Grattius said, the dog didn't move but a growl rumbled from somewhere deep inside.

"Shhhh dog." Caradoc ordered, the animal's head half turned, ears twitching, the others just lay watching. "We use them for hunting and even sometimes in battle Optio Grattius, have you ever seen a man get taken down by a dog?"

"I've seen the results," Varro said, "after the battle of the rivers some of our auxiliaries were attacked by them."

"You were there?" Caradoc asked.

"I was and I went looking for the men in the swamp after the fight, when they failed to return," Varro said, "there wasn't much left of some of them. There were pieces bitten out of them, they stood no chance, it must have been an awful way to die."

"Yes I'm sure it was, nearly as awful as the people they had cut down before they entered the swamps including my brother." Caradoc said. "Death is death though don't you think Centurion Varro and if you are fighting for your very survival, you will use any means necessary?"

"I wouldn't use dogs." He said.

"Really, but you use those giant bows that fire long arrows and impale my people by the handful, if you are looking for a fair fight, I think you've come to the wrong place. After all, it is you and your soldiers who are the invaders here is it not? We didn't ask you to come from Gaul, in fact we didn't want you to come but you came anyway, despite years and even generations of peace between our two people." He paused taking a drink. "In fact I think you will find that we were at peace and there was trade, exchanges of information. Even my traitor of a brother was educated in Rome." There were nods of agreement from the other Britons. "Despite this, your Emperor decided to send his ships, carrying men like you to kill and butcher our people, why did he do that?"

"I'm just a soldier Caradoc and I follow orders, I don't question them, it's not my place." Varro replied, Grattius had given up trying to be friendly to the dog and had returned to his seat.

"Do you not have your own mind Centurion?" Caradoc asked but went on before Varro could reply, "We heard your men refused to board their ships and had to be persuaded, is that true?" Varro looked at Grattius.

"It is true." He replied.

"You were lucky that they delayed you because as it was before, a great army waited to greet you on the southern shores, you probably wouldn't have got onto dry land if you had come when you were supposed to." Caradoc said biting into a chunk of meat.

"We'll never know that now will we?" Grattius said.

"We know what happened before when your great Caesar came to our shores, he was pushed back into the sea when he first came. Then on the second attempt, he was harassed and attacked so much that he gave up and returned to Gaul again and never came back." Caradoc said.

"Are we here to discuss history?" Varro asked, "Or are we here to talk about the present and how we can avoid more bloodshed?"

Caradoc looked up from his meal. "You are the one who has come to us, are you not?" Caradoc said, "We are content to fight to protect our land, our people, after all you have left us no choice, what would you do if the circumstances were reversed?" He asked.

"I'd fight." Varro replied.

"So, what are these words of wisdom that your leader has said that will persuade us not to fight?" Caradoc asked. Varro picked up the bag containing the scrolls.

"They are here. Shall I read them, now?" Varro asked. Caradoc looked around the table at the faces waiting for his response.

"We will hear these words, but not now." He said, "I think that it is probably wiser to discuss this with a head clear of ale. Thank you but we'll talk of it tomorrow, the grog has a tendency to addle the brain and conjure up all manner of things. Please accept my apologies for the talk of Caesar, you are correct, it is history and what is important now is the present. Rome would do well to make an ally of us Varro and we would certainly be more valuable as allies than enemies. It would be of benefit to us all in the long term, I just hope that Plautius has the right offer or we'll find ourselves no further forward." He drained his cup. "We want nothing more than peace with the empire but we won't be subservient slaves, especially on our own land," he paused, "I'm doing it again," he smiled. "Tonight we eat and drink and welcome you to our home, tomorrow we'll discuss your scrolls and their content."

The next morning the sky had cleared and although a thin frost lay on the ground, a warm sun shone overhead. Varro and his party had been housed quite comfortably overnight in a secluded roundhouse and guarded, as was to be expected.

"Gods teeth, my head hurts." Grattius moaned wrapping his cloak around his shoulders. "What did they put in that grog?" He asked of no-one in particular, "You don't think they poisoned us do you?"

Brenna gave him an annoyed look, "If they wanted us dead, don't you think we would be already? Why waste time with potions when they could just overpower us and kill us?"

"Mm good point," He replied, "so today's the day then I suppose, when the fate of Britannia is decided." He bent down to tie his boot laces. "Do you think they'll feed us this morning?"

Before anyone could answer, three young Britons entered the building carrying wooden trays. On plates there was bread, cheese and slices of cooked meat, they placed them down on a table, stared at the occupants and then left without saying a word.

"Ah that answers that then." Grattius said striding forward and picking up a plate and piling it with food. "I'm starving and perhaps this will help clear my head as well."

After breakfast, Varro led them outside into the morning sun, a group of warriors armed with spears and long swords greeted them and they were led back to the hall where they had eaten the night before. Caradoc was waiting for them, he was alone.

"Good morning to you all." He said standing. "Please come, take a seat." He indicated to the chairs that had been occupied the night before by kings and chieftains. "Let us get down to business Centurion. I am eager to hear your general's plan for my people." Varro removed the scrolls from a leather case and he and his companions sat down.

"Won't your war council be joining us?" He asked.

Caradoc smiled and leaned forward, "They trust my judgement and will abide by whatever decision I come to today, they have already left for home." He looked from Varro to Brenna.

"Tell me how you and Lita came to work for the Romans?" Caradoc asked.

"I thought we were here to discuss the proposed treaty?" Varro said before Brenna could answer.

"We have time to discuss that as well but I'm curious to know how a person can turn on their own kind. What is it that causes that to happen?" Caradoc asked looking at Brenna and Lita.

"When they first came with their ships and soldiers," Brenna said, "we didn't know what to do. Our initial response was to fight and to join the others who were resisting, but this man rescued a boy from our settlement. Druids were going to burn him alive as they had done to another to satisfy their gods."

"Their gods, do you mean your gods?" Caradoc asked.

"The druids do want they want, when they want, to who they want, they have no regard for others, just what they believe to be right. They rule over me no more than you, or these Romans. I want to live in peace but greedy men always want more don't they?" She stared at Caradoc her dark eyes boring into his.

"You have some spirit Brenna, I like that but I sense there is something more between you and the centurion here?" He looked at Varro who reddened slightly.

"Are we also to discuss our relationships as well today?" She asked an inkling of anger in her eyes. "You are correct," she said before Caradoc could reply, "I have found Centurion Tiberius Varro to be a man of honour and a man of his word and yes, I have very strong feelings for him, is that a problem for you King Caradoc?"

"No, not for me, but others will not like it that you share your bed with a Roman." He replied.

"Then tell them to say that to my face." She said. "Now can we please talk about what we are here to discuss?"

"Very well," he turned his attention to Varro, "please continue."

Varro laid flat the first scroll and placed four weights from the case on the four corners, they were marked with small images of eagles. "The first detail is a greeting to you, King Caradoc from the Governor of Britannia, General Aulus Plautius, who coincidentally is due to leave these shores soon, very soon and he would like an amicable end to hostilities." He looked up.

"And how does the General propose we go about this when he and his men," he pointed a finger, "such as you, inhabit my land." The atmosphere chilled slightly.

Varro removed the second scroll, "The General wishes to meet you in person to discuss the finer details. He guarantees your safety, if you agree to accompany us back to Londinium." He saw that Caradoc was about to say something but went on. "He proposes that you are to retain the land here and that you will remain King and become an ally of Rome. He says that even the Emperor Claudius respects you and the resistance that you have garnered and demonstrated against his legions." Varro looked up to see how Caradoc was reacting but he sat there impassively, one eyebrow raised, he waved a hand for him to continue. "As a Province of Rome, you and your people will benefit...."

"Province, I have heard this word before." Caradoc interrupted, "Does that not contradict the term ally?" He looked at the faces around the table, Grattius shrugged, he went on, "An ally, within my meaning of the word, is an equal, a partner but this word Province has a different meaning, am I right?"

"There are many Provinces within the Empire, all living happily under the protection of Rome." Varro said.

"And they are all left to govern their own lands, control their own populations? Rome doesn't require payment in taxes, crops, gold and people as slaves? Rome doesn't dig into these people's mountains and valleys searching for rich materials to steal and take away back across the water?" Caradoc asked.

"Different Provinces have different agreements with the Senate. I couldn't say what yours would be. That would be a matter for you and in the first instance the Governor to discuss. These talks would decide that future treaty, hence why he has asked you to meet him in person. General Plautius leaves these islands this year and he doesn't want to return to Rome with a war still raging and Roman lives being lost. It would be to his advantage to return with a peace treaty in place or at least with discussions ongoing, a mutual agreement for both sides, where you and he are happy with the content."

Caradoc sat back in his chair and bit the inside of his mouth, leaning forward he said, "You see Centurion Varro, this is where my people and I have a problem, Rome invaded us, we didn't invade Rome and now because your General is going home, he wants peace. He wants to be received by Claudius, the man who caused this invasion to happen, as a hero, a hero of Rome, is that not true?"

Varro shifted in his seat, "These are the terms I have been asked to put to you. This is how Rome works," he paused thinking, "I cannot change where we are. The rights and wrongs of the invasion of Britannia are not a part of this discussion. You can take that up with the General."

"Albion," Caradoc said, "this island and those around it are known by its people as Albion, not Britannia. That is a Roman word, a word that we do not recognise, maybe that is something else I would discuss in this imaginary conversation with the Roman Governor of the Roman Province of Britannia."

"I'm certain that he would discuss any subject you would wish to be aired, any grievances you may have. Aulus Plautius is a man of honour, he is a soldier first, a politician second." Varro replied.

"A politician, I don't know this word, but I suspect that it means a man who has found himself in a position of power, not through his ability, but to further himself and those around him. If these politicians were there for the benefit of their people, would they tax them so much, work them so hard, whilst they live in luxury? Why aren't all the people of the great Roman Empire equal? You have different levels in your society don't you Centurion Varro? Whilst these people in power eat well, are warm in the winter, dress in the finest clothes and gather with their friends to rule over the greater population, how are the common people living? Is there hunger in your world? I would say from what I am told that there is. Are there entire populations sold into slavery to serve these people and their kind?" Varro attempted to answer but Caradoc continued, "Are families separated and sent to different corners of the Empire? Again the answer is yes isn't it?" He shook his head. "You see, this is where I have a problem, we would never be equal, we would always be regarded as inferior and we would always be used like animals. The young men, what would happen to them? Is it correct you use them in your army, create legions and use them to invade other lands?" He leaned back again frowning, "You see the problems that you and this man of honour have made? Apologies, you are just soldiers as you say, following orders, your Emperor Claudius is responsible for this, he and his

Senate. Tell me, did they believe that this would be a quick victory?"

Varro wasn't expecting the question and searched for an answer.

"Let me tell you what I believe, Centurion Varro and if I'm right you will agree, although you might not say you do." Caradoc looked up at the ceiling as if looking for inspiration, "The Emperor as you call him, we would call him a King, one day decided that he needed a victory over what he regarded as a barbarian people. He consulted with his friends and politicians, these men in the Senate, and looked at his maps. The mighty Roman Empire had expanded in all directions and it was already bigger than any other body of land known to man, at least that we know of. Despite this he wants more, the Senate wanted more and so they stuck a dagger in the land they call Britannia and decided to take it. Now I don't know why you decided to come west, when I say you, I mean Rome. Don't think I mean you because you are a soldier who loyally follows these instructions." Caradoc looked down at the faces around the table once more. "The problem now though, is that it wasn't a quick or decisive victory was it. How long have your boots been on our soil now, nearly four years by my calculations and that's a long time. So if I refuse to meet this man before he goes home, he will be replaced by another, no doubt the same sort of man, another man charged with conquering this land, probably another General am I right?"

"I should imagine so yes." Varro replied.

"This man will, I'm sure, have studied the problems that your legions have encountered so far, but will be arrogant enough to think that he can do better. He will arrive with a head full of ideas on how to defeat us but we will resist, we will fight and some of us will die, but so will a lot of his men, men like you." Caradoc turned and shouted towards the door, "Ardwen, could you please bring some water, my throat is getting dry with all this talking." A mumbled reply was heard from beyond the door.

"The problem for you and your kind now Centurion Varro is that we are prepared for you, we are ready for your legions. I no longer fight with just my own people, I fight alongside the tribes of the west and for that I thank you because Rome has done something they never could; it unified them. They are a proud group of people, a fierce group of warriors and whilst I accept you have ways of fighting in large numbers that we don't, I learnt from those mistakes, and I don't like making the same ones over and over again. I also believe that you would find it a lot more difficult to fight in these valleys and mountains, they are well suited for large scale ambushes of the legions." At that point in the conversation, Ardwen entered the room with two teenage girls carrying water jugs. Suddenly, there was a disturbance of some sort behind him.

"What's all the shouting?" He asked walking quickly back towards the door but before he could get there, a warrior barged the doors open and ran inside panting.

"They're here, they're here." He shouted breathing heavily.

"What are you talking about man? Have you lost your senses?" Ardwen asked.

"Romans," he blurted, "hundreds of them, maybe thousands."

"You've lost your mind, how is that possible you fool?" Ardwen demanded.

"The coast to the west," the warrior panted, "ships, they've come in ships, many ships and they're bigger than anything I've ever seen."

Caradoc stood, his face twisted in rage and pointed at Varro, "What trickery is this? I knew I couldn't trust you."

Varro and those in his group all stood as one, "I know nothing of this Caradoc, you have to believe that." he turned to Brenna.

"He doesn't, I would know if he did, it must be Plautius." She said.

"Seize them and have them guarded." Caradoc ordered of Ardwen, he faced Varro, "Whatever they are doing here, they will fail, is this how Rome negotiates, treacherous bastards." He turned to the warrior who had reported sighting the Roman fleet. "I want to know where exactly and I want to know how many." He grabbed the man's arm and directed him towards the door he had come through only seconds before, then he stopped and turned to face Varro. "I swear on everything that I hold dear, I will crush the men in those ships and then I'll come back and deal with you."

Chapter Seventeen

Valerius leaned over the railing of the ship and vomited into the sea as his hobnailed boots slipped on the wet surface of the vessel's wooden decking. The boat lurched this way and that in the swell as the oarsmen struggled to turn landward against the tide and wind. This ship and the others in the fleet were packed with heavy infantry and only the amount of men crowded together stopped them from falling over. Shields and armour grated against each other as legionaries complained and looked out to the land, so close now. Another spray of salt water lashed over their heads and rained down on them, soaking tunics and weapons as they cursed the sea and the sailors who had brought them here. Looking up along the headland through bleary vision, Valerius squinted and rubbed his eyes and looked again. Did he see a figure up there on the high ground, a running figure? He couldn't be certain as he held onto the rail and felt his stomach churn again.

"Drop the sail." The captain of the vessel bellowed over the sound of the crashing water as it struck the starboard side, sending yet another shower of salt water onto the deck. Sailors struggled through the crowds of bodies and began untying the thick ropes, quickly they lowered the sail and the motion stalled for a moment.

"Row you bastards, get us ashore." He shouted. His face a sheen as yet more sea water was hurled towards the ship.

"Please let it end." Valerius begged the gods of the sea. "Just let me get to dry land that's all I ask." He retched again but his stomach was empty. Pollo's large hand clasped his armour covered shoulder.

"We're nearly there now lad, won't be long." Pollo shouted as the vessel dropped between waves. "Nothing like sailing is there eh? I'm lucky I used to do a lot of it back home. I can't recall the seas being like this though, rough as a barbarians cunny eh?"

Valerius couldn't answer or even acknowledge his friend because he knew that to even try would bring on yet more retching, so he stood wedged against the rail staring up at the green hills beyond the beach.

"What is it, have you seen something?" Pollo asked looking ashore, as the movement of the boat pressed him up against Valerius, their segmented armour scraping together. "I can't see anything except all that lovely earth, even I'll be glad to get my feet on solid ground, I've had enough of this."

The trireme war galley that carried them, was now reaching its top speed and the shore got ever closer as the oarsmen heaved to the encouragement of the captain, who continued to hurl abuse at them. The following vessels had all dropped their mainsails and were turning inland following the lead ship. Valerius looked down at the water that was beginning to turn to foam on the surface and knew that very soon, he would be jumping into it and wading ashore, the idea didn't soothe his nausea but at least he would have a solid surface under his boots.

"Standby Second Augusta," Optio Crispus shouted from somewhere behind in the crush of armour and men, "not long lads."

Two hundred yards out, all eyes were fixed on the beach ahead, it looked to be mostly clear sand, a site chosen by Plautius where he knew the vessels could ground themselves on the low tide. He knew that he was taking a huge risk but a sudden, swift strike to the rear of Caradoc's forces could end the conflict in the west and he would be able to return to Rome a hero.

One hundred yards out now and the trireme had found another gear as it sliced its way through the grey foaming water. The swell here was less significant as the pale faces of the legionaries aboard exchanged hopeful glances that their ordeal would soon be over.

"Row you dogs, like your life depended on it." The captain shouted, his voice cracking through the effort. Men held their pila tight in their right hands, shields hefted up in their left, half above the side rail in the event of attack.

"Get that fucking shield up." Crispus ordered to someone near the bow. "Just because we can't see them, it doesn't mean they're not there you fool."

With an enormous crunch, the ship embedded itself into the beach as men lurched forward at the waist, and then there was a moment of silence as they waited and listened. Another trireme hurtled ashore, its occupants also waited, senses straining for any sign of the enemy, nothing.

"Ashore!" The order was given and troops climbed over the railing, dropped onto the external decking and then into the water below.

"Ugh," Valerius muttered as the cold sea took his breath away, it came up to his chest, "gods that's freezing." He lifted his shield up and over his head as they'd been taught, and angled it downward, the base in the water. It was heavy enough and now the movement of the sea pushed it in all directions. Bodies splashed into the water all around him as he struggled to balance and stay upright. Men shouted, swore and cursed as they began to move forward towards dry land.

Taking large strides Valerius breathed heavily, the strain already showing on his face as he fought against the surging waves. For a brief moment he wondered about the effect the sea would have on his armour and an image appeared to him of it rusting, brown, stained and dirty and then the arrows began to fall.

"Did you know about this, about the attack?" Brenna asked Varro and Grattius after they'd been escorted back to the roundhouse under guard. Varro removed his cloak and threw it down on the table.

"Of course not Brenna, do you really believe that we'd come here knowing that Plautius was planning this? What is the man thinking? There was a real chance that Caradoc would have listened but now…" He slammed a fist down onto the table, "The idiot, why didn't he just wait? A few days, weeks, until spring even, I don't understand."

"He's used us and launched a surprise attack," Grattius said, "in winter, using the sea to outflank them, it's bold I'll give him that." He picked up an apple and took a bite, "The trouble is what do we, do now?" He asked.

"We have to escape, get away from here." Lita said. "You heard what he said, he'll deal with us when he gets back."

"If he gets back, that is." Grattius added.

"If we do that then he'll think we knew all along." Brenna said.

"Ha who cares what he thinks, if we stay here we're dead." Grattius replied. Varro pulled out a chair and sat down.

"We stay," he looked at those around him, "we risked our lives to come here and Caradoc could have left us to die in that village. He didn't he saved us and had us brought here, so he deserves more than an empty roundhouse when he returns." Grattius sat down.

"I'll agree to anything you say, but I don't like it." He took another bite of the apple and chewed.

"How can you eat at a time like this you great stupid lump?" Lita asked angrily.

"I'll eat when I like woman, you heard the centurion, we are staying." He said spitting pieces of apple out in the direction of Lita, "now shut up and calm yourself down before you burst something."

Lita leapt forward and slapped the apple out of his hand, it flew across the room and hit the wall, "You stupid bastards will get us all killed." She tried to hit Grattius but he held his arms up blocking her and then grabbed her wrists.

"So fiery you Britons are in your foreplay." He said laughing as Lita struggled to break free.

"I'll gut you like a pig." She shouted.

"Stop this," Brenna shouted, but the pair carried on fighting and wrestling with each other, Grattius sat laughing, Varro watching not amused and Brenna getting angrier, "I SAID STOP!" She marched over to Lita and grabbed her shoulders and pulled her away, "You are behaving like children, now stop it and shut up."

"Alright Brenna, so what would you have us do?" Lita asked. Her face flushed.

"We stay as Varro has said, it's his decision but I happen to agree with him anyway. Caradoc has shown some trust in us and I believe that we should return it. How were we to know that Plautius would do this? I'm convinced that he was actually beginning to listen and saw that there was an opportunity for peace even if he didn't agree with the initial terms or how it would work." She pulled out a chair and slumped down next to Varro. "All I've ever wanted was peace, I'm sick and tired of constant fighting, death and destruction, it's getting us nowhere. People should live and work together not be at each other's throats constantly, that goes for you two as well."

"I was just eating an apple." Grattius replied, feigning being hurt.

"Shut up." Lita said.

"Enough! Why don't you ever listen?" Brenna added and looked at the door, "I can't even leave to get away from your childish bickering now." She held a hand to her stomach.

"Are you alright?" Varro asked frowning. He reached out and touched her hand.

"I'll be fine if those two will be quiet." She moved his hand away, "I'm going to lie down." She said smiling and got up. Varro looked at Grattius and Lita.

"No more fighting or arguing, understand?"

"Fine by me," Grattius said, turning to Lita, "maybe you'd like to go to bed too? Give me and the centurion time to talk."

"As long as it's not with you." She said standing. Grattius looked back to Varro.

"Are you sure you want us to stay here?" He asked.

"We've got no choice in the matter, the way I see things. If we try to leave and get caught, Caradoc will think we knew of Plautius' plan and probably have us killed. If we somehow managed to escape and get free, he'll still think we knew of the attack." He put his head in his hands. "For better or for worse my friend, we stay…for now."

Above, the skies darkened, streaked with arrows and then they began to land zipping into the water, striking armour and flesh, men screamed in pain or anger. Valerius was mildly aware of the sound of the scorpions opening fire aboard the trireme as the highly wound ropes let fly their own deadly barrage. A few marines launched arrows from bows that were previously stored beneath the ships railing. He pushed forward through the water, now waist high as others joined him. They tried to form a line, to get organised as they would on land.

"Shields, keep em up lads." Someone shouted from the right as they created a jagged wall. He was aware of others behind him and Pollo shouting, "We have to get out of the water." The man next to Valerius suddenly went limp and let out a sigh. He saw an arrow deep inside his flesh, somewhere below his eye line but where exactly, he couldn't see. He fell into the water and disappeared under a swirling blend of blood and froth, he couldn't be helped, not now. Blood swirled up, touching and merging with the cloth of Valerius' *braccae* leggings, cold and warm. The volley of arrows whistled all around as the men of the Second took cover as best they could behind their shields.

They pushed forward tightly huddled together, heads low as sharp barbs buried themselves thudding into the wood of their protective shields, akin to a heavy hail storm. The scorpion crews worked like demons trying to give them cover, archers too, but they were severely outnumbered as more soldiers jumped into the sea to join the mayhem below. Those still on-board the ships could see the lines of enemy bowmen, the top of their weapons at least, as they were raised to fire over rocks, there were hundreds of them, whilst above on the hilltop, riders came into view. A marine centurion ran to the captain of the lead ship.

"Sir, look." He shouted pointing at the dark line of riders as they came lower turning the green hillside black. "We have to warn them, get them back to the ships."

The captain looked upward, horror in his expression, "Gods above, sound the retreat, get them back to the ships and get your men in the water, we can't wait for the tide to turn, we'll have to push off."

The centurion turned and ran to the side of the vessel and began throwing knotted ropes and ladders over the side, "Sound the retreat, get the ropes over the side."

A horn sounded but the noise of the sea combined with the constant hammering of arrows drowned it out almost completely and the men already in the water continued to advance. The centurion ordered the remaining legionaries to stay aboard and to create a shield wall around the deck. He then selected enough to make another around his men who would try to force the hull off the beach.

Valerius grimaced as he struggled with his shield and the swirling water, every now and again his shield would move to the side and he would get a view of the shore and the hail of arrows heading towards them. He grabbed the handle of his shield tighter and pressed it against his helmet, head down and pressed on, Pollo behind him still holding his harness. Men fell when arrows struck them due to the movement of the sea pushing their shields aside, others tried to drag them back towards the boat covering them with their own shields. The water was turning pink now as it merged with fresh blood but the heavy infantry pressed on, the men of the first cohort unaware that the retreat had been sounded.

Caradoc raced his horse down the path leading to the water's edge, a procession of riders behind him, snaking their way towards the battle raging below. His face contorted in rage, he drew his sword and shouted as loud as he could, "Fire arrows, burn the ships."

At first there was no change to the defence of the beach and so he repeated the order again and again until his voice was hoarse, and then he saw a lit arrow take to the grey skies, followed by others. They arched heaven bound and then began to fall, some into the sea but others onto the decks of the Roman ships, where panicked crewmen ran to put them out. Reaching sea level, Caradoc didn't jump from his horse but rode it into the sea still shouting encouragement to his warriors.

"Rise," he shouted, circling the large sword about his head, "rise and kill the invaders." His men roared and whilst horsemen raced into the water, archers moved from behind the rocks so that they had a clear view of the enemy. Now they fired straight, the men in the sea were easy prey, others appeared on foot, carrying small circular shields; they ran after the horses wading into the sea screaming for blood.

Caradoc charged his mount straight into the flimsy shield wall he found before him, men were cast aside, some struck by arrows as they fell, others cleaved open by his mighty sword blows. Water spewed up, engulfing the Romans and reducing their vision as they fought to stay on their feet and fight back. More horsemen reached the enemy line as their riders hacked and slashed at the men below. Cries of anguish merged with those of pain, as the legionaries struggled to punch their swords upward at their attackers.

From the lead ship, the captain could only watch on horrified as waves of riders rode out into the sea and broke through the Roman lines. Onboard, marines and sailors fought the flames caused by the fire arrows, whilst a few archers fired back. The scorpion crews were running out of ammunition now and some abandoned their weapons in favour of defending their vessels by other means. Some leapt into the water and heaved, pushing at the hulls, trying to pry them free of the sand bank. Of those, some were hit by fire arrows that slammed into their unarmoured backs, they fell into the water, the flames fizzing out, dying like their victims.

"Butcher them all." Caradoc shouted, Ardwen now by his side swiping his blade into the invaders.

"Leave none alive." He shouted as other men and women took up their battle cries. Some wore tunics but some had thrown them off when the order had come to enter the water, knowing it would reduce their movement. They had abandoned them and ran half naked towards the advancing lines of the Romans. Taught, sinewy and muscular torsos covered in blue tattooed patterns ran, raising their legs but soon, were waist deep and wading further, screaming, faces contorted in rage pleading with their gods for the death of the enemy.

Valerius stabbed forward from behind his shield, trying to stay on his feet just before a horse hit him and knocked him backwards. Sea water rushed into his open mouth and nose, the salt strong as he struggled to get up, he saw the blurred image of horses legs through the bubbles. His heavy armour seemed to suck him further down with its weight. He heard garbled voices as he felt his back land on the floor of the seabed and then an almighty hoof, pinned him there. Letting go of his shield, he tried to stab out at the leg with his sword but missed, striking only more water. Beginning to panic, his head felt like it was about to burst through a lack of air, he shook his head from side to side. His gladius was knocked from his hand by another hoof and spun away, he grabbed the leg stopping him from moving just as it released him, but another intake of water dulled his senses and he saw the blackness of death engulf him.

The triremes still out at sea, beyond those being attacked, were blocked from getting any closer to the battle, as Plautius had decided upon a relatively small cove for his landing. After exhausting their ballista bolts and conventional arrows, they were rowed closer to the beached vessels and tied onto those not already aflame and pulled them free. The ships had little choice but to abandon the men still in the water, a few lucky souls managed to climb up the ropes of some triremes sides or their ladders, but most were left to be cut down.

Pollo held onto one such rope as the oarsmen struck deep and fast and pulled clear of the avalanche of arrows that were still falling. His fingers were numb with cold as he clenched his teeth against the icy grip of the water. He looked down at the unconscious figure of Valerius he held in the other hand as he began to shout up at those on the deck.

"Stop, stop the boat." He yelled but wasn't sure if they could hear him against the sound of the battle and the crashing of the waves against the hull. The hand in the water now had no sensation, he couldn't feel his fingers and willed them to keep a grip of the strap he held on his friends back. Then, just as he was about to give up hope of anyone hearing him, he felt himself being lifted as he rose higher against the side of the ship. He could just make out heads peering over the edge of the outer decking plate and hauling him and Valerius up.

"Pull you bastards. I've got another man here." He shouted as he was hauled up and over the edge, other hands reached down and grabbed the unconscious form of Valerius and took his weight.

"This is a ship not a bloody boat." The captain said, as he laid Valerius flat on his stomach and began pushing his open palms onto his back.

"What are you doing, is he dead?" Pollo asked shaking his numb hands and staring at the pale face being forced against the wooden ledge with every push. The captain knelt over Valerius' back and kept pumping, ignoring Pollo's question. Suddenly sea water gushed out of his mouth and he began to cough uncontrollably, eyes still closed. The captain kept pumping.

"Come on lad, you can make it, get it all out." He pushed again, shoulders high, arms straight and pushed down again and again. Valerius sounded as if he was choking and then he gasped, spluttered and coughed some more, his eyes flickered open, he was alive.

It was like being woken from a deep sleep, he went from being in a serene place, to one of pain, blurred images and mumbled words. He tried to open his eyes, where was he? Still in the water, trapped under the horse, dead? He coughed and felt sea water rush out of his nose and mouth, it stung, he couldn't breathe, he struggled but something was pressing down on him. Trying to raise his head, he thought he saw Pollo looking down on him, he was mouthing words but he couldn't hear them. He moved his head trying to raise it from something solid, was that the ship's captain above him? He coughed again uncontrollably and felt bubbles of air in his throat and nose, struggling to breath, he blew out through his nose, it hurt but it cleared his airway. The pressure lifted from his chest, but he continued to cough as he was rolled onto his side.

"I thought you were dead." He heard Pollo's voice suddenly clear.

"He was lucky you saved him, unlike those poor swine." The captain said.

Pollo looked back towards the receding shoreline and saw men still fighting for their lives, but they were surrounded, engulfed by warriors on foot and on horseback. White plumes of sea water splashed up as men slashed and stabbed at each other, the legionaries of the Second Augusta had no chance against such odds, but still they fought.

Caradoc, seized by battle rage looked around him, eyes wide with menace and hatred. There were still small pockets of resistance here and there. He pushed his horse forward into a group of surviving Romans, maybe five of them, who had somehow retained their shields. Leaping from his horse, he caught them by surprise as they were concentrating on those to their front. The man underneath him buckled and fell beneath the water level, he stabbed down and felt the reassurance of his blade enter flesh and grate against bone. He got his footing and spun round, the tip of his sword slicing into an enemy's neck, blood sprayed out a red hue in the air. Serenity took over as the scene played out before him as if he were watching from elsewhere, stabbing, thrusting and parrying blows and then all he could hear was his own heavy breathing. Warriors stared at him in surprise and admiration, the enemy dead, sinking under the weight of their armoured shells.

"You bloody fool, you could have been killed." Ardwen shouted, still on his horse.

"Then you would take my place." Caradoc replied fury in his eyes as he looked for more men to kill but those who still struggled were too far away. In moments the resistance died, as did those who had come aboard vessels to attack them from the sea. He turned and began wading back to the shore.

"Strip them of their armour and recover anything we can use." He ordered, "We haven't seen the last of them."

As the daylight began to vanish from the small gap in the smoke hole above them, Varro, Grattius, Brenna and Lita heard horses approaching, riding fast. Pensive looks were exchanged between them but there was nothing they could do. The horses came to a sliding stop outside and there were mumbled commands given, were they to be dragged outside and tortured for information, they didn't know.

The door skin was brushed aside and Caradoc entered quickly, Ardwen behind him. They were both covered in sweat from the ride back to the hill fort from wherever it was they had confronted Plautius' attack. The four of them stood up.

"We killed them, burnt three ships and stopped them getting onto dry land." Caradoc said breathing heavily. "There were more ships, at least five more, but they couldn't get to the beach." He pointed at Varro, "Your friends' bodies line the sea floor. The rest are being dragged ashore as I speak, to be stripped of anything we can use against them."

Varro looked down at the floor, Grattius looked angry and Brenna and Lita stood there red faced.

"We knew nothing of this attack Caradoc, you have to believe us." Brenna said almost pleading, "Why would we come here if we knew that they were planning this? It doesn't make sense does it? Do you think we would throw our lives away for what, just for the possibility of being here? Come on Caradoc, you're a man with a good head, you know we wouldn't do that don't you?"

The barrage of questions seemed to knock some of the anger out of the Celt leader as he stood there contemplating what she had said. Looking at him now they could see faint traces on blood on his face and neck, presumably from the fighting earlier.

"We could hold them captive," Ardwen said, "keep them here and have them to use as hostages later. It would be better than letting them go, so they can work against us."

Caradoc half turned his head and half looked at floor, "We could cousin or we could let them go and show that we are better than they are. That we don't break our promises as they do."

"Promises, what promises have we made, what are you talking about?" Ardwen asked.

"I assured them that they would be safe whilst they were here, inside Silures' territory. As King I have a responsibility not just to my people but to behave as they would expect and set an example. It is a matter of honour cousin, surely you can see that?"

Ardwen stalked forward and stared at the two women, "What I see are two whores, two whores who like the taste of Roman cum nothing more." He laughed, "They probably do both of them together and then each other." He closed the gap between himself and Brenna and stood almost nose to nose, "You might look like something special bitch, but you still bleed like the rest, you whine like the rest and you shit like everyone else. I can see through you, I can see into your heart and it's black, black as pitch." She looked down. "Know this whore," he turned to Lita and approached her, "If I were king and not my cousin, I would have you fucked by my men every way possible and then given to the women. Then I'd have you splayed open, attached to a cart and driven back across the border as a warning to all the other whores who are taking Roman cock." He turned to Varro and Grattius, "And as for you two, even your gods themselves would weep for what I would do to you."

"Enough Ardwen," Caradoc said, "enough, I don't want to hear anymore and whilst I lead, there is no more to be said, I will not harm them, leave."

He turned and looked at his cousin and sneered, venom in his words "Very well cousin, this time I will listen but be warned if anything like this happens again, I may not be so patient. If my man hadn't seen their fleet, we could have all been dead by now, villages and settlements set on fire, women raped, children taken for slaves and men slaughtered. We can't afford to be civilised towards a people who have no honour, a people who smile while talking to you and plot behind our backs, there is only one way to deal with such snakes, remove their heads."

"I hear you Ardwen believe me I do, but I promised these people safety. I also think that they're telling the truth and they have been used as we were, now go cousin leave me to talk to them."

Ardwen stared at each of them in turn, his eyes silently saying that they were lucky their fate lay with Caradoc, he turned, lifted the door skin and left.

"You are a man of honour Caradoc." Varro began.

"Shut up and sit down, all of you." Caradoc ordered, they did as they were told, whilst he paced up and down. "I don't know what your Governor thought he was doing but he has made a grave mistake. I was willing to discuss terms, even willing to go and speak with him, but now after this, this betrayal, I see that there can never be peace with Rome." He raised a hand to his head and wiped at the dried blood. "For decades we lived in peace with Rome, we traded, we bought her goods, yet it was never enough, they always wanted more. I lived my entire life listening to the words of a brother who wanted to bow down, a brother who also betrayed me and my people, is that what it's like to be a part of Rome? Is it such a cesspit of dishonesty, deceit, murder and lies, a place where you can't trust anyone, a place where you are always looking over your shoulder, watching for a blade?" He shook his head. "It is a good thing that Plautius showed his real personality, his real intent after all. He doesn't want peace, he wants domination and he wants my people as slaves to serve Rome, not be a part of it." He pointed at Varro and Grattius, "It won't happen and you can go back and tell him that, as long as I lead, there will be war and if I die another will take my place." He stopped pacing, "He must think me a fool, a fool who lives on raw butchered meat and milk, a barbarian. Isn't that how you regard us Roman?" He looked at Varro. "As a weak, uncivilised people who live in the mud, in a land of constant rain, up to our heads in filth?"

Varro caught his eye but thought better of speaking. He knew that what he said was true, most Romans regarded them as inferior, a people to be governed and manipulated, to be used. His relationship with Brenna and other Britons had showed him that there was a different side to the Celts of Britannia. They were most certainly related to the Celts of Gaul and elsewhere but he had come to learn that was a good thing. Like some Romans there were good and bad in all people. Caradocs' words brought him out of his thoughts.

"You still have my word that you will be safe whilst in these lands, I will provide an escort for you tomorrow. I want you to return to this Plautius, this man of Rome and tell him these words; there is no need for them to be written down like these lies." He pulled the scrolls that they had brought with them out of his tunic and threw them on the fire. "Tell him that I won't be fooled again and that I was so close to giving him the peace the required; the peace that would have allowed him to return to Rome, as a hero, and to have his victory. No more blood would have been shed by our swords and no more sons of Rome would lie rotting on our soil." He walked to the door. "Do you know that Ardwen and I had even said that we would concede certain things if it meant peace, no more war?" He smiled, "How stupid we were to believe that we could trust such a people. No doubt the emperor would have drained our land of its wealth, sold our people into slavery and kept us under the heel of his legions boots. I'm glad in a way that he decided to attack, because now we know where we stand, there can be no peace, we can't live with serpents. Tell Plautius this when you go back, the retribution I have sought and gained so far in raids across the Roman made border, will pale into insignificance compared to what he has brought upon himself now. Burning forts and destroyed villas will be the last of his concerns. Your people started this war, we neither wanted nor desired it, we considered ourselves friends with your empire but still you came to murder and rob." He lifted the door skin, "You won't see me without a blade in my hand again and I won't be talking to you like this, if we should meet. Tell Plautius, I'm coming, if he's lucky he'll be back in Rome, if not, he'll die by my hand." He went to leave.

"Caradoc," Varro said stopping him, "I can't even begin to understand how you must feel, but please know that we knew nothing of the fleet, I promise you."

"In another life," Caradoc said, "we could have been friends, brothers. If your leaders were like you, there would be no war, of that I'm certain. I believe you and I think that you're a man of honour." He looked at Grattius and the others, "Of the company you keep, I couldn't say the same, but I have been known to be wrong, I can admit that." Grattius was tempted to speak but didn't.

"Goodbye Centurion Varro, may your gods go with you, and watch over you and your friends here, but for the others, I will show no mercy. No act will be beyond my reach or conscience now. I will seek to destroy everything that Rome stands for here in Albion. My warriors will strive to strike at the very heart of everything they hold dear." He smiled, "It's probably better this way, no more pretence with dreams of peace. Plautius will either die or return to Rome having failed, empty handed. I vow this will happen on my father's spirit." He took one last look at those listening to his words and then ducked under the door skin and left the roundhouse.

An eerie silence fell over those sat near the table, no-one spoke for a while, Grattius poured some water from a jug into a cup and drank it, not saying a word. Brenna stared at the table, Lita looked at her and Varro gazed at the floor.

"Well," he said eventually, "we'd better get our things packed up and get ready to move out tomorrow."

"Thank Mithras I say," Grattius said, "the sooner we're back behind our lines the better, no offence ladies but you know what I mean."

"None taken," Brenna said quietly, "the sooner we're out of here the better. Ardwen and the others may be content to listen to Caradoc for now, but it wouldn't take much for them to turn and take matters into their own hands."

"Do you think we're safe tonight?" Lita asked.

"I think we'll be safe until we get across the mountains and back into friendly territory, you heard what he said. It's after that I'm more concerned with." Varro said.

"What do you mean by that?" Grattius asked.

"He's already struck at will along the border and deep into Roman occupied lands but now, now he knows it's a fight to the death. He's got nothing to lose, one way or another he that knows Rome wants this land and will do anything to get it. If that means wiping out all those that live here, then so be it. There's nothing to hold him back anymore, or others. Word will spread of the failed attempt by the fleet, of the trick that Plautius tried to employ, even if it's not true. It will give them heart and encouragement to rise against us and they are everywhere we are. If every Celt here decides to rebel, there's nothing, even five legions could do about it and the Governor may have just given them the reason that helps them decide to do it."

Brenna stood up, "What you say is correct, but it won't happen, not with all the tribes anyway, some are more than happy to live this way, under Roman rule, but others will never stop fighting. I've told you before that this war will go on for as long as you Romans are here. Some battles they will win, others you will be the victors, but you will never completely dominate a people that don't want to be beaten. It's not in our nature to lie down and let ourselves be kicked and beaten, we fight back, we always will."

"And yet you work with us." Grattius said.

"I work alongside you Optio, there is a difference, I want peace, but not through any means. I can live side by side with any kind of people, irrespective of where they come from as long as there is harmony, some sort of common understanding. What I will not do is live as a slave or as something thought of as inferior. Centurion Varro has shown me that not all Romans are evil and wicked, we have spoken of this many times and I believe his words, but there is still doubt. Not that he is lying or is trying to deceive me or my people but that those above him, your superiors, have different plans for Albion and her tribes. Your Emperor Claudius clearly thought that invading this island would be easy and yet he's already been proven wrong. Four long years ago, the legions arrived on our soil and still you haven't taken the southern shores entirely, never mind the west and the north. I doubt that we'll ever see an end to the conflict here during our lives if Rome decides to stay. As it is, the Roman way is to dominate and take from others, so it is the way of the Celts to resist and to fight until our dying breath. We are a proud people and will not, cannot live like animals, ruled over by others. This is what you face Optio, we accept the fate the gods have given us and although I want peace and will work by your side to achieve it, others will not, ever."

The rest of the evening was spent in virtual silence, Caradoc had arranged for food to be brought to them and some rations were packed away for their journey the following morning. They ate with little conversation between them, except for Grattius who occasionally spoke about the food they consumed. No-one was drawn into replying however, a depression had fallen over the others as they realised for the first time, there was now little hope of a lasting peace.

THE END

Author's Note

Blood of Rome Retribution is dedicated to Lunt Roman Fort, Coventry, which is situated in the heart of England. It is the fort featured on the cover albeit in flames (sorry), whose employees do such incredible work educating children and adults alike concerning Roman Britain. I would like to take this opportunity to thank all of them for their hospitality recently during a visit. Lunt Roman Fort is unique in its structure and a jewel of Britain's Roman history. It is also the fort featured in the film The Eagle, starring Channing Tatum and Jamie Bell. To learn more visit www.luntromanfort.org

I would also like to take this opportunity to thank my proof-readers, because without their help, this book would not have been released so quickly, so a very big and sincere thank you goes to Anne, Miriam and Shelley Bryham (New Zealand).

I truly hope that you have enjoyed reading, even remotely close to the pleasure I experienced whilst writing, Blood of Rome Retribution, the second novel in the Blood of Rome series. I would like to take this opportunity to thank you for sharing the lives of the characters, some of whom history created, and others who evolved and came to life through my own imagination. Once again, I have tried to stay as close to historical fact as possible with Retribution but here and there, are a few additions for the sake of what I hope, en-riches the story.

The title 'Retribution' came about after various discussions with friends who are also fascinated with the eternal city of Rome, Michael Reed in particular. Thank you Mike for helping the name, 'pop' into my thoughts, I think it's a great title. As Caradoc begins to take the fight to the legions, I thought it was ideal and appropriate for book two.

I decided to 'change' Caratacus' name to the Celtic version for this novel as I believe that's what I would have done if I'd found myself in the same circumstances. The name Caradoc has been used throughout various stories to describe Caratacus and I thought that it fitted quite nicely at this juncture, especially as the latter is a Romanised version of Caradoc.

In Blood of Rome Caratacus, our noble Briton had little time to show his character fully, this was deliberate as the events overtook him as they did in reality. I wanted to try to emulate that story as a form of hurricane, fast and sudden, but now his traits and characteristics are beginning to be revealed. It was always my intention to show more of his background and personality, which I hope I have achieved in this storyline. Also going back to his earlier days, as I did in a couple of chapters, covering the defection of Adminius, who was actually banished by his Father and King, this enabled the younger Caradoc to come through.

Whilst Blood of Rome Retribution also begins to bridge the gap between what Caradoc was doing in the West, in the country now called Wales and what historical records tell us. He must have been a very intelligent and enigmatic man, an individual who had enormous strength of character, absolute determination and resolve and all the qualities of a brilliant leader. He truly was the first hero of Britain or should I say Albion? If I could go back in time and talk to some of the world's historical figures, he would be very close to the top of the list.

Book three is already well underway and has a working title. However I won't say what it is yet, as it may change. The main story or map/framework, as I like to think of it, is complete, but some rivers on that map may change course. Rest assured that the resistance of Caradoc is growing as well as his influence as he continues to defy Rome and all it stands for.

Thank you again for reading Retribution and if you have five minutes to spare, please take the time to submit a review on Amazon and the Goodreads websites. I ask this as it is very important for aspiring authors to receive impartial reviews about their work, thank you.

About the Author

I have always had a fascination and a passion for the Roman Empire, especially when it comes to Roman Britain. Born in Chester, the former Roman City called Deva, I remember visiting museums in the city even when I was small and being intrigued by the models of marching legions, all their stories and campaigns.

At 17 years of age, I joined the Royal Air Force virtually straight from school and spent the next twenty five years travelling the world and serving my country. When I say serving, a lot of it was in the UK but I also had a few 'holidays.' Throughout that time, I read novels and historical texts about Rome and visited as many sites of a Roman nature as possible, which merely whetted my appetite further.

I have always been an avid reader of mainly historical and science fiction stories and once wrote a short novel for the Royal Air Force Star Trek and Science Fiction Association. Another project that is still in its relative infancy is a science fiction story but until the Blood of Rome series is complete, it will be waiting on the back burner.

After leaving the Air Force, I elected to write my own story and chose Caradoc/Caratacus as one of the main characters because he is literally the first hero of these islands that make up the United Kingdom, even before Boudicca came along. I sincerely hope that I am doing his life justice and that of Centurion Tiberius Albinus Varro who is even susceptible to man-flu! Varro of course is my own creation, I hope you like him as much as I do.

The positive reaction to Blood of Rome Caratacus has served to encourage my writing further, and I am honoured to say, so far so good and thank you. Hopefully I'll see you all again in book three, Blood of Rome…!

Best Regards

John

Printed in Great Britain
by Amazon.co.uk, Ltd.,
Marston Gate.